THE JIGSAW BLADE

THE BIZARRE BLADES BOOK 1

STEVIE COLLIER

COPYRIGHT

The amazing proofreading and fantastic story comments (which made this series 10x better) were completed by Lisa Hammann. For more information on getting your own novel/series proofread at: LHammann92@gmail.com

The beautiful artwork you see in this series was also done by him. If you are looking for your own awesome creature drawings, you can email him at: ACollier1121@gmail.com

Need someone to run your Public Relations? Contact Mike @ Kickstandsound@gmail.com or message him on Facebook @ Michael Evans

Throughout this entire series you will discover amazing prehistoric animals such as dinosaurs, fantastic flying reptiles, viscous/hilarious mammals, and, of course, sea creatures! All research and suggestions were taken from Biologist "A" Collier. He is currently studying at the University of Texas to obtain his PhD in Paleontology.

1

THE DEATH CAGE OF FLYING DOOM

Finn Featherstone swung the bag of newly-purchased art supplies over his shoulder, thanked the traveling merchant once more with a nod of his head, and turned to walk in the direction of home. He had a smile on his face, which was a rare occurrence since the death of his mother. Had a day gone by that she hadn't haunted his thoughts?

His boots dropped into the snow with that crunching sound he found so satisfying. People probably thought him weird to walk on the untraversed paths of the city streets but he didn't care. Stepping through soft, thick snow was a simple pleasure of his and he wondered why no one else took advantage of it. Probably because he was the only strange one in the city—or at least, that's how everyone made him feel.

The sudden sound of flapping wings made him duck and cover his head, a habit of all those who lived in the frozen Kingdom of Shimoshimo. It was a land known for its frequent and abundant traveling quetzalcoatlus, the largest species of pterosaurs, and they were even more common in the capital city, Sumetai, Finn's home. It was not uncommon for humans to become quick snacks for these beautiful winged reptiles.

Finn waited a few moments before allowing himself to open his eyes and look at the sky. Nothing. Then where was the sound coming from?

"Oh no...please, no," Finn whispered to himself as he looked down the icy street that headed to his home.

Ahead of him was a crowd of people, growing not only in number but also in excitement. He could picture them surrounding the Death Cage of Flying Doom (which had a more official name, but Finn preferred to call it what it was) as they observed the unlucky souls who had been sentenced to death by pterodactyl, which was one of the more violent species of pterosaurs. Sure, most of those prisoners probably deserved what they had coming to them, but what a way to go. Death by pterodactyl must have been the worst death ever because, well, it wasn't quick. Sure some lucky criminals got taken out fast, but Finn had seen men with plucked-out eyeballs begging for the long beaked animals to finally pierce their throats.

He hated the Death Cage. It wouldn't have been so bad if he didn't have to walk past the damn thing every single solitary day—but today of all days! He'd been given strict instructions by Father to get the supplies and hurry home as fast as possible, as he had run out of paint just when he'd nearly finished his project. If the piece wasn't finished today, then Father would have to reduce the price for having it complete a day late, which didn't seem fair to Finn, but that was the world he lived in. No one had patience for anything, and any good painter knew that fine art took time to create.

Taking a deep breath, Finn made himself walk on. There were other routes he could have taken but all of them would have taken double or more time to traverse. No, he needed to be a man and walk past the Death Cage of Flying Doom. If worst came to worst, he could always cover his ears, which would at least block out most of the screams of the dying criminals.

The crowd of blood-lusting people paid Finn no attention—which he was certainly used to. He recognized many of them. There was Lily, the kind pastry maker whose shop was only a few doors down from his own home. She always had a warm smile on her face...but now her lips were curled back as she swore obscenities at the ones about to die. Her hair, usually in a bun, was undone and flapping wildly in the wind, making her look like a savage—and she wasn't alone. Everyone was there for a show. It was funny what a little bloodshed did to people.

Finn stopped a few feet out from the crowd. A cracking noise came from above and Finn quickly sidestepped just as a large chunk of ice crashed where he'd been standing. He was about to turn away when something sticking out of the snow made him stop. He bent a little closer and...it was a human finger!

Quickly jumping back while trying not to puke, Finn's bag bumped into something hard. He whipped around to see a man he didn't recognize. The stranger towered over Finn, and didn't even bother to look down at him. He had long, ghost-white hair which didn't even compare to the whiteness of his skin. A black bandana covered one eye while the other, blood red and unblinking, stared at the cage. He said nothing, and was so still that Finn thought he might actually have been frozen. Stranger still, he was wearing practically nothing, just a white fur cape and trousers with nothing to keep his hands or chest warm. Who was he? Where did he come from?

Noticing that Finn was staring, the tall man looked

down at him, bore his teeth, and hissed.

"S—sorry about that, mister," Finn squeaked. "I'll just be going now."

Finn walked quickly around the albino, making sure to keep his head down. He could feel his heart beating fast in his chest. Could he go one day without getting in trouble?

He was just about to make it to the end of the crowd. He could see the whiteness of the road ahead and the surrounding homes built on stilts. He focused on them, trying his best not to look at the cage...but he knew he would. He always looked.

From what he could see between the people as he passed, Finn was able to make out four men and two women, all on their bellies and trying to remain as still as possible. This was always the best tactic but, it never worked for very long. The pterodactyls used for the execution were purposely starved, and it wouldn't be long before they would be taking small, excruciating nibbles from their prey.

As for the cage itself, it was made of thin pieces of bendable metal wire which had been molded into tiny circles. These circles were then interconnected to make a wide, see-through metal fence which was then wrapped around four tall wooden beams. Another layer of this metal fence would be placed over the top to make a ceiling. There were safer ways to build cages for pterosaurs, but those would have made watching the executions impossible; and they couldn't have that, now could they?

Turning his head away, Finn cursed himself for this terrible compulsion of his. Why did he always have to look? It never made him feel better. It was that damned superstitious side of him. It told him that if he didn't look, then he would have a bad day—or worse, he would end up in the cage himself.

When his feet hit the snow at the far end of the crowd, Finn let out a sigh of relief. He was in the clear! He bent low and readied himself to run when a sudden change in the cries of the people made him turn around.

The faces of the people were twisted in horror rather than bloodthirsty glee. Finn followed their gaze, and it took him a few seconds to find what they were looking at. He gasped.

A little girl, her skin covered in dirt and her clothes riddled with holes, climbed the side of the cage. She had brown hair which explained her poor hygiene; brown-haired people were on the lowest totem of the hierarchy.

A few men had already taken to the metal-holed cage and were climbing as fast as they could. Of course, all of them had brown hair as well. No other person of colored locks would ever risk their lives for a Spud.

To make things worse, the entrance for the pterosaurs, a trap door situated at the bottom of the cage, had been opened by an unseen hand. The violent and incredibly loud flapping of wings drowned out the noise of the crowd. A flock of desperate pterodactyls pushed themselves through the tiny hole in the ground and took flight inside the cage. Some, however, remained on the ground, stretching their wings while they stepped on the backs of cowering and whimpering criminals. The skin of the reptiles glistened with the redness of fresh blood, most likely that of each other as the mixture of starvation and close proximity had led to cannibalism. There was a reason why there was such a high turnover of these animals. It wasn't because they weren't fed—it was because they killed each other while stored in the pit. Only the survival of the fittest ever made it out of the hole.

Finn's heart was really racing now. He could easily

continue ahead. He could run as fast as he could and make it to his home in just five minutes. But that was the thing: he was fast and he was light. His heart told him that it was he who should have been climbing the side of the cage. He could reach the girl, he knew he could.

But his brain...his brain told him he was a fool. His brain told him it was certain death if he tried something so crazy! So then, why did he drop the bag of supplies? Why were his legs carrying him to the Death Cage of Flying Doom?

Before he knew it, he was climbing up the side of the cage. He could feel the eyes of the crowd, gawking at his speed as he ascended. Finn made sure that he didn't look down but kept his face straight up into the air. His heart was in control, but his brain was catching up fast!

What the hell am I doing?! I'm gonna be beaked to death!

The loud clanging of the chain-link cage had the pterodactyls in a riot. They were flying like mad, crashing into the walls of the cage only to fly to the opposite side and crash there as well. One of them even slammed into the cage only inches away from Finn's fingers. This was the moment he decided to climb back down...but then his eyes caught sight of a hole at the very top of the cage, which a pterodactyl must have ripped open during the last execution. The hole was small enough not to be noticed by the handlers, but just big enough for a little girl to fall through...and the child Spud headed in its direction, a big dumb smile on her face.

Finn double-timed it. He ignored the pain in his fingers as he pulled himself on top of the cage and stood on wobbling feet. The girl had made it to the top as well, had already found the hole, and decided that it must have the best view!

"No!" Finn cried, running towards the girl with his hands extended. The crowd was roaring now but he ignored them as he focused on saving the little girl. He imagined plucking her off the ground, his hands beneath her tiny armpits.

The pterodactyls flinging themselves against the walls of the cage made the ceiling bouncy making it extremely difficult to stay upright. Sure enough, just when the little girl had situated her head above the hole, one of the reptiles flew directly at the ceiling.

Finn saw it in his mind before it even happened and flung himself at the girl who was toppling forward, her eyes wide with fear, her mouth slowly opening. She fell through the hole just as Finn landed next to it, reaching his hand in as far as he could and...and...he felt skin!

Looking down through the hole, Finn saw that he had caught only two fingers of the child. The problem was, he'd always had clammy hands, and today was no different. He tried his best to close his grip on her but it was too late.

The crowd fell silent as the little girl slipped from Finn's grasp and dropped to her death. Finn couldn't take his eyes off her tiny dark brown ones as he watched her fall in slow motion. His hand was still opening and closing when her body crashed into the snow below.

Closing his eyes, Finn let out a curse, his bottom lip trembling from a combination of fear and sadness. He took in a couple deep breaths before realizing that he needed to get off the top of this cage and quick or else—

WHAM!

Not just one, but two frantic pterodactyls collided into the cage underneath him, sending his body a few feet into the freezing air. His hands swam wildly in the sky as he fell forward, his head and half his shoulders landing into the open hole of the Death Cage. Just when he tried to pull himself out, one of the more muscular pterodactyls caught part of his fur coat in its beak and started to wrench him into its domain.

"No, damn you! Let go of me!"

Slipping one hand through the small opening, Finn tried punching at the beast's beak repeatedly, but it was no use. The pterosaur had nothing to lose and a fresh hot meal to gain. It wasn't going to let go no matter what he did—but he still had to try!

Quickly, Finn pulled the other arm into the hole and tried to reach for the thing's beady black eyes, but its bobbing head moved too fast for him to grab. He felt himself being yanked more into the cage and tried to fit his hands back through the hole to pull himself out, but he couldn't. The more he struggled, the more he sank.

With one final desperate move, Finn closed his eyes and swung a right cross at the pterodactyl's head. He felt the leathery skin touch his knuckles as the punch made impact. The reptile opened its beak with a high-pitched scream as it fell to the ground, its wings flapping madly.

Without wasting a moment, Finn brought his hands back through the hole and began pulling himself out. His face was halfway through the clearing when another pterodactyl, flung itself from the opposite side of the cage and directly at him. Its beak clamped down hard on one of his exposed fingers, making him cry out in pain. Immediately, the ferocious reptile pulled at the digit, trying its best to swallow its catch.

Finn had two options. One, he could let the pterodactyl take his finger...or two, he could let go.

He let go and fell.

2

BRYCE SMOLDER

Finn blinked his eyes a couple of times and was about to raise his head but thought better of it. He could feel a lump under his back and assumed it to be the corpse of the little girl. In the background, he could hear the screams of the criminals inside the cage. He glanced to his side and could see that two of them had managed to grab one of the smaller pterodactyls and were busy choking it to death, only for it to turn its head and accidentally slash one of their eyes with the point of its beak.

Should he play dead? Or should he try and climb back up the wall? The second idea quickly faded from his mind as he watched one of the female criminals make it halfway, just to be overwhelmed by four pterodactyls. Finn watched as parts of her skin were nipped off by the tail-wagging reptiles.

A booming noise echoed from the trap door built in the middle of the cage where all the pterodactyls had escaped from. This was followed by a loud exhale of breath. Something was still down there, and whatever it was, it wasn't happy.

Snow flew into the air as whatever lurked underground banged its body against its enclosure ceiling. Finn couldn't help but roll off the girl and scurry backward a few feet, anything to get away from the pterosaur entrance. He looked down at the little girl and expected to see a bloody mess, but what he saw gave him hope, although very little of it.

Her eyes were wide open and her chest rose and fell, ever so slightly. She stared upward at the hole she had just come through. Two pterodactyls landed at her side, their heads angling to the left and right as they tried to figure out what she was. Sure, she wasn't a fish, but she would do.

"Get away from her!" Finn shouted, shooing them with his hand and grabbing the girl by one of her ankles. He pulled her through the snow and into his lap.

The two pterodactyls didn't look scared, nor did they flinch at his attempt to frighten them away. Their eyes bulged from their grey skin, and they slowly turned their heads towards Finn then stopped, going still. Their heads shook slightly, and Finn wondered if it was from a lack of food.

The one on the right took a step towards Finn, and the other followed. To him, it looked as though their eyes were apologizing for the atrocity they were about to commit. Eating human flesh wasn't natural, and he felt like he could sense this in them. They were just doing the best they could. Sure, he couldn't be completely certain of this, but he'd always had a connection with animals. Whether they were mammals or dinosaurs, Finn loved them all. He was fascinated by their beauty and always enjoyed sketching them whenever he could.

Through this love for animals, Finn always believed he could not exactly speak to them, but feel them out. It was like he could sense the emotions of these wild beasts. He called it his sixth sense. But this quirk of his would have no effect on saving his life today.

The pterodactyls were within beak distance of Finn, and he could see the skin on the sides of their faces twitching as they anticipated their attack. And, just when it looked like they were about to make their move, another *boom* came from below. This time, the pterodactyls screeched and took to the sky, smacking into each other as they did so.

"What...is that?" Finn asked himself under his breath.

Whatever it had been, it was silent now, and so was everything else. The reptiles had gone still, not because they were done eating... but because they could sense what was below. The crowd took this as the end of the show, and many now walked away. They'd gotten their fill of blood— and there was a lot of it. The snow of the cage was never white but an orangish-yellow from past executions. Now, it had a fresh coat of red.

It was so quiet that Finn's ears could pick up the soft steps of the underground animal. He could hear its breathing, which was shaky and desperate. It moved slowly through the cage and he could track where it was if he listened hard enough.

"Could it be a ornithocheirus? No, too small... pteranodon? No, still too small..."

Finn flinched as a loud vibrational *screech* met his ears and he knew in an instant what he was dealing with.

"Quetzalcoatlus..."

Finn stopped breathing, and most importantly, stopped talking to himself, as a claw clamped onto the edge of the opening. He could see its bones working under the thin skin as it leveraged itself in just a way that it could pull out its other wing.

"We got us a quetzal over here!" cried one of the observers who had remained by the cage to watch the rest of the bloodbath. The only ones left were him and a few Spuds who were concerned for the little girl with no signs of the parents anywhere.

People excitedly rushed back to the face of the cage as the quetzal managed to pull out its other claw. The ground shook as the beast used its momentum to push more of itself out into the open air. A blue bill covered in thin hairs appeared first, then two pebble-sized black eyes which stared directly at Finn and the girl.

The crowd roared excitedly as the quetzal maneuvered its body, dragging itself out of the underground enclosure in a surprisingly smooth manner. All other pterodactyls had landed and hopped to the opposite side of the cage, getting as far away as possible. One pterodactyl was smashed up against Finn's shoulders, unaware that he even existed. Out of the corner of his eye, Finn could see that its beak was shiny with fresh blood.

Finally, the quetzalcoatlus had fully removed itself from below ground. Its wings were folded to its stomach, but Finn could still see its ribs clearly underneath its light brown skin. The jelly of its eyes flicked all around as it took in its surroundings.

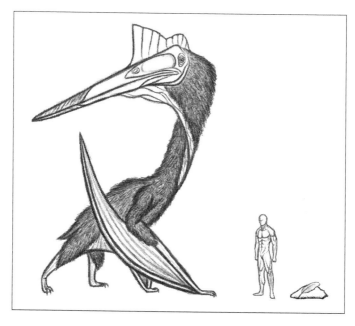

Quetzalcoatlus

If Finn's ears hadn't been blocking all outside noise he would have heard the screams coming from the crowd, pressed tightly against the cage. Carefully, the quetzal extended both of its arms, creating two massive tarps with its wings. Its claws extended through the links of the cage, and clamped down on a spectator's finger and crushed it. The screams of this human snapped Finn out of his hypnosis.

The quetzal lifted its head, which banged against the ceiling of the cage, only allowing it to raise itself to about three-quarters of its normal height. Finn knew from his avid studies of these beasts that they had been known to grow upwards of eighteen feet. He could feel its frustration. He could feel its longing to be free. The four-foot beak opened itself and Finn did the same with his mouth in awe.

The quetzal's long throat wiggled as yet another screech poured from its mouth for what felt like a whole sixty seconds. It sent ripples down its wing, the thick blue veins visible from the sunlight beaming through the skin.

When it had finished its scream of defeat, the quetzal bent its head low, its beak landing only a foot away from Finn. In his arms, he could feel the girl's breath speed up, but she wasn't stupid. She'd grown up in the Frostbite District and therefore knew how to care for herself around these animals. Well, as much as a five-year-old could. Finn wondered how long it would be before she let out a scream of her own. He wondered the same about himself.

Finn dared not move an inch, not even to push himself back against the cage. The pterodactyl on his shoulder lost its nerve and jumped into the air. However, it was no match for the speed of a quetzal. With one lightning-fast whip of its neck, the quetzal caught the pterodactyl in its beak and crushed it flat, the prey going limp without a peep.

The quetzal bent its neck and raised its head, letting its catch slide down its throat. Finn couldn't take his eyes off the bulbous form that slowly eased itself down into the giant pterosaur's stomach. While it was busy feeding, the rest of the pterodactyls had taken to the air, a few of them escaping through the hole in the ceiling while others cowered on the opposite side of the cage.

Finn and the girl were the only edible things left in the giant reptile's vision, and again the quetzal dropped its head towards them. He could hear its wavering breath as it escaped through the two holes on top of its beak. It cracked its mouth open, revealing a rough-looking tongue. The sides of its mouth were glazed with pterodactyl blood and a ripped-off claw stuck out of the edge of its cheek.

Cool air sprayed Finn and the girl as the quetzalcoatlus

performed its scream, and Finn recognized the smell of its breath as the vile smell of dried saliva. Finn was pretty sure he was screaming too, as he held the little girl in a death-grip of a hug, close to his chest.

The quetzal reared its head back for an attack and Finn shut his eyes. Suddenly, there was the unmistakable sound of metal being sliced, followed by the pounding of a body against the cage. Finn's eyes shot open and could not believe what he was seeing.

"Bryce Smolder!" cried everyone, including Finn and the little girl.

Bryce Smolder, the legendary Champion, first in queue for his very own Bizarre Blade, slammed his shoulder hard into the metal-linked cage repeatedly, his head bent low and his face tight in concentration. Finn could see that he'd cut a rough outline of a door into the metal but some pieces of it were still connected.

The quetzal snapped its jaw shut and turned towards Bryce, who was backing up, his teeth gritted. The giant beast squawked loudly as Bryce put all three hundred and fifty pounds and seven feet, two inches of himself into his next power move.

The gate exploded open and the air was powdered with snow, so much so that Finn couldn't see a thing. The girl in his grasp was screaming up at him and he realized he was pinching her tiny arms with his fingers.

"Sorry," he said, his eyes snapping back up to watch the snow clear.

Standing before Finn was the wide V-shaped back of Bryce, his muscles visible through the cracks in his famous Cryolopho-armor which was a mixture of feathers, chain-mail, and dinosaur leather. He wasn't even breathing heavily. His right arm was out and holding a large razor-sharp iron sword, the hilt of which was covered in mammoth fur to keep his fist from freezing up.

The man turned his head, a sideways smile spread across his face. He wiped two fingers over his eyebrows and then pointed them at Finn and the girl, in the customary hello that the lower classes used to greet one another. Bryce was known for this move, even though he was a man of long blonde hair which made him a Highborn. For someone such as him to lower himself to the pleasantries of Spuds, Sprouts, and Sparks made him the legend that he was.

"Are you two okay?" he asked, dropping his perfect smile and turning towards the quetzal. Its head was back and tilted in confusion, which Finn could feel clearly through the air.

"Y-y-y-" Finn tried to say but couldn't get the word out. He needed to piss really badly now.

"Yes!" cried the girl who was trying to pry Finn's hands off her. "Let go of me!"

"Oh, right, sorry," Finn said, releasing his grip on the girl. She fled through the door but not before the quetzal tried giving her a good snap. Bryce sidestepped in front and slapped the beak away. The quetzalcoatlus looked offended.

With no more hesitation, the quetzal reared back its head and tried its best to pierce Bryce through the skull with its beak. Bryce, being the awesome Champion that he was, sidestepped once again and grabbed the beak in a choke-hold, his sword falling flat into the snow.

"Get out of here, young one!" he roared, his voice straining in his effort to hold the quetzal in place.

But he wouldn't last long.

Finn found that he couldn't move. He was paralyzed, awestruck with a good amount of fear mixed in. He'd followed Bryce Smolder's career ever since he was nothing but a Champion's squire. Finn looked up to this man and all of his qualities. He'd drawn pictures of him which were pinned up all around in his room. Now, he knew they weren't accurate. In the past, he'd only gotten glimpses of the Champion as he'd accepted his countless rewards from the king. It was almost impossible to get a good spot during these ceremonies, and even harder for green-haired Sprouts such as Finn. His people weren't very well accepted, even if they were third up from the bottom in the hierarchy; they were basically tolerated.

"Did you hear me? Get out!"

Finn didn't hear him, as he was busy tracing Bryce's veins from his wrists, to his massive arms, to the bottom of his jaw. They bulged and were as big as Finn's fingers.

"GET OUT!"

Finn jumped to his feet and ran through the opening, but tripped and fell face first into the snow a few feet outside of the cage. No one in the crowd laughed, as they were all gone, busy running as fast as they could. There was now a hole in the Death Cage of Doom which meant sooner or later tens of hungry pterodactyls would be free. No amount of amusement was worth the risk, even if Bryce Smolder was performing a miraculous feat.

Finn should have started running for home but he *couldn't*. He had to stay and watch! Bryce might need his help! But who was he kidding? Bryce was a legend for a reason. Finn shook his head in amazement as the Champion wrenched the giant pterosaur's head towards the door. He pushed the beak through the opening and spanked the beast hard on the ass.

The quetzal chirped loudly as it shot itself out from the cage. Finn couldn't help but pee a little when the creature extended itself fully, its head a shadow as it blocked the sun.

Both of its wings opened and Finn had to shut his eyes from the sheer amount of wind that puffed into his face as the quetzal flew off into the sky.

In a matter of seconds, the Death Cage of Doom vomited out all of its pterodactyl occupants, which took off in the opposite direction that the quetzal had flown. Bryce was busy pulling out the only two criminals who had survived: a man and a woman.

"Congratulations, you've survived your execution," Bryce said in his deep, burly voice. "Consider yourselves pardoned."

The man and woman were at his feet, kissing his furred boots and hugging his legs. Bryce flicked his two fingers over his brow and tapped each of them on the forehead.

"Now get out of here before I change my mind!"

The two criminals stood, bowed, and ran. They, too, slipped in the snow and were practically crawling away before they'd even stood back up.

Bryce was putting his sword back into its sheath when Finn realized this was his chance to talk to his hero. He brushed off the snow and clambered up on two shaky legs. He could feel the pee in his undergarments already starting to freeze to his leg hair, but he ignored it, focusing entirely on Bryce.

The Champion was staring at a trail of blood on the ground, no doubt from the person who'd had their finger snapped off by the quetzal's grip. Bryce was just about to follow the trail when Finn worked up the nerve to speak.

"I-I-I-" Finn sputtered. His hair was covered in snow and felt it melting slightly down his back. He was freezing and already he could feel the aches of his spine beginning to make themselves known.

Bryce's face followed the trail up to a nearby street but

caught the open-mouthed stare from Finn. He did the two-finger swipe salute, nodded his head, and bolted in the direction of the wounded person. It was the duty of all Champions to care for the weak but most didn't adhere to this rule.

Bryce, however, was different. He cared for all.

Finn fell to his knees in the snow, pulling his fur cape over his shoulders. He gazed down at the ground, his bottom lip beginning to tremble.

"I want to be like you, Bryce," he whispered to himself.

3

THE GIFT OF THE MONK E

FINN WALKED UP THE STAIRS TO HIS HOME, BEING CAREFUL TO skip the third step which had been broken ever since he could remember and had never been repaired. He pushed on the wooden door and felt relief when hot smoky air breezed over his face. He could smell the scent of cooking fish along with the familiar aromas of different sorts of paint. He slid inside and shut the door quietly behind himself. He wasn't sure why he was being quiet; he still had to give his father the supplies he'd been able to salvage from the road.

"You're late," came his father's voice from the kitchen. "You do realize that now our patron will be wanting half off, if not the whole piece free."

Finn shut his eyes tightly and forced himself to say, "I'm sorry, Father." Then, he added, "I ran into some trouble on the way home."

His father snorted, "Don't tell me it's those bullies again. Did you at least fight back this time?"

"No sir, it wasn't them."

His father rounded the corner, the old wooden floor

creaking under his feet. His long, usually white hair held an array of color from it accidentally dipping into his paints. His face was round and covered in stress wrinkles. He was shorter than Finn, and somehow, he had managed to grow a belly despite their lack of food. He had a rag in his hand and was drying a freshly-washed paint palette. "Then what the hell took so—"

The aging man dropped both the rag and the palette when his eyes fell on his son. Finn looked away, not really sure how he looked, but knowing it must not have been good.

"By God, what happened to you, my boy?" he asked, limping to his son as fast as he could. He never was able to walk right after the accident. He placed both hands on Finn's shoulders and then on his cheeks. "Who did this to you?"

"I did this to myself," Finn answered, his voice muffled by his father's hands.

"This isn't from tripping now, is it? I told you to pick up your feet when you walk and to stay out of the thick snow!"

"No, Dad, it was—"

To Finn's relief, his story was interrupted by a knocking on the door. There was no lock or doorknob, and so with every knock the door opened slightly, soon revealing Lily the baker, her hair retied back into her usual bun.

"Mista Featherstone! I come bearing news!" she cried through the doorway. "It's your son! He was on the cage, I tell you! Saw it with my own eyes I did!"

Father dropped his hands from Finn's face and limped over to the door to let Lily in. Finn took this chance to escape to his room, dropping the bag of supplies on the floor. He could feel tears coming. Once again, he'd failed his father and at the worst possible time. They needed that money.

～

FINN FELT the aches growing stronger in his back as he pushed through the door to his room. He was met with hundreds of flapping pieces of parchment, flying through the air. To his horror, all of his artwork was covering the ground or dancing in the wind.

"Not again," he groaned, as he crossed the room and shut his bedroom window. He had a bad habit of leaving it open.

Finn was just about to bend down and start picking up his work when he caught the image of himself in the mirror. His face had tiny cuts from falling face first into the icy snow and his cheeks were red from windburn. He stood and lifted his shirt, turning at just the right angle to see a nasty bruise developing on the fair skin of his lower back. The mirror was cracked in many places from it dropping so many times to the floor, but he could still see how damaged his entire body looked.

Finn dropped his shirt and rested his hands on the dresser, his head bowed to the mirror. He took a few deep breaths before looking up. Long curly hair in shades of light and dark green fell in his face. The redness of his cheeks brought out the freckles which were usually hard to see. His matching light green eyes stared at themselves.

He loathed the man—no, the boy—in the broken mirror.

"I'll clean this up later," he said to himself as he turned and made for his window. He opened and crawled through it, letting himself drop easily onto the big patch of snow he'd raked up to the side of his house for just this occasion.

He needed some cheering up and he knew just the trick. He would pay his friend Monk Eatsalot a visit. Surely, that crazy oddities merchant would have something for him today. Or, at least something to take his attention off the day's unfortunate events. But, had they even been that unfortunate? He had gotten to see his hero, hadn't he? So, it wasn't *all* bad.

Finn took a step towards the direction of Monk's wagon but stopped to look back at his home. It was hard to fathom that they might lose the place. It wasn't the nicest home a green-haired person could buy, but painting didn't pay well. They were lucky enough to have the two-bedroom wooden box that they did have.

Dropping his attention to the thick wooden stilts the house was built on, he could see that they would be in need of replacing soon. Blizzards had given it hell for years, but somehow the house still stood. However, now Finn doubted it would survive half the night during a storm.

MONK EATSALOT SNORED loudly as he performed his greatest trick of all, which was sleeping while standing up. Finn found him behind his makeshift booth, which was just three pieces of wood crudely nailed together. Monk was a fat man, but today his brown wool shirt looked more bulbous than normal—and it was *moving*. Only when Finn got close did he realize what it was.

Finn made out the form of the overgrown lizard before it even poked its head out of its owner's shirt. The tanystropheus, a half-aquatic animal with an egg-shaped body and four stump legs, poked its thin, long neck out from Monk's shirt. Upon noticing Finn, the reptile moved its shoe-shaped head in his direction.

"Hey, Noodle," Finn whispered, patting the tany on his head. "I'm sorry, but I don't have any treats for you today."

Noodle's face was emotionless as ever and gave Finn a couple of rapid tongue flicks to his nose before pulling its head back into Monk's shirt.

"Hey, Monk…" Finn said softly.

Nothing but snores answered him.

"Monk!"

"Whuh—what's going on? Noodle! Dammit, get out of here you, pesky lizard! Shoo!"

Monk shoved his dirty hand down his shirt and began pushing a reluctant Noodle. The tanystropheus, still in the infant stage, plopped out of the bottom of his shirt and landed softly in the snow. It, too, wore its very own wool shirt that looked exactly like Monk's.

"And you!" Monk said, pointing a finger with a very long yellow nail at Finn. "How many times do I have to tell you? This is an official and serious business! Call me by my full name! Monk Eatsalot!" He squinted his eyes at the ground. "But, seeing as you're my only friend, I'll let you call me Monk E. for short."

"Whatever you say, Monk E.," Finn said with a shrug.

Monk returned with a smile. He had very long and unkempt brown hair which, much like Finn's, was always getting in his face, but unlike Finn's, was never washed. He had big yellow eyes which seemed to never blink. He was the same height as Finn which was odd because Finn was shorter than most.

"You know," Finn said, arching his back from the pain. "I

never asked you this, but how did you go about getting the last name 'Eatsalot'?"

Monk's eyes widened and he put a hand to his mouth. "Finn! It's so rude to ask about one's family name! You know this!"

"Yeah," Finn said, "but I thought we were friends, and friends can ask about family names, can't they?"

Monk nodded his head and played with a make-believe chin beard. "You have a point. Okay! I'll tell you, but on one condition."

"What's that?"

"You tell me how you got yours!" Finn gave his friend the two-finger salute and Monk gave him a devious smile as if he'd just made the deal of a lifetime. "Okay, so you know I was raised in the orphanage, yes?"

"Yes."

"Well, seeing as no one knew my name, obviously, they had to give me a new one!"

"I'm guessing you ate a lot?" Finn suggested.

Monk slammed his fist on his makeshift stand and it fell apart with a small puff of yellow sawdust. His face was bulging with veins when he exclaimed, "You gotta let me tell the story, dammit!"

Finn couldn't help but laugh. although he did try to hide it with his hands. "I'm so sorry," he managed to say. "Please continue."

Monk's face returned to normal, meaning, as usual, he'd forgotten what had just happened. "So, get this! Apparently, I couldn't put down the bottle of milk! The caretakers started calling me 'Eatsalot,' and the rest is history!"

Finn let out a sarcastic gasp. "I never would have guessed.

Monk nodded his head rapidly. "But it's true! And to this day I can't stop eating!"

"That, too, I never would have guessed," Finn said, stealing a glance at Monk's belly, which he was now rubbing.

"Now, it's your turn."

"Oh, yeah, right." Finn scratched his head. "Well, I'm a Featherstone, as you know."

"You are?"

Finn's shoulders slumped. "Monk, you've known me for years, how could you not—"

"It's Monk E. to you! This is a business!"

"Fine, okay, Monk E. Anyway, I'm a Featherstone. My father and I come from a long line of them. He tells me we used to be great in number but that most of us all died off in the Great Plains War."

"But what did your ancestor mother see when she gave birth to you?"

"Well, she saw a feather on a stone. That's what Father says, anyway, but you can never be too sure. Some people lie about it, you know. I mean, come on, have you met the family named Lightningsword? That's just absurd, if you ask me."

Monk was shaking his head. "No, no, no, the surname is sacred! No one lies about it! Trust me." Finn was just about to argue with the man but knew it would be useless. "Tell me, Finn Featherstone, what color was this feather?"

Finn was shocked that he actually knew the answer to this. "Well, it was a mixture of light blue and red. Father strongly believes it came from a Velociraptor."

"You don't say!"

"But again, Monk E., you can never be too sure about these things."

"Not one more word about that!" cried Monk, pointing his finger at Finn. "Have you no respect for your ancestors?"

"Relax, Monk, I was just—"

"Monk E.!"

"Fine!" screamed Finn. "Fine! Just...let's just drop it."

"Have you heard about the Prince?" asked Monk. "He got his first Bizarre Blade!"

Finn nodded his head. "I heard. They're calling it the Chaos Blade but one can't be too sure. It's probably all just false gossip. Besides, I've never even heard of the Chaos Blade before. It sounds made up if you ask me."

"Well, if there's anyone in this world that might have heard of such a Blade it would have been you, Finn Featherstone."

"I do have you to thank," Finn said with a smile. "You always have the best leaflets on the Blades."

Something happened with Monk's face. It twisted itself, and Finn couldn't tell whether he was trying to smile or... well, he didn't know what! The skin was turning red and his yellow eyes practically bulged from their sockets.

"What's wrong, Monk E.? You got something new for me, don't you?"

Noodle could sense the change in his owner's demeanor and scurried through the snow and into the back of their broken-down wagon. It did, however, poke its head out of the curtain doors to watch.

"Do I ever!" Monk finally exploded, his hands bursting into the air. "You won't believe! I! You! I did! You shoulda!" Monk put both of his hands on his groin and bounced up and down as if he had to urinate. "I found the ONE!"

"The one, what?" Finn asked. "You're not making sense!"

"The most important leaflet yet!"

Monk was a lot of things, but he was no liar. Finn had

known him practically all his life and had always bought whatever Bizarre Blade knowledge the poor merchant could get his grubby hands on.

"What's your price?" Finn asked, cutting through the crap. Whatever it was, he knew he had to have it.

Monk's excited dance came to a sudden stop, an open smile appearing on his face, showing off his last four teeth. He turned back to the wagon and whistled. A few seconds later, Noodle burst through the curtain with a ragged-looking leaflet held in its mouth. It waddled through the snow, tail squirming in a serpentine fashion. Monk bent down and scooped up the tany and gave it a kiss on the forehead. He tried to take the small book from the reptile, but Noodle wasn't having it.

"Dammit, you overgrown lizard! Give me the damned leaflet before I feed you to a plesiosaur!"

Upon hearing these words, Noodle released the leaflet and Monk returned the favor by dropping the reptile into the snow. Noodle scurried back to the wagon, and again poked its head out from the curtains.

"I swear, that lizard has it out for my business."

Finn's eyes dropped to the saliva-covered pamphlet and his heart began to race. He hoped with everything in him that Noodle hadn't destroyed it. It wasn't often that good Bizarre Blade information was found.

"How much do you want for it?" Finn asked, his fingers wiggling by his sides. "I just got paid last week. It's not much but—" Monk waved his hand to quiet Finn and offered the leaflet to him. "What's this? What are you doing?"

"You do know what's next week, don't you?" Monk asked him.

"No? What's next week?"

Monk shook his head. "Your birthday!"

"Oh...oh!" Finn smacked his forehead. "I totally forgot."

Monk laughed. "But this time, Monk Eatsalot didn't!" He grabbed one of Finn's clammy hands, opened it, put the leaflet inside, and shut his fingers around it. "Happy early birthday, Finn Featherstone."

4

LIGHTNINGSWORD

ON HIS WAY HOME, FINN HAD THE HARDEST TIME NOT OPENING the leaflet and poring through its knowledge. He never allowed himself to read through a new Bizarre Blade find until he was just about to go to bed. If he did, he figured that he would have a bad day the next day. Or worse—a bad year! And so, yet another habit was added to his collection of superstitions.

As he walked, Finn couldn't help but notice the other Sprouts, those who also had green hair, shutting the doors of their homes. These, too, were built atop wooden beams, but these didn't look as rotted or as cracked as his and his father's. Not only that, but these houses were a lot bigger than theirs. The Sprouts most likely held decent positions in the army of Shimoshimo, or they had other important jobs such as healers' assistants or were even a part of the blizzard rescue teams.

None of these Sprouts were painters.

The sun had gone down and the cold air found its way through Finn's warm clothing. Even his furred cape wasn't having much effect against the freezing winds that were now pelting his already-damaged face.

As he turned onto his road, he spotted her.

"Lola Star," Finn breathed.

Lola lived on the third story of her home, which was the last nice home before the crappy ones began to show up. She was occupied in combing her hair in her window, too busy to notice him. Finn should have hunkered down against the wind and made way for his home, but that's not what his legs did. They carried him closer and closer to her, and there, he knelt. He peeked over the top of the wooden fence just outside the house, making sure to duck if she ever turned to look out the window.

Finn wasn't sure how long he was there, only that his knees had gone numb after the first minute or two. He thought he heard footsteps approaching and turned away for only half a second. When he looked back, the beautiful girl was gone.

"Where'd you go?" he asked under his breath.

Now that she had left his sight, Finn realized that he had yet again given into his seventeen-year-old lustful self. He shook his head, stood himself up, and patted the snow from his wool leggings.

"What are you doing here?"

Finn's heart stopped at the sound of Lola's breathy voice. He shot upward, his back bending in the wrong direction as he pushed his chest outward.

"I, uh, dropped my, uh...book!" Finn dared not look at Lola but waved the leaflet in the air as proof. He was proud of his lie.

"And...you dropped it over here? Right by my front gate?"

"Why, uh, yes! I mean, no...it blew over here."

"I see..."

Finn shot a quick look at Lola's face. Her hair was dyed blonde but the green was visible at the roots. She had a rather chiseled jaw for a girl, but he loved it. Her cheeks were red like his but it suited her more. Her nose was small and pointed and her eyebrows were perfectly shaped.

"Is this sack o'wooly shit bothering you?" came a deep voice from behind Finn. He didn't even have to turn to know who it was.

"I have this handled, Nolan," Lola spat. "Go home!"

"Oh, Lola, is that any way to treat your sweetheart?"

Nolan Lightningsword grabbed Finn by the shoulder and wheeled him around to face him. He was taller than Finn, as were most people, and his green hair was a lot shinier; did he ever have a bad hair day? He had a long face and perfect teeth. If Lola liked anyone, it would be this guy for sure.

"You're not my sweetheart, Nolan. Now, if you're gonna start trouble, do it elsewhere! I'm going to bed."

With that, Lola locked a lock on the other side of the gate and walked back to her home. She slammed the door loudly behind her.

"See what you did, Sprout? You scared her off!"

Finn's face was too close to Nolan's for him to see behind him, but he could hear the chuckling of his two fat goonies coming from nearby.

"You're a Sprout, too, Nolan," Finn said, but sure wished he hadn't.

Nolan's smile faded, both of his white canines showing between his lips. He spun Finn around with one quick movement and shoved his face into the white snow that had built up against the fence. The snow wouldn't have been too bad if Finn's forehead hadn't scraped against the splintered wood.

"Apologize!" Nolan screamed, his voice cracking, which was the only noticeable flaw Finn had ever found in him... well, besides being an asshole.

"Never!" Finn cried through the snow. He pounded at the sides of the ice, trying frantically to pull himself out.

"Oh, you want to fight, do ya?" asked Nolan. "Hear that, boys? Finn Featherbrains wants to fight!"

There was more laughter as Finn was pulled from the snow and shoved out into the street where he tumbled, face-forward. He stood up as quickly as he could and raised his fists just like his father had taught him.

"Oooh, where'd you learn that? I'm shaking all over!"

Nolan's two henchmen matched his height but doubled him in wideness. Finn had always been able to outrun these two, but their gang leader was different. Nolan was a duelist and trained every single day. Finn was so jealous of this; if only he'd had a father who was a duelist rather than a painter.

Nolan's feet crunched in the snow as he walked, rubbing his fist in his other palm. He pulled back his arm and threw a punch. Finn tried his best to block, but it was useless. The fist caught him by the jaw, spun his body, and again he found himself facedown in the snow. He felt something heavy sit on his lower back and push on his fresh bruise. He tried to let out a scream but his face was pressed firmly into the ice, locking his jaw.

He couldn't breathe, and he'd had no air in his lungs in the first place. He could hear Nolan saying words but couldn't make them out. His arms and legs flew spastically around his body as he desperately tried to take in a breath but only succeeded in inhaling snow.

He was suffocating!

He heard the loud crack before he felt it. Whoever was on top of him landed a punch to his temple, and he felt himself blacking out. His arms and legs dipped lazily back to the ground just as he took another shot to his temple, this time on the opposite side.

He wasn't sure when the mammoth of a henchman got off of him. Stars began to cloud his vision, and he realized he was being carried. His head throbbed despite his face and ears being completely numb. He tried to focus on the face of the person that carried him.

"Remain calm, young one!" came the heroic booming voice. "You've had too much action for one day!"

"B... Bryce?"

"The one and only, my good green-headed friend!"

This couldn't be real. The odds of meeting this famous Champion at all were low because, well, he was so damn famous. To meet him twice in one day...no, this must have been a dream. Or, perhaps he'd died. Suffocated under the gelatinous friend of Nolan Lightningsword.

"Where are you taking me?" Finn managed to say, more of his senses coming back to him every second. He was pretty sure that simply being in the presence of Bryce Smolder could heal just about anything.

"Home, my friend. You need to rest."

"But, you don't know where I live, Champion Smolder."

"On the contrary, I know exactly where you live! And please, 'Bryce' is just fine."

Bryce let out a big hefty laugh which was so loud that a big pile of snow from two roofs plopped to the ground, scaring more than one furry trash-eating scavenger.

"But I don't understand."

"Hush, now, Finn. You need your rest. You've taken some

34

damage to that Sprout head of yours. All will be clear in time."

"You...know my name?"

"Of course, I do! Why wouldn't I?"

"Because...I'm a nobody."

Suddenly, Finn felt himself falling, and his back smashed against the ground, knocking the air out of him. A surprised yelp escaped his mouth as his lungs tried to refill themselves.

"I'm so sorry, young Finn. Please excuse this aging man! Your words just shocked me, is all." Finn felt hands curl underneath his body and he tried his best not to flinch when Bryce touched his bruised back. "Never say those words again, young Finn. Everybody is somebody and everybody is the hero of their own story. Well, despite those who ruin their brains snorting tree-star dust; that shit will mess you up! But that's not the point."

"You think I'm important?" Finn asked, the pain making him feel dizzy, as though he himself had just snorted a good two grams of tree-star dust.

"Yes, I think you're very important," said Bryce, his face forward as he walked. "And you should, too. Isn't the Featherstone name connected to an ancient omen? If I remember correctly, great things are supposed to come from your bloodline."

A big, goofy smile spread across Finn's face as his head wobbled to the side. "That's what they say, sir."

"What? You don't believe in omens?"

"I believe that life favors the strong," answered Finn, his smile dropping. "And I'm not strong."

Finn felt hot air breeze over his face from Bryce's exhale of disappointment. The rest of the walk back to his home was a quiet one. As Finn regained complete consciousness, he began working on a list of questions he would ask his hero—but where to start?

What do you eat for breakfast?

How many girlfriends do you have?

How did you get so big?

Can I have a lock of your hair?

Is it true that cryolophosaurus is the tyrannosaurus rex of the ice?

And is it true you killed one all by yourself?

Will you sign my drawings of you? All six hundred and thirty-two of them?

The last question floating around Finn's head was so powerful that it slipped out of his mouth. It was the base of all his fantasies. It's what he thought about before going to bed and when he woke up. This question accidentally slipped out of his mouth, but thankfully in only a whisper.

"Will you train me?"

Bryce stopped walking. Finn realized that he'd been so caught up in his daydreaming that they'd already arrived at his home. Just before Bryce took the first step to the door, Finn was absolutely positive something came out of his mouth. It was one word and he was pretty sure it was "Maybe."

Bryce set Finn down on his feet, and Finn forced them to be strong. He had to look tough in front of his hero, no matter how much his body fought against him. He would NOT be Finn in Bryce's presence. No, he would be Finn the Fantastic! This was the name he'd given himself in his fantasies of being the Champion's personal squire. That... and he imagined himself with flowing blond locks which matched Bryce's thick luscious hair perfectly.

Bryce walked up the stairs first and Finn was flabber-gasted when the man actually skipped the broken step!

It's completely dark now! How'd he see? How'd he know?

Finn ran up next to the Champion, unable to peel his gaze from the legend that was about to enter his home. Bryce smiled down at him as he knocked on the door. Both of them heard Finn's father's loud awkward steps as he rushed to the door.

"Finn? Finn! Is that you?" he called through the door.

"It's me, father. I'm okay."

"Are you okay?"

"I just said I was!" Finn felt his pale cheeks redden as Bryce gave his famous heroic laugh.

The door swung open and out popped the face of a madman—or, at least that's how Finn would have described his father's kooky appearance. His face wasn't the only thing to pop out from the side of the door; his belly followed.

"I believe this young hero belongs to you," said Bryce, pushing on Finn's wounded back. Hearing these words, Finn had to squeeze his legs together to keep from dribbling an ounce of urine in his pants.

Did he just call me "young hero"?!

"H-h-he...he does indeed, Your Highness!" Finn's father's bottom jaw was trembling as if he'd just walked eight miles through a blizzard.

"'Your Highness'? What is with you Featherstones? Please, 'Bryce' is just fine. Oh no, please, no need to—"

Finn covered his face in embarrassment as his father bowed his entire torso a good nine times with his eyes shut. Fresh paint from his hair whipped across the Champion's cryolopho-armor.

"You are most certainly welcome inside, Your Highness, first in queue for a Bizarre Blade. I can make tea! Yes! I've been saving some for a special occasion!"

Bryce put up a hand to stop him. "I'm afraid I have no

time for tea. You see, Mr. Fable Featherstone, I've come bearing a message of either happy tidings or sad tidings, that of which I am unsure. Have you heard of what your son did today?"

Fable's face turned to his son's and glowered up at him. "Yes sir, I have. But wait—how did you know my name?"

Bryce ignored the question. "Then you will know that he has what it takes to be a hero! Your son performed bravely today! I can tell that he holds much courage and heart within him, both traits that make an excellent Champion. This is why I am here. I came personally to let you both know that the king's son, Prince Tarek, has officially instated a Kingdom-wide draft for his army."

Father's mouth dropped at hearing this. "He has? And what is the reason for this?"

"One that I believe in, my good sir. The Mage Scribes, through their mystical writings, have discovered a new Blade just before the boundary of the jungles of Koosah-moorah. These prophets of the page have predicted this Blade to be that of Legendary status."

"Why, we haven't heard of one of those in ages!" Father exclaimed. "How do we know it's true?"

"The Mage Scribes have never once been wrong," said Bryce. "We are unsure what Blade this will be but we know it will be extremely powerful...and I will be its Champion."

There was a mixture of emotions boiling inside of Finn's stomach. This was all just too much for him. First, he met his hero twice in one day. Second, his hero brought top secret news to his home. Third...

"So, I'm being drafted into the army?" Finn asked weakly, all signs of Finn the Fantastic melting out of him.

"You *will* be drafted," corrected Bryce. "By tomorrow's sunrise, word will spread through Sumetai, as well as through the rest of the Kingdom of Shimoshimo, that anyone at or above the age of sixteen will be sent to the armies right away." Bryce must have seen fear on Finn's face, for he placed a heavy hand on his head, tussled his hair, and added, "But do not fret, Finn, because I will be in charge of this army!"

Suddenly, Bryce's face went solemn. His head whipped around to each of his shoulders as he looked for something that wasn't there.

"What's wrong, Bryce?" Finn asked him. "What are you looking for?"

"OBSIDIAN!" Bryce cried out, his voice a little higher than normal. "Where are you?!"

"Obsidian?" asked Finn. "Who's Obsidian?"

A high-pitched screech answered him, along with the loud flapping of feathers, as something black landed on Bryce's shoulder.

"There you are, baby! Where have you been? Daddy was worried!" Bryce pulled out a sliver of meat from the pouch attached to his belt and held it up to the mysterious black creature. As the animal dipped its head low for the treat, Finn caught a glimpse of the face of a young...

"That's a microraptor!" cried Finn.

Bryce chuckled, "You are most certainly right! Little Obsidian here *is* a microraptor. Isn't that right, Obsidian? Isn't that right? Who's a good boy!? Who's a good boy!? WHO'S A GOOD BOY!?" Obsidian chirped. "That's right! You are!" Bryce pulled out another treat and fed the thing.

"Are you sure it's safe to have a microraptor as a companion?" asked Finn, holding back the urge to pet him.

"Of course! Just look at him! Little Obsidian here wouldn't hurt a mosquito!" Bryce exclaimed, putting his hand to his shoulder, atop which Obsidian happily hopped.

The Champion then extended his hand to Finn, bringing close the dinosaur that he had only ever had the pleasure of reading about. He'd seen drawings of them, depicting them to be around four feet long and just under ten pounds. They were rare and mostly only seen in the wilderness, very *very* far from settlements. Finn stared at it in awe as its jet black feathers shined brightly, reflecting the light from the torches inside the house. Finn had always imagined microraptors with beaks, but this one had only a fuzzy snout, its tiny sharp teeth sticking out of the top flaps of its lips.

"Does it have four wings?" Finn asked excitedly, hardly noticing that his father sported a face of bewilderment.

"How can you two talk about this when the Prince has just called for a Kingdom-wide draft?"

Bryce ignored Finn's father and continued, "You know your raptors! Check this out, young hero." The Champion used his free hand to lift first the front wing, the largest. Finn reached out to touch it but Obsidian snapped at his hand. "Oh, sorry about that. Little Obsidian has a hissy fit when he's touched by strangers." Bryce dropped the front wing and pulled out the smaller one in the back. "And this is how they maneuver in the air!"

"Can he fly?"

"Sadly, no. But! Little Obsidian-cinnamon here is an excellent glider. Isn't it true? Aren't you a good glider?! AREN'T YOU DADDY'S LITTLE GLIDER?!" Obsidian chirped. "That's right! You are!" He fed another treat to the microraptor, the dinosaur's light blue eyes never leaving Finn.

Father had his eyes covered with his hand and he breathed heavily. Bryce noticed this and put Obsidian back on his shoulder. "I'm sorry, Lord Fable Featherstone, but this is just the way it is. I don't have as much say in politics as many would believe. I did not ask for this massive draft, nor can I fight against it. However, do not worry, I will take special care of your son." Father's face lit up when he called him "Lord." Finn was sure he'd never been addressed with such an important title.

"Look at the time," Bryce said, glancing up at the stars. "I must be going! Good evening, you two."

And with that, Bryce bowed and took a backward step off the porch. Finn's heart sped up as he searched for the questions he'd prepared earlier, but he could not remember a single one.

"Wait!" Finn cried.

"Yes?" Bryce asked, both his and Obsidian's heads tilting slightly.

"I, um, have a question."

"And what would that be?"

Finn's fists tightened by his sides as he wracked his brain. Finally, only one question popped up.

"Is it true that you singlehandedly defeated a cryolophosaurus?"

Bryce nodded his head. "It had to be done, I'm afraid. I don't know how it managed to capture poor Obsidian under its foot, but it did. I should have kept to my own business, it isn't right to interfere with nature, but poor Obsidian's cries called to me at a deep level...I just couldn't walk on."

Finn looked over at Obsidian who was still staring at him, its long, black, feathered tail flicking side to side with amusement. "Thank you, Champion Bryce. For everything."

"You are very welcome." Bryce spun around to leave but turned his head over his shoulder. "Oh, and it's true what they say."

"What's that?" asked Finn.

"The cryolophosaurus *is* the t-rex of the ice...only, it's

smaller and has light blue feathers. Like this." Bryce ran his hands through his armor, plucked out a feather, and handed it to Finn. "See you soon, young hero."

Bryce jumped over the broken step and disappeared into the chilly night.

LATER THAT NIGHT, Finn sat up in bed, his entire body sore from the absolute best day of his life, except for the fact that he'd forgotten to change his pants after pissing in them. For once, it was easy for him to ignore his disaster of a room. He had yet again forgotten to shut his window and now only one piece of artwork was attached to his wall, while the rest covered the entire floor. It was a sketch of him and Bryce standing side by side, both holding a Bizarre Blade.

He was just about to lay himself down and begin the epic fantasies in his head when a sudden thought came to him.

"The leaflet!" he shouted, his breath turning to smoke in his cold, dark room.

Quickly, Finn fished out the crudely folded piece of paper, opened it, and held it close to his face. He couldn't see a thing, and so he sat back up and maneuvered the first page around until most of the starlight was upon it. He nearly passed out when he made out the title on top of the page.

The Golden Blade

5

THE MASKED MARAUDERS

FINN'S ASS HURT.

For four days he'd sat on the back of a hard, perpetually-bumping wagon, taking in whiffs of a very gassy wooly mammoth. There were eight soldiers—children, really—to each cart. They were told to take turns sitting but most preferred to walk rather than sit on the uncomfortable ride.

It had been less than a week since his memorable night with Bryce. That evening had clouded Finn's brain with more fantasies than it could hold, and so he had to line them up for their chance to be daydreamed. This is what kept him going while breathing in mammoth flatulence.

The day after Bryce's message, Finn's father hadn't had much to say and neither did he. They mostly spoke to each other in mumbles and smalltalk. Neither of them was particularly excited to be separated from each other; they had been together since Finn's mother had passed away.

However, Fable Featherstone did have a good idea that he proposed to his son.

"You do know why Bryce Smolder paid us the visit, don't you?" he'd asked.

"Because he saved my ass from suffocating in dirt-covered snow?"

"No, boy, not that. He wanted to give you the chance to enlist yourself without being drafted. Sprouts who enlist generally get more privileges. If not that, then if I were you, I would do it for the honor."

He had listened to his father and enlisted himself that day. Sadly, there had been no extra privileges. Not only that, but he hadn't even seen Bryce, not even a glimpse! This was not going the way he'd fantasized—not at all, and it was frustrating.

Finn wasn't sure who was more upset about him leaving, Monk or his father. Both had cried when he gave his final goodbye. By the time he was being fitted with armor that was far too large, his nostrils were raw from his constant snot-wiping.

There were two major flaws with the army caravan. One, none of the new recruits had been trained. None of them had swords. Most of them didn't even know what they were there for! Sprouts, Sparks, Spuds, and even Highborns had been uprooted from their homes and placed in the same crazy predicament.

The second flaw was the constant death amongst the new recruits. Finn only had to keep his head turned one direction or the other for ten minutes or so before seeing a young soldier fall face-first into the snow, dead. All of them were malnourished and cold.

What was surprising, but not really surprising, was the number of dead Highborn that lifelessly hugged the snow. These were the young men that lived in the best part of Sumetai. They'd never had to worry about food or clean drinking water. They'd never worried about warmth. These young men had always been taken care of and did not know the meaning of struggle. Finn guessed that so many were dying because they were trying to cure themselves of their parched throats by swallowing snow. This was a bad idea.

All Spuds, Sprouts, and Sparks knew the dangers of eating snow, especially snow that wasn't fresh. This could cause even more dehydration and even hypothermia if the snow wasn't melted first. His suspicions of Highborns eating dirty snow were confirmed when he spotted one throwing up at the edge of the caravan. Finn wanted to help him, he really did, but he himself felt fatigued from lack of water and food.

FINN WAS asleep when the first spear whizzed past him, striking a redheaded Spark in his throat. Loud cries rang through the forest of snow-covered trees, followed by the shouts of the Commanders that rode on top of the mammoths.

Problem was, none of the new recruits knew what these commands meant.

"We're under attack!"

"The bandits have us surrounded!"

"Take evasive maneuver number nine!"

"Use wagon cover!"

"Cut them close, boys!"

Finn's head whipped left and right frantically as he tried to figure out who to listen to. A sudden burst of flames erupted from a cart a little further down the caravan. This scared the mammoth carrying his wagon and it took off, the jolt flinging Finn off and into the snow in the middle of the road. His head banged against a hidden stone and everything began to wiggle in his vision. A loud ringing filled his ears as he lifted his torso up, shaking his head as he did so.

An older man, who he recognized to be the driver of the cart on which Finn had been sleeping, was bent over and yelling something in his face. Finn just stared at him dumbfoundedly, at a loss of what to do. The man slapped him and grabbed him by the collar. He kept spitting words at him until a spear lodged itself through the side of his head. The man let go of Finn and fell to the side.

Two hands clasped around Finn's throat, and he was lifted to his feet. The man before him wore a long wooden mask that depicted some sort of carnivorous dinosaur. The bandit shook Finn, trying his best to snap his neck—and it would have worked, too, if his father's amazing training hadn't kicked in.

Finn's knee shot up and pumped the bandit's balls back up into his body. The man screamed, releasing Finn's throat and clasping his groin. Not knowing what else to do, his brain still a jumbled mess from its meeting with the hidden stone of doom, Finn pulled off the mask from the bandit and smacked him with it.

The bandit flew to the left, his hands still cradling his baby-makers. He was still conscious when one of the Commanders walked over to him and stomped on his throat.

"Way to go, soldier! Here, take this!" The man handed Finn an already-bloodied sword. It was heavy and he had to take hold of it with both hands. The Commander slapped Finn on the shoulder. "You look a mess, kid! Here, take this, too!" He pulled out the long smoking stick from his mouth, put it in Finn's, spun him around and had him face the forest. "Go get 'em!"

The Commander took off down the caravan, cutting

down two more bandits with his sword, a war cry echoing back to Finn's ears. There was chaos everywhere. Fire. Blood. Splintered wood. Roaring mammoths.

And what did Finn do? He stood there, a nasty smoking stick in his mouth and a long sharp heavy object held in his quivering fists.

He turned his head and saw that the wagon in which he'd previously been sitting had turned over—and then, an amazing idea came to him. It wasn't courageous, but damn, it was a good one!

Dropping the sword, Finn fell to his hands and knees and crawled back to the wagon. Then he thought the better of it, turned, and grabbed the sword again. Once he'd made it under the wagon, he tried his best to calm his breath. He kept the sword in both hands and tried to stop them from shaking but they refused! The world began to waver and Finn grew very dizzy. At first, he thought it was from hitting his head, but as the distortion to his vision grew worse he realized that he'd been puffing on the smoking stick.

Colors merged with one another. The screams of dying soldiers, kids, and bandits melted together and changed in pitch. The surrounding trees grew mouths and sang lullabies to him. His father was lying next to him and petting his hair. His mother was on the other side of him. He turned to her.

"Mother!"

This was not a cry of excitement, nor one of love…no, it was a cry of fear, for his mother's face was a wreck. Half her skin was missing, as were most of her teeth. One eyeball hung lazily from the socket, held only by a single red vein. The only reason Finn recognized her was her long, curly, green hair and her two thin eyebrows that always perked up.

After a few seconds, her terrifying form melted into the

snow. Feelings of dread were replaced with feelings of ecstasy. Finn began to enjoy the commotion beyond the wagon. The walking forms holding spears seemed to be dancing. They beckoned for him to come out from under the wagon.

And he listened.

An unknown force spun his body around, while a long wooden spear pulled tightly against his throat. He tried to yell something out but could push no air through his windpipe. The familiar sensation of suffocation overcame him and he struggled as hard as he could but it was no use. The bandit was just too strong.

Two dancing, spear-wielding forms appeared in front of him. Their masks, one a triceratops, the other a tyrannosaurus, sprang to life! The horns of the triceratops jutted in and out of Finn's vision while the t-rex snapped angrily at his face. He was certain he could feel its spittle flying against his cheeks.

The colors of these masks—blue, orange, green, red, yellow, purple—intermingled and danced with one another. The faces of the dinosaurs lunged this way and that. Finn wanted to puke now, or had he already? His stomach was in knots. What was going on?

"Please...stop," he pleaded, his eyelids flickering, his eyeballs floating to the back of his head.

A larger form, one not wearing a mask, fell from the trees and landed softly in the snow. Finn couldn't tell whether it was a male or female, but it was tall and skinny. Very skinny. It joined the dance of the triceratops and tyrannosaurus and, after a few seconds, these two disappeared.

The spear was still pressed tightly against Finn's throat when the strange form, having dispensed of the menacing mirages, turned and began walking towards Finn and his assailant. As it grew closer, the face became clearer.

One red eye. Pale white skin. A man.

A fist whizzed past Finn's face and the spear dropped to the ground a moment later. Finn put his hands to his throat as he tried to pull air into his lungs, still wounded from the harsh smoke of the smoke stick. The person turned and started to walk in the direction of the trees, the black shadow of its body contrasting the fires all along the caravan. This was no Commander. This was no soldier.

"Who—who are you?" Finn choked.

The person's head turned. A soft and whispered voice miraculously made it to Finn's ears.

"Nobody."

6

FINN'S FURRY VISITOR

Only one Commander checked on Finn that next morning. They'd had him laid on a thin blanket under a tent bustling with the wind.

"It's a miracle you're alive, kid," he'd said, and that was all.

Finn had awoken to the sounds of hustling soldiers trying their best to salvage as much as they possibly could from the wreckage. Last night's epidemic was still unclear in Finn's mind—until he heard his personal medic alert the higher-ups that he was still slightly under the influence of tree-star dust. Finn was then thrown in a cage on the furthest wagon down the caravan. There was no debate. He tried three times to argue his case, that it wasn't his fault, but a backslap to his face had him quiet.

Finn would have done anything to smell the gas of his old mammoth, as the one that pulled him now was much, much worse. Something was *wrong* with it. The hot air that came out of its ass told Finn that the animal was sick; either that, or it was dying.

While they had been escorting him to his cage, Finn was

able to get a good look at the damage. Bodies littered the ground, most of which were already partially covered with fresh snow. The soldiers didn't care to bury them, and so they just left them there. For the first twenty minutes or so of the ride, Finn could feel his cart being pulled over the dead soldiers and bandits, and could hear their bones crunching underneath the massive feet of his mammoth.

"So, this is rock bottom," Finn whispered to himself. "Less than a week in and I've already screwed it all up."

"Quiet!" yelled the mammoth driver.

Only a quarter of the caravan had been hit by the attack of the bandits. They had been smart enough to target the rear which held the supplies and, surprisingly, had had the least amount of guards. Well, there'd been a lot of guards, actually, but these were mostly the fresh recruits. The majority of the bodies in the snow belonged to young Sprouts, Spuds, Sparks, and Highborns, with a few real soldiers sprinkled in.

If the bandits attacked again—if there were any more of them left—they would surely attack the rear once more. Finn almost laughed out loud at this thought because *he* was in the rear. There was not a single wagon, mammoth, or person behind him. It was just himself and his wonderful view of red snow.

After a while, the carnage of last night's events was left behind, replaced by the breathtaking sight of beautiful wilderness. Finn had never been out this far, always choosing to remain in Sumetai. Everyone knew the dangers of leaving the protective walls of the city. There were just too many things that could go wrong. Avalanches. Falling icicles. Predators such as the saber-toothed cats. Frostbite. Getting lost. Nomadic savages.

All of these were valid and very possible. Not a week

went by in Sumetai without stories of adventurers dying terrible deaths, floating from mouth to mouth. It was just the way life was in the frosty lands of Shimoshimo.

The thoughts of these horrible things had Finn at the top of his game. Although he was a prisoner, his fear of dying out there in the cold unforgiving wilderness made him the best damn rear lookout the army had ever had.

It was during one of his lookout shifts in the middle of the night that he spotted the tracks.

Or, at least he thought he did. He was pretty sure that his fearful thoughts were playing tricks on his mind and placing false images into his vision, so he ignored them. Still, he kept an eye out, but every once in a while, his eyes would catch a couple of indents in the soft snow. They were too far away for him to see if they had claw marks, so he had no real idea what they were. It wasn't likely that these were saber-toothed tiger tracks—they weren't known to be this close to the jungles of Koosahmoorah.

On his second night locked in the cage, however...he spotted one. Or, rather, it spotted him.

As ALWAYS, a fire was kindled but too far away for Finn to get any real benefit, just enough to keep him alive. Strange black bugs he'd never seen before had found him and attached themselves to his body, adding another element to his misery right along with the bone-chilling cold. It was a constant struggle in keeping the sticky bastards off of him and he doubted sleep would come.

In front of his iron bars was nothing but blackness, and the trees did an amazing job of blocking all light from the stars and moon. If he stared into the darkness for too long, imaginary explosions of colors would begin to appear. Finn would then manipulate these explosions and even form some shapes.

He was in the middle of imagining his mother, the proper way she should have been remembered, when two very faint yellow lights beamed in the night. It would have been impossible for anyone near the fire to see these two yellow dots but to Finn they were so bright that he almost had to shield his eyes.

The two yellow lights grew larger every minute, and as the fire behind Finn's wagon danced, so did its reflection in the two mysterious lights. His heart jumped into his throat as he realized these were eyeballs—and not just any eyeballs. These were the eyes of a predator.

Finn wanted to cry out, but he'd been completely silent for two whole days and he wasn't sure if he could. Did his voice still function properly? Why would he alert the soldiers that a smilodon lurked about? They put him in this cage, didn't they? If anything, they were the ones in real danger; Finn had iron bars to protect him from the predatory cat. No, he should let them die.

Morbid thoughts rushed through Finn's head. His mind wasn't right; he was malnourished and thirsty. He wasn't a shaman, medicine man, or an herbal healer, but he didn't need to be to notice that small traces of mania were settling inside his brain.

And so, Finn did not alert anyone and kept up the staring match with the eyes. They were about the size of two small stones when the pink, upside-down triangle of a nose poked itself through his cage. A thick, nasty scar crossed over the whiskered snout told Finn it had seen its fair share of fights in the past. Condensation formed on the cold iron bars as hot breath moved through wet nostrils and into Finn's face.

Finn raised his hand. He could sense what this beast wanted. It was hungry, just like him. They had something in common. He understood this saber-tooth, he understood it very well. If he could have, he would have mentally told the beast to have at it.

Fresh meat's right around the cage, mister smilodon.

Finn lifted his hand over the white-furred snout and could feel its breath on his wrist as he lowered it. The lips of the saber-tooth raised, revealing a good three more inches of its legendary canines. He'd done a ton of research on these animals—they were one of his favorites. He was pretty sure he even had a drawing of Bryce riding atop a fairly large one.

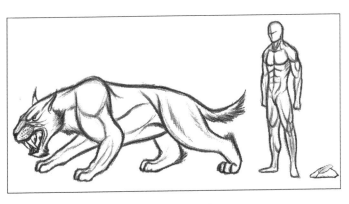

Smilodon (Saber-toothed Tiger)

"Over eight hundred pounds. At least three and a half feet from the ground," Finn whispered to himself, or, at least he thought he did. "You were made to kill, weren't you? You're brave. You're strong...unlike me."

Finn's hand was just about to land on the snout when

the saber-tooth let out a light grumble from its throat. He froze his hand just as the feline pulled its head out of the cage. The smilodon then turned and walked back into the darkness. Finn couldn't help but wave as he admired the shoulder bones work underneath the thick skin with each of its graceful steps.

Most information Finn was able to get his hands on had explained that smilodons were solo hunters, preferring to take down small- to medium-sized prey by themselves. They would then have their fill before abandoning the carrion for opportunist animals to take from the scraps.

However, as Finn's body was giving into his fatigue, the last thing he saw was a good dozen sets of yellow eyes, each reflecting back at him the flickering flames of the dying fire. Everything he'd read had been wrong. They weren't solo hunters after all.

"It's a pride," he said, resting his head on the bars, "and they're hunting something."

7

FINN THE FANTASTIC

THE NEXT DAY WHEN FINN ROSE HE QUICKLY CHECKED FOR ANY signs of smilodons but could not find any. It was as if it had all just been a dream. When the caravan began to move again, Finn kept his eyes peeled for any sightings of the saber-toothed cats but never saw one and nor did he feel their presence in the distance. It was as though they had all vanished.

This might have been because the sick mammoth, the one that had given Finn hell for so many days, had passed on during the night and the pride was busy feasting on its deserted body. Finn, however, highly doubted this. No predator as smart as the smilodon would waste its time on bad flesh.

The new mammoth that pulled Finn's wagon was half the age of the last and not nearly as smelly. They travelled at an incline now as they approached the very outer boundaries of Koosahmoorah. Finn could feel a slight rise in the temperature and he noticed that there was less snow on the tree limbs.

Now that they had reached a decent altitude, Finn was

able to look down upon his city of Sumetai, half of which was built on the face of the largest mountain in Shimoshimo. Although it was beautiful, the city had been devastated multiple times by avalanches. The settlers who'd first built the foundation that would become Sumetai most likely hadn't understood the idea of avalanches. What's worse, even after experiencing multiple catastrophes, the city continued to grow.

But who would be stupid enough to live on the side of the mountain when they could reside safely at the bottom and further away from the deathly avalanches? Why, that would be the working classes. Spuds, Sprouts, and Sparks shared the face of the mountain. The Highborns forced the Spuds to build their homes at the highest point, followed by the Sparks, and then the Sprouts—and this was law. Sometime, years before Finn was born, the evolving people of the snow had realized their mistake and quickly adapted by creating an ingenious class system. It only made sense to push the ugliest-haired people to the top and let them take the brunt of nature's angst. Pure genius.

However, there had only been one avalanche since Finn had been alive, and although it had been deadly, he and his father and mother had survived. The death toll had been enormous, the Spuds taking most of the hit, followed by the Sparks. Although barely any Sprouts had been harmed, Finn remembered his mother standing on the porch every day after that, checking the mountains for any sign of avalanches.

Thought of his mother put a lump into Finn's throat, but over the years he'd found that shaking his head and whipping his hair across his face always helped to push her beautiful image from his thoughts. He continued to focus on the city below.

The two largest structures were that of the royal castle and the Stadium of Athletics (or as Finn liked to call it, the Stadium of Dinosaur Abuse and Needless Death...of Doom). The royal castle was known for its gigantic three pillars made of blue stone. The ancient architects, trying their best to depict the horns of a triceratops, had the three towers narrow the further they raised. At the very top, through amazing architecture skills that should not have been present at the time, the builders were able to angle each of the tips backward, creating realistic-looking horns.

At the bottom of the castle, the depiction of the triceratops continued. The bonyfrill, the top part of a triceratops which protected the neck, was created through one large rectangular building. This building consisted of the courthouse, the dining hall, the royal family's bedrooms, the kitchen, as well as the rooms of the private guards, cooks, and servants. On top of this large bonyfrill building stood a special arena built for games designed only for the eyes of Highborns. Finn wasn't exactly sure what went on up there but he could only guess it was more lancing, duels, and races.

The Stadium of Athletics was not nearly as special. The architects had built it in the shape of an oval and was an eyesore. The outer walls were constructed with cheap materials, and were constantly falling apart. These walls served as the perfect spot for the homeless to relieve themselves, delighting the noses of all those within the surrounding half mile with the smell of dried piss.

Surrounding the Stadium of Athletics, one could find not only actual trash, but trash businesses as well, such as brothels, gaming houses, and underground black markets (which were actually built underground in the very forbidden and very dangerous ice caves). Finn had never been to this area of Sumetai, nor did he ever care to visit.

The view of the city didn't last long, as the trees grew denser, but the wilderness gave Finn more than enough amusement. Before leaving with the army, he'd considered bringing a large wad of drawing parchment, but doubted it would have lasted very long. Instead, he'd peeled off a piece of wood from the bottom of his cage and used it to carve rough sketches of whatever he saw. He made a vow to himself that once he was around proper parchment and ink, he would make real sketches of all the amazing things that he saw. The saber-tooth cat would be the first on his list.

Now that they traveled through the mountains, Finn was suddenly getting fed more food, which made him suspicious. It wasn't just the larger portions that had him on edge, but the sick sideways smile the driver of his mammoth gave him as he handed him his bowl of slop. At first, Finn didn't touch the food, afraid it was poisoned or something. However, it wasn't long before he was inhaling the slop, nearly choking on it as he gulped it down his throat. He was pretty sure it was just stale bread and water mixed together but he didn't care. The hunger and thirst were killing him, and this disgusting crap took the edge off both.

Three days passed of this better-than-usual treatment, and Finn was not only feeling more full but more energized. The negative side to this was he was now aware of how uncomfortable he was in the cage. At least with the hunger he'd been a little too insane to notice.

That night, Finn awoke to the rattling of the lock on the outside of the cage.

"Who's there?" he demanded.

"Keep your mouth shut and do as you're told!" hissed the

voice of the mammoth driver. "You better perform well tonight or I'll leave you tied to a tree in the woods!"

"I don't understand," Finn said.

"Quiet!"

Again, Finn whispered, "I don't understand."

A hand came out of nowhere and slapped Finn across the face but he dared not cry out. He tasted blood as the driver yanked him out of his cage, landing face-first into the snow. Lucky him—there was no hidden stone this time.

"Get up, you little shit! This way!"

The driver pulled on Finn's arm to try and stand him up but the imbecile must not have understood how muscles worked. If you have them crossed for days on end, only allowing them a bathroom break every eight hours, they're not going to function properly!

For fear of being slapped again, Finn forced his legs to work as he was pushed from behind towards the woods. He stopped.

"Keep goin'!" snapped the driver, shoving him in the back. Finn didn't budge.

"I prefer to be left in the cage than left behind!"

"We're not leavin' ya! We're just gonna have us a little fun is all."

Finn's thoughts went to a very dark place in his mind as he was pushed forward. He wasn't sure what this man wanted from him, but if it was what he thought it was, then he would rather die. Even if it meant being picked slowly apart by troodons!

Finn couldn't help but shiver at the thought of these three-foot-tall feathered raptors taking bite-sized chunks out of his body. He could practically feel their serrated teeth sinking into the meat of his arms and legs as he struggled against his bindings. Dying like that would be one hell of a way to go...

The snow grew deeper the further they walked, as did Finn's fears. After ten minutes or so, he caught sight of flickering yellow light, followed by sounds of men talking and laughing.

"Who are they?" Finn asked.

"Not another word!" the driver warned, slapping the back of Finn's neck. "Just do as you're told!"

There were three soldiers standing by a crackling fire, each with a mug in his hands. Finn didn't have to see the reds of their cheeks to know they were drunk. On the ground, by each of their legs, was a lower-caste recruit no older than himself. They looked just like him, too—scared and confused.

"It's about time you showed up," said one of the soldiers, lifting his mug and taking a swallow.

"You know how it is trying to settle down a young mammoth!" said Finn's driver, shoving him one last time. Finn stumbled towards the fire. "They just don't wanna sleep!"

"I'm just giving you a hard time, Verne. What do we have here?"

"This here's Glenn!"

"It's Finn," Finn corrected. He winced as Verne, his driver, lifted a hand to give him another slap but one of the other soldiers handed him a mug of ale.

"He's fightin' for you, ain't he?" asked the soldier. "Why damage the merchandise?"

Finn could feel his hands begin to sweat at the sound of the word "fight." So, that's why he'd been getting fed better than usual. His driver was trying to fatten him up! Or, more realistically, give him enough energy to *perform,* as he had said. Finn couldn't help but feel a little relieved—this was much better than what he'd imagined. However, this didn't last long once he took a look at his opponents.

There were two green-haired Sprouts, one red-haired Spark, and another young soldier sitting a ways from the fire all by himself, a Spud, by the looks of his brown hair. All of them were taller and wider than Finn, except for the Spud. This poor excuse for a soldier looked to be more of a child than anything and belonged less in the army than Finn did. He was half his height and had the face of a baby. There were shiny lines under each of his eyes from past tears and his cheeks were sunken in from malnourishment.

How the hell did this child get drafted?

Verne grabbed the mug and took a big swallow. "Good thinkin', why diminish my chances? He'll get enough beatings soon enough." He laughed and took another drink. Then he pointed the mug at his friends. "You all haven't started bettin' without me, have ya?"

"Five more minutes of keepin' us waitin' and you bet your arse we would've started," said one of the soldiers. At his foot was the fattest contestant for the night's games. His hair was green and cut short, his eyes staring down at the snow. It looked as though he'd done this before.

"Shut your pie hole, mammoth shit," spat Verne. He lifted the mug to his lips but stopped when he noticed the small Spud. "What's with the baby?"

The tallest of the soldiers, one with long blond hair, plopped his hand on Verne's shoulder. "We thought we'd spice things up tonight! This one's going to get the bloodlust going! Get this: whoever kills this one gets triple rations until the Prince sends us back home! Simple and satisfying. If no one kills him, then we simply leave him out here and we continue our game."

Verne squinted down at the little Spud. Fresh tears started pouring from the boy's eyes as his bottom lip curled and quivered. "That's an amazing idea," Verne finally said. "That's why you're head commander. You always have the best ideas, you do. If it were up to me, you'd be the one leading this caravan, not that overhyped Bryce bastard."

The Highborn smiled and nodded. "I wholeheartedly concur."

"Well, you heard 'em!" Verne shouted, finishing his drink and handing it to another soldier for a refill. "Who here wants triple rations?"

Finn snorted silently. Who in their right mind would kill one of their own just for more food? The soldiers were out of their minds if they thought—

The fat Sprout stood up, his head still facing the snow. He walked over to the Highborn and lifted his hand.

"I—I will."

"Of course, you will!" cried the Highborn. "Who would have guessed the fat-ass would be the one wanting triple rations? I sure wouldn't have!"

The Sprout didn't even flinch at being called fat. Finn didn't doubt that he'd been called that all his life. Obesity was rare in the lower-class people who didn't have the funds to afford mounts— if they wanted to go anywhere, they had to walk. Not only that, but Spuds, Sparks, and Sprouts usually held manual labor jobs such as foraging, farming, hunting, building, and, well, foot soldiers. Not many of them were fat.

"Don't just stand there," said the Highborn, spinning the Sprout around to see his foe. "Go get him!"

Finn couldn't help but gasp when the young fat soldier stomped towards the cowering Spud. He gasped again when the Sprout didn't hesitate to send a roundhouse to the young soldier's face.

"Stop it! Please!" cried the Spud, covering his face as the fat boy sat on his stomach, raining down upon him a flurry of punches.

Finn covered his eyes as drops of blood flung into the air as the Sprout lifted his fists over and over again. Once again, Finn wasn't even aware of what his legs were doing. He just opened his eyes and there he was, standing over the Sprout who was giving him a confused glance over his shoulder.

"Get off of him," commanded Finn. These words were certainly not his own. Borrowed, most likely, from the fantasies of him being a Bizzare Blade-wielding Champion.

I am Finn the Fantastic. I am Finn the Fantastic. I am Finn the Fantastic.

The fat Sprout stood up from the boy, his face emotionless, his eyes dead. Finn understood this face; it was the face of survival. Underneath his legs was the boy who lay motionless, eyes shut. Red snow covered his body, his hair matted down with his own blood. He wasn't moving and Finn couldn't tell if he breathed or not.

"You don't have to do this," Finn whispered to the Sprout. "We aren't savages."

"What the hell do you think you're doing?!" shouted Verne. "Why, I outta—"

"Wait," said the Highborn Commander, putting his hand out to stop Verne from walking over to Finn and kicking his ass. "I have an idea. You like being a hero, boy?" he called over to Finn.

With no answer readily available, Finn just stared at the commander.

"I know you're not deaf, soldier. What's your name?"

"His name's Finn," Verne answered.

"Did I ask you?" The Highborn glared at Verne, who hunched his shoulders and looked away, running his fingers anxiously through a strand of his red hair. It seemed that even outside of Sumetai, out in the wilderness where there was no one watching, the rules of the caste system still applied. A Spark was still nothing but a lousy, red-headed human.

"I'll ask you again, soldier, what is your name?"

"Finn," he answered, trying to straighten himself up with a little more confidence. It wasn't working too well.

"Finn? Finn what?" The Commander walked up to him and Finn nearly gasped at his height. He must have been six foot five!

"F-F-Finn...Finn..."

"Spit it out!" The Highborn raised a hand to slap him.

Without knowing what he was saying, Finn shut his eyes and shouted, "Finn the Fantastic, sir!"

A large gust of wind flew through the trees. The fire flickered dangerously, nearly extinguishing itself. The patrons of the camp went quiet and all eyes were on Finn. *Finn the Fantastic.*

8

THE MIDNIGHT GAMES

"Finn...the Fantastic?" asked the Highborn Commander. He bent himself to Finn's level and put his face in his. "And what makes you so fantastic?"

Again, Finn was without words. His head began to shake without him telling it to. That was all he could muster. The best he was able to do was to keep his teeth from chattering. Was it him, or did it just get colder?

"Well, if you're so *fantastic* then I don't see why you can't take on all these young soldiers. However, that would be unfair, wouldn't it? I mean, if you're fantastic then these chumps will be nothing to your mighty fists!"

Finn bit his bottom lip, refusing to make eye contact. Instead, he looked over at the baby-faced Spud who was now rolling on his side and coughing. The fat Sprout kept his eyes on the snow while sniffling, and wiped his pudgy nose with his knuckles.

"What do you say, Finn the Fantastic?"

"I don't want to."

"What's that? I can't hear you."

"I said I don't want to fight!"

"Ha! Well, that's too damn bad, isn't that right, boys?"

The rest of the Commanders nodded their heads but said nothing, tending to their ales instead. Tension was tight around the fire, even for those who were in no danger. Just who was this Highborn? Finn forced himself to look up at him and found that one eye was green and another blue. He was a very beautiful man, and beautiful people never had to work a day in their lives. Why would this one choose to join the army?

The Highborn sighed and walked back over to where he'd placed his mug in the snow. He extended his hand and one of the Commanders picked it up and gave it to him. The Highborn took a very loud slurp, squinting as he looked up through the conifer trees at the stars.

"Tell you what. You want to save the little boy, Finn the Fantastic? I'll give you a chance. Soldiers!" The Highborn looked at the remaining three young recruits. They didn't look back up at him. "I will triple the rations to whomever can kill the Spud. By the looks of it, our fat friend here has already done most of the work. And! Whoever doesn't at least try, and I mean really try, they will be left out here to die. Do I make myself clear?"

Silence.

"DO I MAKE MYSELF CLEAR?!"

"Yes, sir!" the boys cried, each standing up as quickly as possible. They turned to the Spud, but their eyes were on Finn.

What do I do? What do I do?! I just can't abandon him...but where does that leave me? What options do I have?

An idea came to Finn.

"Don't any of you touch him!" he shouted. "I'm a master martial artist! If any of you so much as lay a finger on this soldier, I will break it!"

67

"Oh, you've got to be kidding me," said the Highborn Commander. "Don't be stupid, soldiers! He's bluffing!"

"But sir, what about our betting game tonight?"

The Highborn whipped around to the Commander who'd had the gall to ask a question and hissed at him. The Commander gulped and returned his gaze to the ground.

The fresh recruits looked at Finn, their eyes drooping along with their bodies as they turned and dragged their feet toward the wounded boy.

"I'm warning you!" Finn called out. "I'll hurt you!"

He didn't know what else to say. It took everything in him just to push out those lies. What else could he do now but watch?

But if I don't join in...I'll be left out here too...

The first kick came from no other than the fat Sprout. The second punch was thrown by the Spark. His red hair was long and tied in a bun, giving Finn a good look at his trembling lower lip and snot-covered mustache.

The other Sprout, the thin one, wrapped his hands around the Spud's throat and began to strangle him. Finn turned his head away, but he could still hear the gurgling of the little Spud. He was still having his coughing fit but the coughs couldn't go through a closed-off windpipe, which made his body convulse. The Sprout raised his head and screamed out his grief at the moon before bowing his head into his victim's shoulder as he continued to choke out his life.

Tears rolled downs Finn's eyes as he tightened his bite on his lip, drawing blood. He paced in the snow, his head hunched over. He coughed a few times of his own as shame imbedded itself into his heart.

I'm a coward...I'm a no-good coward!

"He-help!" squeaked the Spud. It was a miracle that he could even utter a single word.

And that was that. Finn's heart shoved his brain out of the way and took control of his body. The tears of sadness turned to tears of fury as he charged at his fellow soldiers. They were busy hunkered over the Spud and didn't see him coming. As Finn passed the observing Commanders, an audible "*Woah!*" escaped someone's mouth.

Finn rammed his body into the fat one, who lost his balance and fell sideways into the snow. Next, he charged at the Sprout who had his hands around the Spud's throat, and kicked him right in his face. Blood shot out in a line from the soldiers nose as his head snapped backward, only the whites showing in his eyes. The Spark, who was just standing and watching, raised both of his hands and backed away in surrender.

The adrenaline began to fade and Finn tried to imagine how he must have looked to anyone watching—like an animal, no doubt! His back was hunched over, his hands out with fingers extended like claws. He breathed heavily through a mouth full of spit making him sound like a rabid beast!

"Why are you just standing there?" demanded the High-born. "Kill them both!"

The Spark held one arm with the other, looking away from Finn and out into the woods. The thin Sprout leaned up on his elbow, crying as he wiped the blood from his nose. He looked up at Finn and quickly crawled away.

Finn let a confident smile appear on his face. He'd done it! He'd saved the Spud! He was a Champion after all!

Suddenly, bright yellow fireworks went off in his mind's eye, complemented by a loud *cracking* sound coming from the back of his skull. As he fell, Finn caught sight of the fat Sprout standing behind him, a large stone in his hand.

All Finn could think as he dropped beside the Spud's body was, *Is that...is that the Hidden Stone of Doom?* By some crazy miracle—or bad luck—Finn was still conscious. He pulled himself over the Spud, putting as much of his thin body over him as he could. It didn't take long for the kicks and punches start to roll in.

Everyone was crying; even the fat, emotionless Sprout wailed as he punched his fists into the side of Finn's face. One of the punches did an amazing job of loosening one of his teeth and he could taste the blood running down the corners of his mouth.

They tried to pull Finn off the Spud so they could get to his head. Their dirty fingernails wreaked havoc on Finn's face, but he persisted to keep his head atop the boy's. Finally, a punch made it through and smacked the Spud's face, hard.

All seemed lost when a deep voice boomed through the dark, frozen woods. All things went still; even the light snowfall seemed to pause its powdering of the ground. Again, the voice came.

"HALT!"

Finn knew who it was, but doubted the reality of it. The stone to the head must have finally done the trick. He'd lost his mind. Either that or he was dying, although dying didn't seem too bad right now.

What made him open his eyes was the lack of pain—the raining down of punches and kicks had stopped. He saw the three boys sitting in a line in the snow. They had their hands on their faces as they cried their eyes out. Hovering over them was none other than Bryce Smolder.

"I don't blame you, soldiers." he said. "It was by poor

leadership that you had to endure such terrible, terrible abuse." Bryce turned his head to Finn and gave him the two-fingered salute. "Are you okay?"

Finn returned a poor salute of his own.

Bryce nodded his head and Finn watched as he turned his attention to the Commanders. All except the Highborn cowered beneath a tree; Verne was practically hiding himself behind his comrades. The fire had gone out and now all Finn could see were shades of blue from the moonlight.

Bryce took two giant steps so that he was in front of the Commanders. He extended his large, hairy hand and gripped the Highborn by the throat, raising him and slamming his body into the rough bark of the tree.

"Explain yourself, head Commander Constantine Firefurnace."

Constantine opened his mouth to speak, but only spittle made it past his lips. Bryce must have released his grip a bit, as after a moment he was finally able to say, "Just having a little fun is all, Bryce."

"You call this fun?" Constantine shrugged his shoulders but still kept his hands on Bryce's thick forearms. "What was this game you had them playing?" Constantine didn't answer, so Bryce turned to Verne, who gasped and turned his head away quickly.

"They'll never tell you," Constantine hissed.

"You, tell me!"

"Yes, sir!" Verne shouted immediately, and he did tell him. All of it. Every last detail.

Bryce turned back to Constantine, and even in this dim lighting, Finn was able to see his face turning purple. "That doesn't sound like fun to me." Bryce let the Highborn go and he fell to his knees holding his throat. He sputtered a few times as he tried to catch his breath. "You three, Commanders Verne, John, and Benjamin, you are hereby under arrest for your crime. And as for you, Commander Constantine Firefurnace, I have a special proposition for you. A game, as you call it."

"Oh yeah?" said Constantine, his voice harsh. "And what is that?"

"Oh, I'm sure you will find it very amusing, as it is basically the same game as yours—except you won't be fighting a four-foot Spud, but me, Bryce Smolder."

Constantine spat, "And if I refuse? Will you tie me up to a tree and leave me to the troodon raptors? That's cruel, Bryce, so very cruel."

"You're right," agreed Bryce. "That's why, if you refuse to fight me, I will allow you to run off in any direction besides the one back to the caravan. You will be named a deserter and will never be able to show your face in any large city in Shimoshimo without getting your head chopped off at Rolling Heads Plaza in Sumetai."

The Commanders all gasped—all but Constantine who was still on his knees. He looked up at Bryce with a poisonous glare. Finn doubted his frown could deepen any more than it already had.

"Well," said Bryce. "What say you?"

Constantine kept his eyes on Bryce as he stood. He was only an inch or so shorter than Bryce but about two feet less in width. He spat at the soon-to-be Bizarre Blade wielder's feet and walked around him, hitting his shoulder with his own.

"I expected better from the Second in Queue," Bryce said, shaking his head.

Constantine ignored this, and as he walked passed Finn, he let a small whisper float into his ears.

"I'll find you."

Bryce walked over to Finn and watched as Constantine disappeared into the woods. He bent over slightly and gave Finn his hand. "Are you okay?"

"I'm fine," he said. "Just a little banged up. I got hit in the head with a rock, I think." Finn put his hand to a wet spot on his head and pulled back a bloodied palm.

"We need to get you and this soldier to the medic immediately!" Bryce stooped over quickly to scoop up the Spud but paused. He put his hand to the boy's raw neck and left it there for a few seconds. After that, he stood, shaking his head. He swiped two fingers above his eyebrows, pointed it at the Spud, then back up to the sky.

9

THE MEETING OF TWO FANATICS

BRYCE HAD TO CARRY FINN BACK TO THE CARAVAN. NOT BECAUSE he couldn't walk by himself, but because he wouldn't leave the Spud's body. His name turned out to be Mathew Firepoker. Finn knew the family name, as did many who lived in Sumetai. The Firepoker family was not only huge in number but were kin to the legendary Bizarre Blade wielder, Frank Firepoker. He was the only known Champion to wield the Poker Blade which allowed the Champion to not only cover his body in quills, but to shoot them out at will. Some said that, when he'd mastered the Blade, he was able to lace the tips of the quills with poison.

Until Frank had gotten his hands on it, the Scribe Mages hadn't known the Poker Blade existed. They gave the Blade its name in his honor, which made the story even more awesome.

To think such a strong bloodline had created such a small weak boy, one who couldn't protect himself. If only Finn had reacted faster, if only he'd made a move sooner!

They'd put Finn back in a cage, not because he was in trouble but because Bryce feared that he would harm himself. Bryce remained by Finn, sitting in the wagon next to him. The Champion remained silent for two days until Finn was ready to talk. This was also the first time he'd asked for a meal.

Bryce had a hot plate of potatoes and mammoth meat brought to Finn, and also pulled him out of the cage. The food only lasted a few seconds before it rested at the bottom of Finn's stomach. He felt ready to talk. He told the Champion everything. From the lack of training, to the bandit attack, to his accidental inhalation of tree-star dust, to his imprisonment, and finally, to the midnight games out in the woods.

Bryce apologized thousands of times for not coming to check on Finn after the bandit attack, saying that he would never forgive himself. He'd been busy using his strength to rebuild the wagons that had been destroyed by the bandits, and even had lent a helping hand in bandaging up a few harmed mammoths.

Finn just nodded his head and sat in silence. He didn't need the Champion's apology. It's not like Bryce was responsible for his wellbeing. In fact, he'd done more than enough for Finn. He'd saved him not once, not twice, but three times. It seemed that fate would always have Finn as the one being saved rather than being the savior, and some part of him started to resent Bryce for this.

After another day of riding, Bryce told Finn that he needed to head to the front and check on some things, but that he would be back. As he was leaving, Finn realized he'd forgotten to tell the Champions of his encounter with the saber-toothed cat. However, he remained quiet and let Bryce leave. He just didn't feel like complaining anymore to him—he felt like a tattling child.

If only he'd known what a huge mistake it was to keep things from Bryce.

FINN WAS NO LONGER at the back of the caravan but still he kept his eyes open for any sign of smilodon tracks. It had been two days since his talk with Bryce and his physical wounds bothered him less. As for his mental wounds, that was another story. Growing up so close to one of Sumetai's pterosaur execution cages, Finn had seen his fair share of death, but seeing it so close...that was different. When had the life of Mathew breathed itself out through his lips? Had Finn been on top of him when his soul had left him or was he dead before he got there?

The image of Mathew's smashed, bloodied face kept popping up into his mind. He would go a good half hour without thinking about the boy, only for him to creep back into his thoughts. It felt like guilt had taken on a physical form, and was repeatedly plunging a dagger into Finn's gut.

If I'd only acted sooner. If only I wasn't a coward. If only...

Finn was placed in a wagon with six other soldiers, all much older than him. They did not speak to him, most likely afraid that Bryce would have a word with them if they did. Finn didn't care about not being spoken to. He was more upset with the fact that he had to be protected—that he couldn't protect himself.

Unlike the newly-drafted young soldiers, these soldiers had actual uniforms. They wore a combination of chain-mail, plate, and lots of leather. They wore large mammoth wool capes which had silk sheet sewed to the outsides, dyed with the royal colors of blue and purple. Depending on the rank of the soldier, the color of the outer edges of this silk changed.

Finn had seen a few soldiers walking around with capes that had gold coloring and he figured these must be really high-ranking men. As for the men he was stationed with, the outsides of their capes were dyed red, which probably made them a little more important than a foot soldier.

There was a positive side to being pretty much invisible, and that was that Finn got to listen in on some very interesting conversations.

"Cut them right off!" said one of the soldiers, his long, light red hair bouncing with the wagon.

"How could a father do such a thing to his son? I don't believe it," said a Spud walking behind the wagon. His breath wasn't heavy at all; he was clearly used to these sorts of long hikes.

"I'm tellin' ya! My own brother told me and my brother doesn't lie. His theory is that King Leon's gotten crazy with age and that he was afraid his son might usurp him before his death. So, what does he do? Cuts off his boy's boys is what he does. And to think, this man's running all of Shimoshimo!"

"Bullshit," said the Spud, shaking his head.

"I'm not so sure it's bullshit," said another Spud who was seated on the side of the wagon and gazing out into the woods. "My father was the man cleaning up the royal throne, if you know what I mean. He's seen his fair share of shit, literally. Anyways, he tells me—"

"That's enough. Can't we just ride in peace?" said the walking Spud.

"Let him talk," said the Spark. "I'm curious now. What did your father see?"

The Spud scratched his head. "Well, now that I'm about

to say it out loud it does sound kind of mad. Father says he caught a glimpse of a young boy during one of his cleaning duties. Described him as bald as a babe's asscheek. No hair, no eyebrows, not even a single eyelash! But that's not the worst part."

The walking Spud sighed loudly and took a drink from his water sack.

"I'm almost through. The worst part was his mouth! Father says it was sewed up tight with black lace."

"Okay, no more of this shit," said the Spud. "I've heard enough."

"Oh, you're no fun, Mason," said the spark. "We're just passin' the time! Sure, we don't know any of this is for real but somethin's up, I just know it."

The stories of what had become of Prince Tarek continued, despite the groans of this so-called Mason. Finn hadn't even gone through the trouble of memorizing all of their names because it seemed every other hour the soldiers rotated to some other wagon. Finn, however, stayed put. He'd all but blocked out the talk of the soldiers until his ears caught the word "*bizarre*."

It was the Spark who'd started up the conversation about the Prince. Now, he was going on about what Blade he'd inherited from his sick father.

"But I thought you can only get a Bizarre Blade if the owner dies?" asked a soldier who'd been passing by but found the conversation to be more interesting than patrolling.

"Exactly!" said the Spark, nodding his head excitedly. "Although, I've heard there are other ways."

"Oh, come on, Saul. Are you telling me that you honestly believe Prince Tarek killed his father, who is his king, and claimed a Bizarre Blade? That just sounds ridiculous!"

"Don't stick around this wagon too long," warned Mason, who happened to just be walking down the caravan, checking wagon wheels. "Saul's stories have been known to rot the brain."

"Like you haven't heard the stories of the Chaos Blade!" Saul shouted at Mason as he was walking away.

"Chaos Blade?" Finn asked aloud, making Saul jump. "What about the Chaos Blade?"

"You—you talk?" Saul asked him, his hand over his heart. "You frightened me, boy!"

"I'm sorry. What you said just took me by surprise, is all."

"Do Bizarre Blades tickle your fancy or something?" Saul asked him.

"Sort of," said Finn with a shrug. He didn't want anyone to know he was a Bizarre Blade fanatic and so he played coy. "I guess I'm as interested in them as anyone else."

"Doesn't seem like it." Saul pointed to his forehead. "Then why're you sweating?"

"Uh, because of this damn mammoth wool. I'm wearing too much of it, I think."

Saul rolled his eyes. "Sure, kid. Honestly, I'm shocked you haven't heard the rumors about the Prince and his newly acquired Chaos Blade."

"Do we know for sure that he has it?"

"Think about what you're saying, Sprout. The only way to get a Bizarre Blade that already has an owner is to kill said owner. Or, at least that's the popular idea. Anyway, if the Prince does indeed have ownership of the Chaos Blade, then that means—"

"He killed his father..."

"Right," said Saul. "And the Mage Scribes, who in my opinion are the real people running the show, won't tolerate anyone killing His Majesty. Not even his son. But, like I said, there could be more than one way to transfer a Blade. Who knows."

"What do you think the Chaos Blade does?" Finn asked.

Saul took out a piece of jerky from one of his pouches, took a bite, and offered some to Finn, who took it gratefully. He tried to bite off a chunk and as he did, the tooth that had come loose from his beatings finally came out. Blood poured from his bottom jaw like a river.

"What's wrong with you?!" yelled Saul, picking himself up from the wagon and scooting himself a little further away. "Haven't you ever had jerky before?"

"Sahwee," Finn tried to say through the blood in his mouth. He bent over and spit a wad of red into the snow, into which it sunk at least a foot. He swished his tongue around until he found his tooth and let it fall through his chapped lips and into his palm. He put it in his pouch. There was a good amount of pain aching through his jaw but his interest in learning about the Chaos Blade masked it. Finn pulled the corner of his mammoth cape and bit onto it to stop the blood flow.

Saul used his pinky finger to scrape away jerky that was stuck in his teeth. "What were we talking about? Oh yeah, the Chaos Blade. I've heard only stories, and who knows for sure what's true and what's false? As far as I know, when the king obtained it, he never showed anyone what it was capable of. I doubt it's even called the Chaos Blade!"

"So," Finn said, keeping his cape pinned to the top of his mouth, "you don't have any idea?"

"Of course I do! They don't call me Saul the Storyteller for nothing!"

"Is that your last name?"

"Of course not! That would be stupid. My name's Saul Chandelier, pleased to meet ya."

He gave a lazy two-finger salute and continued chewing on his jerky. After a few seconds, he said, "Well? Aren't you gonna tell me your name?"

"Finn."

"Finn what?"

"Featherstone."

"Featherstone...where have I heard that before? That's a pretty ancient name, isn't it? Isn't there some sort of omen attached to it?"

"That's what they say," said Finn with a shrug, but he really wanted to change the subject. "Can you tell me about the Chaos Blade?"

"You outta count yourself lucky there, Finn Featherstone. Most people can't say they have last names with history. It seems nowadays people are changing their last names from the original and that's a damn shame! I think it's fascinating to have a name based on the first sight our ancient grandmothers saw when they gave birth to our ancient grandfather. I'm not really opposed to the idea of a mother breaking away from the tradition and changing it to *her* first sighting, that's fine. However! It's when people start faking the first sighting at birth that really gets me. Have you heard of the Lightningsword family walking around? Give me a break!"

Finn couldn't help but laugh at this, and it felt so good! How long had it been since he laughed? The last time had been with Monk, he supposed. He'd forgotten how soothing it was. It made him feel as though he wasn't on the back of a dirty stinking wagon heading to God knew where.

"I have heard of them, actually."

"Wanna know their real last name? The one that preceded the amazing Lightingsword name?"

"Oh yeah! Tell me!"

"Get this: the Lightningsword family used to be no other than the Snowshovels! Ha! Not sure I blame them in changing the name, but come on! Lightningsword?"

Finn could feel his shoulders relaxing now. He'd been on edge for so long, but something about this man, something was authentic about him. This was a real person, not just some overly authoritative Commander or immensely tough soldier.

"Alright, you want to know about the Chaos Blade? Or, I mean, what I know of it anyway?"

Finn nodded.

"Well, it ain't much. I've heard rumors that the Chaos Blade creates terrible confusion in its victims. Others say it's a Blade that can cause nearby catastrophes, which is pretty vague if you ask me. I've also heard it could control the minds of others!" Finn didn't know it, but he was leaning in closer and closer to Saul, who was leaning further and further away. "And, uh, the last thing I heard the Chaos Blade may or may not be capable of is causing malfunctions in the body of the targeted enemy."

"Woah," was all Finn said, pulling himself back in his seat as he took it all in. His hand raised to his breast pocket where he'd hidden the leaflet on the Golden Blade. He hadn't read it yet and was afraid to brandish it in front of the other soldiers for fear that they would steal it. However, his instincts told him that he should show it to Saul. It was a crazy and risky idea as this was the best piece of knowledge on Bizarre Blades that he'd ever received. Still, he found himself pulling out the leaflet and handing it to Saul.

"What's this?"

"Read the first page," Finn said, pulling the mammoth wool out of his mouth to check if he was still bleeding.

Saul opened the leaflet, saw that it was upside-down, rotated it and…snapped it shut. His head shot upward as he checked his surroundings like a nervous herbivore. Then, he ducked down and pulled Finn down with him.

"Where did you get this?" he hissed.

"Uh, uh, a friend. Why? What's wrong?"

"What's wrong!" Saul yelled. He realized he'd yelled, rechecked his surroundings, then whispered, "This is Mage Scribe property! Feel that?"

Finn let his fingers slide over the paper and felt something odd. He brought the leaflet closer to his face and found extremely tiny hairs on top of it. When he ran his fingers over the parchment, the hairs seemed to extend themselves to his skin.

"I never noticed that before," he said in awe.

"If you're found with this, then you're dead, kid, you hear me? Dead! This is some highly classified shit you've got your hands on…and I want to read the whole damn thing."

"You're not gonna take it from me, are you?"

"What?" Saul asked, his face twisting in confusion. "You mean, steal it? What do I look like to you? A dirty beggar?"

Finn said nothing.

"Your silence disturbs me…anyway! I would never think of it. First of all, *I* don't want to be caught with it. Secondly, I'm no thief, I just love juicy information. You will let me read it, won't you?"

Finn thought about it a moment. "If I do, will you tell me how veritable it is?"

"What do you mean?"

"Like, when I buy these sorts of things I never know for sure if the information on the Bizarre Blades is true or not."

"Oh, you're a Blade Guru, are yeah?"

"I mean, I wouldn't say that...okay, well kinda—"

"Cloud Blade!" shouted Saul.

"Allows the wielder to take on a gaseous form and cannot take physical attacks unless it's electricity! Easy!"

"Oh, I'm just getting started!" exclaimed Saul, rubbing his hands together. "The Switcheroo Blade!"

"Known to replace objects in the opponent's possession with nearby objects chosen by the wielder! Come on, give me a hard one."

"Don't get cocky, I got one for ya. Let me think...ahah! This one I know for a fact you won't know. Tell me about... the Growth Blade!"

"OH!" Finn said, clapping his hands excitedly. "OH! OH! OH! I know this one, I know I do! It's, um, it's..."

"Give up?" asked Saul, raising an eyebrow.

"Hell no! I know I know it..." Finn snapped his fingers. "Wait, isn't the Growth Blade one of the low potential Bizarre Blades? Yes! Yes, it is! I remember now. The wielder can grow his or her body hair and nails at will! 'Growth Blade' is a misnomer. It was thought that the owner could grow to be a giant. It was made famous by a savage king, who, as the story goes, searched for years to find it. If I remember correctly, he wanted to, um, grow...a certain appendage, as he was born with a less than ideal-sized...appendage."

"And when he finally obtained it," continued Saul, "he quickly realized that it was useless! I'm impressed, Finn Featherstone, really, I am. Do you know the ending of the story?"

"Wasn't he killed by another king or prince who wanted it for the same reason?"

"Yes! Or, like you said, that's how the story goes. It's true what they say, isn't it?"

"What's that?"

"That wars are basically dick-measuring contests."

Finn buckled over, laughing so hard that no laughter came out at all. Saul just chuckled, but it quickly became awkward.

"Alright, boy. It wasn't that funny."

After Finn had finally settled down and was wiping his eyes, Saul asked, "How long have you been studying Bizarre Blades?"

Finn looked up into the trees. He couldn't see the sun through the grey clouds but he guessed it was almost evening. "All my life."

"And what of the Champions?"

"Them too. Not going to lie to you, Saul, I'm a little addicted."

"Then you heard about what happened to Constantine Firefurnace, the Second in Queue. Shame, isn't it?"

Finn tried to keep his face as deadpan as possible. "Yes," he said. "It's a shame."

"You're not alone, Finn; I'm also addicted. Not only with Champions and Bizarre Blades, but anything out of the ordinary, really. If only I could find a job where I could get paid for crazy stories and odd rumors."

"Like the city criers?" asked Finn.

It was Saul now who laughed. He slapped Finn hard on the back, nearly shoving him off the wagon. "That's a good one, Finn! We're a good team, we are. We have a good back and forth."

"I agree. It's good to know someone here in the—"

"How long have we been stopped?" Saul interrupted, looking behind them and down the line of wagons.

The mammoth carrying their wagon was flicking its tail to the left and right, and Finn could feel anxiety steaming out of its thick brown fur and into the air. He didn't know how he felt it, he just did. Something was wrong.

"Something's wrong," said Saul, as if he could read Finn's thoughts. "I'm going up to the front. You wanna come with?"

Finn placed the leaflet of the Golden Blade back into his pouch. Finn had always been the curious type and so, of course, he agreed.

10

MAN VERSUS BEAST

FINN AND SAUL WALKED TOGETHER BESIDE THE CARAVAN. THIS was the first time Finn realized just how tall Saul was. He wasn't a particularly handsome man but had a better attitude than most Sparks. There was a reason why the redheaded people had gotten the nickname "Sparks."

Each time they passed a mammoth, Finn could feel a wave of stress coming off of it; animals were always the first to feel disturbances. As they walked further up the caravan, the tension in the animals became more pronounced.

"Something's got the woolies worked up," Saul said, his eyes focused on making sure he didn't trip in the snow.

"I noticed."

They made it about ten wagons from the front of the line when they were stopped by a few golden-caped soldiers.

"That's far enough," one of them said, holding up the palm of his hand.

"What's going on?" asked Saul.

"It doesn't concern you, soldier. I suggest you report back to your post or—"

"We have a right to know! What's going on?"

"Soldier, if you don't turn your ass around and get back to your wagon, I'll be forced to—"

"Do we have an issue?" asked Bryce, appearing from around the side of a wagon and placing his hands on the shoulders of two of the golden-caped soldiers. He was easily twice their height. When he caught sight of Finn he grinned broadly.

"Suh—sir! I mean, Champion Bryce, First in Queue! We have two soldiers here who will not return to their wagon."

"They not need worry you, Commander. I'll take them from here."

The Highborn Commander returned his gaze back to Saul and sneered. However, this sneer turned into a look of jealous surprise when Bryce welcomed Finn and Saul to join him up at the front.

"But sir!" protested the Highborn.

"Is there a problem, Commander?" asked Bryce, his face showing authentic concern.

"I—uh, no sir. No problem at all."

"Good! Come along, Finn, and...I'm sorry, but have we met?"

"We have not had that pleasure!" exclaimed Saul, who gave the Highborn a real nasty look before passing him. "I'm Saul Chandelier, at your service. I must say, I'm a huge fan of yours!"

"You're too kind, Saul Chandelier. I appreciate your support! If only we could have met in better times..."

"What's happening, Bryce?" Finn asked him. Saul looked at him as if he were crazy for addressing a Champion without his last name. "Oh, don't worry, we've already met."

Saul shook his head in shock as they continued walking.

"It's not good, Finn. You'll see for yourself soon enough."

Finn was going to ask what he meant, but went quiet as

they were forced to squeeze through the narrow passage. The trees had grown very dense and pushed themselves against the road. Bryce had to suck in his chest and stomach and walk very slowly to get through the tight spaces. It was also a tight fit for Saul, but Finn didn't even have to turn sideways to make it through. The sound of roaring water became louder the further they walked, the road becoming more and more icy. Just when they made it to the end of the caravan, Finn gasped as his feet slipped from underneath him. If it wasn't for Bryce's quick reflexes in grabbing his arm, he would have tumbled over the edge of a cliff.

"Careful there, Finn. Wouldn't want you falling down into that ice river."

Finn's eyes grew wide as he stood himself up carefully. Bryce released his wrist slowly and put a hand on his shoulder as he looked over the edge. The source of the roaring water was a half-frozen waterfall which gushed gallons upon gallons of clear, ice-cold water. Every once in a while, Finn caught a glimpse of a flopping fish sailing over it. He would listen for a few seconds, but could never hear the final splash of the fish hitting the river.

Ahead of them hung a wide wooden bridge, covered completely in ice. There looked to have been rope hand-holds in the past but those had clearly frozen and broken off years ago.

"Mr. Smolder, sir," said Saul. "The people running this caravan can't possibly think we can get the mammoths over this bridge, can they?"

Bryce's mouth formed a tight line as he furrowed his eyebrows. He put his fist to his jaw as he thought. "I don't have much control over this, Saul Chandelier. It's up to them." He pointed to a covered wagon, painted red and adorned with all sorts of dangling purple and blue jewels.

From a window, Finn could see that the inner walls of the cart were covered in cushions. "As a Champion, I have no choice but take orders from the Mage Scribes."

"What?!" exclaimed both Finn and Saul.

"You're telling me that there are Mage Scribes in that fancy wagon?" asked Saul.

"Yes," Bryce nodded. "Two of them. Unfortunately, I cannot give you their names, but what I *can* tell you is that they're the best at what they do. They've informed me that the legendary Bizarre Blade we've come for is somewhere around here. If luck is with us, we may not even have to cross the bridge."

Something rustled the leaves in one of the trees, and all three of them snapped their heads towards it.

"What was that?" Finn asked, squinting.

"Probably nothing," said Saul, turning back.

Bryce's face said otherwise. He was looking into the woods suspiciously, and for once, had nothing to say for a while, so Finn and Saul remained quiet.

"I'll be right back," said the Champion finally, turning to the regal wagon holding the Mage Scribes and walking over to it.

"But what of the mammoths? What's got them acting all crazy? Something isn't adding up, isn't it Finn?"

"No," Finn agreed. "Something *is* wrong, but I just can't quite put my finger on it. But...I've felt this sort of energy before. Or, maybe I've just dreamt of this energy before."

"Energy?" Saul raised an eyebrow, crossing his hands over his chest. In the chilly air, his breath was extra white. "What energy? What the hell are you talking about? You're scaring me."

Finn shook his head, not really wanting to talk about it. He'd never explained his gift with animals before, not to anyone, not even to his father. Not because he felt embarrassed or anything, but because he wasn't even sure if it was a real gift or not. He could just be making it all up in his head.

Saul was about to say something, but Finn shushed him and pointed across the bridge. Out from one of the snow-covered shrubs poked out a pink nose attached to the white furred snout of a saber-toothed tiger.

The familiar yellow eyes caught sight of Finn and rested there. He could see the puffs of air spouting out of the smilodon's nostrils as it took in the many scents in the air. He watched it lift its head once it caught a particular odor it had been looking for.

It recognizes me.

"What are you doing?" asked Saul, putting his hand in front of Finn's chest. "Where are you going? We should probably stay here."

Finn didn't know what he was doing, only that his legs had taken on a mind of their own as they usually did when the heart took over. He felt no fear, only a strong pull forward, as he took a few steps towards the bridge. He shoved Saul's arm out of the way. Something, some force, pulled him in this direction. He swore he could hear his name being called somewhere off in the distance as a strong trance took over him.

"Don't be crazy, Finn! Stop right there! It's not safe!" Saul tried to grab hold of Finn but it was already too late.

He stepped onto the icy bridge. His eyes glazed over as the world melted around him. Something beckoned him to continue walking, some power that could not be reckoned with or ignored.

"Stop! Finn! You're gonna get yourself killed!" called Saul, his voice frantic.

Finn answered by taking a few more steps.

"Bryce!" cried Saul. "It's Finn! He's on the bridge!"

A few moments later, Finn could barely hear the deep shouts of Bryce coming from behind him. He couldn't make out what the Champion yelled at him, nor did he really care. He was more focused on the energy that called upon him. At first, he thought that it might have been the smilodon's eyes that had hypnotized him, but was it? Or was it something else that pulled him further onto the bridge? Something inside his gut told him his destiny rested just up ahead; he only needed to worry about walking onward and that was all.

When he'd made it halfway across the bridge, something switched off in his brain, and it was like the world plummeted back into focus. He swiveled his head around and gasped when he discovered where he was.

"What's going on? What happened?" he asked himself.

"Finn! Finn!" came the cries of Bryce and Saul.

He turned around to see them pointing, but not at him.

"Turn around!" he heard Saul shout.

Finn slowly turned his head back around to look at the end of the bridge and there, standing a few feet away, was none other than the saber-toothed tiger. It looked much more mangy than it had that night it had visited Finn in his cage. This beast no longer showed any more signs of its majestic aura, and had replaced this with a more animalistic one. Its ribs showed through its white and grey coat. Multiple scars covered its face, its teeth were a nasty yellow, its gums were red with infection. Its mouth hung open and it breathed heavily. Every few exhales, it lowered its head as a low growl escaped its throat.

The smilodon stood almost as tall as Finn. Its long, white whiskers extended far beyond the width of its body and shook with its breath. It took a step forward and Finn took one backward.

"Finn!" cried Bryce. "I'm coming for you!"

He could hear the Champion's footsteps pounding on the bridge, making it bounce and causing most of the ice to crack. Saul was shouting in the background for him to run but Finn couldn't. He was paralyzed with fear.

The smilodon gave no hint of its lunge towards him, and did so without sound. The beast moved through the air in slow motion and Finn could make out the protective membrane slide over its eyes as its claws slid out of its furry paws.

Finn bent his knees and brought his forearm up to cover his face. A gust of wind flew through his hair as Bryce jumped over his body. The Champion sent a back kick into Finn's chest, sending him flying as Bryce took his place to accept the embrace of the saber-toothed tiger. The sound was that of meat smacking meat. The smilodon roared as Bryce popped it in the jaw with one of his oversized fists.

Finn hit the side of the bridge hard, knocking the air from his lungs. His head popped the hard ice and ricocheted back into the air just in time for him to see Bryce take a nasty slash to his ribs. Finn tried to dig his fingers into the ice but it was no use; he was sliding to the edge.

"Grasp onto something!" came the voice of Saul but there were no ropes for Finn to try and grab. "Hold on, Finn, I'll save you!"

"Stay there!" shouted Finn, just as his legs shot over the side of the bridge. He scratched frantically at the ice and finally was able to slip his fingers into one of the cracks Bryce's heavy footsteps had made.

It looked as though the smilodon and the Champion were evenly matched as they pounded each other with blows. This, however, was an illusion, only what Finn wanted to see. In reality, Bryce's body had been torn to shreds slash after slash by the smilodon's razor sharp claws, easily tearing into his armor. No matter what Bryce did, his punches and knee strikes went completely ignored by the eight hundred pound cat.

In a single, unbelievable moment, it was all over.

The smilodon slapped Bryce across the jaw, forcing his face towards Finn as the cat sunk its teeth into his exposed neck. With one aggressive jerk, the inside of Bryce's throat was exposed to the world.

Finn didn't realize he was screaming as his Champion, his hero, his friend, fell to his knees. The smilodon pounced off its prey, understanding instinctually that the fight was over. It turned its back to the Champion as if to let him die with dignity.

Bryce, with astonishing fortitude, stayed on his knees a while longer. His body convulsed as blood sprayed from his neck with each of his trying breaths. He gave Finn one last red-toothed smile and even managed to perform a sad two-finger salute before face-planting into the ice.

Bryce Smolder, Legendary Champion, Hero to the People, and First in Queue...had fallen.

11

DESTINY FINDS A WAY

IT HAD ALL HAPPENED SO QUICKLY THAT FINN COULD BARELY register that it had happened at all. It was the pain in his fatiguing fingers that brought him back to reality. He wouldn't last much longer; he needed to pull himself up, and quickly! He could mourn later.

"I'm coming, Finn! Hold on!" cried Saul, and Finn could see him taking a few cautious steps onto the bridge.

Finn couldn't waste any more breath on telling him to stay away. He needed all of his energy if he was to pull himself back up. He tried swinging a leg over the edge but only succeeded in making his left hand slip. Now, he dangled from only one hand, his head barely able to look over the edge. He tried replacing his hand back on the bridge but couldn't find the same crack in the ice.

Finn felt them before he saw them coming. Vibrations danced up his arm as the full pride of smilodons sprang from their hiding spots in the foliage on the other end of the bridge. Their footing was perfect, their claws extended, keeping them firmly stuck to the ice as they ran towards the alpha male, the one that had ended the life of Bryce.

The alpha turned back towards them, its white-furred mouth dripping fresh crimson. It opened its jaw and raised its head, letting out a terrible roar. The saber-toothed cats returned this roar with deep growls of their own as they passed the alpha and galloped towards the caravan.

They're going for the mammoths! Finn thought desperately. *I need to get up! I need to help Saul!*

But it was too late. Saul had tried to turn and run but he just wasn't fast enough. The first smilodon to cross the bridge batted the redheaded soldier on the side of his torso. There was so much strength behind the animal's strike that Saul was sent flying out of sight. The man didn't even have time to cry out.

There was nothing else Finn could do but hang there and watch as he tried his best to keep from slipping. No matter what he did, he just couldn't get his left hand to grip. Screams echoed in his ears as the pride of saber-tooths wreaked havoc on the caravan. He could hear the cries of the mammoths and the sound of their panicked footsteps. Finn caught a glimpse of wagons overturning as the mammoths stampeded backwards, no doubt crushing hundreds of soldiers to death.

All but one of these mammoths ran backwards. One, a juvenile, judging by the lightness in its fur, got confused and began trotting in the wrong direction—towards the bridge! The alpha male saber-tooth stood its ground as the disoriented wooly charged forward.

The entire bridge rocked up and down a good two feet each way. It was a miracle that Finn was still hanging on. He waited for the inevitable slipping of the last four fingers that were keeping him alive.

The alpha lunged into the air, crashing into the side of the mammoth's face. The wooly squealed, popping up on its back two legs and punching wildly with the front ones. It tried hitting the smilodon with its trunk but it couldn't reach.

When the mammoth's front legs landed on the bridge, Finn was sent flying into the air, both of his arms flailing as he tried to grab onto anything that would keep him from falling. He landed on his stomach, both arms spread out as wide as possible. He thought he might actually have a chance to pull himself up, but that dream of his quickly vanished when the damned mammoth reared onto its hind legs once again.

This is it, Finn thought. *This is where I die. This is where my journey ends.*

The smilodon hopped back onto the bridge and jumped once more at the mammoth, this time sinking its claws into its belly. The mammoth screamed as it fell backward, the saber-tooth riding upside-down on its stomach. The landing sent a colossal quake across the bridge, and Finn's luck had run out. He was shot backward into the freezing ice water of the waterfall. As he plunged down the breathtakingly frigid waterslide, Finn felt slashes against the skin of his back as broken icicles etched their way through his wooly cape and dug into him.

His body spun a few times in the air, his thoughts nonexistent as he fell to his death. He wasn't truly aware of when he actually...stopped. Freezing water splashed heavily over his head while his legs dangled once again underneath him. Opening his eyes, Finn found himself looking through a light blue window of falling water. He shook his head, trying to defrost his brain.

Blinking water out of his eyes, Finn looked up to see what he'd grabbed hold of to stop his fall, but what he saw didn't make sense. Somehow, he'd grabbed hold of a metal rod wrapped in what looked like orange-dyed leather. This strange object jutted out from the inner coal-grey stone wall of the waterfall. Hanging at the tip of this rod swung three metal chains, each of them sliding over his face as they drifted in the breeze.

Finn turned his attention to finding some sort of foothold he could step onto to relieve his aching grip. He grabbed the rod with both hands, and as he did so, both of his hands vibrated, so much so that he was nearly forced let go.

What the hell was that?

The rod looked to be connected to something wider, but was hidden underneath a thick layer of green algae. Finn let go of the rod with his right hand and began dusting some of it off.

"Ow!" he cried, pulling back a bloodied finger.

He looked back at the algae and saw that he'd uncovered three sharp, triangular metal teeth on the underside of the rod. He replaced his hand back on the rod and tried swinging one leg over it. It took him a few tries, but soon he was sitting on top of it. He let his shoulders fall as he tried to catch his breath. That's when the shivers started.

"I'm duh-dying..." he said to himself. "I cuh-can't believe I'm dying. I'm guh-gonna freeze tuh-to death."

As the cold set in, half of him wanted to give up. To just let the icy cold water consume him and freeze away all his pain. He thought about how funny he would look when someone discovered his rigid body beneath the waterfall—*if* they ever found him, which he highly doubted.

Finn tried shaking the thoughts out of his head once again, but his neck no longer responded. His entire body was becoming numb fast, and it wouldn't be long before he slid over the edge of the rod and fell to his death.

He let his head droop to the side as he searched for something he could grab onto, or perhaps even a platform he could jump to, but there was nothing. The only escape from the waterfall was what looked to be a two hundred foot drop into the water, which alone was enough, not to mention the river of ice that would meet him.

His sight began to blur as his eyelashes froze over, making it nearly impossible for him to blink. His breath grew shallow until he wasn't really sure if he was breathing at all. Finn had always imagined that freezing to death would be painful, but he'd been mistaken. The pain only lasted a minute or two before it was just him and his thoughts, floating in a frozen husk.

Luckily, most of the waterfall fell directly in front of him, but that didn't keep a steady smaller stream falling on top of his head. Finn made sure to keep his lips open so that the water didn't freeze his mouth shut. Both of his nostrils had already frozen over, leaving only the small hole of his lips to breathe through. He wondered how long it would be before the waterfall sealed it up as well. As death approached, the blissful feelings he'd heard from adventurers who'd survived near death experiences never arrived. Instead, fear came knocking at the door.

"I duh-don't wuh-want tuh die..." he moaned airily through his mouth hole without the use of his tongue. "I wuh-want tuh see father...I wuh-want tuh guh-get down..."

Suddenly, the rod he sat on jerked, hitting him hard in the groin—which he was glad he didn't feel.

What's going on?

The rod moved again, then again, then again, creating a motion that seemed to be speeding up. There was the dim sound of metal screeching on metal. This terrible sound grew louder as the gyration of the rod grew more intense.

Finn had thought he was numb to all pain, but the sheer loudness was killing his ears.

Finn yelped when the rod dropped down a foot. His hands and butt were both frozen to it, and his entire stomach lurched as the rod fell yet another foot. The screeching noise grew to an unbearable level as the rod continued dropping, rocking Finn back and forth as it did so. Pink and red powder filled the air, some of it making it into his mouth.

Is that...iron? No...it's rust!

Finn could feel the hair that wasn't frozen to his neck float in the air as his chaotic ride descended to the water below. He wouldn't hit the water with enough force to kill him but it was going to hurt...it was going to hurt very badly.

With one last puff of rust dust and remembering the fact that he couldn't swim, Finn closed his eyes and his legs submerged into the river. As he toppled forward, he sucked in as much breath as he could just before his face dipped into the running water. He'd thought his entire body had been numb but he had been so terribly wrong. It was like getting pricked by millions of thick needles with no end in sight. His heart rate jumped from hardly beating at all to feeling like it would explode from his chest. Panic began to wash over him and it took all of his mental strength to keep from breathing in the water.

Finn spun head over heels, his body still attached to whatever it was that had been stuck in the waterfall wall. In fact, the damned thing was still gyrating underneath him.

It felt like hours, but was in reality probably only a few seconds, before his lungs forced whatever they could get through the hole in his lips. Freezing cold water ran down his throat, making his eyes bulge as he tried to cough it back up, only to take another watery breath.

And then, it was bliss. All was numb and all was good. Mother and Father were holding hands in front of him at the end of a very dark tunnel, both of them extending their free hands to accept him into a big hug. Finn couldn't help but laugh at the familiar sight of his mother towering over his father. He'd always wondered why he hadn't inherited her amazing height.

Finn ran towards them, and just as he opened his arms to embrace his parents, he was stopped by a hulking shadow.

"Where are you going, young hero? It isn't your time yet!"

"Bryce?" Finn asked. "Is that you?"

"It isn't your time yet, young hero!"

"Bryce...Bryce! Where am I?!"

The shadow lightened, revealing a soaking wet version of Bryce Smolder. He stood strong, his chin in the air in his usual heroic pose. He had no visible damage to any part of him, not even his throat. He performed the two-finger salute, then pointed his fingers at Finn and left them there.

"Please, will you take care of my Obsidian-Cinnamon?" Bryce asked, a single tear falling from his eyes and curving around his shaking smile.

"I-I will, Bryce, but...I still don't understand!"

"You've literally fallen into a pool of great responsibility, young hero!"

"What?" Finn asked. "You're not making sense!"

"Your journey doesn't end here, young hero, as it has only just begun!"

Finn gave up trying to ask the Champion what he meant and just stood there in the dark tunnel staring up at him. Tears of his own began to fall down his face. He was warm, so very warm.

"Train, and train hard, young hero! I knew the universe brought us together for a reason. It was you the Blade wanted. Not me. It was never me. I was only its guide. It's time for the Featherstone omen to come to fruition! Let me just say what an honor it was to meet you, Finn the Fantastic."

Bryce put both of his hands on his waist and gave a deep laugh. Finn ran forward and hugged the Champion tightly, burying his wet face in the soft fur that covered his legendary armor.

Bryce bent low and spoke softly. "Oh, and Finn?"

"Yes, Bryce?"

"Wake up!"

Finn's eyes shot open.

12

A BIZARRE AWAKENING INDEED

THERE WERE HOLES IN THE CEILING, AND IT WAS THROUGH these holes that sunlight shined. Sparkling dust filled the air, making the light bend ever so slightly. The room smelled of metal and honey, and it was silent. So very silent.

Finn blinked a couple of times. His head was pounding, and when he tried to sit up he found that he couldn't. He looked down to see three thick leather belts stretched across his body, keeping him stuck snugly to the soft bed he was lying on. He felt something wet on the upper part of his arm. He turned his head painfully to the right and screamed when he saw something—someone—with their tongue in the crease of his armpit!

"What the? Get away from me!" he yelled, trying to move himself away, but the bands were making it impossible.

The person, a girl around his age with soft pink hair and wide green eyes, lifted her head from his. Her tongue dangled out of her lips for a few seconds before she sucked it back up into her mouth. She raised her eyes to the ceiling as she swished around her saliva before performing a dramatic swallow. She raised one finger into the air, and in a high-pitched voice, she said, "That tasted like polka-dots!"

"Who—who are you?" Finn asked, his mouth twisted in revulsion at the girl who'd just licked his armpit.

"Who is she?" asked the girl, pointing to herself. "Who are *you*?" She pointed her finger at him.

Finn was about to answer her when a wave of pain shot across his body, making him tense up. He squeezed his eyes shut as hard as he could until the pain went away. When his body finally relaxed, he said, "No, you first. Who are you? Where am I?"

"Areola will give you all the answers when you first answer hers." The girl tilted her head, her eyes growing wide as she studied him.

"Who's Areola?"

The girl gasped. "How did you know Areola's name?"

"Are you Areola?"

"Are you a mage?"

"No," Finn said, shaking his head. "I'm not. I'm—I'm... who am I?"

"This is to be expected," said an old female voice.

Finn's eyes darted to the foot of his bed, where a very small and even more frail-looking elderly woman sat. Her eyelids were squinted shut so tightly that he couldn't see any part of her eyeballs. She looked to have a permanent smile on her wrinkly face as she massaged his feet.

"Who are you? And why can't I feel my feet?"

"Which question do you prefer me to answer, Mr. Featherstone?"

"Is that who I am?"

The old lady nodded. "Classic case of severe hypothermia, I'm afraid. You're suffering from a tad amount of amnesia. I'll have my student here cook you up a concoction that will cure that right up."

The girl smiled and bowed her head. "Areola is expert in all things cooking!"

Finn's eyes moved from the older lady, to Areola, and back to the lady who'd turned her attention back to rubbing his feet.

"Am I going to survive?" he asked her.

"Oh, I would hope so! You are in very capable hands, dearie."

"Who are you?"

"Why, I'm Nora Nibblefingers, but everyone here just calls me Nibbles."

"And where is 'here'?"

Nibbles chuckled and shook her head slightly. "All in good time, young one. Just know that you are safe. You will be well-taken care of and, if you choose to stay, there is a place for you amongst our people."

"You're joking, right, Nora?" came a deep hissing voice from the darkest corner of the room. "We trained Jade for seventeen years, turning him into the perfect Champion in every way imaginable." The figure walked out of the shadows. Finn couldn't place where he'd seen this person but he definitely looked familiar. "Five of those years we spent searching for this particular Blade, Nora, and all for what? For a single green-headed screw-up to accidentally claim it when..." The man, who had white hair, turned his head and stared at Finn with one wide red eye. "When he should have died."

"Oh, hush now, Silver. You know as well as I do that destiny is more in control than we are of who gets what Blade and who doesn't. It just wasn't the right Blade for Jade, that is all. We have other options, you know."

Silver didn't take his gaze off of Finn. "I still say we kill him and take back what's rightfully ours."

Nora's tiny grey eyebrows came to a point, and Finn could feel her grip tighten around his legs. "Hush, Silver! You're gonna scare the lad to death with that kind of talk! He's been through a lot in the past few days, and besides, the poor thing doesn't even know who he is yet."

"That's even better," snarled Silver, walking more into the light. "He's a nobody. We could all feel a little less guilty about feeding him to the dire wolves."

Finn pulled his head further back into his pillow as he took in all that Silver was. He was tall, definitely over six feet. He had a terrible slouch and his arms hung lazily at his sides. He wore tight black pants and a shirt that was cut open in the front, showing off skin that was even whiter than his hair, which had silver streaks running through it. A black bandana covered one of his eyes, pushing the hair out of his other eye and straight into the air.

Areola made her way back to Finn and she bent over him, putting her face close to his. Her skin was tan, too tan for her to have been a native of Shimoshimo. Her nose was one of the tiniest he'd ever seen, her nostrils angled slightly upward. Her light green eyes sparkled as she studied him, and he did the same to her. Her chin and jawline were more chiseled than they should have been for a girl.

"What are you looking at?"

"Areola does not understand your question."

"Are you referring to yourself in third person?"

"She does that," said Nibbles, releasing his feet and standing up from her chair at the foot of his bed. She looked to be an astonishing four feet tall, maybe four foot and three inches. Her grey hair was tied in the bun on the top of her head, and she wore a light yellow button-down shirt made of yarn that covered her entire body and dragged on the ground. Her most striking feature, however, was the thick scar that started at her chin and ended below her left eye.

"Shoo, shoo," Nibbles said, shaking her hands at Areola. "Go on, go make that concoction like I asked."

"Yes, Mother Nibbles," Areola said, shutting her eyes and bowing her head. Finn had never seen this sort of sign of respect before.

When the girl opened the wooden door and left, Finn asked Nibbles, "Is that your daughter?"

"Oh, my, no."

"Then, why did she call you 'Mother Nibbles'?"

"That's just a nickname the children all call me. Really, honey, you can call me whatever you like. Nibbles, Mother Nibblefingers, it's all the same. I'll respond to most anything, but that's not important. What is important is—"

The door opened again, and in walked yet another tall figure, though not as tall as Silver. He looked down at Finn, shook his head, and walked over to the corner of the room. The sunlight from outside blinded Finn, and it took a few seconds for his eyes to adjust.

"So this is it," said the stranger. His voice was young and male, clear and laced with attitude.

"It?" Finn asked.

"Yeah. *It*," said the person.

"What has gotten into you all lately?" asked Nibbles incredulously. "Have I not taught you all better manners than this? I'm talking to you, Jade Whetstone!"

"Sorry, Mother Nibbles."

"Like I told your Master, Jade, we will find you another Blade. You should know as well as anyone else that occurrences like these do not happen for no reason! Let us say you did claim ownership of this Blade, tell me, what would have happened?"

Jade lowered his head. He was a black male and he too was also around Finn's age. The sides of his head were shaved but he had long dreadlocks on the top of his head which hung over his left shoulder. "If a Blade isn't a perfect match to its wielder, then mastery of the Blade is impossible."

Nibbles nodded her head. "That's right, Jade. So, instead of being a meanie to our guest, you should really be thanking him!"

"Thanking him? Why the hell would I do that?"

"Language," spat Silver from the other side of the room.

"Sorry, Master."

"Because!" exclaimed Nibbles. "If Finn hadn't been so in-tune with his instincts, he never would have answered the call of the Blade! And if he hadn't claimed the Blade then you most certainly would have, and do you know what that means?"

Jade slouched even more, in an imitation of his Master. "I wouldn't have been able to master the Blade."

"Righty-o!"

The door slammed open, smashing against the back wall and sending a few jars that had been resting on a shelf to fall and shatter on the floor.

"Areola has arrived! And she has brought Grim his concoction."

"Dearie, it's *Finn*," corrected Nibbles.

"And how many times do I have to tell you?" said Jade, turning towards her. "Your name isn't Areola, it's Ariel."

"Yes, Ariel knows all these things," said Ariel, looking at both Nibbles and Jade like they were crazy. She walked over to Finn and tried handing him the concoction which was a small vial with a bubbling blue liquid inside of it. However, it was impossible for Finn to even grab the vial as his arms were currently pushed against his body from the leather bindings. "Do you not want your concoction? Ariel made it especially for you! It will bring all memories back to your brain!" A toothy smile formed on her mouth, a little bit of spit drooling out the corner of it.

Finn nodded his head the best he could and wiggled his sore fingers at his sides. "I can't really grab it at the moment."

Ariel tilted her head. "And why not? You don't want Ariel's concoction? Fine!" She lifted the smoking vial of blue liquid over her head and was about to throw it against the wall when, with amazing acrobatics, Nibbles jumped onto the bed, then into the air, snatching the vial out of Ariel's hands.

Finn could not hide the surprise on his face—his jaw hanging open. It just wasn't possible for a lady of her height and age to have done something so miraculous! What was going on? Where was he? Who was he?

"Ariel, that temper of yours is going to get you into trouble," warned Nibbles.

"That's what I keep telling her," said Silver, his back leaned against the wall. He was watching something outside one of the square, glassless windows.

"And you're one to talk," said Nibbles, dipping a finger into the blue liquid and popping it into her mouth. "Mmm! It's perfect, Ariel. You are so talented, sweetie."

Ariel bowed. "Thank you, Mother Nibbles."

"Now, let's try this again. Please, Ariel, pour the concoction into the boy's mouth, but do so slowly, my dear. We don't want to have to resuscitate him twice, now do we?"

The girl took the vial and walked over to Finn's bedside.

Finn tightened his lips, not really sure he wanted to drink whatever the blue liquid was. Foam leaked over the edge of the glass, and smoke puffed out of the small hole on top like a chimney.

"Open wide!" Ariel cried in an even higher-pitched voice. "Ariel has some good yum-yums for you!"

Finn shook his head and sucked in his lips.

"Open your damn mouth or Ariel will open it for you!" roared the girl, her face turning a deep shade of red.

Finn's head sunk into the pillow as Ariel reached out and grabbed him by the jaw. He tried to shake her off but her grip was strong and starting to hurt him.

"Easy, Ariel! Easy!" cried Nibbles. "I swear, must I do everything myself?" Ariel let go of Finn's face and backed up. Nibbles extended her open palm to the girl and she handed her the vial. "Now, Finn, I want to explain to you all that has happened but I cannot do so if you don't even have your memories, dearie. Don't you want to know where you are? Who you are?"

Finn nodded his head.

"Well, then, please oh please will you drink this medicine? I promise you will feel much better."

At first, Finn turned his head away, making sure to keep his mouth shut tightly. However, something in his gut told him that these people had it in their best interest to keep him alive. Besides, did he even have much choice?

Finn turned his head and opened his mouth slightly.

"There we go," said Nibbles, reaching up the bed with her wrinkled hand and pouring the vial's contents into his mouth.

Finn grimaced as the concoction hit his tongue. It burned a little at first, but when that subsided he was left with a delicious blueberry taste, the smell rising through his nose with a minty, cooling effect.

Icy smoke poured from his mouth as he let out a relaxed breath. Finn allowed himself to loosen up a little. He turned over to the old lady but flinched at the horrific face she had on. Her warm smile had changed to an ugly, low-hanging frown. "You idiot, boy! Don't you know not to take food from strangers? Tell me, Finn, do you feel the poison coursing down your throat? How about through your veins? Ha! I can't believe you fell for it!"

"What have you done to me, you old bag?!" Finn screamed, fighting as hard as he could against the leather bindings. He pulled himself up with all his strength but the leather would not give, it wouldn't even stretch! He was doomed!

That's when he heard the hysterical laughter coming from the floor. He leaned over to see the old lady on her back, kicking her feet in the air and holding her chest. All the eyes on the room were on her as she had her fit of laughter.

"What did you do to me?" Finn asked her.

"Hahaha, oh my, I'm so sorry, Finn, my dear." A couple more laughs came out of her before she could continue. "I—I just couldn't help myself!" Silver was by her side and offered her a hand, which she took. She was wiping tears out of her eyes as she walked over to the bedside, still chuckling as she did so.

"You think poisoning people is funny?" Finn asked her. "I'll have you know that I am friends with a Champion and he'll—"

Memories flooded back into his brain. Thoughts of his mother, her funeral, his dad's cheaply performed leg surgery, painting, drawing, his fascination with animals and his connection to them...then came the memories of him leaving father to join the army. He remembered his encounter with Constantine...meeting Saul...Bryce...Bryce!

"Where's my friend?!" screamed Finn, once again fighting the leather keeping him attached to the bed. "Where's Bryce?!"

The smile on Nibbles' face fell away. She and Silver looked at each other. He shut his one eye and bowed his head slightly, as did the old lady.

"I know this is all a lot for you to take in, Finn. The concoction has already started working to repair all of your memories and it will take a few more minutes for everything to become clear. However, I'm afraid that the Champion Bryce Smolder is no more. I wasn't there to see it, but my top student was."

"Student? What are you talking about?"

Silver raised his head. "I saw your friend, the Champion Bryce Smolder. He died protecting you from a smilodon. I was in the area, searching for the Bizarre Blade, trying to get my hands on it before the army of Prince Tarek got to it."

"Then what happened?" asked Finn, not entirely sure he believed what this man was saying. It was impossible— Bryce Smolder was immortal!

"How can you not remember?" asked Silver, shaking his head in disgust. "The smilodon and wooly fought it out— too bad they'd chosen the wrong place to do it. After you slid off into the waterfall, I assumed you were dead. I was going to continue my search for the Blade while the army was distracted by the mammoth stampede. That's when the bridge snapped, sending both the wooly and the smilodon to their deaths."

"But we never *found* the saber-tooth," interjected Jade.

"Right. We didn't."

"And where was I?" Finn asked. He tried to concentrate as hard as he could, struggling to remember the very last moments. All he could bring to light was the feeling of freezing to death, rushing water, and the taste of rust.

"It seems my student Silver here has gotten softer with age," said Nibbles, looking up at the tall man with a kind smile. She patted him on the forearm.

Silver gave no comment on this, but continued his story. "The chaos of the mammoth stampede took turn after turn for the worse. I figured it best to retreat and come back later. The army was in such disarray I figured they would need to return to Sumetai to resupply and grab another Champion to lead the search. I believed the Bizarre Blade would be there when I got back. But..." Both Jade and Silver turned their heads away, their lips puckering as if they'd tasted something sour. "But, when I rechecked my Foretelling Fabric, the black dot indicating the whereabouts of the Blade was—"

"You stole my Blade!" interrupted Jade, one thick vein pulsing on his forehead. He was bent over and pointed a nasty finger at Finn's face. "It was supposed to be mine!"

"Manners, Jade!" cried Nibbles, turning to the boy. "Silver, please, take your student out of the room."

"No need, I'm leaving." Jade spun on his heel and was just about to walk towards the door when Finn heard him whisper, "Sorry, Mother Nibbles." Then, he left.

"You were saying, Silver?" asked Nibbles, acting as if nothing was wrong at all.

Silver's face was without emotion as he stared out the window, the sunlight gleaming into his red eye. And then, Finn recognized him. He was the man he'd bumped into in front of the Death Cage of Flying Doom! The man who had been barely wearing any clothing! The man with one red eye! This spontaneous memory hurt his head and so he decided to shut his eyes and not say anything.

"What's Foretelling Fabric?" Finn asked. "And, can I please be released from this bed so I can sit up?"

"Oh dearie, I'm sorry! I forgot! I'll go ahead and undo these for you, but I suggest you remain laying down. I can tell by the scrunching of your forehead that you are trying hard to regain your memories. Please, don't do that, it will only give you a nasty headache. Just relax and"—she snapped three latches in succession and the bindings went loose—"*just* relax. Like I said, you are in good hands here. As for the Foretelling Fabric, we will talk about that later, *if* everything goes well in your transition."

"Wait, what transition?"

Silver cleared his throat. "As I was saying," he said, a hint of annoyance in his voice, "when the dot disappeared I knew someone had claimed the Blade, which at the time seemed impossible. I'd been staking out and searching the area for days. No one had gotten past me without me knowing about it. Then, it hit me." Silver turned towards Finn, his red eye wide and his fists slowly clenching at his sides. Nibbles walked over to him and placed her liver-spotted hand on his forearm. Silver relaxed instantly. He took a few deep breaths then sighed. "Then, I knew it must have been you who'd claimed the Blade. I figured you were some top-trained Champion's squire or something like that. All I knew was that you must have known something that I didn't."

"I assure you that I didn't," said Finn. His palms were sweaty just looking at this freakishly tall weirdo.

"Don't worry," said Silver, his eye twitching slightly. "I'll find out if you're lying. I have ways..."

"Ahem!" coughed Nibbles. "Tell him where you found him, Silver."

"You washed up ashore, about half a mile away from the falls. It's a miracle you didn't get caught in the debris of the broken bridge. You weren't breathing, but what was more insane was me deciding to revive you with my own breath. I feel I'll regret that for the rest of my—"

"AHEM!"

"So, I breathed you back to life. I got most of the water out of your lungs but still, you were dying. The only reason I brought you back here was because of the thing between your legs."

It was Finn's turn to widen his eyes. He scooted himself back as far as he could until his backside touched the wall. His breathing intensified as he scanned the room and found the only means of escape was the window. He *knew* something was wrong with these perverts! He just knew it!

I gotta get out of this freak house! Before...before...they try and touch my gooch troll!

Silver squinted his eye at Finn, clearly not registering what he'd just said. It took the chuckling of Nora Nibblefingers for him to finally understand Finn's reaction, and it was the first time actual emotion appeared on his face.

"What? No! I didn't mean it like that, you sick bastard! Children these days! Their minds always stuck in the moat... I meant the Bizarre Blade! It was frozen to you between your legs...you really thought? That's sick." He turned away from Finn, mumbling something about how he hated his generation.

"Bizarre Blade? I don't understand..."

"Honey," said Nibbles, walking over to him. She grabbed one of his cold hands in her warm ones. She pulled him closer to her, and for some reason, he allowed it. She pushed his curly green hair out of his eyes, just like his mother used to do. "Honey, I don't know how to say this but...you're a Champion."

Finn's face went blank. What was she trying to say? "I'm —I'm a what?" he asked, his mind growing foggy. He felt like he was about to pass out.

Nibbles chuckled as she patted his hand.

"You're a Champion, Finn Featherstone."

13

THE UGLIEST BIZARRE BLADE

SILVER TIGHTENED HIS ARMS ACROSS HIS CHEST. "HE STILL doesn't get it. Are our words not making sense to you? You stole our Bizarre Blade."

"Hush, Silver! He did no such thing! The Blade was never ours in the first place, it was never destined to be. Reevaluate the events from that day, and you will see that the Blade put all things in alignment for Finn to grasp its hilt."

Silver snorted but said nothing.

Finn could not believe his ears and did not trust what these strangers were saying. They must have been up to something! This was all just too strange, too...amazing. If it was true and he had accidentally obtained a Bizarre Blade, then why wasn't he happy? He'd dreamed and fantasized about this very thing happening since, well, forever! Wait, that must be it...he was dreaming! It was the only logical explanation. Either that, or he was dead.

"If I truly did obtain a Bizarre Blade, then where is it?" Finn asked.

"'Where is the Blade?'" asked Nibbles, raising her

eyebrows, "Well, honey, it never left you! Go on, take a look under the bed."

"Under the bed? What for?"

"Just do it already," snapped Silver.

Finn's eyes switched between the two odd characters in the room and slipped his feet off the bed oh so cautiously. He did not take his gaze off them as he put his knees on the ground and lowered his head. He used his peripherals to take a quick look under the bed and...there it was!

Forgetting completely about Nibbles and Silver, Finn lifted the fallen sheet that covered half his view and looked upon—

"That is the ugliest thing I've ever seen," he said, looking back over his shoulder at Nibbles. "What kind of joke is this?"

A soft purr resonated from under the bed and the ground shook slightly beneath Finn's knees.

Nibbles wagged her finger in the air. "Uh, uh, uh! If I were you, Mr. Featherstone, I would watch my tongue."

Finn narrowed his eyes at her before returning to look back under the bed. However, before he could get a second glance at the Blade, the purring intensified to an all-out roar! A thick cloud of red dust blew into Finn's face, sending him onto his back, sputtering.

This taste of rust sent a memory through his mind, and snapped his brain back to normal with a single jolt of pain through his skull. He suddenly remembered everything.

"Bryce! Saul!" he yelled, standing up and wiping the rust dust out of his eyes. "I-I—"

"Honey," said Nibbles calmly, "we have your Champion friend here...my people are readying him for burial as we speak."

"But, no! He's not, he can't be...he's—"

"Dead," said Silver. Nibbles tried to speak but Silver spoke over her. "He's dead and it's time you got over it. There are more important things in this world than Finn Featherpebble." The tall albino looked at Nibbles, then back at Finn. He scoffed and stormed out of the room, slamming the door behind him.

The room fell quiet a few moments. Both Finn's and Nibbles' eyes looked at the ground as they let the words sink in.

"I'm sorry about him, he can be—"

"No, he's right," said Finn, tightening his fists. "It's time I stopped being...me. It's time I did something. It's time I made a decision." He was talking tough but could not stop a tear from falling all the way to his chin. His bottom lip was trembling when he said, "I won't let Bryce Smolder's death be for nothing. I—I will take this Blade and master it!"

More purring came from underneath the bed in response. Nibbles tilted her head with a smile. Even though her eyes weren't visible through her tightly-shut eyelids, Finn thought he could see tears.

"And, Mr. Featherstone, how do you plan on doing that?"

"I...I don't know. My, um, my fantasies never really got this far. I just sort of always envisioned myself with a Bizarre Blade, but never really what I did with it."

Nora Nibblefingers nodded her head. "Do you know what Bizarre Blades are used for?"

"Normally?" Finn asked, and Nibbles nodded. "They're used for war. The greatest of the past Champions, no matter what kingdom they were from, would charge the front lines, using his or her Blade to vanquish massive amounts of enemy troops."

"And why not see yourself doing this in your mind?"

"I don't know. It's not really my thing, I guess." Finn shrugged. "I'm not very patriotic when it comes to Shimoshimo. Never did agree with what our Kingdom was doing."

"And if you were king, what would you do?"

"Why ask me these things? I'm a nobody."

"Nobody's a nobody," said Nibbles, pointing a finger into the air. "Everyone is someone. Bryce was a nobody before he became a Champion—or, more accurately, on his way to becoming a Champion. I'm a nobody, but I'm a somebody to me. Does that make sense?"

Finn's mind was in a jumble and he had to think for a second to understand what the old lady was talking about. "I think so," he finally said. "So, 'nobodies can make a difference' is what you're saying?"

Nibbles opened her eyes slightly, showing Finn her grey irises that matched her grey hair. She blinked a few times before asking, "What happened to that confidence I just heard?" She poked him in the chest. "What happened to you wanting to see that Bryce's death wasn't for naught?" She poked him again, this time harder. "What happened to you wanting to master your new Blade?" She poked him harder still. Finn was backing up and trying to guard his chest which was getting sore, but still the little old lady persisted. "You"—poke—"are"—poke—"a"—poke—"CHAMPION!"

"Okay, okay, I get it!" Finn's back was against the wall. "It's just, it's hard being confident when you're scared!"

Nibbles dropped her hand and nodded her head. "So, the truth comes out, does it? You're a coward?"

"I, well, that's kind of harsh—"

"But it's true! But, have no fear because now we know where to start!"

"Where to start? What do you mean?"

"What I'm saying, dearie, is that fear is a great place to start when building character! Do you know why?" Finn shook his head. "Because bravery cannot be present unless the person is fearful. When there are things we must do, even though they terrify us, and we do them anyway...that is bravery. Not hoisting a Bizarre Blade over your head with a half-naked damsel at your feet!"

Finn didn't think it appropriate to admit that he had sketched that exact image of himself and had hung it above his bed back home.

"So, now what do I do?" Finn asked.

"You have two options as I see it," said Nibbles. "You could leave and head back to Shimoshimo with your Bizarre Blade. You could even abandon it if you wanted I suppose, but...I do have an offer for you. We can train you here, you know. If you really want to be a Master at the Blade you've just obtained, then this would be the place to do it. However, we train a different class of Champions here. We do not fight for glory, but for balance. I assume you've heard the terrible tales of those with rotten hearts who have gotten their hands on Bizarre Blades?"

"Of course," Finn said. "There was Tarvo the Terrible, Abnor the Appalling, Icarus the Incinerator, and—"

"Yes, yes, but that's not the point," interrupted Nibbles. "The point is, who do you think combats these ignorant and twisted Champions, if you can even call them that?"

Finn tapped his nose with his finger. He usually knew anything and everything when it came to Bizarre Blades and their Champions. Never before had he been stumped! "I don't know, I've never actually thought about it."

Nibbles grabbed Finn by the waist and turned him around to face the window. His mouth dropped at the sheer beauty upon which he now looked. The sun was setting and yellow blinking insects filled the air. There were dozens of homes built into the trees with grey smoke bellowing from their clay chimneys. Below the trees he could faintly hear someone calling out, "One! Two! Three! Ah-hah! Very good! Gavin, watch your form on the thrust." Finn looked down to see four lines of children, each with a wooden practice sword in his or her hands. A tree limb was in the way, blocking his sight of the person training them.

"It's us, Finn. We are the arbiters. We are the peacekeepers. We keep the balance."

Finn watched as water moved smoothly through bamboo slides that ran throughout the entire village, through the trees, and connected to each of the houses. This was...amazing! Breathtaking! This village had plumbing! How had he not heard of this place before?

"I'm going to give you some time to let all of this sink in," said Nibbles. Finn could hear her tiny footsteps walking away. He turned to see her head poking out from the door. "You're welcome here, Finn. You have a good heart, I can tell. We need Champions like you. Think it over. If you have any questions, I will be more than happy to answer them.

As she shut the door, Finn glanced over at his bed. It was time he got a good look at the Bizarre Blade he had accidentally connected with. He took a step towards the bed and the purring started up again. He took another step and it grew louder. When he was finally at the bedside, he almost had to cover his ears as the Blade chattered loudly. The linen cloth lining the bed fluttered and the wooden bedposts started to move due to the vibration.

Excitedly, Finn dropped to his knees again. He looked under the bed and quickly pulled away his face for fear of another puff of rust dust. But nothing happened. He looked back under the bed and saw the charcoal iron of his Blade, but still he could not get a good look at it from this angle. It was time to grab it.

Finding the orange, leather-wrapped hilt, Finn scooted himself down the side of the bed and carefully slipped his hand underneath. The Blade was roaring now as he readied himself to grab it. His heart was beating fast and he flinched when his hands touched the softness of the leather.

The Blade fell silent.

Finn took in a big deep breath, wrapped his hand around the hilt, and dragged the Blade out.

14

A HERO HAS FALLEN

FINN HAD SEEN DRAWINGS AND DIAGRAMS OF AT LEAST ONE hundred different Blades. Each of them had been so very impressive, having its own awesome qualities and quirks. For example, Blades that had something to do with the element of fire would have flames brandished on the side of the steel, with actual tiny flames flickering up and down at the hilt. Blades that could give the wielder awesome mental abilities usually had some sort of magical colored aura covering the entirety of the sword, as well as intricate etchings of ancient runes.

This Blade, however, had none of that. It was ugly. Not only that, but it was extremely heavy.

Finn kept the Blade flat on the ground but held onto it firmly by the hilt. Although it wasn't aesthetically pleasing, it was still a sword that would draw the eye of anyone around. He'd never seen a Bizarre Blade in person before, and was not expecting its massive length—he figured it must have been eight feet from the tip to the end of the grip, not counting the three one foot chains that hung from the very bottom of the hilt.

The Blade itself was more like three blades side-by-side, each with serrated triangles, making the Blade look more like a giant three-layered saw than a sword. The outside two blades held the larger of the triangular teeth, while the inside held the smaller ones. Finn didn't need to touch the serrations to know that they were razor-sharp. No Bizarre Blade would ever need to be sharpened, as they magically never lost their edge. However, what was strange was the fact that this Blade had succumbed to the water and had actually rusted. Already, Finn had decided that this must belong to the class of the lesser-tier Blades, given that something so stupid as water could damage it.

About five inches from the end of the Blade the sawlike teeth ended. From here, there was one long upward angle in which all three blades pressed together into one sharp tip. This part of the Blade would be useful if Finn ever needed to slice something rather than rip it to shreds.

To Finn's disappointment, there was no cross-guard but instead it had a large sized hole just above the Blade's hilt. Covering this hole on both sides of the Blade were four metal strips making it look like some sort of vent. As for the hilt, it was wrapped with yellow-orange leather straps which overlapped each other tightly at an angle. Squishing this soft fabric led Finn to believe that there were more than two layers of padding, but why? Wouldn't one layer of leather be enough to keep the Blade from slipping from his grasp?

"Okay," Finn said, breathing in through his nose and out through his mouth, "time to stop being a baby and pick it up."

With one hand, Finn pulled upward, barely budging the Blade, which purred softly in response. It made this noise by the movement of its serrated blades. The outer two swords would rise while the middle lowered. He gripped the hilt with two hands and the Blade seemed to growl at this, the teeth sliding against each other faster now. Still, he could not budge the damn thing.

"Come on, you gotta help me out here."

He gave it one last tug and the Blade seemed to come to life! It exploded into movement and somehow flung itself straight into the air. Finn could barely hold onto it as it slid easily through the wood of the ceiling. Without him telling it to, his Bizarre Blade thundered into action, sawdust raining down atop him as he sawed through the house. The vibrations of the Blade were so strong that it sent tremendous amounts of pain flying up his fingers and down his forearms. He tried to let go of it but something, some power, did not let him. The pain grew worse and worse until he could not stand it any longer.

"Stop! Stop! Stop!" he cried, but it was too late, his hands were broken.

The gyrating monster finally came to a halt, the three serrated blades seeming to give a wheezy exhale. The door on the opposite side of the room burst open, revealing a furious looking Silver standing in the doorway.

"What the hell is going on here? Explain yourself!"

The Blade was stuck in the ceiling and Finn was finally able to let go of the damned thing. His hands were red and swollen completely, and horrible pain throbbed through his arms as if he were still holding onto the pulsating hilt.

Finn held out his hands to Silver, trying his best to keep back the tears from the pain. He didn't want to cry, certainly not in front of this man.

"By God, what happened to you?" asked Silver with the tiniest amount of concern in his voice. He walked over to Finn and grabbed him by both of his wrists in one long-fingered hand. He pulled them to his face and eyed them with his one freakishly large eye. "You've been awake in our camp for what? Ten, twenty minutes? And already you've dislocated all of the joints in your hand."

"It. Wasn't. Me," Finn snapped, keeping his mouth almost closed while he spoke for fear the tears might spring up. "It. Was. The. Blade."

Silver threw down Finn's hands and stared down into his eyes. He kept them there for a moment before spitting, "You will never make it here." He turned and walked to the door. He paused and said over his shoulder, "I'll be back with Ariel. She'll heal you."

He shut the door hard, causing more dust to pour down onto Finn's filthy hair.

THEY HELD the burial of Bryce Smolder that night. It was dark and no fire was lit. The only light these people—these secret Champions in training—had were thousands of captured fireflies in jars. Actually, they weren't really even captured, the jars simply had drops of honey at the bottom, giving the flies incentive to stick around.

Bryce, even in death, held his famous smile. However, the usual dark tone of his skin had turned a pasty white. Only half of his face was revealed and the bottom half of him was covered in twigs. They had washed his face, and even polished his armor. A white cloth had been placed over his neck which made Finn believe that these weird people actually cared.

A choir of children stood to Bryce's right as they sung a song Finn couldn't understand. This made him wonder if a lot of people died here in this village. How else would they have been able to organize such a beautiful ceremony so quickly?

The funeral took place in the middle of the main road, which was the widest clearing without trees. On each side of this road stood buildings such as the armory, the barracks, and the storage houses. Finn wasn't quite sure, but since there was still a small amount of snow covering the leaves, he guessed he was somewhere between Shimoshimo and Koosahmoorah. This might come in handy if he ever needed to escape. If it ever came to that, he would just head in the direction of the snow.

The thoughts of escape were pushed aside as Mother Nibbles walked down between the rows of seated guests. She wore all black clothing, and a matching hat. When she got to the very end of the aisle, where Finn was seated, she turned to him, gave him a small smile, and nodded her head in respect. She continued to the front, where a carved wooden podium had been set up.

Finn's back ached and he tried readjusting himself on his wooden stool. He had been given a seat that didn't have a back because Silver had forced him to don his Bizarre Blade over his shoulders. They'd attached it to him using a Bizarre Baldric, a device crafted by Mage Scribes to hold Bizarre Blades, as they were impossible to craft sheaths for due to their complex nature. Finn couldn't help but wonder where these villagers had found this Bizarre Baldric and decided that they'd probably stolen it.

Finn hadn't dared argue with Silver about wearing the Bizarre Blade for fear that the man might kill him right then and there. On the bright side, earlier that day, Ariel had given him yet another concoction (this one tasting like peaches) which had sped up the process of healing his damaged hands and soothing the pain. She'd then wrapped both of his hands tightly with white linen gauze. The worst part, however, was when she'd stuck one of her fingers in his ears.

"It took one ounce of Ariel's earwax stash to make this concoction, and it's only right you pay your dues!" she'd said.

Finn shook his head, trying to rid himself of the memory of his ears being milked for fresh earwax.

"Greetings students, professors, and"—she looked down at Finn—"guests. We are gathered here today to give our respects to an almighty and gold-hearted Champion. You may be wondering why I give this man this title even though he was not blessed with a Bizarre Blade of his own. You see, students, you don't need a Blade to be a Champion. All that is needed is heart and soul. If you live a life of generosity, goodwill, and kindness, then you too are a Champion, no matter what anyone says."

The students, who ranged in age from what looked like five years old all the way up to Finn's age, began talking to one another. Finn expected to hear a lot of ridicule of the old lady's words and was surprised when he heard nothing but positivity.

"Mother Nibbles is right! I'm a Champion already!"

"Me too!"

Finn took this chance to steal a peek at the other so-called professors, which he assumed to be the older ones in the back. There was one woman who wore big, bulky, plate armor despite her face being extremely thin and petite. She looked nice enough. The man to her right looked very sickly as he wiped his long, pointed nose with a stained handkerchief. He sneezed and wiped an allergy tear from under his large circular glasses.

Next to him was none other than Silver. He was

slouched in his chair with, yet again, both arms crossed over his chest. He wasn't even looking in the direction of Nibbles as she spoke.

Finn's heart stopped in his chest when his eyes met two bulging white ones. This man was wrapped head to toe with the same gauze that was wrapped around Finn's hands. Even the guy's mouth had been covered shut!

Snapping his head forward, Finn tried to calm his breathing. All of them had Blades attached to their backs, all except for Silver who carried no weapon. He tried to decide if any of the Blades looked familiar to him, but it was too dark to get a good look at them. He did, however, notice that all of their Blades were huge, just like his.

How are they able to look so comfortable! My back is killing me!

It was true. Finn was having a terrible time trying to keep himself from falling backward. Perhaps this was why they had the seat directly behind him empty—just in case.

"I kept my eye on Mr. Bryce Smolder for most of his life," said Nibbles. "As I do all Champions. It is my job, as you all know, to make sure no Champion gets out of line. However! Bryce never once gave me worry. He was one of the few I could count on to not abuse his natural God-given strength. If I'm not mistaken, he even adopted the Shimoshimo lower-class pleasantry and used it on a daily basis. Bryce Smolder, among many things, was a good man. It is with a heavy heart that we must see him off to paradise, where he will surely be dueling Blade-to-Blade with all the past good-hearted Champions." The old lady paused here to wipe a tear from the corner of her eye. When she spoke next, it was obvious she was having trouble keeping her voice steady. "Finn, would you care to do the honors?"

Nibbles reached below the podium and pulled out a

torch. She tapped it with one finger and a flame burst out of nowhere.

How did she perform this magic without a Bizarre Blade? Finn thought to himself. *She must be a Mage Scribe! Of course! That's it!*

"Yes, yes, I would," Finn said, trying to stand up, but he could not. He tried to swing himself upward, but not even that worked. The damned Blade was just too heavy!

Two students around the age of twelve walked over to him and pulled him up by the shoulders. His knees popped under the weight of the Blade and he bent himself forward to keep from falling back onto his seat. "Thank you."

The Bizarre Blade purred softly, sending weird tingles over his body. Sweat poured down his face by the time he made it up to where Nibbles stood. She handed him the torch and bowed her head. Finn returned the bow and grabbed the torch awkwardly between his two bandaged hands, making sure not to catch the linen on fire.

Holding the torch above Bryce's face was his limit and he could no longer hold back his tears. Seeing the flame flickering over his lifetime hero was just too much for him. He'd only just met Bryce and now...now it was time to say goodbye.

"Thank you, Bryce. Thank you for showing me what it takes to be a true hero. It isn't the Blade, but the person. I'm... I'm so sorry I got you killed..." Finn lowered the torch, holding it only inches from the wood. "I promise you, I will do all in my power to uphold everything that you were. You will not have died in vain."

Finn let the torch drop onto the wood, which caught immediately. In a matter of seconds, Bryce Smolder was literally smoldering.

"I will become the best Champion that I can possibly be."

Not a second later, a loud familiar screech echoed throughout the secret village. Everybody's heads looked up and scanned the trees for the source. Even Nibbles had her eyes peeled, looking for whatever had caused the interruption.

Finn found it right away.

"Obsidian?"

The microraptor leapt from its place high up in the tallest of the trees, its wings swooping elegantly as he found his way to Finn and landed on his shoulder. All of the guests, including Mother Nibbles, gasped.

Obsidian cawed sadly in Finn's ears, and together, they watched their friend burn.

15

THE BLADE WITH THE FIERY ATTITUDE

OBSIDIAN SLEPT WITH FINN THAT NIGHT.

After the funeral had ended, Finn was shown to his own private house, which was the size of his room back in Sumetai—a strange comfort to him. Inside stood only a bed and a nightstand, each hand-carved, no doubt from the surrounding trees.

They brought food for him, a delicious clay bowl of warm salty potato soup, a few pickled vegetables, and a half loaf of bread. He'd scarfed these down like a starving dire wolf, using the bread to soak up any remaining juices from the soup.

During the first part of the night, sleep did not come and gave no hint of ever showing up. Thoughts raced through Finn's mind as if it was the middle of the day. He thought of his father and how he missed him. He'd finally obtained a Bizarre Blade, something he'd dreamed about all of his life... but at what cost? In the past few weeks he'd seen enough death for a lifetime, and it was starting to really wear on his mind. Flashes of the Spud, Mathew's disgusting bloodied face kept popping into his thoughts, reminding him that he was indeed a coward.

Why didn't I move faster? Why did I freeze?

It was no surprise to him that his mother visited his thoughts that night as she did every night. He didn't mind this. He'd rather lose sleep than lose his memories of her sweet face. Sometimes he could feel her soft touch on his chin. Sometimes he could hear her lullabies. Sometimes he could hear her telling him that everything was going to be alright, which was the most comforting of all. He wondered if this was really his mother's spirit watching over him or if this was just his imagination, a human failsafe mechanism to keep him from going insane.

The Bizarre Blade wouldn't shut up. Finn had leaned it against the wall behind the door, hoping that its powers would not activate. He'd already destroyed one home, better not destroy a second. Silver and his student Jade had already made it very apparent that he was unwanted here; one more mistake and they may really kick him out.

It was the middle of the night when the black feathered dinosaur showed up on his windowsill. Finn watched him, and the raptor watched Finn. He could see the feathers under his neck flutter as he cawed at Finn quietly. Finn found it funny that even the raptor knew that others were trying to sleep.

Every time Finn blinked, Obsidian would hop a little closer to him, his head cocked to the same angle as it studied him. When he came close enough to touch, Finn reached out and, to his surprise, Obsidian lowered his head for a pat.

"You miss him, don't you?"

Obsidian just stared.

"I do, too. What's worse is the guilt that I feel. He gave

his life for me and I'm not so sure I was worth it."

Obsidian stepped closer and pecked him hard on the forehead.

"Ow! Hey! Okay, I deserved that." Finn rubbed his face. "He'd be upset if he heard me saying that, huh?"

Obsidian answered him by lowering his head, waiting for another pet. This time, Finn was brave enough to caress the microraptor's down. He felt very soft and just a little bit oily feeling. The raptor let this petting continue and Finn couldn't tell whether it was more as a comfort for himself or for Obsidian.

He did this for an hour or so, the dinosaur getting closer and closer to him until he rested his feathered body against his. Finn would doze off every once in a while, only to be awakened by Obsidian standing in the middle of the room crying out. He would hop to different corners of the room, searching, searching for his lost partner. Finn watched this with a broken heart, beckoning for the dinosaur to come back to him, only for the process to repeat itself. He wasn't sure how long this went on but at some point they must have fallen asleep together, as a knocking on his door woke him with a start.

The door creaked open, revealing a tiny white nose. "May I come in?" Nibbles whispered.

Finn yawned as he sat up. Obsidian pecked at his fingers, reluctant to lose his warm spot. "Ow, cut it out! Uh, yes, come in."

Nibbles entered and shut the door behind her quietly. She wore all black which meant she was still in mourning. How well had she known Bryce?

"I see you've made a little friend," she said with a kind smile. She was leaning on a wooden walking stick today, which was barely a foot tall.

"Yeah, I guess I did. Not that I asked for it or anything." He looked down at Obsidian who returned the glare. "And he has a bad habit of poking people!"

Obsidian cawed an argument at him.

"Is he domesticated?" Nibbles asked.

"Not by birth, no," answered Finn. "Bryce saved him from a predator, a cryolophosaurus to be exact. Not really sure how Bryce got him to like people."

"Well, he certainly seems to like you!"

Finn looked down at Obsidian who was still pushed up against his leg. Hs eyes were shut —this conversation had nothing to do with him and the raptor would apparently rather get in a few more minutes of sleep.

"I guess so. Not so sure I make such a great replacement for Bryce."

"Hush!" Nibbles commanded, popping him on top of the head with her cane. "Hush!" Bop. "Hush!" Bop. "HUSH! Another word like that out of you and I'll feed *you* to a cryolophosaurus!"

"Why is everyone hurting me this morning?" complained Finn, rubbing the top of his head. Nibbles cocked her stick back and looked ready to bop away. "Okay, okay! No more feeling sorry for myself, promise...geez." Then he whispered, "Damn crazy-ass old lady."

BOP.

"OWW!"

"Say, where is this Bizarre Blade of yours? I'm afraid I haven't really gotten a good look of it as of yet. I spent years tracking it through the Foretelling Fabric, and it's always nice to see it in person. Mind if I...?"

"Go ahead," Finn said, flicking his wrist towards the corner of the room while rubbing his aching head. "I don't think it likes me very much...nor I it."

"Oh, come now. All Bizarre Blades take some time getting used to their new wielders! Imagine if you were the Blade. Imagine that you watched your previous Champion die, only to be stuck hidden somewhere for years! That wouldn't be fun, now would it?"

"Why are you talking to me like a baby?"

"Because you're acting like one."

"That's fair."

"Now come on, let's get you two acquainted. Besides, it doesn't even have a name yet! You can't expect to get close to, say, a pet if you haven't even named it!"

Finn pulled himself out of the bed, dodging all of Obsidian's pecks as he did so. Nibbles tried to hide her snickers with her hand, but was not successful. They walked over to the Bizarre Blade which breathed through its vents as they approached. Finn thought he saw a flicker of flames between the grills, but he wasn't sure. It could have just been a trick his mind was playing on him.

"Hey there!" Nibbles said to the inanimate object. "I'm Nibbles! You probably recognize my energy, don't you? I'm the one who persuaded you to let me find you!"

The Blade purred, its teeth moving up and down slowly.

"Wait, you *talked* to this thing?"

"Yes, through the Foretelling Fabric which is, long story short, a very rare magical Fabric that we Mage Scribes use to find Bizarre Blades. It's a difficult process but I happen to have a certain knack for it."

I knew it! Finn thought. *She is a Mage Scribe! I was right!*

Nibbles winked, but then popped him again on the head with her stick. "And it's not a thing, Finn! If Bizarre Blades hate anything its being called a *thing*. This is why it's so important we find a name for it."

"Okay, okay, please stop hitting me! And why do I have to name it? Don't all Bizarre Blades already have names?"

A coy smile developed on Nibbles' face as she rolled her walking stick in her hand.

If she's not using the walking cane, then why bring it? wondered Finn. *Just to beat me with it?*

"That's the interesting part, Finn. That's why it took me so long to find and persuade this Blade to give me its where-abouts. You see, Blades only let Mage Scribes know where they are hidden when they *want* to be found. That is, unless, you are like the Mage Scribes of today who have found a way to yank the knowledge from them without their permission. This may be why your Bizarre Blade is acting up."

Nibbles turned to the Blade. "Shame on you!" The Blade hissed at her through its vents, and this time Finn did see fire! "Oh, don't take that attitude with me! You practically spilled where you were to me! You knew Prince Tarek was coming for you and you chose the lesser of two evils!" The Blade's hiss turned to a sputtering purr and it reminded Finn of a child who'd just been scolded.

Nibbles extended her hand to the Blade but Finn grabbed it and pulled it away. "Wait, don't! We don't know what it's capable of! You saw what it did to the roof!"

Nibbles raised an eyebrow and used two fingers to pluck Finn's hand off hers. "I've been doing this longer than you've been alive, dearie." She put her hand to the face of the Blade, letting her palm slide down it as if giving it a good pet. The Blade's purr turned to a hum, a hum that sent good-feeling vibrations through the body. "There we are! Who's a good Blade? Huh? Who's a good Blade? WHO'S A GOOD BLADE?!" The Blade's humming grew louder. "That's right! You are!"

That's when Finn knew. "You were more than just

friends with Bryce," he said. "What exactly was your relationship with him?"

Nibbles pulled back her hand, her face falling to look at the wooden planks. Finn could tell she must have been replaying old memories in her head. "You're smarter than you look," she said, a tear dripping from her crease of an eye. "We made the right choice in reviving you. You just never know what you might pull out the icy cold river." She tried to laugh but it was a pathetic attempt, and quickly turned into a fit of sobbing. She turned to Finn and fell into him with a warm embrace.

Finn bent and returned her hug. He could feel the heaving of her back as emotions poured from her eyes, her nose, and her mouth. After only half a minute, Finn joined her in crying. He'd tried to keep it together, but it was no use. He needed this.

Minutes later, they sat across from each other, sniffling and wiping their eyes.

"Who's the baby now?" Finn asked her.

"Oh, shut up. I'll let this go, just this once. The Champions of Arbitration don't train babies, you know."

"Champions of Arbitration," Finn said to himself. "That has a nice ring to it."

"Doesn't it, though?"

"Will you tell me how you knew Bryce?"

Nibbles sniffed one last time. "Yes, yes I will. I knew him very well, actually, better than anyone else."

"But how? Are you his mother?"

"God, no! I was closer to him than a mother." Nibbles' eyes drifted from Finn and over to the now quiet Bizarre Blade—it was as though it was listening. "I was his *Master*."

16

HOW TO NAME A BIZARRE BLADE

FINN'S JAW DROPPED, DESPITE THE FACT THAT HE WAS TRYING not to be rude.

But how could that even be possible?! Finn thought. *She's shorter than a tree stump! There's just no way she could have trained someone as amazing as Bryce Smolder, Legendary Champion and First in Queue! No, she's lying...she just has to be.*

"Judging by the look you're giving me, I'd say you don't believe me."

"It's not that, it's just—"

"Looks can be deceiving, young one! Well, not for Bryce, his looks were pretty spot on! However, as for me, I may not look it, but I'm a grandmother to be reckoned with! I may be old but I still know my way around a Blade, trust me. Although, I do spend less time with weaponry as my joints don't much care for them."

"What was he like?"

"What was who like?"

"Bryce!"

"Oh yes...what was he like? You mean, at your age?" Finn nodded. "Well, not to be rude but he stood a good two feet taller and three feet wider. He ate like he was starving and no amount of food could satiate the boy. He was talented in all forms of martial arts and favored larger swords made of bone. He had a heart made of gold and would lend a hand to anyone in need."

"Wow, he sounds amazing."

"Well, you knew him, didn't you?"

"Yes, I did. He was just the way you described. I—" A thin layer of sweat appeared on his forehead—he had just stopped himself from saying something embarrassing.

"You want to be like him," Nibbles finished for him, nodding.

Finn looked away. "Yes, but how did you know?"

"Because everybody wants to be like Bryce Smolder. But you're different, Finn."

"How so?"

"Because, you're more like him than you think."

SMALL SANDWICHES WERE BROUGHT into the room as Nibbles told stories of her adventures with young Bryce. Apparently, he'd been very sympathetic towards all animals. He'd even shown mercy to predator dinosaurs such as allosaurus, tyrannosaurus, and carcharodontosaurus, only killing them if absolutely necessary for things like food or if one got too close to camp and he couldn't scare it away.

She just finished a story of Bryce returning a stolen triceratops egg back to its nest when Finn said, "I knew you were a Mage Scribe, by the way."

Nibbles leaned back, stroking her chin. "Oh yes, and how's that?"

"The way you lit the fire with your fingers."

"Clever boy," she said, raising her hands and snapping her fingers. A small blue flame appeared atop her index finger before she blew it out. "Not extremely useful but good in a bind—literally, if you're bound by rope. It's more of a trinket power, if you ask me."

"If you're a Mage Scribe, then why aren't you in one of the palaces of one of the four kingdoms?"

Nibbles finished off one of her sandwiches, chewed, and washed it down with a sip of her hot tea. "Ahh, that's good stuff." She put the cup of tea down, and her face became serious. "Remember when I said it was possible to force Bizarre Blades to give you their whereabouts?"

"Yes."

"Well, it's a relatively new power to the Mage Scribes. It's also highly unethical and very, VERY dangerous."

"How could writing on pillowcases be dangerous?" asked Finn, but as Nibbles lifted her cane and readied to swat him with it he quickly added, "Sorry, sorry, just a joke, please continue."

Nibbles dropped her stick, her eyes even more pressed together than usual. "AHEM! As I was saying, it's a very dangerous process, this pulling information out of Bizarre Blades. You see, it requires blood—and lots of it—to perform this sort of magic. Not only that, but it puts tremendous amounts of strain on the Blade, which can leave it unlikely to bind with any wielder properly. Not only that, but it has been known to shatter them."

"No way!"

"Yes way!" Nibbles exclaimed. She was getting excited now. "I once belonged to a king in a Kingdom far, far away. He tried to get me to use blood magic but I said no! Well, I didn't say no. I said yes then escaped in the night. Think I'm stupid enough to just plain out say 'no' to the king? No...I'm a survivor! Anyway, we call these blood-utilizing creeps 'Crimson Mages.' Pretty clever, huh? Came up with it myself."

"And so you formed the Champions of Arbitration to combat these Mage Scribes?"

"No and yes. The Champions of Arbitration already existed, I just outlived the previous owner."

"And I'm guessing Prince Tarek got his information on my Bizarre Blade by using the Crimson Mage Scribes?"

"Right! I was working for years to get your Bizarre Blade to open up but it was so damned stubborn!" The Blade hissed. "That's right, I'm talking about you! It kept insisting on the right person not being ready for its powers. I kept pushing Bryce on it, but it would only push back! Imagine that! Bryce Smolder, declined by a Bizarre Blade. The Blade finally gave in and gave me what I needed to find it, because Prince Tarek had sent his Crimson Mage dogs on its trail! But, now I know that was only half true. It told me where it was because it knew *you* were coming, Finn. It was waiting on you this entire time!"

"Wow..." Finn felt a little lightheaded. A Blade that declined Bryce but chose him instead? It just didn't sound possible.

"Speaking of which, it's time to name your Blade!"

"Oh, right. Well, you may not know this but I've never named an ancient and power-wielding Blade. Especially one that doesn't like me."

"Oh, it's not hard, dearie! Come on, take a hold of it."

"I'm okay."

"What did I say about being a baby?"

Finn's cheeks grew red. To think that a little old lady was tougher than him...well, he wouldn't stand for it. He walked over to the Blade and was about to take hold of it when Nibbles grabbed him by the arm.

"Not like that! Be gentle! Ask for its permission and you'll get much further with it!"

"Really?" Finn wasn't sure whether Nibbles was messing with him or not.

"Yes, really. Try it."

"Okay...Mr. Blade, sir, I'd very much like to hold you."

The Blade hummed softly.

"Go ahead, now, Finn, take it."

"It's too heavy to hold upright."

"Then let's lay it on your lap."

And that's what they did. Carefully, Finn laid the Blade on the ground and slid his legs underneath it. He could smell some sort of gas coming from the vents as it rumbled on his thighs. It, too, seemed like it was being cautious around him.

"Okay, what names come to mind?" asked Nibbles, rubbing her palms together, her tongue sticking out the side of her mouth.

"Are you sure it isn't already named?"

"I'm very sure. Its name would have appeared on the Foretelling Fabric. Since it did not, I'm assuming this Blade hasn't been wielded in hundreds—if not thousands—of years. It's been waiting that long for you."

"That's insane."

"But true!"

"What about the Hissing Blade?"

The Blade on his legs let out a big puff of black smoke from its vents making Finn cough.

"Guess not," said Nibbles, waving the smoke from her face.

"Okay, what about Cutter Blade?"

More black smoke.

"The Sharp-Teeth Blade?"

Even more black smoke. Nibbles was coughing now. "Please, for the love of God, find one before we die of smoke inhalation!"

"Uh, uh, uh, I don't know! Why is this so hard? The Vibrating Blade! The Smoke Blade!" Smoke poured out of the Blade in a constant flow now. "Come on! Work with me! Uh, uh, uh, okay! Okay! How about, the Saw Blade?"

The smoke stopped with a sputter; the Blade now hummed. Every few seconds the sword would puff out a tiny cloud of smoke.

"Hey! I got it! It wants to be called the Saw Blade!"

Another puff of smoke.

"No, something's wrong," said Nibbles, chewing on one of her knuckles. "It's close, but I don't think that's exactly the name it's looking for."

"Then what am I supposed to do? I can't think of any more names!"

"It's not that, Finn." Nibbles looked away, her face scrunched up in thought. "Hmm, I'm curious...I want to try something."

"What's curious? What do you want to try? I'm so confused." A black puff of soot shot out from the vents and slapped Finn's neck. "Ahhh! I'm so sick of this Blade!"

"Hush, Finn! We are close, so very close." Nibbles fished out of her pockets a rectangular piece of white linen, much like the one Finn's hands had been wrapped in the night before. Miraculously, Ariel's concoction had healed his hands by the time the funeral had ended. "Sometimes, Bizarre Blades, especially ones that are old, VERY old, will take on the name of their first wielder. It's rare, so rare that not even I have come across a Blade old enough to take on this ancient tradition. It's worth a shot, am I right?"

"Sure," Finn said, wiping the soot off his sweaty neck. "But how do we do it?"

"By using this Foretelling Fabric!"

"That's Foretelling Fabric? It...seriously looks like a regular piece of fabric."

"To the untrained eye, yes, but look closer!"

Nibbles laid the fabric on the wood floor, and at first Finn could see nothing special. He was considering faking that he saw something...but then, he actually did! The fabric had tiny little circular waves pulsing through it, much like those that would occur after dropping a stone into a pond. Nibbles tapped the fabric in the middle and the linen behaved like water!

"What the—"

"Language, Finn."

"I was gonna say 'heck'!"

"Sure you were. Now, here's your first lesson. A Foretelling Fabric is like a medium between Bizarre Blades and people. Only Mage Scribes can use it, as the ability to use Foretelling Fabric is determined by birth. Often, relationships must be formed with a Bizarre Blade before you can speak with it. Now, since we have the Blade right in front of us, the effects are strengthened, especially if I do this!" Nibbles picked up the Foretelling Fabric and laid it gently on top of the Blade, which vibrated in response. "Now here's the fun part." She pushed her pinky finger out and stroked the fabric with it, a black line trailing behind it. With her finger, she wrote the words *Saw Blade* which disappeared a few seconds later. Then, she asked out loud, "Who was your first wielder?"

Nothing happened and Nibbles looked visibly hurt.

"Who was your first wielder?" Finn asked it.

Again, nothing happened, and Finn was just about to ask it again when black lines began to stroke themselves into the Foretelling Fabric from an unseen hand, making them both gasp excitedly.

"It's working! Oh my God, it's working!" Nibbles shouted. "I didn't think it would!"

The Blade wrote: *Jig-awa Roasting-Spit Saw Blade.*

"Okay," said Finn. "That's ridiculous. I'm not calling it that."

The Blade answered him with a hiss and another shot of black soot, this time to the face.

"I agree, that is a bit ridiculous," said Nibbles. "Work with us a little, Mr. Jig-awa Roasting-Spit Saw Blade."

The Blade went silent for a moment, and even stopped its vibrating, much to the relief of Finn's legs. The black-inked words written on the Foretelling Fabric began to waver until all of them disappeared. More strokes appeared on the fabric, this time finishing in a question mark, as if the Blade was asking for their approval.

Finn wiped the rest of the soot from his eyes and said, "Well, that's a little better."

"It sure is!" agreed Nibbles. "I think we can make this name work."

Finn rested his hand on the Blade and was surprised when the Blade reacted with a soft hum.

"Well, it looks like I'm your new Champion," he said, petting its face. "It's good to meet you, Jigsaw Blade. Sorry to keep you waiting."

17

FINN GETS BRANDED

THE ONLY TIME A NON-MAGE SCRIBE COULD WRITE ON THE oh-so-ancient-and-powerful Foretelling Fabric was when a Mage Scribe allowed it. This was usually when a serious contract was written and a normal, non-magically gifted person was asked to bind themselves to said contract. Finn had been unaware of this because all knowledge of Mage Scribes was very hard to come by—so hard that even the great Secrets Selling Merchant Monk Eatsalot never had anything to sell on them. The only reason Finn knew this now was because he was surrounded by at least a hundred Champions in training, all watching him as he readied his pointer finger to sign his name.

"I, Nora Nibblefingers, former Mage Scribe of the Shimoshimo Kingdom, current overseer of the hidden Society of the Champions of the Arbitration, do cancel out all rules in favor of an amendment allowing one over the age of eleven years old to join the ranks of this prestigious school of likeminded and talented students. This will be the seventh time in the history of the Society of the Champions of Arbitration this has occurred and it will not be the last as we are an ever-growing people with open minds. We see you, Finn Featherstone, as a means to keep the peace from the shadows, a person who can stand for what is right, for glory that is hidden from the eyes of the public. We see you as selfless and one who has a heart worthy of our title. We see you as a Champion for the greater good, a Champion above all others, with a Bizarre Blade in his right hand and a book of justice in the left. We neither lean towards evil nor towards good, but understand that if a powerful creation such as Bizarre Blades exist, then we must as well. However, as a student Champion of Arbitration, you must realize that it will often have you putting your life on the line as the evil rises up higher than the good on occasion." There was a metal rod sticking in the fire, half of its shaft turning a bright orange. Finn had his eye on this while Nibbles talked and he could feel his undergarments pour over with sweat when she pulled it out of the fire, revealing it.

A brand.

"Do you, Finn Featherstone, accept these words into your heart, mind, soul, and blood? Do you accept your life-long position amongst our people? Do you accept your destiny as a Champion of Arbitration?"

"Is...is that a brand?"

"DO YOU?!" screamed out the entire populous that had attended the ceremony, causing Finn to about jump out of his boots.

"Yes! Yes, I accept! I will become a Champion of Arbitration. I will put my life on the line! I will accept this cause into my heart, body and...and...what was the other thing?"

Nibbles rolled her eyes and pressed the brand into his right shoulder without warning. The sting was the worst pain he'd felt in his life but only lasted seconds before the nerve endings burned away. What was left, however, was the smell that could be described as a three-month old rotten corpse's ass. Hell, to be more precise.

"You may now sign the Foretelling Fabric," announced Nibbles in a deeper voice than usual.

Finn's body was a little shaky from the pain, and he was trying his best not to gag from the smell of his skin as he lifted his finger and touched it to the fabric. A black dot appeared below his finger and he swore he caught a raised eyebrow from Nibbles as she touched his forearm. Together, they spelled out his name on the magical linen, which was the softest thing he'd ever touched. With a flick of his finger, he'd done it. He'd signed his soul over to a cause that superseded his lifetime by thousands of years.

"Congratulations, Finn Featherstone, you are now one of us. LET'S PARTY!"

The darkness erupted with the sound of banging drums as students playing wind instruments walked inward from the shadows. People shouted excitedly as they pushed themselves forward to touch Finn as well as the excruciatingly heavy Jigsaw Blade on his back, which hummed loudly in tune with the instruments.

What is going on? he thought.

Finn was hugged by so many strangers, including the other professors, not to mention so many pretty girls his age —which was not helping the sweaty underwear situation. The Jigsaw Blade on his back shook with excitement; it must have been feeling all the positive energy surrounding it. As if on cue, the fireflies left their places in the glass jars and buzzed into the air, creating a cloud of yellow light. It was so beautiful that Finn almost forgot about his brand. Almost.

Nibbles grabbed him by the hand and led him out of the crowd, somewhat to his relief. Never before had he been celebrated—well, if you didn't count his mother and father on his birthdays. He wasn't exactly sure how to act around all of these people, so he stuck to the basics: saying thank you, shaking hands, and performing the two-finger salute, which made him feel very much like Bryce.

"I want you to meet some people, dearie," said Nibbles, leading him out of the crowd of people, most of whom were still reaching out to touch him. Someone accidentally brushed his wounded shoulder and he just about fell to his knees in agony.

"I'm kind of tired," Finn said, trying to get out of it. "Maybe I should just go to bed."

"Nonsense! You're one of us now, and the ceremony wouldn't be complete if you didn't meet the professors!"

On the outskirts of the crowd were the three Bizarre Blade wielding Champions he'd seen the night of the funeral. The sickly man was busy blowing his nose, and the woman in plate was chatting loudly to the man wrapped from head to toe in white strips of cloth. They all went quiet as Finn approached.

"Champions," Nibbles addressed them, "meet our newest recruit! Finn Featherstone! Finn, meet Doctor Steve Skeleton."

The man with the nose of ever-running snot wiped his hand on his leggings and extended it towards Finn. Finn tried his best not to hesitate and shook it almost immediately, but the sideways smile the woman gave him told him she'd noticed, and didn't blame him.

"Hi," he said. "Please, Doctor Skeleton is fine."

He was about Finn's height with short blond hair and circular-lensed glasses that were far too big for his head. Now that Finn was up close, he saw that this man had one lazy eye that pointed off in another direction. He wore simple, white cloth clothes with a few dried bloodspots on them. The only distinctive thing about him was the massive Blade on his back.

Doctor Skeleton caught Finn eyeing his weapon and said, "I guess it would be rude of me not to introduce you to my Virus Blade."

"Virus Blade?" Finn asked. "I've never heard of that one!"

"That's the point," said Doctor Skeleton, his lazy eye swimming to look up. "Most people don't know anything about the Blades our little society bears."

"That makes sense," said Finn. "Mind if I ask what its power is?"

"It makes you really sick," said the woman. "The name says it all!"

Doctor Skeleton's body stiffened. "I beg your pardon, Miss Flowerfield! It does more than that!"

"Don't tell me," said Miss Flowerfield, who pointed at Finn, "tell him!"

Doctor Skeleton took his glasses off his face and used his shirt to begin wiping them. He looked flustered. "The Virus Blade is very dangerous. So much so that even I am not immune to its effects. From nausea to terminal illness, I can use the Virus Blade to cause death to an individual, havoc to a few, and incredible discomfort to the masses." He replaced his glasses back on his head, swung his hand behind his back and pulled out his Blade with a strength Finn never would have guessed possible from such a scrawny man.

The Blade was long and extremely thin. The metal was silver, with a sewage-green gloss that dripped from the Blade's edge and sizzled softly in the grass. The hilt was long, just like all hilts on Bizarre Blades, and wrapped in purple leather with black stitch work, which made the grip look like a sewn-up forearm.

"Doctor Skeleton is not only a talented man with medicine," said Nibbles, "but he also plays an important part within our society. It would be a complete catastrophe if anyone with ill heart got hold of the Virus Blade. Think of what death it could bring to its people!"

Doctor Skeleton nodded. "Unfortunately, the cold that I have is permanent. A bad side effect of being this Blade's owner, I'm afraid. Sometimes I wish this burden wasn't on my shoulders, but, what can you do?"

Upon hearing these words, the Virus Blade grew upset and slopped its Master's white shirt with a green glob of goo. "Oh come on! I just washed this!"

"And I'm Mary Flowerfield," said the woman, extending her gauntleted hand. Finn shook it, and she about broke all of his fingers with her grip. "And I'm the owner of this here beauty! The Tamer Blade!"

Mary whipped her Blade out just as fast as Doctor Skeleton, if not faster. Shining before Finn was a pale white Bizarre Blade crafted from a rather large femur bone. Much like Jigsaw, this Blade also had teeth instead of an edge. However, the Tamer Blade's teeth looked to be *actual* teeth, possibly from an assortment of meateaters. Thick brown fur covered the cross guard that worked to protect the top of the wielder's fist, and the grip was wrapped tightly in a dark, scaly leather.

"The Tamer Blade's abilities are quite simple really, I can tame a shitload of animals!"

"Language!"

"Sorry, Mother Nibbles," Mary said quickly before continuing. "Anyway, I can communicate with animals and have them do whatever I wish. It's more powerful one on one, and the strength of its abilities lessens with the more animals I try to tame at once."

Finn tightened his fists, shaking with excitement. "That's amazing! I can't wait to see it in action! To be honest, I wasn't expecting the owner of the Tamer Blade to be wearing such an awesome set of armor. Does it protect you from predators if the taming abilities wear off?"

Mary Flowerfield lifted her armored arm and flexed, smirking as she did so. "Nah, I just like the way it looks." Doctor Skeleton shook his head at this as he wiped his glasses again on his shirt. "What? Just because this girl's a Champion, doesn't mean she can't look good!"

"And last but certainly not least," said Nibbles, gesturing to the man wrapped in bandages, "we have our very quiet and very gentle Alan Avalanche. However, he prefers to be called 'Gauze,'—it's what his students call him."

"Woah!" Finn exclaimed. "Did one of your ancestors really get their name from their mother seeing an avalanche at their birth?"

The man stared down at Finn with his eyelid-less stare. Finn could see the red veins bulging on the whites of the eyeballs and took a step back when the man pulled back the bandages from his mouth, revealing cracked lips which spread into a big creepy smile.

"Aside from his neat name," said Nibbles, "he's also the owner of the Combustion Blade."

Gauze nodded again, his grin growing even wider, his eyeballs seeming to pop out even more.

"Go on, show us the Blade, Alan," said Nibbles. "We don't have all night."

Gauze's eyes shot down at Nibbles then back at Finn. "Yes...Mother Nibbles..." he whispered through his wall of white teeth. Finn had to strain his ears just to hear him.

Unlike the other two teachers, Gauze took his time in brandishing his Combustion Blade. Nibbles bent down and whispered into Finn's ear, "We have to be very careful with this Blade. You think the Jigsaw Blade has a bad temper? You really don't want to set this one off. Literally."

The Blade's outer skin didn't look like steel at all but more like dried volcanic lava. Between the crusty cracks, Finn could make out the bright orange oozing of magma. On the outside of the rough black exterior, small mushroom clouds exploded in random spots up and down the Blade. Gauze couldn't help but flinch with each crackle.

"As you probably figured out," said Flowerfield, pointing at the Blade with her thumb, "this Blade has a talent for spontaneously setting people on fire, including..." She stopped there, looking up at Gauze.

Gauze's eyes whipped over to her and he finished her sentence in a whisper. "...its owner."

"You know what I just realized?" exclaimed Nibbles, her head turning around to look behind her. "We're missing Master Silver! Where could he have gone to?"

Finn knew exactly where he wasn't—at his ceremony of induction. The man hated him and Finn completely understood why. He'd stolen his prized student's Blade and he wanted nothing to do with Finn, not even if he was now a Champion.

"That's disappointing," said Nibbles, shaking her head. "The nerve of that man!"

"What Blade does Silver, er, Master Silver wield?" Finn asked. "I haven't seen his attached to his back like the rest of us. Is it invisible?"

"I don't think he has one," Nibbles said nonchalantly as she continued her search for the tall albino. "If he does we haven't seen it."

"Then why is he a professor here?" asked Finn.

"Because he doesn't need one," answered Flowerfield. "The man's dangerous enough without it."

Doctor Skeleton and Gauze nodded their heads at this.

AFTER FINN SAID his goodbyes to the teachers of the society of the Champions of Arbitration, Nibbles led him back to his room. He could barely keep his excitement to himself and about talked Nibbles' ear off with ideas he had on how the others could use their Blades for combat. He went quiet when Nibbles said to him, "These are thoughts you should be having about your own Blade."

This got Finn thinking. He honestly didn't know exactly what it was his Blade *did*. He would never say it out loud, but he was pretty sure his Blade was useless, most likely the lowest of the low-class Blades. Sure, he could probably cut down a few trees, maybe a few wooden houses, or so but he couldn't really think of anything else the Blade could be useful for. After meeting the other Champions, Finn couldn't help but feel a little jealous. A Blade that could put a deadly virus in someone's body, a Blade that could control animals, and a Blade that could seriously cause someone to blow up! And what did he have? A Blade that was more like a saw than anything.

All this Blade is good for is being a literal pain in the back, he thought.

"Have a good night, Finn," said Nibbles at the door. "Tomorrow is when the real fun starts!"

Finn entered his room and turned to asked what she meant by this but the strange old woman had disappeared.

"That's weird," he said. "Is no one in this village normal?"

He shut the door and found Obsidian standing in the middle of his floor. It looked up at him, cawed loudly, and flapped over onto his shoulder. He flinched, expecting the microraptor's wings to slap him in the face. Instead, the raptor landed on his shoulder with grace. However, he gasped when the raptor dug its claws into his brand.

"Ahh! Down, get down!" he said, trying to yank Obsidian off his shoulder but the animal just wouldn't budge. Instead, Finn pulled one of its black claws and moved it a few inches to the side—not without getting his hand pecked a few times, of course.

He undid the leather baldric and carefully peeled the Jigsaw Blade off his sweaty back, letting the tip of it drop heavily to the ground. In doing so, the Blade stuck itself a few inches into the wood floor.

"Oops."

He let go of the hilt and the Jigsaw Blade remained standing straight up; he decided to just leave it there as a sudden wave of fatigue washed over him. He took a few tired steps towards the bed before falling face-first into it, Obsidian screeched loudly as it flew off of him, trying to avoid being crushed.

Finn pulled the rest of himself into the bed, his back pulsing with the pain of his sore muscles. The brand, thanks to the unlucky grasp of the microraptor, had reawakened and was causing painful havoc across his whole shoulder.

Obsidian hopped into bed beside him and curled up next to his body. The raptor's butt pointed at his head, but Finn felt too tired to even move it. So, with a dinosaur anus in his face, an aching back, and a brand that felt like it was on fire, he fell asleep.

If he thought this was pain, then tomorrow would be a true nightmare.

18

I LIKE THAT BOULDER

THE SUN HADN'T EVEN SHOWN ITS FACE WHEN A KNOCKING came to Finn's door. He was pretty sure it was just part of his dream until it turned from knocking to pounding.

"Coming! I'm coming!" he cried, pushing one foot out from under the covers. "Geez, doesn't anyone sleep in in this village?"

His back felt doubly sore compared to yesterday and Finn could barely lift his arm to grab hold of the doorknob. He pulled the door open just half an inch before it was shoved from the other side with such force that he fell onto his back, the top of his head slamming into the face of the Jigsaw Blade, only inches from its teeth. The Blade woke with a start, pushing out a gust of smelly black smoke.

Finn sat up rubbing his head and was just about to yell at whoever had done this to him...but then he realized who it was.

"Silver?"

"That's Master Silver," he spat. "Get up."

"But what are you doing here?"

"No questions. Either get up or I'll pick you up."

Finn knew this was more than a threat—it was a promise. Quickly, he picked himself up from the floor despite the pain in his back. He stood as straight as possible. "Can I help you, Master Silver?"

"Yes. Yes, you can," he said, his slight smile visible in the moonlight. "You can strap on your new Blade and follow me."

Finn looked back at the Jigsaw Blade. "I-I—"

"You what?"

"I—I don't think I can," he managed to say.

"You can't what?"

"Put—put on the Blade."

Finn turned his face away from Silver as he approached him, Silver's one eye not giving away any emotion at all. With lightning speed, his palm flew towards Finn's cheek and smashed against it, sending him yet again to the floor. Silver bent down, his mouth to the side of Finn's face, and said, "Strap. On. Your. Blade. And. Follow. Me." He let his breath flow into Finn's ear. "Or else."

Finn stood himself up on shaky knees. He turned to the Jigsaw Blade and grimaced. He couldn't imagine how badly this was going to hurt, but still, he did as Silver said and strapped on his Blade. He tried to use his legs to pull Jigsaw out from the wood but it wouldn't budge.

Silver sighed, walked over to the Blade, grabbed it by the hilt, and yanked it out of the floorboards. He put his face in front of Finn's and said, "Follow me. Don't fall behind."

Finn took a few steps and nearly fell, but caught the side of the doorway and managed to keep himself upright. Silver didn't turn around but kept walking toward the ladder that would take him down to the ground floor. Finn made it halfway down the rungs before falling.

MASTER SILVER WAS relentless with his pace and didn't even turn around once to make sure Finn was still following him. He'd done one last favor by picking him off the forest floor with a grip that nearly broke his wrist.

Finn struggled to walk with a hunched over posture, trying to use the muscles in his legs rather than those of his back. Hours seemed to pass by as the sun rose higher in the sky. Silver moved further and further ahead but Finn kept trailing behind, afraid of what would happen to him if he got lost.

Finn had slowly entered into a hazy state, not really knowing where he was anymore. The pain disappeared as did his thoughts, his subconscious taking over and moving his legs for him. He didn't know how long they had been walking, only that suddenly he ran into something hard and yet again fell backward, landing flat on his Blade.

"Here we are," announced Silver. "This is where we start training."

Finn blinked his eyes a few times as reality set in. "Training? What training?"

"Nibbles didn't tell you?" Silver asked, his hand over his eye to block the sun.

Wherever they were, it was cold and snowy, which meant they must have walked back into the Kingdom of Shimoshimo. If Silver had told Finn they were coming this way he would have worn something a little warmer than his thin leggings and cloth shirt.

"No, she didn't."

"No, she didn't what?" asked Silver, looking down at Finn with his evil eye.

Finally, it dawned on him. "No, she didn't, *Master* Silver."

Silver nodded his head. "Unfortunately for you and unfortunately for me, I am to be your Master."

"You're what?!" Finn asked a little too loudly.

"Do you have a problem with that, *squire*?"

Even though Finn had a Bizarre Blade, in Silver's eyes this must have meant nothing. Sure, he had a Blade but he didn't know how to use it, not even in the slightest. Finn had skipped all the steps, the years of training that a Champion would normally have, and had accidentally and literally fallen into this responsibility.

"Uh, no sir. None whatsoever."

"Good. Just to let you know, I'm going to do my best to have you killed. I'm not in complete agreement with Nibbles and believe Jade a better potential wielder than the likes of you. Prove me wrong." Silver pointed at something in the distance. "You see that boulder over there?"

"No," Finn said, straining to lift his head to see what Silver was pointing at. "I mean, no sir, I can't see it."

"Well, believe me, it's there. You'll find a tattered blue flag at the summit of it. Retrieve that flag and make your way back to our village. Don't return without it or I *will* kill you. Do you understand?" He said all of this without even looking down at his newly-obtained squire.

Finn wanted to ask how it was possible for him to be a squire to someone without a Bizarre Blade, but he dared not. Not only that, but his fast-beating heart made him doubt he could say anything else but, "Yes, sir."

"Good," was all Silver said as he stepped over Finn's body and strode off back towards the road they had just come from.

A gust of wind pushed snow into Finn's face and mouth but he felt too miserable to do anything about it. The weight of the Bizarre Blade attached to his back made it impossible for him to stand up, so he decided to unlatch it. Putting his frozen hands on the buckle, Finn fiddled with it for a time until finally giving up, his fingers too numb to even unlatch his burden. He tried calling out to Silver but no response came. He tried a few more times but was met with silence.

A high-pitched screech came from one of the trees and Finn spotted Obsidian standing on one of the tallest limbs staring down at him, its tiny black head angled to the side, as if wondering why its new owner was lying in the snow.

"I'm going to die out here," Finn said aloud. "I'm... going...to die."

Finn rolled himself over, his back beyond repair. He didn't know where he found the energy for this, other than that his desire to live was stronger than the pain in his back —which was so bad that he'd completely forgotten about the brand on his shoulder.

Obsidian hopped up and down at him excitedly, pecking at his sleeves as it pushed up his body with its trembling arms.

"Stop! You're not helping."

"CAW!"

Finn looked up and found a tree ten feet away and crawled toward it, one agonizing foot at a time. A lifetime later, when he finally reached the trunk, he pushed his back against it and let himself rest a few minutes. Obsidian took this chance to crawl into his lap and curl into a ball.

"Don't get comfortable, Obsidian-Cinnamon," Finn said, his breath heavy. "I'm gonna stand up! I'm gonna do it, dammit! I'll show him! I'll show him that I'm tough! I won't die...not now! Not like this!"

However, he didn't quite believe his own words, despite how good they felt coming out of him. He tried to think on the positive side: at least Silver wasn't there with him. If he had been, Finn couldn't imagine how much worse it would be.

Once he caught his breath, Finn told himself he would try to stand up in ten seconds, and counted it out loud. At ten, he pushed a very reluctant Obsidian out of his lap and pulled his feet in as close as he could. He let himself count to another set of ten before pushing.

It was nearly an hour later that he was standing up, his head rested against the rough bark of the tree. Despite the cold around him, his body felt steaming hot and was drenched in sweat. Obsidian had been no help at all, just watching him and occasionally pecking at his feet. No matter how many times he'd tried to shoo away the microraptor, it always came back to mock him.

"Okay," he said. "Where is this boulder Silver was talking about?"

Finn was afraid to let go of the tree and so he kept both of his hands on it as he swiveled his head to the left and right, but saw nothing. Carefully, he bent a little to look behind the tree.

"You've got to be kidding me."

He could see the boulder, alright, but it wasn't just an ordinary boulder, of course it wasn't. Not only was it as tall as the trees but it was also covered in snow—and no doubt, ice—giving the boulder the appearance of a small mountain. At the very peak of this boulder of doom stood the blue flag Silver had been talking about. It was attached to a stick which was stuck, most likely, into a crack in the ice. There was no wind at the moment, and the flag hung lazily on its wooden pole.

"There's no way," Finn said, feeling himself sliding down the bark of the tree. "There's just no way. No possible way in hell I could get up there, not with this heavy-ass, bulky, burdensome Blade on my back!"

The Jigsaw Blade came to life with a roar, filling the air with smoke and shaking Finn's body with an extreme intensity—so much so that he lost his balance and fell backward onto the magical sword. Smoke poured from the Blade's vents beneath him, rising from the sides of his body and into the air. The Blade did not engage its teeth, which was lucky for Finn because that would not only have torn his skin to shreds but, as they were so far from any sign of civilization, would probably have killed him.

"I'm sorry! Geez, you're so sensitive."

Jigsaw burped one last big blast of smoke underneath him before going back to sleep, or whatever Blades did when they weren't acting up.

"If we're gonna survive out here, we're gonna need to work together," Finn said, resting his hands over his chest. The cold was starting to set itself back into his body, which was still sweaty and therefore not helping the situation.

The Bizarre Blade growled and somehow managed to prick the skin of his back with a single tooth.

"Ow! Hey, cut it out! But, you're right. My mouth isn't really helping the whole teamwork thing is it?"

Jigsaw hummed.

A flake of ice tapped Finn's nose as it began to snow. His priority at the moment was not getting the flag—that was the least of his concerns. What did concern him, however, was staying alive. If he was to survive, he would need shelter and a fire. How he was going to do that with a Blade on his back that weighed a ton was beyond him.

So, as he rested his body, he made smalltalk with the Blade. Obsidian hopped out of a bush, its normally black beak red from a recent kill. The raptor stepped over to him and curled himself against the side of his ribs. If anyone was watching from a distance, they would have looked very odd.

"You were waiting a long time, weren't you?" Finn asked Jigsaw.

The Blade hummed its answer which sent a pleasant feeling through Finn's body.

"Must have been lonely."

Jigsaw agreed.

"I can't really compare to thousands of years without people, but I can relate to the lonely part. As if being a Sprout wasn't enough, I just never was good at making friends, especially with the opposite sex."

Jigsaw said nothing and Finn wondered if it went back to sleep or if it was still listening. The snowfall had grown more intense, falling from the sky in thick white blankets, and Finn's head was now mostly covered. It tickled his nose, and he sneezed a big cloud of it. Obsidian screeched and dove for the tree, using its claws to climb up its bark. This gave Finn an idea.

He imagined putting his back—yet again—to the tree. He envisioned himself adjusting his back so the teeth of the Jigsaw Blade were connected with the bark. When the Blade came to life, it helped pull Finn back up on his feet by using its saw teeth to climb the tree, much like Obsidian had done with his feet.

Finn was just about to ask Jigsaw if this was possible, but before he could he felt another soft hum spread up and down his spine.

"Can you hear my thoughts?" he asked it.

The Jigsaw only continued its purring.

"Okay, well the only way we can find out is if we try!"

With great effort, Finn rolled himself onto his stomach and crawled back towards the tree. It took him another good fifteen minutes before he had himself set up to ensue his plans.

Okay, Jigsaw, let's see what you got, Finn thought, wiggling his shoulders and readying himself for his slow and careful ascent.

Finn was pretty sure he'd maneuvered the Blade's teeth into the tree. He took a deep breath and imagined the Blade pulling him upward with the most detail he could manage. For the first few seconds, nothing happened. He was just about to reimagine his idea of how things should work when Jigsaw roared to life. If Finn had gotten one thing right, it was that Jigsaw's teeth were definitely stuck in the bark.

Before he knew it, Finn was yanked off of the ground! The Blade carried him higher and higher, so quickly that he didn't even have to time protest. Tree limbs and pointy leaves slapped him in the face and shoulders as Jigsaw screamed with effort, smoke bellowing and trailing behind them at his feet. Before long, he dangled at the very top of the tree, the mountain's wind kissing his face with its icy breath.

Finn was at a loss for words. He dared not look down, terrified that at any moment the baldric around his shoulder might come unlatched. Just the thought of suddenly falling made him produce a good amount of nervous sweat on his palms and forehead.

"What...was that!? Are you trying to kill me? No, wait, don't answer that," he said, putting his hands out as if to stop someone. "Don't do anything crazy, Jigsaw. Just, slowly take me back down and place me on my feet."

Finn was too afraid to picture his instructions for the Blade, but through this fear he couldn't help but accidentally produce these images. Once again, Jigsaw awoke and took him on yet another ride. This time, however, the Blade did Finn a justice by not smashing him into the ground but coming to a complete halt just when Finn's feet hung an inch from the snow.

Finn was holding his breath, his eyes pressed firmly shut. All feelings of pain had left him momentarily as he was much more preoccupied with retrieving his intestines, which he was sure he'd left somewhere at the peak of the tree. He tipped one toe down and when he felt the ground he allowed himself to open his eyes.

FINN HAD ANOTHER GREAT IDEA—WHICH meant it would probably get him killed this time. However, seeing as he would definitely die if he didn't take action, he decided to go through with it. He really couldn't come up with any other option, and he had most certainly tried to think of one. He'd rushed into this idea because his hands had gone almost completely numb and it wouldn't be long before he lost control of them. Not only that, but he could feel the cold creeping into his boots as well.

Having used his armpits as a source of warmth for his fingers, Finn was able to finally remove Jigsaw from his back, giving much relief to his legs. However, the heavy Blade had acted as a sort of dam, keeping the pain from his back muscles at bay. Now that Jigsaw stuck out of the ground a few feet away, his back was an assortment of pulsing cramps and fiery agony. It took everything in him not to fall to his knees and cry out. He imagined what Nibbles would say if she stood nearby. No doubt she'd pop him on the head with her cane and tell him to "suck it up, baby."

The temperature began to fall with the slow but eventual disappearance of the sun. Finn no longer allowed himself to think, and instead grabbed the hilt of Jigsaw and pulled it towards himself. Once it leaned on his collarbone, he used the little remaining strength he had to drag it over to the base of the tree, where he laid it down. He sat next to it and used his feet to push the teeth into the trunk.

He again grabbed ahold of the hilt and thought, *Okay, let's cut this tree down!* He barely had to imagine anything before Jigsaw powered through the wood sending a cloud of sawdust into the air. Finn could feel the cheeks on his face and on his ass jiggle as he tried his best to hold onto the Blade. Lucky for him, the job was completed in only a few seconds. In fact, Jigsaw had cut through the trunk so quickly that the tree still remained standing!

Finn shook his hands, trying to put feeling back into them. The aftereffects of the Jigsaw had left his teeth rattling, as well as giving him the feeling that his hands were still connected to the vibrating Blade.

"I'll admit, that went better than expected," said Finn. "Is this the first time that I actually used you correctly?"

The Jigsaw said nothing.

The fact that the tree still stood was a blessing in disguise. If it had fallen just anywhere then it might not have made the best ceiling for his shelter. Now, however, that his brain was awake with the excitement of actually using his Blade somewhat correctly, he noticed a boulder (this time, regular-sized) which would give his shelter the perfect height off the ground.

"That is a nice boulder," Finn said, putting his hands to his mouth and breathing into them.

Using the last bit of his strength, Finn placed his shoulder against the tree and began pushing it in the direction of the boulder. It didn't budge. He put a little more strength behind his push and still, nothing happened. Getting frustrated, he put his hands to the bark and found that they were slow in opening and closing. His teeth no longer chattered from the aftereffects of the Blade because he was freezing to death.

The thought of death being realistically close—literally breathing onto the back of his neck—caused adrenaline to rush through his veins. This numbed the pain in his back and gave him that little extra oomph he needed to complete the job. Digging his heels into the snow and reaching the dirt beneath, Finn pushed with all his might.

The tree creaked as it leaned in the proper direction. A few seconds later, Finn no longer needed to push—the wind doing the rest of the job. Finn gave himself a mental clap on the back for not flinching when the tree slammed into the boulder.

He walked over to where the tree had fallen and couldn't believe his luck. The very end of the tree only extended past the boulder by a foot; had it been any shorter, the tree would have fallen short of its destination. However, seeing as that wasn't the case, Finn felt very proud of what he was able to accomplish. The tree and boulder combination made for an excellent start to his shelter.

Too bad his hands no longer functioned. The night of doom was upon him.

19

FINN VS. WILDERNESS

Finn had no more options. He would just have to take his chances through the night.

He used the very last of his energy to push the Jigsaw Blade up to the base of the tree where he would sleep. Not even with death close behind him would his body produce any more adrenaline for him to use. Apparently, it would rather watch him shut down.

Laying his back into the snow, he was pleased to discover that his skin was so cold that the ice chips now running down the back of his shirt didn't affect him. Obsidian cawed at him from somewhere in the woods but he was too tired to look for it. Instead, he pointed his nose upward, facing the bottom of the fallen tree, and prayed that the wind would not figure out a way to push it onto his head. He started to picture his brains exploding from his ears but quickly focused his energy elsewhere, as he was afraid the Jigsaw might take it as a literal command and saw his head in half.

The sound of air flowing through the vents of the Jigsaw Blade made a sweet whistling noise that was surprisingly not annoying. The Blade paired its hum with the whistle to make a song which sounded much like a lullaby to Finn's ears.

Obsidian hopped over to Finn and pecked his forehead, but he didn't feel it and didn't even have the energy to blink. The microraptor pecked him a couple more times before giving up and disappearing. Finn didn't know how long Obsidian had been gone, as he soon fell asleep. He awoke with the sound of Obsidian pulling something towards him. He couldn't quite see what it was—it was pitch black now. The whistling of the wind through Jigsaw's vents hadn't stopped but the humming had. Did this mean the Blade had fallen asleep?

Finn's breath was dangerously weak, and he was positive he wouldn't make it through the night. Obsidian pulled whatever it was towards him, carried it over his body and left it between him and the Blade. The microraptor then hopped over his stomach and ran back into the trees only to continue the process for God knew how long as Finn again drifted off.

Finn woke up one last time, his breath practically non-existent. His lips had stopped their trembling as they were far beyond that point now. His hands and feet ached terribly, and his eyeballs felt as though they themselves had frozen. Still, he was able to move them slightly, and he looked to his left.

There, Obsidian slept on top of a giant nest it had manufactured throughout the night. Somehow, he sensed that Finn had awakened and opened one of his eyes, and Finn could see the reflection of the moon on its watery surface.

The whistling was yet again beginning to put him to sleep. He was just about to give into the calls of his fatigue when the whistling brought a crazy idea into his mind.

"Fire," he wheezed through his open lips. To his ears, the sounds he made didn't sound anything like the word.

He remembered his first few encounters with the Blade and how it had produced fire within its vents whenever it was angry with him. Perhaps pissing the Blade off would be the only way Finn would be able to survive the night. If only he could get his mouth to function.

He began flicking his tongue up and down as best as he could, trying with all his effort to put blood back into it. He did this for a couple minutes before switching its movement from side to side. He practiced shoving air out of his throat and tried to form words that made no sense.

"Butt cheeks," he said, and was happy with how it sounded, and tried not to wonder why these were the first words to come to his mind. Who knew that the words "butt cheeks" might save his life? As Finn continued saying words, Obsidian raised and cocked its head, confused. "Gooch troll. Tuh-tuh-tyrannosuh—saurus!" He paused to think of more words. "Nuh-Nibbles. Nuh-Nora Nuh-Nibblefingers!" It turned out that Nibbles' name was perfect for warming up the mouth.

He continued spouting off nonsense until he felt confident in his reestablished ability to speak. When he figured he was as ready as he was going to get, he began formulating sentences, sentences that he was sure would anger the overly aggressive Bizarre Blade.

"Huh-hey, Juh-Jigsaw."

The Jigsaw purred itself awake.

"Huh-how's this? Yuh-you're nuh-nothin' buh-but an oh-over guh-glorified shovel!" The darkness was interrupted with a flash of orange light as the Jigsaw's hum turned into a low growl. Finn didn't know whether to be excited or terrified, but he continued. "And—and, nuh-not just any shuhshovel! Buh—but one yah-used for dih-digging holes! Huh-holes for shuh-shitting!"

The Jigsaw's hum was earsplitting now, its teeth digging aimlessly into the snow. In the corner of his eye, Finn could see flames licking from the depths of the vents, and they were continuing to grow!

Obsidian turned around and squawked loudly, hopping out of its nest and directly onto Finn's face. The orange light in the air grew larger as the sound of crackling limbs meant that the fire had spread into the microraptor's nest. It was the sweetest music Finn had ever heard. However, now he had a new problem.

As the flames spread, his shoulder came back to life and began to burn. Obsidian now stood in the snow to his right, screaming at him to get up—but that was the problem. He couldn't get up. At least, not yet.

The entire left side of him was now burning up and he could feel a slight trickle of energy come back to him. He tried moving a finger and found that he could. He tried leaning himself up, but it was no use.

Obsidian was frantic now, screeching and puffing out its feathers. Finn wondered if his last sight would be a micro-raptor that had fluffed itself up to two times his original size.

Then, something amazing happened.

Obsidian stopped its complaining and grabbed the top of Finn's shirt with his beak, albeit with a good chunk of skin as well. It pulled Finn with a surprising amount of strength, that, combined with what little energy Finn had, was able to pull him far enough away from the fire that he wouldn't be burned alive.

He faced the fire now, his breath a little stronger than what it had been. He could taste the salt of his sweat dripping from the upper corner of his mouth.

"Thuh-thanks, Obsidian. Yuh-you're a lifesaver."

Finn fell asleep wondering if he had just about been the first ever Champion to get killed by their own Bizarre Blade. Somehow, he doubted it.

～

FINN DIDN'T KNOW who was surprised more when he jolted awake, he or Obsidian.

The raptor lunged into the air, shoving its red tongue out of its mouth as it squawked in fear.

Finn raised himself, rubbing his warm face with his palm. "Sorry about that," he said.

The fire had gone out, but it must not have been that long ago as he still felt relatively warm. The side of his clothes had turned black from the smoke, as was the bottom of the tree that served as his ceiling. His stomach growled loudly for a breakfast that would doubtfully come anytime soon. If only Finn had practiced more survival skills. Sure, he knew more than many as he was a commoner from the lower class, but he was nowhere close to having the skills of a savage from one of the nomadic tribes of Shimoshimo.

No, there was a really good chance he would die out there in the woods. If it wasn't from freezing to death, than it would be from starvation.

Well, if I'm going to die anyway, then I might as well try!

Standing himself up, he was shocked to find that his back was only slightly agonizing and not to the point of debilitating him like yesterday, so he went to work in finishing up his shelter the best he knew how. He took a tip from Obsidian and started pulling brushes from the ground to cover the ceiling of his fort. He ran out of brushes and low-hanging limbs, and was forced to search at a wider radius.

This took about half the day but he was happy with what he had accomplished. The shelter was now mostly covered, and he'd even managed to position some of the brushes in a way as to let smoke escape from the top. He felt very proud of this clever addition.

The entire time he had been building, Jigsaw remained on the ground. It was still red with a constant fire that crackled within its vents and it seemed to be breathing in a heinous manner. Was it really still mad from the night before? Could Bizarre Blades hold grudges? If anyone was acting like a baby, it was certainly Jigsaw.

Now that the shelter was complete (which, it still looked like crap), he thought it best to start looking for food. While he had been out searching for shrubs to create his shelter, he had come across a frozen river and figured he might be able to come up with a way to catch a fish. He knew the basics of how to do this, just had never done it himself. The worst part was, in order to get to the water below, he would need to use Jigsaw—and this meant he needed to apologize.

Treading carefully, Finn sat himself next to the Blade which produced a growl that rumbled the ground. Now that the fire had gone out and he had stopped his physical work, the cold was starting to set itself back into his body. Not only did he need to eat but he also had to find something to wear as Silver hadn't provided him with any warm clothing.

"Look, Jigsaw. I'm really sorry about last night," he said, feeling slightly stupid that he was talking to a sword with attitude problems. "I didn't mean what I said, I just said it so we could make the fire together."

The Blade roared its hurt at Finn.

"Don't you realize that if I hadn't said those things that I could have died?"

The Blade's growl disappeared, as did any signs of life.

"Don't act like that! Wake yourself back up! I'm trying to apologize to you!"

Nothing.

Finn sighed and lay next to Jigsaw which grunted at him but did nothing else. "I'm dying, Jigsaw. I'm freezing. I'm hungry. And, I'm dying. Did I mention that I'm dying? I don't know about you but I don't really *want* to die. If we're going survive out here we're gonna have to work together, no matter how much we don't like it."

The Blade said nothing.

"And you know," said Finn, looking at Jigsaw out of the corner of his eye. "If I die, then who knows how long it'll be before someone comes along who is as suited for you as I apparently am? Could be years, Jigsaw...could be years."

At first, Jigsaw remained playing dead. Slowly, however, the Blade woke up and produced a soft purr.

"Can I count on you to be more of a team player?" asked Finn. "I know I'm one to talk, but I'm ready and willing to make this work. Whaddayasay?"

The Jigsaw continued to make soft sounds.

"Great. I saw a frozen river just beyond the boulder of doom. It's probably the one we nearly drowned in, but it's our only option. You ready for this?"

Jigsaw gave a small roar of its agreement, its teeth flinging off some of the snow that had drifted onto it.

Finn nodded his head and started to make preparations. He decided he must rid himself of some the cold before his hands froze up again, leaving them useless. He grabbed onto Jigsaw and dragged it over to a pile of brush he'd saved for just this occasion. Carefully, Finn grabbed the top of the Blade and lifted it up on its side.

"Okay, Jigsaw, I need fire and I'd rather do it without insulting you, so—"

The Blade shook, and fire spat out of both sides of its vents, sending a flame right through the middle of the brush pile. Unlike the night before, it took a few tries before the fire caught.

Black smoke rose in the air and he welcomed the smell of it. As he was warming himself back up, his boots and hands extended outward, he said to the Blade, "So, I can give you verbal commands?"

Jigsaw purred.

"And somehow you can read my thoughts, but I'm guessing it may not always be clear to you exactly what I'm thinking, or else you wouldn't have dragged me all the way to the top of the tree yesterday. We're going to have to work on all this."

Jigsaw agreed.

Once Finn was as warm as he was going to get, he snapped off the straightest limb he could find from his shelter and went to work using the top edge of Jigsaw, which was the only part of the Blade without teeth, and started making his spear. The Blade was extremely sharp and it took only a few minutes before he had a point. He was just about to stand up and head to the river when an excellent idea came to him. He sat back down and instead of having the single point, he used the Blade to slice the tip into three tips. He figured this would give his thrust more radius and increase his luck.

"Sometimes I amaze myself with my genius," he said, standing up and wiping sweat from his brow. He looked across the fire and at his shelter and couldn't help but feel a little proud of what he'd accomplished. "If only Father could see this. From painter, to soldier, to Champion, to now, a man of nature."

Finn was about to grab hold of Jigsaw by the hilt and drag it to the river but decided to carry it instead.

If I'm going to get strong out here and become the best Champion I can be, then I need to stop taking shortcuts. I need to get used to carrying this weight.

Laying himself down on the face of the Blade, Finn snapped Jigsaw into place on his Bizarre Baldric, then proceded to take forever to stand up. After he'd caught his breath, Finn made his way towards the river, noticing that the Blade was just slightly less heavy than yesterday.

Once he'd reached the boulder, Finn took time to observe it. It was a good forty, maybe fifty feet tall. Falling from that height definitely had the possibility to kill him. He blew on the snow and cursed at what he saw. Just as he thought, the boulder was covered in a thick layer of ice, which would make it nearly impossible to get a good handhold on any part of it. He looked up at the blue flag which flapped in the wind, taunting him. There was no writing on it, and it was stained and torn in many places. Finn wondered how many times it had been used in the past for Champions just like him.

"If the freezing climate doesn't kill me," he said, giving one last look at the flag, "then this damned boulder will."

As he walked towards the river, Finn realized that he'd nearly been killed by two stones already. Would this boulder be the rock to finally put him down?

20

AN UNWELCOME VISITOR

Finn had Jigsaw all set up with its teeth stuck in the ice above the river, and was ready to give the order. He thought it best to give a verbal command rather than a mental one just to make sure the Blade didn't do anything crazy. He had no room for error—he'd prefer not to go swimming a second time.

"Alright, Jigsaw. It's showtime. Let's cut us a nice circle and—"

The Jigsaw's teeth buzzed to life and cut through the ice like a hot knife through butter. The Blade slid straight into the ice, and nearly slipped through Finn's grip. It would have, too, if he hadn't been prepared.

With both feet spread out wide, Finn kept his back straight and held the Blade upside-down with two hands. Sweat trickled into his eyes upon seeing how close the sawing teeth were to his legs. Carefully, he took a step onto the ice, and then another. He pulled Jigsaw with him and began cutting a terrible excuse for a circle. He'd left the patch of ice connected by just a sliver when he ordered Jigsaw to stop.

Powdered ice floated in the air as Finn pulled the Blade out of the water, its steel already beginning to freeze over as its wetness touched the air. Finn dragged the Blade off the ice and laid it into the snow. He picked up his spear and walked back to his freshly-cut hole. It took only one kick of his boot for the ice to fall into the water. He hadn't expected to see fish right away, but the flowing water before him splashed with activity!

"Wow, just look at all of them!"

Every few seconds to half a minute, a silver tented fish would swim by, taunting Finn with a flip of its shiny tail. The fish ranged in sizes from tiny babies to huge adults, but he didn't care which one he caught—only that he caught one. If and when he caught his first fish, he wasn't sure if he could wait long enough to put it over a fire. He might just have to eat it right then and there, bone and all.

Finn, with a growling stomach, put his spear at the edge of the hole and waited.

It took almost an hour for Finn to spear himself a fish. He swore the bastards figured out what he was up to after the first few failed stabs as they started to avoid the hole altogether. Finn had to wait extra long for fish to swim by that hadn't seen his strike, but it was all worth it in the end: he now had a two-foot sturgeon wiggling on the side of his shoulder.

"Look at what I got, Jigsaw! Dinner!" he cried. "I! Am! Fisherman! Fisherman! Is! I!"

The wind had picked up and Finn couldn't hear the Blade purr. He did, however, see a faint glimmer of orange in the snow as it breathed its congratulations at him. Well, that's what he imagined it was saying, anyway.

On the way back to his camp, Finn chose to drag the Blade rather than carry it. He was going to attach the Blade to his back but figured he'd done enough for one day. If he was going to survive then he needed to be smart, not feeding his ego. He figured the only way to get stronger was by letting his back muscles heal, and he couldn't do that with a three-ton Blade over his shoulder. Besides, the flopping sturgeon was more than enough trouble. Its pointed snout kept smacking Finn in the face, and a few times he'd cut himself on one of its many fins that poked out of its back.

He was passing the boulder of doom when he caught sight of someone in his camp. Finn fell to his stomach, prone, dropping the Blade and the fish into the snow. The sun had fallen behind the trees, and Finn could barely make out the person rummaging through his belongings—which, to be fair, was really nothing.

Judging by the man's wide girth and slouched, short stature he was most likely a savage, perhaps one that got separated from his tribe. He was easily almost double, maybe triple Finn's weight, his body juicy with thick hair-covered muscles, muscles that could tear Finn in half. His long brown hair fell to his shoulders in complete disarray and blew in the wind. Suddenly, the monster of a man stopped what he was doing and put his nose into the air, grunting as he did so.

He's caught my scent!

Finn lay as still as he could as the savage sniffed the air, taking a step in Finn's direction. He saw him stick his tongue out of his mouth and lick his lips as he turned to face him. The savage's eyebrows were connected into one and hung over his eyes, giving him a very primitive look.

He's smelled the fish! He's smelled the damned fish!

Finn began to panic. There was no way he could fight one of these...these...monsters! Sadly, he was going to have to abandon the fish if he wanted to survive. He could always catch another one, but he could never get a new, un-crushed windpipe.

Finn grabbed the fish by the tail and tossed it as hard as he could off to his right, praying the savage didn't see him stand up. The beast of a man did, however hunker down when it heard the THUD noise in the snow. He turned to the direction of the sound and began walking towards it.

There was no way Finn could drag the sword with him into hiding, so slowly and quietly he covered it with snow. Then, he log-rolled himself to the left until he was behind the boulder of doom and out of sight. Still, he couldn't help his curiosity, and peeked one eye out from the corner of the rock.

The wind blew hard now but it wasn't enough to hide Obsidian's famous annoying squawk.

Finn's heart leapt into his throat as he made out the black figure of Obsidian, trapped in a net and hanging over the savage's shoulder. The overgrown and overly stupid humanoid bent down and grabbed the fish by the tail, then took a big raw chomp out of its gut. Even from behind the boulder, Finn could hear his grunts of delight.

"There's no way I'm letting you get away with my raptor. There's just no way!" Finn whispered to himself, but what could he do? There was nothing he *could* do. The savage could—and would—kill him with one punch if he wanted to! He could snap each bone in Finn's body if he so desired. Savages were known for their barbarity. Finn had heard horror stories of adventurers coming into contact with these monsters and they never had fairytale endings. In fact, the endings usually involved soup bowls being crafted out of skulls.

Finn put the back of his head to the boulder, his breathing intensifying. He could feel tears swelling up in his eyes as he realized he was about to lose his little friend.

What would Bryce do? But Finn knew exactly what Bryce would do. He'd kick this savage's ass! But Finn wasn't Bryce. He was Finn, Finn with a Blade he could barely pick up.

He heard the crunching of snow as the savage made its way back into the woods with its two prizes, never to be seen again. If Finn let him go now, then there would be no way to track him, as the woods were *their* territory. Savages were usually only found when they wanted to be.

The savage was disappearing into the woods, and with each step Finn could hear less and less of Obsidian's cry. At that moment, a memory seeped into his mind. He remembered how terrible he'd felt for hesitating when it came to saving Mathew Firepoker. Well, he would not make the same mistake twice.

Finn didn't need his heart to take over this time, as he had already made up his mind. He would not hesitate any longer, and he would save his raptor friend or die trying... but probably would die trying. As he stood up and walked around the boulder, he saw that the savage was almost out of sight. He needed to get his attention or risk losing him in the woods. If this happened, then Obsidian would be gone forever.

"Hey! You! Get back here!" Finn found himself yelling out as loud he could, which came out high-pitched and weak.

However, it worked! He could see the savage's shadow turn and...and...it was running away!

"Oh no you don't!" Finn cried, running over to Jigsaw

and uncovering it from the snow. "Quick, Jigsaw! We need to go after him!"

Finn grabbed the Blade's hilt and dragged as hard as he could. He closed his eyes and put all of his strength into running with Jigsaw, but he knew he would never catch up to the savage—who had most likely sprinted out of his mother's womb and had never stopped running.

"NO!" Finn screamed as he watched the savage's shadow grow fainter and fainter. "Come back!"

All seemed lost until an idea that was not his own forced itself into his mind. It came to him in the form of imagery. He could see Jigsaw Blade pulling him, his body sliding behind it in the soft snow.

"Did you just—?" Finn asked, looking down at the Jigsaw Blade which roared loudly with its teeth, its flames kicking out the sides of its vents. "Alright...alright!" Finn yelled, psyching himself up. This was his only option. "Let's do it!"

Finn spun the Blade around, placed its teeth into the snow and lay down behind it. He was just about to yell out the command when they shot off! The Jigsaw Blade screamed as snow slapped Finn in the face, making it impossible to see. How would he know when to stop? Not only that, but Jigsaw moved so fast that it was hard to hold on! A few times Finn's body had bounced off the ground, flapping in the air like a flag blowing in the wind.

Jigsaw even took control of turning left and right, dodging tree after tree with only a few inches to spare. Finn was just about to let go, his fingers now drained of all of their strength, when they hit something hard and came to an abrupt stop. Snow covered Finn's eyes but he could hear the horrific shrieking of the savage.

A splash of warmth whacked Finn in the face, some of it

getting into his mouth. He let go of the Blade with one hand and used it to wipe the snow out of his face. He looked down at the ice flakes in his palm and saw that they were red. That's when he realized the Jigsaw Blade was still sawing—right into the savage!

More blood splattered onto Finn, his face soon completely covered in it. The cold air was filled with the gore of the savage and Finn was soaked from head to toe in it. He dared not look at the work Jigsaw was performing but yelled out, "Alright! That's enough!"

The Blade slowly quieted down, its teeth sinking back into the snow. Finn dared not look at the mess, but he couldn't help himself. It only took one glimpse and he vomited stomach acid over his shoulder.

The savage, if you could even call it that now, was no more than a pile of bone and pureed meat.

When Finn had finished his vomiting and his thoughts had slowed, he stood up, trying his best to wipe the blood from his face and spitting it out of his mouth.

"Obsidian!" he cried. "Where are you?" He took a step and something squawked at him from under his boot. He looked down to see the microraptor nibbling furiously at the rope net. "There you are! I thought Bloodlust Blade over here forgot that the point of this whole thing was to rescue you!"

The Jigsaw Blade protested behind him, but he didn't care. Finn lifted the net, and out popped Obsidian who squeaked happily, acting as if nothing was wrong.

Unfortunately, Finn had to look back at the pile of savage to retrieve Jigsaw, which he had to activate once more just to get itself unstuck from a piece of bone.

"This night is not going as planned," he grunted, giving

Jigsaw one last yank. The Blade came free and Finn fell on his ass in a puddle of savage blood.

Finn let his head fall back into the softness of the snow as he stared at the blinking stars that had begun to appear. Of course, Obsidian had to ruin this beautiful moment by trying to use his face as a nest.

So, this is what it's like to be a Champion.

21

THE BOULDER OF DOOM

Seven Months Later

Finn soared out of his tree shelter, the Jigsaw Blade following behind him in his right hand. They fell halfway down, both of them screaming out their excitement.

"And...now!" Finn commanded, swinging Jigsaw out in front of him so it could sink its teeth into the usual thick tree limb, which now held hundreds of scars. Jigsaw snagged the tree, swinging Finn forward. "Release!" Jigsaw lifted its teeth and Finn flew a few more feet before plopping into the snow, rolling as he did so to lessen the fall. He stood up, stuck Jigsaw into the snow, and lifted his arms into a wide stretch. His mouth opened and he gave a big yawn as he faced the rising sun.

"Good morning, frozen land from hell! What horrors will you bring me today?"

Over the months that Finn had been stranded out in the woods, he'd defied death multiple times. It was as if whoever had created this frozen world was sending problem after problem his way, testing him and making sure he was fit for the Blade. Whether by luck or a gradual increase in his skill, Finn had overcome everything, from infected cuts all the way to falling bare-ass-first into the hole he'd just defecated in. It had certainly been a ride.

Finn stood as long as he could with the chilly wind blowing onto his bare chest and legs. This not only woke him up and energized him, but he liked to think it also toughened him up, which either it did, or he was seriously toying with hypothermia. Still, he did this every morning and he hadn't died yet.

When he couldn't take it anymore, he lifted Jigsaw out of the snow and snapped it onto his Bizarre Baldric attached to his back.

"Alright, Jigsaw, warm me up!"

Jigsaw sputtered to life. With a little black smoke rising into the air, Finn felt the heat from the Blade's vents wash over him, warming his entire body. He'd grown a pretty decent-sized callous on his back where the heat always hit him, which had taken some getting used to. However, this was the only way he knew how to get warm. Sometimes, if he was feeling really cold, he would tie brushes to his waist, his knees, and at both of his shoulders, finding that this helped to contain the warmth against his body. Nevertheless, today he felt chipper and hungry for some breakfast.

Finn jogged half a mile to where he knew he could find some berries. He'd experimented with all kinds, and had nearly died from many cases of dehydration due to what he liked to call "Diarrhea of Doom". It went without saying that the undergarments he wore now were not the ones he started out with. He'd had to make good use of the shirt he was stranded out there with.

He'd slapped himself across the face when he discovered an abundance of bushes covered in cranberries as well as crowberries, which were tiny and blue. So, he'd basically had the worst diarrhea of his life for no reason.

You live and you learn, he thought as he plucked a handful of crowberries and shoved them into his mouth. He always waited to assort them in lines up and down his mouth and pop them in unison, sending sweet and tart flavored juices all around his mouth.

Only eating berries didn't cut it, so he'd had to become rather good at catching fish. Using the Jigsaw Blade, he'd cut several holes in a line across the frozen river, and shoved very thick brushes into each of them. By that afternoon, he could have two or three sturgeons entangled in these brushes and ready for him to cook.

Other than all of that, life was pretty boring out there in the tundra woods. Luckily, Obsidian brought him an assortment of dead animals—which he dared not guess what they were, but just stuck them on a stick above the fire and ate them. He would try his best to talk to Jigsaw, but it was always hard, if not impossible, to make conversation with it. The purrs could mean it was agreeing with you or that it was just in a pleasant mood. Roaring and earsplitting shredding noises of its teeth could mean it was mad...or just really excited. There was one exception, though, which was when the Jigsaw sung. It had only happened a few times, but Finn knew the Blade did it when it felt truly happy, which in turn made him feel happy. One time he'd even whistled along with it and felt more connected to it then he ever had with another human, besides his father, mother, Bryce, and Monk, of course.

Finn had never gone a month (or even a day) without talking to someone, only to go seven (or at least he felt pretty sure it was seven) without hearing another human's voice. Without Obsidian and Jigsaw, he was convinced he would have gone mad long ago.

He never saw another savage, which was a good thing, not for his sake but the savage's. Finn had become quite handy with his Jigsaw, nowhere near mastery, but at least he could pick up the damn thing and swing it. He could control its basic functions with his mind and he'd even gotten used to Jigsaw's suggestions that popped up as mini-visions every now and then.

Finn was feeling chipper today because today happened to be a very special day, one that would either leave him paralyzed, or would have him leaving these Godforsaken frozen woods and heading back to the Champions of Arbitration's village. Today, he would conquer the boulder, grab the flag, and head home.

Now, he could have completed this task a good four months ago. All he needed to do was stick Jigsaw into the ice and have it pull him up with its teeth. But there was a good ego-filled reason as to why he waited four more months to go for the flag: he didn't feel right in Jigsaw doing all the work. Finn had decided that he would not only be like Bryce Smolder, but he would be better! Bryce would not have died in vain. Finn would give the people of the world a reason to call him Finn the Fantastic.

So, Finn began climbing the boulder with his bare hands.

Finn had studied the boulder for countless hours, figuring out the best way to climb it without Jigsaw's help. The boulder seemed to be almost unscalable, all except for the very VERY thin slits in the outer shell of ice that were randomly spread across its face. Finn thought that if he could somehow get his fingers strong enough to hold up his and his Bizarre Blade's weight, that he could make it to the top. It took him the remaining four months of training to prepare his fingers, forearms, and the rest of his muscles for the climb.

His daily routine was exhausting, but he was diligent and creative. First, he would wake up and, on an empty stomach, would run several miles around his camp. Despite it being excellent exercise, it served two other purposes: one, he was tired of eating fish and tried his best to capture small animals as they ran away. To that day, he hadn't caught a single one. Obsidian, on the other hand, was an excellent hunter, and surprised Finn on occasion with half a carcass —and sometimes even a full one.

The second reason for his jog was to check for any signs of predator dinosaurs or savages that were wandering a bit too close to camp. Only one time did he spot tracks of a meat-eater and was relieved when he found that the tracks led far away from his camp.

Next, after his run, Finn would climb back up his tree for breakfast, carefully selecting the jutting pieces of bark that would be strong enough to hold his weight. At the beginning, climbing seemed hopeless; he would try all day long and not even make it halfway up the tree. Thank God the snow was thick at the bottom or he would have long ago broken his neck from all his falls. Climbing the tree now, however, felt almost as simple as walking. He did not rely on Jigsaw to climb for him anymore. If he was tired and doubted he could make it to his shelter, he would sleep on the ground that night.

Next came his hanging meditation. Once he'd had his breakfast he spent another hour, sometimes two, hanging from a tree by his fingers alone and meditating. He took this time to clear his mind, but he did allow himself to revisit his fantasies. He often thought about his father and how much he missed him. He wondered if Father knew what had become of him. Did the army inform him that his son had died? Or had they not even bothered?

After meditation came the last part of his training, which was swinging his Jigsaw Blade a hundred times from the right of his body, and a hundred times from his left. He also used Jigsaw to cut logs of varying weights so he could practice lifting them, squatting with them, throwing them, and even running with them.

Most of the day, Finn did not need Jigsaw to warm himself up, but did so himself by producing his own body heat. In fact, the cold of the climate was sometimes even welcomed! There were drawbacks, however. When he was getting really good exercise and his breathing had grown heavy, the cold wind would often leave his throat raw. Not only that, but he learned the hard way that even if he felt cold, he could still be sweating profusely—he'd come close to dehydration a couple of times and had gotten very sick from drinking the cold river water too quickly, but he'd learned and he'd learned quickly.

These woods had grown too easy for him to live in, and he felt he was now wasting his time. He needed to get that flag and head back to the village to see what Silver had next on his agenda. Surely, it couldn't be worse than what he was already going through, could it?

"Alright, Jigsaw, time for the moment of truth."

Finn reached around and pet Jigsaw's leathery grip, and the Blade breathed onto his back softly. Finn turned in the direction of the boulder and ran towards it. He ran everywhere, as he saw it not only as a chance to increase his endurance but that it made him feel more like a Champion. If Silver left him out here to get stronger, then by

God he was going to use every minute of it to train his body.

Finn breathed calmly as he reached the boulder. Not only was he going to climb the boulder with Jigsaw attached to his back but he'd also left his shirt back at the shelter, further adding to the severity of today's test. Obsidian had met them there and was perched at the very top of the flag, busy lapping at the underside of one of its wings with his black tongue.

The raptor, much like Finn, had undergone his own sort of training. No longer did he wake up in the middle of the night in search for Bryce, but kept himself as close as possible to Finn's body. During the day, Finn barely ever saw the microraptor, and he knew the raptor was out hunting game or simply gliding from tree to tree for the sheer fun of it. Obsidian had grown at least another foot making it around three feet tall with a wingspan that looked to be also around three feet when spread fully.

"Go ahead and bring me down that flag, will ya?" Finn called up to Obsidian jokingly. His heart almost stopped when the raptor started fluttering his wings, his feet connected to the flag as it tried to rip it off the pole. "No! No! Stop! Don't do that! If Silver finds out that you brought me the flag he'll kill me!" When Obsidian persisted in trying to pull up the flag, Finn rolled up a snowball and accidentally-on-purpose smacked the annoying raptor right in the face. He listened to the sound of Obsidian plopping into the snow behind the boulder, followed by a loud frustrated screech.

"I told you to stop! But, no, you didn't want to listen. You deserved that—"

The microraptor glided around the boulder, its beak pointed straight at Finn's head. With perfect timing, Finn ducked and snatched the raptor by his two legs. The bird flipped and flopped in his hand as Finn lifted himself back up.

"How many times do we have to go through this? I'm bigger and stronger than you. You can't—"

Obsidian pecked him on the forehead, forcing his hand to open and drop him. The raptor then proceeded to peck at his exposed legs a couple of time before running to the nearest tree and disappearing.

Finn rubbed his forehead and didn't even look down at his legs. He knew the raptor had pecked just hard enough to hurt slightly, never drawing blood. If he had to describe his relationship with the feathered dinosaur he would say loving but...complicated.

Rubbing his palms together, Finn did as he usually did before something that scared him and counted to ten. He knew once he got to ten there was no going back, and it was all up from there...literally.

"Ten!" he shouted, jumping as high as he could (which wasn't very high, thanks to Jigsaw.

His right hand snapped into place in the bottom hand-hold (if you could call it that) while his left took a much higher-up hold. His body hung in a very awkward position, his skin and muscles pulled taut. He knew that he would have to ascend quickly if he was to make it all the way to the top lest his hands grew too tired or slipped.

Probably should have made a big pile of snow before doing this, Finn thought as he reached for the next handhold. *Live and learn.*

With his right hand firmly in place, Finn pulled his left off and had to pull himself up slightly with his right fingers to reach the next spot. He knew this was dangerous and he didn't want to put any more strain on the ice then he already was, and so he stuck to fluid motions rather than that of snapping his body upward.

His left hand brushed the next handhold, but it felt too thin for him to hang off of. He must have miscalculated this one—it was hard to really see this high up from the ground. Good thing he'd practiced thumping the bark of trees with the pads of his fingers! That, and he'd let his fingernails grow out for just this occasion which allowed him to pick at the ice. He went to work, scratching the ice horizontally then popping it with the pads of his fingers as he tried to make a new handhold.

His right hand grew tired quickly and slipped not a moment after Finn gripped his new handhold with his left. He looked down at the pieces of ice that had sunk into the snow below. He wasn't very high right now, not enough to really hurt him that much if he fell. He gave one last look at his dangling legs and continued his climb.

He made it about halfway up before he heard Obsidian cry out. By this time, Finn had heard all the different squawks that the microraptor could make. He could judge the dinosaur's emotions not only by these calls but also by the energy that flowed between them. What he'd heard just now...it wasn't good. Something was wrong.

"Obsidian!" he cried. The wind blew hard this high up and he had to keep his eyes closed so his long green hair didn't whip into them. "Obsidian! Where are you, boy?!"

Another cry, but this one came from much higher in the air, and Finn relaxed. Whatever was wrong it didn't matter anymore, because Obsidian must have escaped. Whether or not the raptor was injured, he didn't know. It looked like he was going to have to abandon this climb and go searching for Obsidian. There was always tomorrow.

Finn looked one last time over his shoulders and then

back down at the boulder to find the lowest handhold he could grab onto. His eyes caught something black at the very top of the trees and he looked up to see Obsidian perched at the very tip of the highest limb which bent under its weight. The raptor screeched at him, with the same troubling squawk. Even from this distance, Finn could feel the disturbance in the energy the raptor was giving off.

"What's wrong?" he shouted over the wind. He knew dinosaurs couldn't understand his words but somehow Obsidian could tell what he was saying just by his intonation and body language. Or, at least that's what he decided to go with. Anything to keep himself from believing he'd gone crazy.

Obsidian kept up his distressed calling and Finn just could not figure out what the hell was going on and, seeing that Obsidian was okay, he decided to keep climbing up. He was just about to go for the next handhold when the entire boulder shuddered.

"What was that?" he asked himself, looking to the left and right. More sweat rose from Finn's forehead as he realized that Obsidian's screeching wasn't a cry for help...it was cry of warning.

Then came the sound of something scratching on ice, and Finn slowly dipped his head downward to see what it was. Every single hair rose on his body, including the ones on his ass, as his eyes were greeted by a pair of hungry ones. The scar running across the smilodon's nose told Finn all he needed to know.

This was the same saber-tooth that had visited him that night in the cage. This was the smilodon that had taken down the legendary Bryce Smolder. This was the smilodon that had come back to finish the job.

But something looked wrong with it. The bright yellow

eyes Finn had first met had turned a shade of green. Its cheeks had sunken inward, and its ribs were exposed. The smilodon fell back to the ground, then tried again to run up the ice boulder, this time getting only a foot away from Finn's boot. It then dug its claws into the ice, keeping itself stuck to the boulder.

Finn couldn't take his eyes off the monstrosity that was desperate to get at him. Dirt-covered foam bubbled from its mouth with each breath, and only one set of whiskers stuck out the left side of its muzzle. The same black bugs that had pestered Finn for days in the cage now clung to its body.

Jigsaw snapped an image into Finn's mind of him using the Blade to climb the rest of the way to the top.

"No!" Finn cried, grabbing at the next handhold, but did so too quickly and his hand slipped. He tried it again and was successful. "I can do this!"

The smilodon pawed itself up another foot and tried swiping again at Finn's boot, its claws extended for maximum reach. Again, it missed, and again Jigsaw pestered Finn with more thoughts.

"Stop! I'm trying to concentrate! I can do this on my own! I can do it!"

Looking up, Finn saw that there were no more handholds to grab onto within reach. He would have to start building his own, so that's what he did. Working as fast as possible, he shoved his fingernail into the ice and chiseled as fast as he could. Then, using his calloused fingers, he popped the ice until a handhold formed. However, the ice fell a little too easily off the boulder which made him wonder if this next hold would be strong enough to support his weight.

The smilodon pulled itself up another foot and this time was able to paw the very bottom of Finn's boot making him yelp and lift his legs. This, in turn, caused a cracking sound from the ice. He faced the boulder and found hundreds, if not thousands, of lines spreading across the ice.

With one last try, the Jigsaw Blade, rather than pester Finn with another one of its ideas, shoved an old memory into Finn's mind. Somehow, in some way, Jigsaw had pulled a memory from Finn's brain and sculpted it. The image was a drawing Finn had done of himself, his foot raised on a barrel and big smile on his face. In his right hand he extended out towards the sky his very own Bizarre Blade. Somehow, Jigsaw had implanted itself into the sketch that Finn remembered, taking place of the rather basic sword that Finn had drawn.

The boulder of doom had had enough of Finn's weight and, finally, shattered the portion of ice he held onto with one loud clap.

Finn the Fantastic fell.

22

THE OVERGROWN BIG-TOOTHED SLOTH

As Finn fell backward, the saber-toothed cat pawed at him with so much force that it sent him soaring to the left of the boulder. Pain erupted from his ribs but Finn had no time to pay attention to it. With lightning-fast and well-practiced movement, Finn swung the Jigsaw Blade off his baldric and shoved it into the ice of the boulder.

"Let's go!" Finn shouted at Jigsaw. "Climb! Climb! Climb!"

Flames exploded out of the Blade's vents and up they went. The scarred-nosed smilodon lunged from its position on the boulder, both its front limbs spread wide as it tried desperately to slash at any part of Finn's body but it was too late! The Champion was already reaching for the stars.

Finn launched into the air, Jigsaw's smoke bellowing beneath him as he landed perfectly on his feet. He lifted the Blade into the air and gave a war cry! The smilodon returned this cry but much louder and...well...scarier.

Finn looked down at the cat and spat at it. "Ha! Try and get me now you...you overgrown, big-toothed sloth!"

Finn thought to himself, *Really? Overgrown big-toothed*

sloth? Are we really down to the level of insulting animals?...I need to get out of these damned woods.

Unfortunately for Finn, however, there would be no leaving the woods that day as the smilodon looked prepared to wait him out. It gave one last angry look at him before limping to the nearest tree. It curled itself up into a ball, resting its head at an angle facing him. If Finn got off the boulder the damned cat would know.

Finn was about to start coming up with ideas of what he could do when the pain finally caught up to him. He fell to his side, his teeth gritted and his neck tight as a spasm of white-hot pain traveled from his ribs to the rest of his body. He dared not look down but did it anyways.

Dammit...lots of red stuff.

The smilodon had done him in. With no water to clear the blood it was impossible to see how many holes there were on the side of his torso. He wasn't a shaman or medicine man but he was pretty sure all his organs remained safe and sound. That wouldn't matter, however, if he couldn't stop the bleeding. He didn't have anything to put pressure on the wounds besides his hands, so that's what he used.

Why, of all things, did I decide to climb this wretched boulder without clothes on? he thought as he pressed his hands into his side. The pain was so intense that it was nearly impossible to pinpoint the source of the spilling blood, and so, agonizingly, he had to use his palms to find it.

He found three gashes, the widest one in the middle. He scrunched himself upward and used both hands to cover them up as best he could. In his panic, all he could think to do was to rip out his hair and use that as a bandage. Either that, or he could roll himself onto his side, pushing the wounds against the rock.

Who was he kidding though? Neither of those options

would save him. Whoever found his corpse would laugh at the half-naked bald person lying on his side strapped to a Bizarre Blade.

This thought made Finn laugh, and a glop of blood pushed through his fingers. He looked down and about vomited.

"Oh God, oh God, oh God, what do I do...what do I do!" Jigsaw planted an idea into his mind and Finn shook his head. "No, no...I don't want to do that. I DON'T WANT TO!"

But he had to. It was the only way.

The Jigsaw roared to life, fire licking out from its vents. The snow around the Blade quickly melted leaving a wet, greyish-green rock underneath. After about three minutes, Jigsaw re-sent its idea to Finn's mind, letting him know it was time.

"But I don't want to," groaned Finn—but then why was he using his free bloodstained hand to drag himself to the Blade?

He sniffed as tears of fear dripped from his eyes as he lifted his wound just above Jigsaw's vent, from which a little trickle of fire flickered out every few seconds. Without giving it more thought, Finn screamed and dropped his torso onto the vent. The blood fried instantly, creating a black smoke that smelled worse than the hole into which he'd released his diarrhea of doom.

Finn screamed as he tried unsuccessfully to pull his body off the Blade's vents, but he was stuck. Finally, after an immense amount of effort, he ripped himself off of it...only to find that still more blood trickled out of two of the smaller gashes. He had to take care of those as well.

He bit into his bottom lip, drawing blood as he raised his body yet again over the vent. Jigsaw blew more fire through its vents to reheat the metal. With his eyes rolling into the back of his head, Finn dropped once more, screaming out, "FOR BRYCE!"

He did this one more time before falling flat on his back, the ice melting underneath his wounds. There were stars out now and they were not only blinking and twinkling at him, but also spinning. He felt like he might throw up—not from the pain but from the smell coming off of the fried cakes of blood attached to his body.

He let the vents of Jigsaw cool down before rolling himself on top of it. The Blade took in air from beneath them, flushed it over Finn's body as the Champion fell asleep.

IT WAS STILL DARK when Finn opened his eyes. He didn't move but let his eyes drift to the tree where he'd last seen Obsidian. The microraptor was still there—he could see the moon reflected off of its eyes. Only three times had Finn seen such a massive moon during his stay in the woods, and each time it was just as awe-inspiring as the last. Even now with three cauterized saber-tooth claw wounds over his ribs, he couldn't help but stare at the craters of the moon, counting each one. He lifted his hand and pretended to pluck it from the sky.

How magnificent it would be to walk across that, he thought. *I wonder if it's as cold as here...kinda looks like a circular block of mammoth cheese.*

His stomach growled at this. He was hungry and in a lot of pain. The Blade was doing an excellent job of keeping him warm, but his feet weren't getting a lot of the heat and had gone halfway numb.

I need to get off this boulder while I still have my strength.

Finn adjusted himself over Jigsaw until he heard the snap which meant the Blade had attached itself to the Bizarre Baldric. Then, he rolled onto his stomach and crawled to the edge of the boulder. The smilodon was awake.

Of course it's awake! he thought. *If it was asleep then that would be too easy! And we can't have easy, no we cannot.*

There would be no sneaking around the overgrown big-toothed sloth, so Finn made a choice. He would face the smilodon head-on just as Bryce did. There just wasn't any other option.

Finn stood himself up, puffing his chest out as much as he could. The saber-tooth must not have found this impressive, as it also raised itself and gave a good stretch and yawn.

"I'll show you," Finn promised, and was just about ready to lower himself to the ground when he realized he'd almost forgotten something.

He walked to the blue flag, tore it from the stick, and shoved it into the undergarments on the side of his leg but readjusted it so that it was sitting in front of his groin.

Well, I may not have plate armor, but at least the gooch troll is protected!

His head was still swimming from the pain as he tried using humor to keep his right mind from spiraling away. He only had one shot at this. If the smilodon managed just one single hit on him, then he was finished.

Finn pulled Jigsaw from his back and laid it onto the ice, teeth first. Before giving himself any more time to consider what he was doing, he and his Bizarre Blade were whizzing down the ice, sending a white powder into the air. Looking down, Finn could see the smilodon running towards where he would inevitably touch ground—but this was not his plan.

The saber-tooth flexed its claws as it waited for its dinner to arrive. Finn, using his instincts to let him know when, kicked the boulder as hard as he could, flipping backwards while pulling Jigsaw free from the ice. The smilodon roared as Finn flipped over it, preparing his legs to land just as he had practiced so many times before. Sadly, this wasn't like those times. He was wounded, so of course his feet slipped out from underneath him, and he fell onto his back.

The saber-tooth was on him in less than a second. Finn, trying to catch his breath and bring his mind up to speed, did the only thing he could do, which wasn't much. He whipped Jigsaw out in front of him and used it as a shield. The smilodon leapt onto the Blade, its front two paws landing on the face of Jigsaw. With a crazy amount of luck, Finn maneuvered the Blade left and right at the exact moments the smilodon slashed at him.

Jigsaw pushed an excellent idea into Finn's mind, and he gratefully agreed. The Blade buzzed alive and Finn swung it to the left, being careful not to chop his legs off in the process. The Jigsaw sliced through a few of the toes of the smilodon, sending it backwards with a cry of pain. Blood squirted over Finn's face but he didn't even care to wipe it away; he was too busy trying to breathe and checking that the oversized sloth didn't break his ribcage.

The smilodon retreated back to the boulder, its eyes on Finn as it licked one of its paws. It looked as though it was reevaluating its target. Should it attack? Or should it flee? Of course it would stay and fight, because that was just how Finn's luck worked.

Standing up on two shaky legs (more from fear than from pain), Finn held the Blade up with two hands, pointing it at the smilodon that had taken his hero away from him. He checked his stance and found it lacking confidence. He bent more at the knee, but not too much, and squared himself up to face saber-tooth properly. He tried making himself look as large as possible without falling forward from the weight of the Blade.

"Come and get me!" Finn cried at it. "You're gonna make a very fine throw rug for my tree fort!"

Well, at least my taunts are improving, Finn thought.

The saber-tooth called his bluff and charged, jumping left, then right, then left again. Finn didn't have the strength to maneuver the Blade to mirror the beast running towards him, so instead he kept himself pointed forward. He knew that the best attribute of the smilodon was its amazing agility and that was something Finn just didn't have, not even when he wasn't wounded.

It took a millennium for the saber-tooth to get close enough for Finn to swing at him, but his attack missed terribly, leaving him wide open. The saber-tooth launched itself in the opposite direction without wasting a moment and pawed at Finn's revealed ribcage. Finn was sure it was over, that the smilodon had won, when Jigsaw blasted out a black sludge right into its face!

The saber-tooth jumped backward, pawing at its eyes to rid itself of the black goo. Finn took this opportunity to swing Jigsaw behind his back and bring it down on the head of the beast. Without him having to tell it to, the Blade's teeth were in motion, its vents creating a humongous roar along with two long lines of shooting fire that arched back with Finn's swing.

Somehow, the saber-tooth knew what was coming as it tried to evade, but it couldn't escape in time. Finn's Blade sunk itself just above the tiger's left paw, right above the joint. The Jigsaw made quick work separating the limb completely from its owner. Finn's mouth fell open, not from his excitement, but from his confusion. The blood, it was... black...and not just black because it was night, but because something was wrong with this animal. Very wrong.

The smilodon did not cry out, but swiped yet again at Finn's side. It wasn't the most powerful attack but it still sent Finn to his side, the ground smacking his wounds and making him cry out. Still, he spun around just in time to catch the saber-tooth trying to awkwardly pounce on top of him, the claws on its remaining front paw pointed right at his head.

Finn pulled his Blade over his face. There was a loud crunch as Jigsaw pressed against Finn's nose under the weight of the smilodon, sending pain all up and down his skull. A crazy idea came to Finn just then. He swiped the Jigsaw out of the way to the right and the smilodon's foot fell directly onto his face. Finn, with his mouth full of cat fur, swung back the Blade and sawed off the paw, pouring tons of the black blood all over him. He tried his best to cover his mouth but it was no use. It was not like any blood he'd ever tasted. There was no hint of iron, but a mixture of bitterness and sweetness with the smell of three-week-old milk left out in the sun...and he had it in his mouth.

Finn hadn't considered where the smilodon's face would go when it no longer had any front paws. The saber-tooth's head fell flat on Finn's, but it did not snap at him, likely because it was just as confused as he was. Finn pushed up on the Blade to get the smilodon's head away from his, having to use all of his strength to do so.

The beast was whimpering now, but still kept fighting!

What in the actual hell is going on? How is it still alive? Why does it not run away?

The cat snapped at his face, getting closer each time, shooting thick saliva into his hair. Finn watched as its movements began to slow as its life poured into the snow, melting it. When the smilodon had finally gone limp, Finn lay in an odd, bloody snow angel of death.

It took him ten minutes to leverage the smilodon in such a way that he could pull himself out from under it. His heart raced like mad and the pain in his side was coming back to life, as was the pain in his nose. Whenever he tapped it, the excruciating pain made him want to vomit. He could tell that it was bent the wrong way, and did not look forward to fixing it, especially because he would have to do it on his own. He could no longer breathe out of either nostril—not because of the blood gushing from them, but because the cartilage had collapsed in on itself.

Finn, sitting on his knees and bending his face into the snow, screamed as he grabbed onto his nose and yanked. It was too slippery, though, and this did nothing but torture him. He pulled the flag out of his pants and used it to wipe some of the blood off before trying again. His head throbbed from the pain and his ears popped when he clasped his hands onto his nose again and gave it yet another good pull.

CRACK!

The nose cooperated this time and came halfway back to its normal position. Finn blew through it, and two circular blood splatters shot onto the snow in front of him. Tears of pain fell down his face and he sniffed a few times.

It had to be done, Finn. It had to be done. Can't expect to make it back to the village if you can't breathe!

Finn fell to his side, his body convulsing. He pulled his legs into his stomach as his mind went through a mini panic attack. He'd nearly been killed! He'd seriously nearly been eaten alive by the very beast that had torn out Bryce's throat.

But you did it, Finn. You did it. Everything's going to be okay. You're alive. You're alive...

Jigsaw rested behind him and blew out a steady stream of hot air to warm him. Finn found comfort in the sensation of his body descending into the snow. He didn't know how long he stayed out there, recovering from the shock of all that had happened; all he knew was that the sun was finally showing its face.

Finn was not strong enough to pull the saber-tooth back to camp, so instead he carefully stuck Jigsaw through its body, using its ribs to keep the Blade in place. Then, he commanded Jigsaw to pull both he and the saber-tooth back to camp.

Once he'd gotten something to eat and drink, Finn decided that he would not start his return back to the village that day. Instead, there was something else he wanted to do, that he NEEDED to do.

Looking down at the smilodon, he noticed that something had changed. There were no more black bugs crawling all over it. Its eyes no longer had their tint of green, but had changed back to their normal shade of yellow. The skin's patchy fur was now full and even looked healthy. The bloody stumps were not black but a bright red, in contrast with the white snow.

Did I just imagine all of those things?

Well, there was nothing he could do about it now. There was work to be done. He sat down beside the carcass and began using the top edge of Jigsaw to skin the smilodon.

Finn's heart stopped as he heard the crunching of snow coming from the edge of the woods. His head shot upward to see Silver walking towards him. He looked even skinnier and paler now then he had all those months ago. Anger bubbled in Finn's gut and he could feel his skin growing hot.

None of these horrible things would have happened to him if the albino hadn't left him in the woods in the first place. Finn had never been the apprentice to a duelist or fighter before but he knew there had to be safer and perhaps even more efficient methods of training people than stranding them out in the woods.

Finn pulled his eyes back to his work and kept going.

Silver stood above him a moment, watching him work. Then, he pulled out a knife of his own, sat next to Finn, and helped him skin the beast that had ended the life of the Legendary Bryce Smolder.

23

SILVER EXPLAINS HIS INTENT (IT'S NOT NICE)

OBSIDIAN CHIRPED HAPPILY ON FINN'S SHOULDER AS HE AND Silver made the walk back to the village. The microraptor found its owner's newest cloak made from the fur of the smilodon to be extra comfy. However, wearing this new cloak made Finn feel a little silly, especially because he felt like he didn't deserve it. Killing the saber-tooth had been a feat of accident and luck, rather than one of actual skill. Still, he did feel sort of like royalty wearing such a beautiful cloak. He carried more of the smilodon's skin in a pouch at his hip and he wondered what he would craft it into.

"How long were you watching me?" Finn asked Silver, breaking the silence that had lasted from last night.

"As long as needed."

"So, the whole time?"

Silver nodded.

Finn didn't want to ask this next question but he kinda wanted to. He needed to know. "Were you going to step in at all?"

"What do you mean?"

"If the cat had gotten a hold of me or if it looked like I

was about to get eaten or something. Would you have come to save me?"

"No," Silver said simply, but, seeing as Finn was just staring at him, he continued. "It wouldn't have mattered anyway. If something had gone wrong, then the smilodon would have killed you long before I could have made it."

"But the entire thing went wrong," Finn protested.

Silver said nothing, a very small hint of a smile flashing across his face. This freaked Finn out. It was as if this man *wanted* him dead—which he probably did.

They walked on for a few moments in peace...well, sort of. There was no peace in Finn; instead there was molten hot anger, an anger he dared not show because he knew if he did Silver would kill him right then and there. So, he waited until this hotness passed before asking, "How did I do?"

"I'm not following you," Silver said, keeping his eyes on the road.

"You know, being in the woods. How did my training go?"

"Training? What training? You thought that was training?"

"Well, yeah, I assumed so," said Finn, scratching his forehead. "Of course it was training! You left me out there to toughen up and—"

"I left you out there to die," Silver objected.

Finn choked, only being able to spit out a simple, "Oh... well, then, what about the flag? You told me to bring the flag back to you and then we'd continue the training or whatever."

"That was to speed up your death," admitted Silver. "I needed that Jigsaw Blade as soon as possible, but..." Silver snapped his eyes to the Blade then back at the road. "It looks like Nibbles was right, as she always is. As much as I hate to admit it, you and that Blade are a proper match. Depending on how well you do during the real training, you might even make an okay Champion, or maybe even a decent one. Jade will just have to find another Blade."

"I don't think Jade likes me."

"You're wrong," Silver said, crossing his arms over his chest and breathing out a white cloud. "He absolutely despises you. You took his chance away to become a Bizarre Blade wielding Champion. Now, who knows how long it will be before Nibbles catches the attention of another willing Blade in the Foretelling Fabric?"

"But," said Finn, raising a finger. "Nibbles said that Jigsaw wasn't willing." Silver didn't answer but only sighed, which Finn took to mean that the conversation had ended.

They walked on for hours to camp, only this time Finn wasn't in agony because of fatigue but because of his lacerations. The skin of these wounds kept opening back up with his movements and his healing nose made for a constant reminder that a smilodon paw had nearly crushed his skull.

"Oh shit," Silver said all of a sudden, his posture straightening so perfectly that any Princess's teacher of etiquette would have approved.

"What? What is it?" Finn asked, looking up and snapping out of his daze.

Silver did not answer but sprinted at an incredible speed, a speed to which Finn would not possibly be able to keep up with. Then, his eyes caught it: the small wisp of smoke coming up from above the trees, more smoke than would come out of the chimneys. Something was wrong.

Finn took off running behind the Master who wanted him oh-so-badly dead. Obsidian chirped loudly and glided off of his shoulders and towards the trees. Finn watched the raptor disappear into the woods. He turned attention back to running, grimacing as the warm sensation of blood trickled out of his wounds and down into his undergarments. Jigsaw reduced its heat on his back as he warmed himself up from the run. His stamina had increased dramatically and, although Silver had disappeared up ahead long ago, Finn figured he was doing as well as anyone could when chasing that freak of nature.

What could have happened? Could the village be under attack? Who in their right mind would invade a village that held at least, to Finn's knowledge, four Bizarre Blade-wielding Champions? It just didn't make any sense. There was no way the village could be under attack; most likely it was a fire set by one of the younger students who wanted to cook some meat and lost control of the embers.

Finn was just about to clear the hill from which he knew he would be able to get a decent look of the village when an ice cold hand gripped him by the upper arm. He was yanked into a bush filled with thorns that tore into his skin.

"Ow! Why'd you pick this bush? Why not one of the other ones without—" Silver's hand slapped against Finn's mouth, silencing him. His one red eye made it clear that he wasn't afraid to snap Finn's neck if he kept talking, and Finn nodded his understanding.

The two of them sat in their highly uncomfortable hiding spot. Silver stood as still as a statue, his eye focused on the road, his ears twitching with any little sound he heard. Finn jumped when Silver finally moved and pulled himself out of the thorn bush, the paleness of his back covered in fresh red cuts.

The two of them crept forward, their bodies hunched forward as much as possible to keep from being seen. The village was now clear to Finn as they made their approach, sneaking from bush to bush. Suddenly, Silver shot out his hand and smacked Finn's stomach hard, then pushed his head down into the snow and hovered over it.

Finn turned his head slightly under the man's strength just in time to see him snap forward with incredible speed. Two people had appeared without Finn having noticed. Silver had both of their heads pushed into the ground, just as he had had Finn's only seconds earlier. The two men must have been so shocked that they didn't even have time to cry out. Silver released the man on the right, grabbed hold of the head of the man on the left, and snapped his neck. He returned both hands to the other man's head and snapped his neck as well. Then, as if nothing had happened, Silver stood back up and continued his sneaking approach to the village.

Finn was laying on his side looking at the two dead men in horror. The one facing him wore a large wooden mask, the same mask the bandits had been wearing the night they had ransacked the caravan. Somehow, Constantine must have come in contact with these bandits and had hired them for his own purpose.

Finn stood up, being careful to keep himself hunched over. He looked one last time at the dead men. The one facing him still had his eyes open and his tongue had flopped out of the mouth hole on his mask. The sight of these corpses raised the hair on the back of his neck, but he had to keep going. He had to stay tough! Besides, this really had nothing to do with him. Surely, Silver and the other Champions would take care of this problem and everything would go back to normal.

And then, a loud voice rang through the village, "FIND ME FINN FEATHERSTONE! I KNOW HE'S HERE SOMEWHERE!"

Silver looked back at Finn from his hiding spot with one wide eye. That's when Finn knew, if it came down to it, this man would easily sacrifice him for the sake of his village without a second thought about it.

In fact, he'd probably be happy to do so.

24

SINISTER TWIGS

"What do you mean you can't find him?!" said a voice that was all too familiar to Finn. "He's the only damned Sprout with a Bizarre Blade! Look again! This time, don't be afraid to rip up the floorboards if you have to! The bastard is more cockroach than human, so I wouldn't be surprised if he's hiding in a crack somewhere!"

Hiding behind the bushes, Finn stared up at Silver and swore the man never blinked. The widening of Silver's pupil showed that he was thinking, maybe even considering something. Finn was about to break the silence when his Master did instead.

"Do you know him?" Silver whispered.

"I—I don't know. His voice sounds familiar but—"

"Get a good look. I'll tell you when to raise your head."

Silver turned his face into the bushes and looked through the leaves towards the main road of the village. He raised his hand and, after a few minutes, dropped it which Finn took as his signal to look.

Constantine Firefurnace's face was a mess of scars and scabs, his teeth visible through chunks of cheek that had been bitten off sometime in the past. When he blinked, only one eyelid closed, while the other was either missing or no longer functioned. Chunks of his once-luscious blonde hair were missing, and both of his hands were gloved with a couple of the finger slots missing a digit. Whatever had happened to this man in his time in the wilderness, he hadn't been nearly as successful as Finn. It looked as though he'd been dinner to more than one type of dinosaur.

Finn was just about to drop back down to the bushes when he caught sight of the massive Blade strapped to the back of Constantine; he knew instantly which one it was.

The Nullify Blade.

The Nullify Blade was a Legendary Blade known for its amazing ability to cancel out the magical effects of all other Bizarre Blades at a very far distance. It was also famous for always being wielded by Champions of—more or less—ill intent. Now that Finn understood that Blades had personalities and chose their wielders, it made sense that the Nullify Blade was always in the hands of the corrupt, and why it had chosen Constantine.

"What?! What did you see?" Silver asked, grabbing hold of Finn by his new cape with both hands.

"I know who he is," answered Finn. "He was a Commander in Shimoshimo's army. And—"

"And what does he want with you?! And tell me why I shouldn't feed you to him."

Finn swallowed but wasn't nearly as scared as he would have been several months prior, and he calmly told Silver all he wanted to know. He explained about Constantine's banishment by Bryce and how he was kind of responsible for it, even though the man deserved it. Silver listened to this story without saying a word. The only part of him that moved was his twitching eye.

When Finn had finished the story, Silver let go of his cape and they both sat back against the bush.

"How do you know it's the Nullify Blade?" Silver asked.

"I know about most of the Blades that have made themselves visible to the world," Finn said. "This one was one of my favorites because..." Finn stopped himself because he had just been about to reveal that he'd often imagined himself fighting against another Champion who wielded the Nullify Blade. It was the perfect Blade for the antagonists of his fantasies. He quickly changed this story. "...Because of how powerful it is. Not only that, but its features are unique. The Blade is known to be visible for five seconds, then invisible for another five seconds. It is said that when its owner dies, the Blade disappears until it's claimed again."

Silver looked straight ahead and nodded. "We need to get closer."

"Closer than we are now? But we'll be seen!"

Silver responded to this by rolling from the bush to behind a tree, then again rolling to another bush. Finn watched him as he moved through the shadows with grace, a grace Finn did not have possession of. Maybe he could have been half as proficient but certainly not with the Jigsaw Blade on his back. Somehow the Blade must have sensed the severity of the situation and had gone completely quiet. It did not hum, nor did it produce any fire or smoke. It was like it was pretending to be dead.

If only it could shrink itself to a smaller size! Finn thought, standing up from his aching knees and starting for the tree. He froze when he felt movement on his back. He did not move a muscle as Jigsaw made slight noises, but noises nonetheless, that sounded liked metal sliding against metal. Through the brush Finn could see that Silver had heard his

Bizarre Blade, and glared back at him with a gaze that said, "If we get caught, you won't have to worry about *them* killing you."

A few seconds later, Jigsaw went still again, a small puff of smoke exiting from its vents. Finn grabbed for the grip, but his hand clasped only air! He searched for the Blade and found that the grip had not only dropped to below his shoulder blades, but that it too was smaller in size. He pulled Jigsaw out in front of him and almost squealed with excitement.

Jigsaw had unlocked a new power! The Blade must have decided that Finn, with all the progress he'd made, had deserved to have access to a new ability!...Or the Blade might have done it just to protect itself...yeah, that was probably it.

Jigsaw had magically reduced its size by half, and it looked exactly the same, only smaller. It was more of a shortsword or large hunting knife now. The craziest part of all was that the weight had remained exactly the same, making it still incredibly heavy to wield.

Why didn't you show me this back in the woods? Finn thought, knowing the Blade was listening. *You do realize how useful this could have been!*

The Blade answered with the slightest puff of hot air that breezed past Finn's nose.

We'll talk about this later but...thank you.

Finn snapped the Blade back to his Bizarre Baldric and continued with his poor excuse of trying to be stealthy, but at least there wasn't four feet of sword sticking out from the bushes now! When Finn reached Silver, his Master snapped his hand with lightning speed and gripped him by the throat.

"What. Was. That?" he hissed, his red eye bulging and his grip tightening with every passing second.

Finn tried his best not to cough and used his thumb to point back to the small Blade on his back. Silver looked over his shoulder, looked at Finn with an ugly face, and pushed him backward.

They waited in that spot for a few minutes, listening to the sounds of footsteps. None of the bandits spoke, not even a whisper! The village was dead silent. Finn and Silver stood behind a massive tree and seeing anything past it was impossible. Silver was busy mouthing words and moving his fingers up and down like a crazy person. Finn already had enough anxiety as it was and whatever Silver was doing it was driving him insane.

Well, he could be listening to the footsteps of the bandits, counting how many there are, Finn thought to himself. *Then, he could probably figure out which to kill first. Yeah, definitely either of those.*

Without warning, Silver leapt from their hiding place and put his back against the next tree. Finn started to follow but Silver put a hand up to stop him. They stayed like that for a few moments before Silver jumped to yet another tree, again with his hand up. Finn now understood what he was doing. Somehow, his Master could tell the whereabouts of the bandits just by listening, and was able to judge his sneak moves accordingly.

Who is this guy?

Finn saw Silver's face tighten up. His eye, which was usually wide with anger or frustration, grew less intense. He looked...sad. Maybe scared? Still, he kept his hand up for a while, until finally dropping it. Finn had been waiting for this and tried his best to perform the same jumping and somersaulting technique.

It did not go well.

"What was that?" asked one of the bandits.

"You hear something?" asked another.

Finn was laying on his back where he'd landed. His heart beat so hard and so fast that he could have sworn that the whole world could hear it. He could feel Silver's gaze burning into him.

"Yeah. A twig snapped or something."

"Something? Darrel, these are the woods. Twigs snap all the time in the forest and I suggest you snap out of it lest you want to feel the wrath of that Canister Firefurniture guy."

"His name's Constantine Firefurnace," said the Bandit with disgust. "How the hell did you get—ah, never mind. I'm gonna go ahead and check on that twig snapping. You never know."

"Please, Darrel, Firefurniture doesn't pay us enough to be chasing after sinister twigs."

"Go to hell," snapped Darrel. "It's like you don't even listen. If anything, Constantine is paying us *more* than enough to go twig hunting. I suggest you start working hard or you may get yourself tied up right next to the prisoners."

Finn's beating heart stopped dead, a flash of sweat rising on his forehead. Prisoners... Constantine must have taken the entire village hostage! The only way Finn could possible conceive the man doing so would be by him using the Nullify Blade to null the powers of the Blades of the professors. Then, using the brute force of his mercenary bandits he took control of the village.

But why go through with all this trouble? Why chance getting killed? Was getting revenge on Finn really that important? No, that couldn't be it. There had to be something else. How did he get the Nullify Blade? He didn't seem the kind of person to be smart enough to search for an invisible Blade only to find it within months, while simultaneously organizing a miniature army. Something was missing.

"Whatever you say," said the other bandit. "I'm gonna keep acting like I'm doin' stuff important."

Finn listened as one pair of footsteps trailed off while another started walking in his direction.

"Gonna get himself killed is what he's gonna do," grumbled Darrel. "Not me, I'm playin' it safe. Do what I'm told, get paid, go home."

The sounds of footsteps grew closer and closer. Finn prayed with all of his might that the bandit would stop, listen, then give up the search, but of course not. He had to keep heading in the direction of the cowering, green-haired Champion.

Finn tilted his head back and saw a somewhat concerned Silver. The man was bent low and apparently miming what he wanted Finn to do, which was to pull out his Jigsaw Blade and shove it upwards, probably into the bandit's throat.

With shaky hands, Finn reached behind his back, unsnapped his Blade, and held it to his chest. He looked back at Silver, who nodded his head and stood back up, his back to the tree. He raised his hand, ready to signal Finn when to strike. Thing was, Finn didn't know whether or not if he could do it. Sure, he'd already killed a man—well, a savage, really—but he'd killed him nonetheless. But that had been an accident! He never wanted to kill anybody or anything. Well, besides the smilodon.

So, thought Finn. *This is to be my first real kill as a Champion...but it doesn't feel right! It just—*

There was no more time to think. The footsteps had stopped just behind the bush that Finn lay behind. He held

Jigsaw tightly in both hands, ready to plunge it upward on Silver's command.

I don't want to do this. I don't want to do this. I DON'T WANT TO DO THIS!

But he had to.

The suspense of waiting for Silver to drop his hand was killing Finn. He flinched every time the man's pinky finger flinched. He could feel his butt cheeks tightening as sweat ran into his eyes and stung them.

Silver's hand never dropped, and Finn's butt cheeks relaxed slightly. He let out the breath he'd been holding when the footsteps started to walk away.

Finn, still holding Jigsaw to his chest, let his elbows drop to the ground out of relief. His right elbow fell onto something stiff and thin.

SNAP!

"Who goes there!?"

25

BETRAYAL

THE SINISTER TWIG HAD ALERTED THE BANDIT, AND HE NOW charged towards Finn's hiding spot.

A head popped over the bush. The man wore the usual wooden mask, this one with a painted pterodactyl on it. Through the mouth hole, Finn could see the man's mouth open wide as he readied to cry out, "Intruder! Intruder!"

That never happened. Instead, through the opening of the mouth, Finn watched as a shining piece of metal slid in and out of the back of the man's throat. The eyes behind the mask turned to the right, and Finn followed them to see Silver kneeling right beside him, pulling his bloodied dagger out of the bandit's head.

Blood was slow to come, but boy did it come. Red drops rained onto the top of Finn's face and he tightened his lips to keep from any getting into his mouth. He started to gag and Silver slapped his hand over Finn's mouth just before an explosion of half-digested berries could escape from his mouth in a disgusting fountain. Instead, the vomit remained in his mouth and he was forced to swallow it while more blood poured onto his face.

If there was a hell, Finn imagined it would be like this.

Silver grabbed the bandit by his shirt and pulled him over the bushes. He landed on his back still alive, both of his hands going to his throat as he choked on his own blood. Silver did the bandit a service by lifting his head up off the ground, putting the man's chin on his chest to close off his windpipe. Finn, on the other hand, was busy wiping blood from his mouth.

Silver bent low, his lips touching Finn's ears. "If we get out of this alive, I'm going to kill you myself."

Finn nodded his head. Wait, why did he nod his head?

Silver pulled his face away from Finn's and let go of the bandit's head which lulled over to the side dead. Silver then shoved the corpse into the side of the shrubs, pulling as much of the foliage down over the body as he could. He then turned and tried his best to wipe the blood into the creases of the grass, but it wasn't working.

"No more somersaults. No more noise. No more mistakes," Silver warned, pointing to the tree he'd just come from. "Stay close to me and move when I move."

"Okay."

"SHHH! Not another word!"

Finn was able to make the run to the tree without being spotted and was given no commendation from Silver. This was to be expected of Champions. This wasn't something they were taught, it was just something all Champions could do: they were good at moving their feet in stressful situations; they were good with their bodies and always knew what to do. All but Finn, of course. Sure, he could swing from trees but he was still not worthy of the Bizarre Blade he had attached to his back.

"Take a quick look when I say so," said Silver, his one eye at the side of the tree. "Now."

Finn peeked out from behind the tree. He swallowed hard. In the center of the road laid a pile of bodies, all with their ankles and wrists tied together. Most all of them looked to have rags shoved down their throats.

Everyone had been captured.

The children. The young adults. Jade. Ariel. The Champions. Even Nibbles lay flat on her stomach, her chin resting in the dirt, her legs and wrists tied together into the air. The hostages were all arranged in a giant circle and, on the outskirts of this circle were piles of wood. Constantine must have had the intent to burn them alive!

Finn looked back at Silver who mouthed the words, "Your fault."

The guilt inside Finn was strong and he wasn't sure why. Silver could say it was his fault all he wanted, but the truth of the matter was, he didn't ask for this, not any of it! It wasn't his fault that Constantine had tried to get young soldiers to fight to the death in the woods! And it certainly wasn't his fault that Constantine had been caught!

"I've waited long enough!" came Constantine's voice. His footsteps grew louder.

"But sir!" said a bandit. "You've waited only half a day and—"

"SILENCE! When I say I've waited long enough, then I mean I have waited long enough! We have four Bizarre Blades, which should be more than enough to suffice Prince Tarek in whatever scheme he's planning."

"And what of Finn, sir?"

"Bah! I'll find him, don't you worry. As for now, we need to relinquish ownership of our newly-obtained Blades. Douse the wood in oil and set this pile of filth aflame. I'm tired of looking at them. No one will miss the Champions of

Arthritis," Constantine said, directing his serpentine smile towards Nibbles.

"Uh, sir, I think you mean 'Champions of Arbitration'."

"Correct me one more time and I'll see you added to the human bonfire! Do you understand?"

"Yuh-Yes sir! I understand!"

"Clearly, you don't. Now, do as I say!"

Silver twitched, his body ready and itching to move. He was completely ignoring Finn which was for the best, as Finn was aware that he was basically useless. He would only get in Silver's way, that much was evident. No, it was best he stay out of the way.

Fifteen minutes later, one of the bandits alerted Constantine that the wood was ready to be lit.

"What? Are you awaiting my order? Just do it! Dammit, it's like I have to hold everybody's hand around here. When I hired your guild I thought I was hiring heartless killing monsters! But no, all I got were babies to babysit." Constantine paused, and then added, "Instead of calling your guild the 'Masked Mercenaries', I would have gone with something more like the 'Guild of Mindless Morons'. Ha! That one's pretty good...I'm writing that one down."

Finn could see some of the bandits giving Constantine some evil glares behind his back while lighting the tip of a very large stick. As they walked towards the pile of villagers, Finn was shocked to see that none of them squirmed. None of them screamed or even looked at the stick that was about to bring them their doom.

Silver had sidestepped from the safety of the tree and was preparing to run when one of the prisoners stood up. This person, who was none other than Jade himself, turned his head and spat the gag to the ground.

"I can get you the Blade you seek!" he yelled in a voice that he'd obviously deepened for effect.

"Wait, what?" Constantine sputtered. "What's this child doing out of bondage? Does anyone, I repeat, do *any* of you idiots know how to tie a damned knot? COME ON!" Constantine was breathing heavily. He took a big breath in, pushed his shoulders back, and released his breath slowly from his mouth as he calmed himself. He turned to Jade and said, "What did you just say? I was a little busy expressing my frustrations. I paid good money for these so-called mercenaries, and, well..." Constantine gestured to the bandits walking around, some aimlessly, some kicking in doors of houses already searched, and some picking their noses. "You understand what I mean."

"I said I can get you the Blade you seek, but not only that... but I can bring you its wielder."

Silver backpedaled behind the tree. He reached out and gripped Finn's wrist tightly, making sure he didn't try to run off. Like it would matter anyway. Finn knew he shouldn't have trusted these people. It hadn't even been a year and they were already throwing him to the fire...literally.

Constantine brought his fingers together and drummed them together in the way all villains did in the stories told before bedtime. "This sounds too good to be true. What do you want in return? Your freedom?"

"That, and the Blades you have nulled and stolen."

"So, you're saying you want me to trade four Blades for one?"

"Finn's Blade is of Legendary status, I assure you."

Constantine snorted. "That's pretty funny, I have to hand it to you. You really think I'm going to fall for that?"

"No," Jade said, bending down towards Nibbles and pulling out her gag, "but you'll believe her."

Constantine's face went serious. Nibbles looked down, her face scrunched in frustration. Her eyes were non-existent.

"So, the Mage Scribe traitor...is it true? Is this Blade of Legendary quality?"

Nibbles didn't say anything for a while, but Constantine was patient. He paced while he awaited her answer. "Yes," she said finally. "The Jigsaw Blade is a Legendary Bizarre Blade."

"Oh, you've named it already? Very nice. I like it! The Jigsaw Blade! It has a sort of ring to it, doesn't it? Odd, but unique. Tell me, how is it you know this Jigsaw Blade is a Legendary Blade?"

"Because..." Nibbles' words trailed off. She let her face fall into the dirt.

"Because, why?" Constantine pursued. "Tell me or I'll burn you all!"

"Because it took the use of blood magic to finally get it to respond to me!"

The pile of Champions of Arbitration had been quiet, even in the face of death. This, however, made them all gasp through their gags.

"My, my! And here I thought you ran away from the Mage Scribes *because* of their use of blood magic!"

Nibbles said nothing.

"Why'd you do it? Why turn to blood magic to awaken this Blade?"

"Because it would not listen to me no matter what I threw at it. Year after year, I spoke to the Jigsaw Blade. Every day I would give it my attention and wrote to it as if it was my journal. I knew from the instant I found it that it was the Legendary Blade that could change the world... but no matter what I tried, the Jigsaw Blade remained distant."

"And so you coaxed it with blood magic?"

"I did."

"And then what?"

"I…I didn't have to use much blood. I was unaware of its power and ended up stealing random pieces of information from the Blade. Some of that information explained that it was of Legendary status. As to how it became such or what it does, I do not know. I did not get that far."

"And why not?" asked Constantine, walking up to Nibbles' head and looking down at her. "Why stop there?"

"Because it was no longer needed. I tried once more to speak to the Blade without blood and it wrote me its location—in all capital letters. It was as if as it was excited to give me its whereabouts."

"I'm surprised," said Constantine. "Usually, Blades forced by blood to give up their destinations are never so willing and happy to do so."

"Well, that is because I believe the Jigsaw may have forgotten that I did so, as it was preoccupied with finally finding its perfect match after hundreds—if not thousands —of years of searching. Plus, it knew Prince Tarek was after it."

Constantine looked up at Jade. "Are you sure you want to put your life on the line for this woman? Now that you know she is a traitor? I wouldn't mind if you walked away right this moment. You could leave and never turn back."

Jade looked down at Nibbles and paused before shaking his head. "Never would I put my back to my people. I *will* bring you Finn and the Jigsaw Blade. All I ask is for our freedom and our Blades. Besides, it is impossible for you to take our Blades—you haven't gone through the proper ritual."

Constantine chuckled at this. "Obviously you don't

know the powers of the Nullify Blade. Not only does it allow me to cancel out the powers of other Bizarre Blades, but also to nullify their connection to their previous wielders." Constantine licked one of his fingers and fixed both of his eyebrows. "Your friend Finn isn't the only one with a Legendary Blade these days, I assure you."

Jade let out a deep breath through his nose and bit his bottom lip. He waited a few moments before saying, "I will give you half the Blades we own, but I get to choose which ones we keep."

"Done."

Constantine walked up to Jade with a wide grin on his face. "My boy, you are an excellent negotiator. Now, when can I expect my Legendary Blade?"

"No more than ten days," said Jade, shaking Constantine's extended hand. "But I will need help. There's no telling how strong Finn has become in the past months of his training."

"Oh, he's been training has he? This is turning out to be more and more interesting! Okay, and who will you take with you?"

"Ariel."

"Who's that?"

Jade pointed to the girl with pink hair.

"The dumb one? You're sure?"

Jade balled up his fists. "She's. Not. Dumb."

"Calm down! Calm down! No need to ruin the deal with your fists, because you and I both know who would win that little scuffle." Constantine waited until Jade relaxed. Then, he threw his hand into the air as a sign of dismissal. "Take the girl. You have ten days." Constantine turned and began to walk away.

"And I need her Blade."

Constantine stopped and chuckled. "Oh, I see your little plan now. This Ariel must be your little girlfriend, huh? Well, I won't be fooled! Tie him back up!"

The bandits swarmed Jade at once and readied themselves to tackle him. "Wait! We had a deal!"

"No more deals! And to think I almost let you two get away. Do you really think I'm that stupid?"

The bandits grabbed Jade and pushed him down to the ground. At that moment, Silver let go of Finn's hand and walked out into the clearing, dropping his daggers which clanged together loudly on the ground. He put both hands into the air just as Constantine turned towards him. The Highborn flinched and about fell onto his backside in fright.

"Who—who are you? What are you doing here?"

"I'm Silver, the Master of Jade and Ariel. Let those two go in search of this Finn Featherstone and I will sit in their place."

26

THE CREATURE OF A THOUSAND LEGS

It was a miracle that Finn made it from the tree and back into the middle of the woods without being detected. His heart hammered in his chest as the Jigsaw Blade rumbled on his back.

He decided that the best course of action was to head towards the jungle of Koosahmoorah. Jade would most likely think him cowardly and that he would try and make it back to his home in Sumetai. Well, Finn was too smart for that. He would go the opposite direction and try his luck in the forests.

It took the rest of the day to circle around the village. He kept himself a generous distance away from it just in case the bandits had spread themselves out wide. It took him half the night to cross through the hybrid lands into the full-on jungle. Even though the sun had disappeared, the jungle still held an incredible amount of humidity in its air, and sweat poured down Finn's back. However, he didn't care about the humidity—he was preoccupied with the abundance of terrifying jungle noises that surrounded him.

He found himself a spot between two thick roots that

had grown aboveground, and placed his back against the tree. Now, no one could sneak up on him. If they wanted to capture him then they would have to come from the front. Usually, Finn would have congratulated himself on such smart thinking, but at that moment he was far too scared.

There were so many things to consider. Thoughts rushed through his mind, shoving each other away as they tried their best to gain Finn's attention. Residing above all of this was his fear. He had a hard time slowing down his breath, and he put his hand on his rapidly rising and falling chest. If anyone was out there, then they would easily hear him and find him.

Leaves blew on the ground making Finn jump and turn towards the sound only to twist his head in the other direction at the sound of scurrying animals. The roars of big dinosaurs in the distance echoed through the trees. Finn could not place what kind of dinosaurs these were, but his imagination was quick to pop up images of the most bloodthirsty and ferocious ones.

The jungle of Koosahmoorah was loud with activity, and Finn knew there was no way he would be able to catch any sleep. Not only was he being hunted by other Champions, but now he was at the mercy of this climate's predators. The jungle was very much awake, and to Finn, who was used to the cold and quiet of his own woods, this was a haunting experience. He wished that Obsidian was by his side; then, at least, he wouldn't be alone. He hadn't seen the pesky microraptor since his journey back to the village and this worried him. What if a predator got to him?

The moon shined down its cream-colored beams through the thick leaves from above. The moisture in the air allowed Finn to see these rays and, even though his knees knocked and his teeth chattered, he couldn't help but admire their beauty.

One thing didn't make sense. Why didn't Silver just push Finn out from his hiding spot and give him away right at that moment? Unless...Silver didn't trust Constantine to keep his word about letting them all go free. In letting himself get captured, Silver had secured the survival of his two students.

Something moved in the jungle—but this time it was different. Goosebumps flared on Finn's skin as he let his head drift up to the source of the sound. It was so dark that the tree he rested up against was completely black. The limbs were covered in a thick mass of leaves which blocked most of the moonlight, leaving Finn in an intense darkness. The positive side to this was it would be hard, if not impossible, for anyone to see *him*. Unfortunately, that also meant that he couldn't see what was coming towards him.

The sounds of footsteps and hushed whispers brought Finn's head back down to scan the field of moonlight rays. He watched for any black shadows that crossed his vision but was distracted by the crackling noises that were getting closer to the top of his head. Finn had no idea where to look! What should he do?! Should he keep his head facing forward? Or should he make a run for it?

Too late.

Tiny moving arms connected to something wide and heavy crawled onto Finn's left shoulder. He was just about to scream but popped his hand over his mouth before he could. Whatever it was, it seemed to have felt Finn's movement, and slid its head to Finn's hand to check it out. Tiny wiggling sticks tickled the outside of his hand as the monster—for that was surely what it was—brought its face closer. Two wet pinchers nibbled on his entire hand softly, and Finn could tell they had the potential to crush bone.

As the dark monster crawled further onto his body, the more Finn could feel himself sinking into the dirt below. Whatever this thing was it was getting heavy, heavy enough that it was actually starting to hurt. Not only that, but the monster had hundreds, if not thousands, of thick fingers that were constantly poking him as more of it slid over him. Just how much of this creature was there?

Finn dared not move, as the beast's pinchers still poked at his hands. Finally, it decided that Finn was either dead or that he wasn't a desirable meal, and dropped its head into Finn's lap and remained there. That's when Finn took action.

Slowly, Finn moved his hand from his mouth and to his back, his fingers reaching for the hilt of Jigsaw. As soon as he clasped his hand over the grip, a hand clutched his wrist tightly. This time, he did scream.

The monster picked its head up and flung it onto Finn's head, its tiny fingers slapping his face in a frenzy. Although the underbelly of the beast felt soft, most of its weight was directly on top of Finn's half-broken nose, sending streaks of pain down his face and neck.

"Don't you dare," said a soft voice. "Ariel doesn't like when animals are harmed."

Someone lifted the beast from Finn's face and directed it back to the bark of the tree, onto which it gladly clung. With the same scratching noise, the monster retreated into the darkness.

"She doesn't like it when we kill insects," came Jade's voice, wiping his hands together.

"It's not an insect," corrected Ariel. "It's an arthropod."

Jade snorted. "It's all the same."

"Not to Ariel it is not," said Ariel, her grip tightening to a painful level on Finn's wrist.

Finn lifted his hand and tapped her fist, his teeth clenched together in an effort to ease the pain.

"Oh, Ariel is so sorry! Ariel did not mean to hurt you!" She released his arm and Finn fell to the ground on his side, his head resting on top of one of the roots.

Finn was still catching his breath when he asked, "What was that thing?"

"A millipede," answered Ariel.

"Is it poisonous?"

"Ariel thinks you mean 'venomous', and no they are not."

"What you have to watch out for is them falling on your head and crushing you," said Jade.

Everyone remained quiet for a moment as Finn took his time to calm himself. Once he'd lifted himself back into his crossed leg position, he said, "Okay you found me, but how about this? I let you take the Jigsaw Blade and you two let me go free. No need for me to die."

Jigsaw exploded into life, fire brushing past Finn's upper back and making him yelp.

"Your weapon is right. You never just abandon your Blade." Jade shook his head. "You really are a disgusting person and a poor excuse of a Champion if you're already willing to just give up your Blade."

Finn had finally had enough. He stood himself up, nearly fell over, then straightened himself. "Look here!" he said, pointing his finger at Jade. "I didn't ask for this! None of it! Jigsaw was an accident! If you're so damned strong and tough then why didn't you find it for yourself? Oh wait, because it didn't want *you*, it wanted me!"

"Why, you son of a—" Jade walked forward, raising both of his fists.

It was Ariel who stepped in between them. "Cut it out, both of you! If we are going to make this work then Ariel believes it best we all work together. As a *team*."

"You really think this plan is going to work?" asked Jade, gesturing to Finn. "Look at him. He's pathetic. Worthless. A babe with a Blade and nothing more! It should've been me!"

"Well, it wasn't," snapped Finn with more courage than normal. He was seriously just tired of all this crap. "The Blade chose me and that's that. Get over it and find your own damn Blade."

"I'm seriously about to rip your head off," warned Jade through gritted teeth.

"Oh yeah? Well, you might as well get in line because I'm pretty sure you're number three."

"Three?" asked Ariel. "Ariel only believes two were going to kill you."

"No," Finn said, sitting himself back down between his roots. "Silver, your Master, wants to kill me as well."

"*Our* Master," corrected Ariel. Finn couldn't exactly see facial impressions, but he did see Jade turn himself away at this. "Mother Nibblefingers put you under Silver, so that is where you belong! Ariel just knows it."

"How can you trust Nibbles?" asked Finn. "She betrayed you all, did she not? She used blood magic!"

"And so what?" asked Jade. "At least she isn't abandoning everything she cares about! So what, she used a tiny bit of blood to break through to a stubborn Blade? This is a tough world, Finn. Our job isn't easy and we need all the help we can get."

"He means you," Ariel said.

"That is certainly *not* what I meant."

Ariel sighed. "And you're wrong about another thing, Finn."

"Doesn't surprise me."

"It's four."

"Four what?"

"It's four people who want to kill you," Ariel whispered.

"PRINCE TAREK KNOWS WHO I AM?" asked Finn, astonished that someone so powerful actually knew his name. He wasn't sure whether this was a great honor or a great tragedy for him...probably the latter.

"Ariel thinks you are misunderstanding the impact that owning a Bizarre Blade has," Ariel said, walking between the large roots and sitting down next to him. There was hardly any room, and they were crushed against each other. Who was this girl? "To some people, people like Prince Tarek, Bizarre Blades are worth thousands of acres of land, maybe even kingdoms," continued Ariel. "So, it is no surprise to Ariel that Prince Tarek hired his Second, now First in Queue to hunt you down."

"And it just so happens your worthlessness was tracked to our village," grumbled Jade.

"Ariel believes that is enough out of you."

Jade grunted and turned away again.

"Why waste your time telling me all of this? Why not just hit me over the head with a stone and knock me out? Trust me, it wouldn't be the first time."

"Can you really not figure it out for yourself?" asked Jade. "We aren't taking you back to Constantine. The Champions of Arbitration do not deliver prisoners. We were trained for occasions like this."

"Not as terrible as this," argued Ariel. "Jade doesn't show it, but Ariel knows he's afraid."

"Of course I'm afraid! Our professors and our mother have all been captured by that Highborn idiot, and now it's all up to us to take back the village!"

"Wait," said Finn, putting up his hands. "Wait, wait, wait...let me get this straight. You two aren't delivering me to Constantine?"

"No," said Ariel.

"Of course not," added Jade.

"And now you want my help to take back the village?"

"Yes," said Ariel.

"Obviously," said Jade. "You were present for your own initiation ceremony, were you not? Or were you not paying any attention?"

Finn tried his best to ignore Jade but still he could feel blood rising up to his face. He reminded himself to breathe. "I'm sorry, I just think we're a little outnumbered, especially seeing as I'm the only one with a Bizarre Blade."

Ariel chuckled. "Who says you're the only one?"

Finn was about to ask what she meant when she showed him instead. She reached behind her back and gripped onto a Blade that Finn had not been able to see in the darkness. However, now that it was being awakened, the Blade lit up, a violet hue wafting over it. Two translucent wings were attached to the top of the crossguard and flapped a few times as Ariel adjusted her hands around its haft. The Blade itself was long, but not as thick or broad as Jigsaw was, and looked as though it was a lot easier to lift and swing.

"What the...how the..." stammered Finn, reaching out to touch it—but drew his hand back when he saw what Ariel had become.

The girl's face, once petite and beautiful, was now a

horrifying mess. Her lips protruded from her head and were making some sort of wet suctioning noise. Her eyes were the worst! They had grown at least four times their original size, bulging from the eye sockets. Not only that, but there was no iris, nor was there any white. Instead, both her eyes resembled those of an insect's, only enlarged to an unnatural degree.

"I—I have no words," said Finn, unable to take his eyes off the creature before him. He slowly pulled his head away, as he did not want to be too close to this...thing.

"Ariel is the owner of the Flutter Blade," said Jade. "Which, as you've probably guessed is under the domain of Animal Bizarre Blades."

"And what animal does she resemble?"

"Ariel is a dragonfly!" she said cheerfully, her voice a lot higher than it was normally.

"There is a downfall though," said Jade, letting his finger slide down the face of the Blade. "With the Flutter Blade comes the effects of, well, having a fluttery mind."

"So, she becomes more stupid?"

"Careful with your words, Finn, or I might just hand you over to Constantine."

Something buzzed through the darkness, and Ariel's small fingers snatched it from the air. Before Finn could protest—as he had an idea of what she was about to do— she shoved the black dot of an insect into her mouth. She swallowed without even chewing.

"Not to be rude but..." Finn stopped, trying to figure out the best way to put this.

"Spit it out," said Jade. "I know what you're about to say."

"Even without the Blade...Ariel is kinda—"

"The Blade's effects, although more powerful when

wielded, still influence the wielder's mind even when it's not in use."

"I've heard of Blades implanting certain traits into their owners," said Finn. "I just didn't know they were this...potent."

"All Blades affect their wielders' minds," corrected Jade. "Some more than others. The Flutter Blade just happens to be one of those 'more than others' Blades."

Ariel's tongue flopped out of her mouth and she proceeded to try to touch Finn's exposed shoulder with it. Jade came to the rescue and gently pushed her away. Ariel sniffed the air, one of her eyes reducing to normal size and staring at Finn. Two antennae protruded from her head and twitched a few times.

"Ariel smells blood!"

"Is he wounded?" Jade asked her.

Ariel took a few more sniffs and nodded. "Ariel smells blood on his face, his and someone else's. Also, there is blood on his torso."

"Where are you hurt?" Jade asked, turning towards Finn. "We have much to do and it's best we start healing you as soon as possible. I won't have you slowing me down."

Finn just stared at Ariel a few moments, pulling his hanging jaw back up to its locked position as he watched the pink-headed girl's normal eye swell back to its dragonfly form. "I'm, uh, I have a broken nose, and, uh, three puncture wounds on my ribs. I've cauterized them, though."

"Are they infected?" Jade asked Ariel, who pushed her head and antennae closer to Finn's body.

"The nose is not, but Ariel smells the beginnings of infection on his ribs. He can be saved, though, Ariel is sure of this," she said, nodding her head confidently. "One thing

Ariel doesn't understand is how you made it all this way. Your injuries, they are of the serious variety."

Finn scratched his head. "I guess I didn't have much time to think about it. Silver brought me out of the woods and I was expecting to be healed at the village, but then we saw the smoke and everything just happened so fast after that. You won't believe how much the pain deadens when your life is on the line. Trust me, I should know."

"Ariel must know where you got these wounds."

"A smilodon. The same one that killed Bryce."

"How the hell were you able to escape the clutches of a smilodon in one piece?" asked Jade, crossing his arms and taking a seat.

"Well, I didn't escape. I, uh, sort of killed it."

"Impossible. You're lying." He reached out and gripped Finn's saber-tooth coat between two fingers. He rubbed the material and, finding that it really was smilodon fur, let go and mumbled something about Finn still being a liar.

"You can call me a lot of things, Jade, but never EVER call me a liar. My mother hated that word."

"At least you *have* a mother," said Jade, plucking a piece of grass and messing with it. "People like you don't know how well they have it and it makes me sick."

"You're wrong," said Finn, biting his lip and begging his eyes not to tear up. "I *had* a mother."

Ariel turned to Jade and popped him in the chest with the back of her hand.

"How was I supposed to know!?" he demanded. Ariel said nothing, only nodded her head towards Finn. When Jade didn't do whatever it was that she requested of him, she nodded her head again, this time clearly threatening to smack him again. Jade's eyes stared at the ground, peeking up at Finn as he said, "Look, I'm sorry. I didn't mean to say those things. I didn't know."

"It's okay," Finn said, winning his battle against his tears. "I'm used to it."

"If it's any consolation for Ariel's rude brother here," Ariel said, and Finn noticed Jade flinch at the word "brother," "all of us Champion of Arbitration trainees come without family, or very little family."

"Well, I do have a father," Finn said. "One that's probably worried about me."

Ariel and Jade looked at each other. Ariel's eyes reduced back to their normal size, and through the moonlight Finn could see worry in them.

"What?" Finn asked. "What's wrong? Is my father in trouble?!" He wrenched himself out from the roots, the burn wounds on his side hurting like hell. He stood up and balled his fists. "Tell me! What have you heard of my father?!"

Ariel sheathed her Flutter Blade on her back, which then shrunk a few feet much like Jigsaw could now do. She raised her hand as if she was about to put it on Finn's shoulder, but thought better of it. "Finn, if Prince Tarek knows you own the Blade he is after, then what do you think he would do?"

Finn's voice lowered to a whisper as thoughts of his father being captured by Shimoshimo soldiers flashed into his mind. "He would threaten the life of my loved ones."

"Ariel thinks you are right on this. Only more reason we should hurry."

Jade nodded and stood up. "But first, you're useless with those wounds. Come over here."

Finn did as he said, his eyes staring off into the distance as the thought of his father being taken prisoner really set in. He didn't know what to feel at that moment. Should he be furious? Should he be cautious? Should he be scared? Perhaps he should feel resentment? Well, the answer was clear...he felt all of these things.

"This is going to hurt," Jade said, drying his fingers on his pants and placing them on Finn's nose. "Are you ready? Or should Ariel make a concoction to put you to sleep?"

"Just do it," Finn said, his mind elsewhere.

CRACK!

Pain rushed into his face and tears welled in his eyes, but Finn did not cry out. He felt blood run down his throat, and thought he could even taste some of it. He tried breathing in through his nostrils and found that it was a lot easier now. He would never take breathing through his nose for granted ever again.

"What's our plan?" Finn asked bouncing on his heels, trying to take his mind off of the pain.

"Ariel thinks there is no plan until Finn is all healed up and ready to go."

"I've told you, I've already cauterized it."

"I'm starting to think you're deaf," said Jade. "Did you not hear her before? Your wounds are infected."

"Ariel will make a quick concoction using the ingredients of the jungle." Ariel pointed at the pouch on Finn's hip. "What do you have in there?"

Finn shrugged. "Just a few berries and the rest of the smilodon skin."

"Perfect! Give Ariel the berries!" Ariel held out her hands as Finn handed her the last of his crowberries. "These are exactly what I needed!"

"For the concoction? Really?"

"No, silly! Ariel was just hungry." She then shoved all the berries into her mouth and popped them all at once. Blue juice ran down her chin as she chewed, humming the entire time.

"You are odd," said Finn.

"Ariel knows this," she said through a mouthful.

"Your smilodon cape needs work," Jade said. "Give it to me and I'll make it more suitable for battle."

"You know how to do leatherwork?" Finn asked him, not able to hide the surprise from his voice. What did these people not know how to do?

"All Champions trained in the village know how to do most things that revolve around survival. This is why you don't belong with us. You started too old."

Finn took off his saber-tooth coat and flung it over Jade's head who quickly pulled it off, returning Finn a furious look.

"Well, like it or not, I'm here to stay."

27

TROLL SNOT AND TOENAIL CLIPPINGS

The three young companions walked further into the jungle while Ariel looked around for the ingredients she needed to concoct the healing concoction. Once she had gathered everything needed, she explained that she would need a fire in order to complete the process. With the help of Jigsaw's flame, they built a roaring fire in less than five minutes. Finn couldn't help but feel pride in his heart at the sight of Jade's jealous scowling.

While the concoction was brewing, Jade had pulled a needle from his survival pack and was using it to craft Finn's new armor. The Champion-to-be worked wonders with the needle, and was able to make an awesome set of armor. Finn was fitted with smilodon leather vambraces, a coat that fit snug around his neck, two doubly thick shoulder pauldrons, a flapped skirt that allowed free movement, and, of course, leather boots that replaced his old, worn-out ones.

The best part of all, however, was the helmet made from the head. Jade had been extra careful with this, washing it thoroughly with water and using his knee to pop up the helm to give it the desired shape. It took him only three tries to make the perfect fit for Finn's head—and it didn't even smell!

"The armor may fit loosely now," said Jade, adjusting one of Finn's vambraces on his arm. "But tomorrow's sun will bake it until its stiff."

"They seriously teach you this stuff back in the village?"

"And more."

"I can't wait to learn," Finn said eagerly.

"You will... *if* there is a village to go back to."

Ariel stood next the crackling fire, a waterskin filled with the concoction's ingredients held a good four feet above the flames. She reached out and popped Jade on the top of the head. "Don't say that, Jade! You know Ariel does not want to hear these things."

"Why does she speak like that?" Finn asked.

"Like what?" asked both Ariel and Jade together.

"Well, I don't know." Finn felt a little stupid now that it wasn't obvious to everyone else. "Why do you use your name to refer to yourself?"

Ariel scrunched her eyebrows at him then looked up at the stars as she pondered his words. "It has never occurred to Ariel why this happens. Ariel thinks it would be odder to say it the way your people say it."

"Our people?"

Finn was answered with soft snoring. Somehow, the girl had fallen asleep standing straight up, her face lifted towards the sky. What was most unbelievable was that her hand was still extended in the air.

"She does stuff like that," said Jade, sitting himself next to the fire, much closer than Finn cared to be. Jade and Ariel were used to hotter climates and needed to be warm, but Finn was an ice and snow type of person through and through.

"But why does she do stuff like that? Is she, um…slow, or something?"

Jade didn't look up from the fire, only shook his head in disgust. "Why a Bizarre Blade would choose you over me or Bryce, I will never understand. No, she's not slow. On the contrary, she's very intelligent. So intelligent that she's weird."

"I don't think just being smart makes you that weird," Finn said, readying himself just in case Jade decided to attack him.

"Well, she's half fairy, so there's that."

"Half fairy?"

"Yeah, you heard me. Half fairy. You know, the flying miniature people with dust shooting out of their asses? That kind of fairy."

"But I thought those were just stories."

"They are—for people of Shimoshimo. For the rest of us, in the other kingdoms and whatnot, fairies, although rare, are very real."

"I'm not so sure I believe you. I mean, look at her!"

"What about her?" asked Jade, putting his hands closer to the fire.

"Well, she's tall! Almost taller than me, and like you said, fairies are short."

"Usually," corrected Jade. "They are *usually* very short. They can increase their size and blend in with humans very well, though. They're probably less rare than we think but are just good at keeping their identities a secret."

"So, how do you know she's a fairy?"

"Because I found her in a cage about the size of my fist." Jade made a fist and showed it to Finn. "I was ten years old."

"What was she doing in a cage?" Finn asked, scooting

himself a little closer to the fire as if he was about to be told an epic tale.

"Her father killed her mother once he found out she was a fairy. Then, he put his daughter in a cage. End of story."

Finn could feel himself deflating. That wasn't a good story, not a good story at all. In fact, it was downright depressing. Did anyone in the Champions of Arbitration have a normal backstory? He guessed the answer was most likely a big fat no.

"And what about you?" Finn asked.

"What about me?"

"Where do you come from?"

Jade sighed as if he'd been waiting for this question. "Royalty."

Finn cracked up at this. "Yeah, and my father shot out of a mammoth's ass...oh wait, you're serious."

Jade stood up and walked away from the campfire, leaving Finn alone with the girl who was standing and snoring. He watched him walk away and wondered where he was going but dared not follow. He let Ariel sleep a little longer until he started to smell something sweet coming from the waterskin. He thought it might be best to wake her.

Finn pushed her lightly on the arm and she snorted herself awake. She looked around in a daze, then said to Finn, "You aren't going to cut off Ariel's ear, are you?"

"What? No! Is that what you were dreaming about? Me cutting off your ear?"

"If you do, cut off my right ear."

"What are you talking about? Wait, why would I cut off your right ear?"

Ariel shrugged. "Because my left ear is my favorite."

Finn's eyes floated off to the side and he sat down slowly. Who in their right mind had a favorite body part? What kind of person thought this way? Jade couldn't be lying about her being a fairy. Either that, or she was just plain crazy.

"Oh!" Ariel shouted. "It's ready!" She pulled her hand from the fire and opened the waterskin. She blew into the sack and white steam floated into the air. Then, putting her nose close to the opening, she took a big whiff. Finn watched as her eyes rolled to the back of her head as she took in another deep and slow draw. "Ahhh, perfect! You," she said, pointing to Finn with her nose, "drink this." She bent down with the waterskin and held it out to him with both hands.

Finn now knew better than to argue with her or else risk triggering her temper. Besides, whatever she brewed smelled delicious! He caught scents of banana berries, sweet leaves, cinnamon, tree syrup, and even a little bit of spice for a kick. He took the skin and took a big swallow.

It did not taste how it smelled.

Ariel was ready for his reaction and pulled the waterskin from Finn's hands before he could throw it. On his tongue he tasted dingleberries rather than banana berries. Ass wiping leaves instead of sweet leaves. Toenail clippings instead of cinnamon. Troll snot instead of syrup, and there was spice, only there was TOO MUCH OF IT!

Finn fell to his side, his mouth a furnace with mucus running from his nose. He tried wiping dirt onto his tongue but he could not get the horrible burning sensation nor the terrible taste off of it. As if that wasn't bad enough, white hot pain radiated on his side where the saber-tooth had snagged him. The outside of his nose stung so badly that it felt like he was having his back teeth removed through his nostril.

It seemed like ages until the pain and the taste finally began to subside. He tried to make himself relax, breathing heavily by the fire. He could tell his face was a hideous red, his green hair matted to the sides of his face with sweat and snot.

"What—what was that?" he asked, his voice a little hoarse.

"Ariel likes to call it the *Back From the Grave* concoction. Get it? Because it can save your life!"

"Yeah, well, I'm not so sure what is worse. Death, or drinking that crap."

"Hey!" Ariel yelled. "It's not crap! Ariel worked very hard on that. You should be grateful to Ariel!"

"But why not warn me!"

"Because you wouldn't have drank it, that's why!"

Finn worked some saliva through his mouth and spit it out to the side. "You're right! I wouldn't have! I would have much rathered taken my chances! Let me guess, you made it smell like that on purpose, didn't you?"

Ariel nodded.

"But why!"

"Because you wouldn't have drank it! The real concoction smells of—"

"Sweaty ass, I'm sure."

Ariel's eyes widened and Finn could make out the beginnings of the dragonfly effects on them. "How did you know this? Are you also a concoction maker?"

"What? No, it's just common sense."

Ariel looked away to think about this for a moment before nodding. "Yes, Ariel thinks you are right." She moved the waterskin closer to Finn. "Okay, now you must drink the rest."

Finn shook his head and pushed the skin away. "I'd rather die."

"Oh, you will!" Ariel agreed. "If this concoction is only

half consumed, then the beverage drinker will surely die a most terrible and painful death."

Finn stared at her unblinking eyes to see if she was lying, but she looked serious. From what all he'd seen up to this point, he didn't doubt that the concoction could and would kill him, so he took the waterskin and prepared to drink it. He put the skin up to his lips—he'd have to do it quick or he'd never do it. He had his eyes closed while he counted to ten, and on ten opened them to see Ariel smiling a trickster's smile.

He threw the waterskin to the side.

Ariel burst out laughing, falling onto her backside with her hands on her stomach. She laughed so hard that she was having a hard time catching a breath in between the fits.

"That's not funny! You nearly killed me!"

"Haha! Sorry! Ariel could not help it! You are so ignorant! It's too easy to abuse!"

Finn let her have her laugh, as he was scheming a plan of revenge. If and when she fell asleep, he would pour the remaining concoction into her mouth and see how she liked it. However, before that, he had a few more questions, so when Ariel had finished laughing, he said, "Jade tells me he comes from royalty."

Ariel nodded, wiping a tear from the corner of her eye. Her pale cheeks burned a bright red from her hysteria. "This is true."

"Then why did he join the Champions of Arbitration? Why not stay and enjoy the life of royalty? You know, getting fed grapes and stuff like that."

"That is something Ariel thinks you should ask Jade about."

"Like he would tell me."

Ariel nodded. "This is true."

"Was he banished or something?"

"No, it was the opposite. He left. However, now that he has left, he is certainly banished."

"But again, why leave something so wonderful?"

"To Jade, it wasn't as wonderful as you say. He wanted nothing to do with inheriting the throne."

"Jade's a Prince?!"

"Yes, well, he *was*."

"From what Kingdom?"

Ariel looked away. "Ariel really should not be saying so much, but...since we are traveling there tomorrow, Ariel guesses it cannot hurt."

"Where are we going?"

"Kimidori."

"Kimidori? The capital city of Koosahmoorah?"

"That's the one!"

Finn took a moment to let all of this new information sink it. At this point, he didn't know who to believe. Ariel was supposedly a fairy whose mom was murdered when she was younger, and Jade was supposedly a Prince who didn't want to be a Prince. Yeah, that all sounded perfectly believable.

Finn would have remained skeptical, but the memory of Nibbles using Jade's last name came to his mind. It was when he first woke up and so he wasn't really thinking straight. She'd called him Jade Whetstone—as in THE Whetstones that ruled over all of Koosahmoorah. They were known to be the oldest family to ever rule over a Kingdom without ever losing rule to another bloodline. Finn could understand now why Jade would be banished from his home. To break a thousand-or-so-year-old tradition would not be taken lightly by anyone, especially not by a king.

"Jade Whetstone," Finn said. "That's his name, isn't it?"

"Yup!" said Ariel, grabbing her knees and rocking herself on her butt. "You figured it out!"

"But I don't understand, why—"

"Ariel wants to help you understand," she interrupted.

"Okay? What I don't understand is why we are going back to the place Jade left and was banished from. It sounds like it would only add to our problems."

"Ariel agrees. It will most certainly bring us misfortune."

"Then why go?"

"Because," Ariel said, pointing her finger into the air. "Do you not know what is passed down from king to king in the Koosahmoorah Kingdom? You know the name, but not the most important tradition of all?"

Finn thought a moment. "You're talking about the Bizarre Blade?"

"Exactly!"

Finn grabbed his face with his hand and pulled on it in frustration. None of this was making sense to him. "See where I'm coming from, Ariel. You're telling me Jade left his chance to get a Blade passed down to him and instead chose a harder life with the possibility of not getting a Blade at all."

"There's more to it than that," said Jade from behind making Finn about jump out of his skin. "I see your nose has healed. What about your ribs?"

Finn had forgotten about his wounds, the disgusting concoction having taken his mind off them. He moved his hands to his nose and carefully touched it. There was no pain. He felt the shape of it and was relieved that it felt to be back to normal. He stood up, threw the cape over his shoulder, and lifted his shirt. The cauterized holes, once swollen and full of pus, were now mere purple spots and looked more like bruises.

"That...is amazing."

"Thank you very much," said Ariel with a bow. "And don't worry about your missing tooth. Once we save the village, Ariel will be able to craft you a new one!"

Finn, having forgotten he'd broken a tooth while chewing Saul's dried meats, let his tongue find the vacant hole in his gums and played with it. He didn't know that his missing tooth was so obvious and couldn't help but feel a little self-conscious about it. He'd always been proud of his teeth because he'd always taken such good care of them, unlike most people in Sumetai, or anywhere else really. It seemed he had finally joined their rotten-mouthed ranks.

Out of all of his fantasies of becoming a Champion he never once realized how hard it would be on the body.

"The sun is almost upon us," said Jade, stamping out the fire with his boot. "We need to get going."

"But I haven't gotten any sleep!" protested Finn.

"That's because you've been talking this whole time. Should have thought about it."

"Don't worry, Finn!" exclaimed Ariel. "Ariel got quite enough sleep!"

"You slept for like one minute! And you were standing up!"

Ariel didn't seem to hear him as she turned and walked away with Jade, leaving Finn by the fire alone, confused, and exhausted. He let out a sigh, kicked dirt over the remaining flames, and hurried to catch up, as there was no way in hell he was going to fall behind, not in this jungle of doom. They walked at a brisk pace, dodging limbs and vines with ease. Finn, however, did not fare so well. Any limb they bent out of their faces was sent flying into his. After only five minutes of walking, he'd tripped over countless roots and jumped at a dozen different animal noises.

When the trail cleared up slightly, Finn asked, "So what exactly are we going to do when we get to Kimidori?"

Jade answered without any sign of fatigue in his voice. "I will accept the Bizarre Blade that is rightfully mine."

"But aren't you banished? What if they don't give it to you?"

Jade shrugged. "Then we steal it."

28

GOOCH TROLL TROUBLES

If it hadn't been for Finn's seven long months in the woods, he never would have been able to keep up with Ariel and Jade. The two never stopped for a single break, not even to relieve themselves. Finn, on the other hand, stopped three different times, and each time he'd nearly gotten himself lost. It was as if they wanted to rid of him. Did Ariel have some sort of concoction that made pissing and crapping disappear? Or was training the bladder and colon to stop functioning part of the teaching regimen of the Champions of Arbitration?

Here he was, with two people his own age, who outdid him in every way. They were physically in better shape than him, and probably even smarter. They were most likely even more mature than him, as they probably were thinking about other things besides defecating. Jade was right, Finn just did not belong. The Jigsaw really was bizarre...why choose him?

"We're here," announced Jade, stopping and pushing down a waxy-looking leaf, revealing a running river.

"Where's 'here'?" Finn asked, trying his best not to sound as exhausted as he was.

"Take a guess," answered Jade. "It's the most famous river in all of Koosahmoorah."

Finn shut his eyes and shook his head in disbelief. "Oh, no...no, no, no, no, no. Nuh-uh. This isn't Snapper's River. It can't be."

"Oh, it is," said Ariel excitedly, sticking her face very close to Finn's. "Wicked and terrible things swim in these waters!" She put her hands together, her fingers bent as she formed a mouth full of teeth. She moved her hands up and down while making juicy snapping noises with her mouth.

Finn gulped. "Is it true, what they say about this river? That there really are nasty things in there?"

"That, and more," admitted Jade, walking towards the river with Ariel by his side.

"Doesn't it make sense we keep our distance then?!" Finn called out to them, but they didn't answer him. He cursed and followed behind them.

The river looked to be very wide, but it was impossible to see the other side as a thick white fog had formed a few feet above it. The green murky water sped by as if it was in a hurry to get somewhere. Not only did Finn have a fear of rivers, seeing he'd nearly drowned in one, but now he was afraid that his secret might get out, one that might force Jade and Ariel to leave him behind.

He couldn't swim.

Hardly anyone in the Shimoshimo Kingdom knew how to swim, and the ones who did had likely been born in other Kingdoms. There simply wasn't any body of water in Shimoshimo that was warm enough to dip oneself into. Bathing water had to be warmed in large iron tubs, held over fire with thick ropes. Those who couldn't afford their own iron tubs could use the public tubs for a fee. If one couldn't afford the public tubs, then one simply did not bathe. This was why most Spuds walked around with dirty faces and brown fingernails.

Finn shuddered at the thought of never being able to bathe. At some point down his family tree, someone had been wealthy enough to buy an iron bathing tub. Too bad that the wealth had disappeared somewhere down the line, but at least the tub had made it to him and his dad...as well as the house...and, well, anything else they had that was considered "nice". Painting didn't exactly pay a ton of ammonite chips, which were hard to come by for anyone in the lower classes of Shimoshimo.

There were three ways to get ammonite chips. One was by selling items or performing a service. The second was by stealing them. The third was by collecting the spiral-shaped shells oneself, through complex harvesting with boats and nets. This was a highly dangerous job, as the oceans were notorious for their more-than-aggressive sea animals, as well as pirates.

However, it wasn't that anyone in Shimoshimo didn't want to do the dirty work; it was just that there was no ammonite in the coastal waters. The mollusks hated cold water, preferring to live in the more tropical climates. Therefore, Shimoshimo relied on getting its currency from foreign trade, which meant that other Kingdoms held most of the power.

In the past, Shimoshimo had tried to adopt other currencies friendlier to the freezing cold environment. Past kings had tried everything from mammoth ebony all the way to icicles, but nothing ever stuck. Getting messages from village to village in Shimoshimo was difficult already, due to freak blizzards and frozen lakes. Not only that, but the people of Shimoshimo were a stubborn folk and as cold as the weather. If you told them that ammonite chips were no longer used for trading for goods, they'd only laugh (or spit) at you and continue on with their business.

Shimoshimo was stuck under the boot of all the other kingdoms that had a healthy supply of swimming ammonite to collect and lay out in the sun to dry out. This was one of the main reasons that Shimoshimo was known for starting so many wars. The present king, King Leon Hailstorm the Ninth, was the first king in years to not have started a single skirmish with the surrounding kingdoms. In fact, he would be forever known as the first king to actually negotiate for better prices and higher quality goods. Although the negotiations hadn't gone well, as King Leon had no choice but to accept what the other Kingdoms would give him—it was a start.

Jade and Ariel were in the middle of discussing something when Finn walked up to them. Although he was only a few feet away from them, he could not hear what they were saying, as the crashing rapids were far too loud. His eyes were planted on the river as he waited for an enormous crocodile to spring out of its greenish depths and swallow all three of them whole. He was so preoccupied with his daydream that he didn't hear Jade's warning cry to stop moving.

Finn's boot slipped under a vine and he tripped forward, his face planting into a pile of soft mud. He turned his filthy face into the air to see a plump and bulbous pink plant belch a yellow dust into the air. Both Jade and Ariel tried their best to jump out of the way but it was too late. All three of them were bathed in this flower's bitter smelling pollen.

Finn sat back and sneezed. "What was that?!"

"A Paralysis Pouch Plant," said Ariel, using both hands to wipe the yellow debris from her face. "They're carnivorous, known for eating fist-sized bugs."

"Are they dangerous to humans?"

Jade walked up to Finn and put his boot on his chest, pushing his back into the mud. Jigsaw vibrated awake and shot Finn an idea of sawing off Jade's leg, which Finn quickly dismissed before he let himself give into the temptation.

Jade bent down. "The plant's gonna be the last of your worries if you don't start to watch where you're going." Jade pushed one last time on Finn's chest before walking back to Ariel. "We need to wash this shit off our bodies."

"Ariel agrees. We have one hour before the paralysis kicks in."

"How long does it last?" Finn asked, wiping the mud from his lips. He stood up and shook the yellow dust out of his hair.

"Jade and Ariel will be paralyzed for over twenty-four hours, as we got most of the pollen on us. You, on the other hand, were protected by the mud. Good thinking!" She gave Finn the thumbs up, and he, out of habit, performed the two-finger salute.

"Oooohh!" cooed Ariel, walking up and grabbing Finn by his hand. She smelled his fingers. "What was that?" She sniffed again. "And where have these fingers been? They smell amazing!"

Jade rolled his eyes and turned towards the river. Placing his hands on his hips he surveyed the best and safest place they could rinse off.

Ariel's face moved yet again close to Finn's, and for the first time he got a full look of her. She was absolutely beautiful. Her green eyes paired perfectly with her light pink hair. On the tops of her perky cheeks were triangles of freckles, which brought out the pointy-ness of her small nose. Her lips were thick and full and her teeth shined an arcitc white.

"Well, I, uh," he babbled, before shaking the lustful thoughts from his head. "We, um, call that the two-finger salute. It's something the poor people of Shimoshimo do to one another."

"But why?" Ariel asked, using her hands to rotate Finn's fist around as she studied it.

"I kind of think of it as a way of us telling each other that we understand the other person's woes. Maybe even to show one another that we have each other's backs. Honestly, I never really thought about it, I just kinda grew up doing it."

"So it's a positive gesture?"

"Very," Finn said.

"How interesting! Ariel will take this up herself!" She wiped her brow with two thin fingers, pointed them at Finn, then brought them back to her nose and gave them a big whiff.

Jade walked back from the shore and, ignoring Ariel's loud sniffing noises, said, "If I remember correctly, this way down the river there is a waterfall that splits into four sections. We can use these natural showers to wash the paralysis pollen off of us. Let's get going." Finn stood and started to walk but Jade pushed against his shoulder, his eyes very serious. "Next time, watch where you're going." He looked up at the trees. "This jungle isn't my friend and it's certainly not yours. It wants to kill us, do you understand?"

Finn nodded his head quickly and Jade let go of his shoulder. Grabbing Ariel by the wrist, Jade spat on the ground and pulled her in the direction of the waterfalls.

THE PARALYSIS EFFECTS were stronger than Finn had expected. At first, he felt the skin of his neck begin to tingle, until finally going numb. A few minutes later, he could no longer flex his calf muscles, meaning that some of the powder had found its way underneath his smilodon cape. When Jade tried explaining who would get what waterfall, Finn had a hard time understanding what he was saying as Jade's lips had started to freeze up. Not only that, but the crashing water made it almost impossible to hear anything.

"Got it?" Jade asked, and Finn nodded his head yes even though he didn't catch which waterfall he was supposed to go to.

They walked for half an hour until Jade spotted a tall grey cliff, situated on the other side of the river. From here, Finn could get a full view of the water rushing over the cliff-side and colliding onto a giant boulder. Over the years, the water had eroded a little pond on top of this boulder. From here, the water splashed over the sides, creating four different showers of clear, clean-looking water. Too bad that this freshness was lost when the water mixed in with the greenness of the rushing, crocodile-infested river of doom.

Finn felt a little more useful when he came up with the idea to cut down one of the larger trees using Jigsaw to use it as a bridge to get to the showers. With Jigsaw's speed, this only took a few minutes, and soon they were crossing the bridge. During the very last five feet, Finn slipped, but Jade caught his hand just in time. He didn't say a word when he jerked Finn over the rest of the bridge and didn't offer a hand to help him up. Well, at least this meant that he wasn't going to kill Finn, as that would have been an opportune time to let him die. They must have really needed his help... or they were just desperate.

Jade tried yelling over the roaring of the waterfall, but gave up when Finn and Ariel shook their heads at him. Jade then rolled his eyes and made for his waterfall. One of his legs had seized up and he now walked with a limp. The boulder stood on a circular disk of stone which stuck out about five feet. Jade had gone to the left as it was the side that connected to the river. He most likely did this so Finn could take the safe side.

As Finn pulled the smilodon leather off his head, he cursed when he noticed that Ariel had already disappeared into the falls. He had meant to watch her to make sure he didn't end up in her shower.

Looks like he would just have to guess.

Finn slipped off his armor and walked into the falls. The pollen had mixed with his sweat and started to sting his eyes. He wondered if it was possible for eyes to get paralyzed...but these thoughts melted away when he realized he stood naked outside for the first time. He made sure no one was looking at him, then raised his hands to the sky and let the mist of the falls wash over him. Without the saber-tooth armor, the jungle wasn't all that hot, especially next to the falls.

The water temperature surprised him. It wasn't freezing cold, but it wasn't hot like he expected either. It was the perfect temperature, a little cooler than the heat of his skin. The water that crashed onto his head was heavy but soft as it ran through his hair. The water felt so smooth and dense that it covered his entire body like a thin layer of water armor. He lifted his arms at a slight angle and the water poured from each of his fingers. He stuck out his tongue and let the water fall into his mouth. It tasted crisp and delicious.

He walked further into his shower with a hand covering his eyes. He felt happy but slightly disappointed to not find Ariel there waiting for him...but that was probably for the best. He didn't need any more trouble with Jade and, besides, he was pretty sure the man had a thing for her.

Finn ran his hands through his hair, his pits, his groin, and his butt. He scraped vigorously, making sure that all the paralysis pollen was off of him. He bent down to clean off his feet when he felt pressure on his butt cheeks. Slowly, he turned around to see that his ass had connected with none other than Ariel's ass. They now stood ass to ass.

"Oh my God, I'm so sorry!" Finn shouted, but his words were lost in the falls.

Ariel turned around, exposing her full nudity to him. She smiled and continued bathing herself. She opened her mouth and looked like she was asking him a question, but Finn couldn't hear her. Besides, he was pretty sure he had no blood in his ears at the moment, as it was all rushing somewhere else. Uh-oh.

Oh my God! Am, am I really? Right now? Oh no!

Finn began to panic. He spun himself around to hide his growth. Ariel walked around him but didn't seem to notice anything. She was busy wiping her own butt when she bent and yelled into his ear, "Ariel wants to know if you've guessed why Jade was banished!"

"I—I don't know!" Finn shouted into her ear. At this moment, he wasn't thinking about Jade, nor did he want to. For the first time in his life he'd seen breasts! Actual breasts! And not just breasts he used to craft on his excellent snowmen...err, snowwomen.

"Because of Ariel!" she yelled, pointing at herself.

Having finished her shower, Ariel walked out from the falls, giving Finn an excellent view of her backside. He felt shivers crawl up his spine as she shook the water out of her hair before walking out of sight.

It took Finn another ten minutes to finish up his shower. Not because he wasn't clean, but because he didn't want to walk outside with his gooch troll standing at attention.

"What am I, twelve?" Finn asked himself, walking out from under the water. "Can't even control myself. Now she probably thinks I've never made it with a woman..."

Well, I haven't, Finn admitted to himself.

"Have you seen Jade?" Ariel asked him as he walked up to grab his armor.

Even though Ariel wasn't looking down at his groin, Finn still hid his manliness with a banana leaf. He'd specifically chosen a very large one, just in case she did look down.

"No, have you? He could still be in the falls."

Ariel shook her head. "Ariel doesn't think so. Jade never takes this long."

Finn felt a little bit of jealousy rise in him. Did they take showers together or something? He'd kinda hoped that Ariel had *chosen* to enter his shower because she'd found him attractive...but it was probably because she was just clueless when it came to boundaries.

Ariel finished pulling her leather jerkin over her stained cloth shirt before rushing past Finn and back into the falls. When she had gone, Finn rung his hair out, the green curls already showing signs of life even though they still dripped water.

He slipped on his last smilodon leather boot when he heard Ariel's bloodcurdling scream come from the waterfall.

He stood up as fast as he could and nearly tripped as he sprinted for the falls. He found Ariel on her knees, her hands lifted to her face. At her feet lay Jade on his back with eyes wide open.

He wasn't moving as the water poured over his nose and into his open mouth.

29

THE HUMAN INSTRUMENT

"HE'S DROWNING!" SCREAMED ARIEL SO LOUDLY THAT FINN heard every word over the crashing falls.

No, Finn thought. *He's already drowned.*

Finn rushed over to Jade and pulled his body out of the water, then bent down and pulled Jade over his shoulder, lifting him with ease off the stone ground. All that time in the woods had really paid off —the old Finn would never have been able to lift anyone onto his shoulder and jog him out from under the falls. There was just no way. Maybe he was becoming a Champion after all? ...Even though it was sort of his fault that Jade had drowned in the first place.

Finn set Jade down carefully onto his back in the grass. The first thing he did was close his eyes, as they were starting to creep him out. Ariel stood over his shoulder yelling at him, her face red from crying.

"You have to help him, Finn! He's dying!"

Finn dared not tell her that he might already have been dead. He put his hand to Jade's neck and waited for a pulse but felt none. He was about to pull away when he felt the slightest of thumps.

"He's still alive!" Finn cried. "What do I do?! What do I do?!"

"Make him breathe!" shouted Ariel. "Make air come out of his mouth!"

Finn clenched his fists. "Shit! Shit!"

He had to think! He had to calm down! He could do this, he could! He just needed to think! But no ideas came to him! He had no idea of what needed to be done as he'd never done anything like this before! People rarely drowned in Shimoshimo—they usually froze to death before they could drown.

In frustration, Finn pounded on Jade's stomach, making Ariel cry out. When he did this, a good amount of water surfaced from Jade's mouth and Finn felt a little tingle of hope.

"Hold his mouth open!" Finn demanded of Ariel.

"What?!"

"Just do it!"

Finn went to work right away. He pushed on Jade's stomach with both hands, and water just would not stop pouring out of his mouth. Finn looked up at Ariel as he worked. Her lips curled inside her mouth while tears streamed down her already wet face. She let her hair brush over Jade's head and Finn was going to tell her to move it when he decided it might actually help. Who knew if Jade was unconscious or not? The pink hair might just give him the little bit of will to live that he needed.

When the water stopped gurgling out from Jade's lips, Finn turned him over and let the remaining drips of water run out of his mouth. He then rolled him back onto his back and put the back of his hand to Jade's mouth, feeling for air.

There was none.

"He's still not breathing!" Finn shouted.

"Make him breathe!" Ariel cried back. She grabbed Jade's head and started to shake it. "Wake up, Jade! Wake up! Ariel needs you!" Ariel's cries turned into babbling sobs. "Puhleeeassee wake up! Ariel can't go on without you!"

Finn bit his bottom lip as he thought. Ariel was right, he needed to force Jade to breathe. But how?! How, dammit?!

In one last drastic action, Finn put his lips to Jade's and pushed air into his mouth. He felt his breath on the side of his cheek as it escaped Jade's nose. Finn then pinched Jade's nostrils and tried again, this time feeling the man's stomach rise with air. He pulled his head back and used his hand to push on Jade's stomach to let the air back out. He did this over and over again for what seemed like forever without any success. It was like playing a strange instrument with a person's body.

He lifted his head and looked at Ariel. Her eyes were barely open, and she could bring no more tears to her eyes as she'd cried them all out long ago. So, instead, she just choked on the air that she breathed in. Finn was about to tell her the bad news that she already knew, but thought he'd give it one more try.

Finn blew one last breath down Jade's throat. This time, he visualized Jade waking up and imagined breathing life into him. When he pulled his head back, Jade's eyes were open and staring right up at him.

"He's alive!" screamed Ariel. "He's alive! He's alive!"

Jade started to cough, and more water sprinkled into the air and onto his cheek. Finn turned him back onto his side and slapped on his back. Jade continued to choke and cough for another ten minutes before his body finally began to relax under Finn's hands. He curled up into a shivering ball and both Finn and Ariel covered him with their bodies as they rested.

FOR THE REST of the day and half the night, Jade slept. Finn worried about the fury that would come with the awakening of the beast, but still he sat by his side while he rested. Occasionally, Finn would check Jade's pulse, as well as made sure air flowed from his nose. When he did wake up, it was in a peaceful manner.

"Is Ariel asleep?" he asked Finn.

"Yeah," he said. "She's been asleep. I think seeing you almost die really drained her."

"Really? She was that upset?"

"You have no idea."

Jade nodded his head slowly, watching Ariel as he crossed his legs and sat up. "You do realize that was your fault. I never would have drowned if you hadn't tripped that paralysis pouch plant."

"I do realize that," Finn said. "And I'm sorry." Finn thought a moment and added, "And I'm sorry I took your Blade."

Jade shook his head. "You didn't take my Blade. It was never my Blade."

"But it could have been."

"No. I want a Blade I can grow with and master. I never could have done that with the Jigsaw Blade."

"So, this Blade you're trying to get from your father, do you believe it will bind with you?"

"Easily. When I was younger, I swore that it would speak to me in my dreams, beckoning me to come and wield it."

"But if it's your father's Blade, then how is it possible that you receive it?" Finn asked.

"There are rituals that can be performed to transfer ownership, some harder than others," answered Jade. "I've heard it depends on the relationship between the two who are performing the exchange. There are rumors that some rituals require a blood sacrifice, but honestly, I don't know a whole lot about it myself."

Finn tried to hide his excitement that came with learning more about Blades but couldn't keep his feet from squirming. Although he had his own Bizarre Blade, he still found the thought of them exhilarating, even if his Blade was almost useless when it came to abilities. It was more of a tool than a sword, in his opinion.

"What Blade is it, if you don't mind me asking? No one outside of your family knows the name. Trust me, I've asked my sources."

"And there's a reason for that. My family has kept the Blade's powers in the shadows because it creates a sort of fear factor. It's a tactic, if you will. Armies may think twice before laying siege on our city because they do not know what awaits them. I don't even know what its powers are, but I do know its name."

"Well?" Finn asked, feeling antsy. "What's the name?"

Jade looked at him and through the light of the fire Finn could see his eyes squinting at him. Judging him. "I will tell you the name, but not because we're friends. We're not. But...you did save my life."

"I did," Finn agreed.

"But it was your fault."

"It was," Finn also agreed.

Jade sighed. "The Blade I was supposed to inherit is named the Phantom Blade." Finn squeaked and Jade gave him a concerned look. "You okay?"

"Yes! Ahem...yes, sorry. And you say you don't know what it can do?"

Jade shook his head, "Nope. Not a clue."

"It has an awesome name, though."

"That it does."

Finn paused before asking his next question, wondering if he should even ask it. This probably wasn't the right time, but when would there be a right time? "So, why *did* you get banished?"

Jade pointed at Ariel without looking at her. "Because of her."

"What happened?"

"Why do you want to know?"

Finn shrugged. "Well, for one, it seems important that I know what I'm getting myself into. Secondly, if we're gonna be spending a lot of time together we might as well get to know one another."

"I could do without getting to know you."

"You're really blunt, you know that?"

"So I've been told."

Finn had nothing else to say, so he just sat back on his elbows and looked up at the starry night. Yet again, the jungle remained wide awake with all sorts of strange noises, but they weren't nearly as horrifying as when he'd been alone. He hated to admit it, but he felt a lot safer with Jade and Ariel next to him. They could probably whip anything or anyone's ass that tried to sneak up on them...well, apparently not Constantine and his minions.

Staring up at the stars brought up the image of his father sitting with him on their roof back home. He would point out the constellations and make up stories for each and every one of them. Every night the constellations would have a different story and a different connection to other constellations. Now that Finn was older and looking back, he realized that his old man sure had a great imagination. The trips to the top of their roof stopped after the accident, when his father could no longer make the climb. It hurt Finn's heart to think that he may have put his father's life in jeopardy.

A loud caw rang through the trees, lifting Finn's saddened heart from its dark place. Jade's ears perked up and put his hand to his belt which held his daggers.

"Obsidian?!" Finn called out. "Is that you?"

Obsidian answered him with another caw. Finn heard the raptor's wings before he saw the black dinosaur glide over the fire and into his lap. Jade quickly pulled himself away from Obsidian, a small amount of fear on his face.

"Don't worry," Finn said, "it doesn't bite." He patted Obsidian on the head and the raptor snapped at his fingers. Finn should have known better than to stroke his face feathers. No, Obsidian always preferred from the shoulder down, and no more than five strokes. "Well," said Finn, sucking on his finger. "Not always."

"You named a raptor?" Jade asked, staring at the midnight black microraptor. The fire reflecting off his eyes made for an excellent fearful effect.

"Yes," said Finn. "Well, not really. He was Bryce's microraptor, not mine. He just sort of adopted me, I guess."

"You do realize that is incredibly stupid. Microraptors aren't pets, they're dangerous dinosaurs."

"I never had a choice in the matter," said Finn, finishing up his fifth pat. Obsidian looked up at him, daring him to try for a sixth. But he knew better. "I tried shooing it away, but it just wouldn't go. Besides, it was my friend for seven months while I was in the woods. Say, how did you and Ariel fare when Silver stranded you guys?"

"I don't understand your question."

"I'm asking how you and Ariel did when Silver left you two in the woods."

"Oh...he never did that."

"What?" Finn asked, his hand accidentally dropping back down on Obsidian, who gave him another nip on the finger. "Ow! Stop that! And what do you mean he never stranded you out in the woods?! Then why'd he do it to me?"

"He doesn't like you," said Jade simply.

So he wasn't joking when he said he wished I'd died out there, Finn thought.

Now that Jade was awake, Finn felt like it was safe for him to get some sleep. He lay down on his side, Jigsaw starting up a very relaxing purr that sent soothing vibrations down his spine. As usual, Obsidian curled up on top of his hip bone, only to poke its head out to watch Finn. Obsidian would then wait for Finn's eyes to shut before it would shut its own. Finn had discovered this one night and had done a few tests to see if the microraptor really was waiting for him to fall asleep first. It was something to do when you were dying of boredom.

"I was on a hunting expedition with my father and his best soldiers when we found Ariel," Jade said, still sitting up and looking at the stars. "Her cage hung from the bark of a rotten tree overhanging a long-abandoned camp. She'd been starving and was nearly crazy with famine. The cage she was in must have had some sort of curse on it, for it would not allow Ariel to grow to her full, normal size." Jade held out his palm into the air. "I remember being able to hold it up with just one hand."

Finn said nothing, hoping Jade would continue the story. He could feel his eyes beginning to grow heavy and fought off his sleepiness with all his strength.

"My father ordered me to leave her be. He said it was

best for all magical things to die, as they were unnatural and dangerous to our world."

"But Bizarre Blades are magical," Finn argued.

"Don't you think I told him that? Nothing worked. His soldiers laughed at me for wanting to save some deranged pixie out of a filth-infested cage. There was nothing I could do at that point but wait until everyone was asleep back at camp before returning to her. When I opened the cage and lifted her out, she quickly grew to a regular size, pinning my hand beneath her foot. I gave her the food I'd saved from dinner which I'd smuggled in my pockets. She wouldn't take it from my hands and so I had to throw it on the ground. She ate the food like an animal."

"Her father just left her in the cage like that?" Finn asked, his sleepiness slowly draining away. The story was getting good.

"We think he did. Ariel doesn't have much memory of it. Or, if she does, it's been pushed far back into the shadows of her mind. But, seeing as though he killed her mother for being magical, it only makes sense that he wanted to do the same to her. My theory is that he couldn't bring himself to drop the knife on his own blood, so he left her to starve to death. A worse death, in my opinion."

"Then what?"

"Hold on a minute. Have some patience, I'm getting there. Anyway, when I brought her back to camp, Father arrested her and beat me with a piece of reed. When he was leaving my room I asked him where he was going. He said he was going to whip Ariel. Being the Prince that I was, I knew our laws frontwards and backwards. I knew that I could substitute myself for the punishment of others, and that's what I did. That night, my father beat me until his hand grew tired. Then, he had his second in charge finish the job. I couldn't walk for a week."

Finn had his fingers in his mouth and was busy chewing on the nails. Jade didn't see this, however, as he was in a different world.

"When my wounds had healed enough so that I could walk, I snuck to where they had caged Ariel. Again, she was kept in a cell that was far too small for her. I'll never forget that my people had the audacity to put a young girl in the same cage we keep livestock in. Her skin and hair was covered with her own filth and she was speaking to herself as if there were two of her. I remember sitting in front of her prison, crying while asking how it was possible for humans to be so cruel. I then stole a key from the same second in charge who had beat me. When I opened her cage, I thought I was going to have to knock her out and carry her away, but no, she came right up to me. Together, we escaped the camp and ran into the jungle. That is when Silver discovered us. We were huddled under a tree, both of us living off bugs and dirty water."

"And you did all this when you were ten years old."

"Yes," said Jade, "and I'd do it all over again. There, you happy? You got your story."

"Thank you," said Finn, his sleepiness returning like a punch to the face. "Goodnight."

Jade snorted and laid himself down on his back, both arms crossed over his chest. He probably thought the crackling sounds of the fire hid his returned, "Goodnight," but Finn heard it loud and clear.

30

THE CITY OF WATERFALLS

THE REST OF THE JOURNEY TOOK NO MORE THAN TWO DAYS, but what a two miserable days they were! The three travelers walked along the river, swatting at relentless suicidal mosquitos that were desperate to get just a drop of blood—they knew the palms was coming to crush them, but they bit the travelers anyway. The Champions had covered themselves in mud to try to keep the disease-carrying insects off of them, but it didn't make a huge change. Finn literally slapped himself when he discovered that the smoke from Jigsaw had a one hundred percent success rate in keeping all buzzing things far away from him.

At one point, the mosquitos had gotten so bad that Jade's head was almost completely hidden under the layer of bloodsuckers attached to it. By the end of that day, Finn was hugging Jade from behind and Ariel was hugging *him* from behind while Jigsaw covered all three of them with its life-saving smoke.

"This never leaves the jungle," Jade had threatened.

"You think I would ever tell this story?" asked Finn.

"Finn, the Champion, humps fellow Champion from behind to save him from the mosquitoes of doom."

Jade hadn't appreciated the joke. Not at all. Ariel, however, was having too much fun with their circumstance. She kept threatening Jade that she was going to tell the whole village of their humping adventures. For hours, Finn was stuck between the arguing two. It was like they were brother and sister or something...well, they kinda were. Or were they more? The whole thing was complicated, and it hurt Finn's head to think much of what was going on with his life. He did find Ariel's humor to be a great distraction from his sad thoughts about his father. He just kept telling himself that everything was alright and that he was doing the best he could to get back to him.

As they walked down the river, Finn never took his eyes off the rushing water. The entire time he was on edge, expecting a crocodile to spring out at any moment and swallow their human sandwich whole, but this never happened. Instead, it was actually quite a boring trip with not a single dinosaur to be seen.

At one point, Ariel broke away from the safety of the smoke and dashed through the mud to what looked like a hole in the ground.

"What are you doing?" Jade asked. "Get back here! We need to keep moving forward."

"Look what Ariel's found!"

"What is it?" Finn asked, now curious himself. He pulled off of Jade, who groaned.

It took Finn a few seconds for his brain to figure out what he was looking at. An incredibly large dinosaur print lay imbedded in the mud, puddles of mosquito-infested water already forming at the bottom of it.

"What dinosaur is this?" Finn gasped. "Don't tell me it's a—"

"Tyrannosaur," Jade said, confirming his fears.

"But, but, but, look at it! It's too big to be a tyrannosaurus! No meat-eaters have prints like these."

"This t-rex is special," said Jade.

"Ooh! Ooh! Is this the t-rex you've told Ariel about?" asked Ariel excitedly. "Is this Jewels' footprint?"

Jade's eyebrows drew together as he scanned the jungle before them. "Yes...yes, it is."

"What kind of name is Jewels?" asked Finn. "Doesn't seem very fitting for a tyrannosaurus, if you ask me."

"No one asked you," snapped Jade. "Now hurry up, we need to keep moving."

The three of them walked back to the river, reconnecting themselves and forming once again their human sandwich.

"Ariel is so happy she got to see Jewels' footprint before she died!"

"You may see more than a footprint," Jade said from the front.

"Wait, what do you mean by that?" asked Finn worriedly, his eyes jumping from looking for crocodiles in the river, over to the forest for the t-rex that would inevitably charge out from the trees.

Jade didn't answer but only snickered.

They reached Kimidori late that afternoon. Finn nearly shouted when Koosahmoorarian soldiers began to appear, walking quietly from the jungle's edge. They all had long shiny black hair pulled back over their ears. They wore rust-red plate armor that covered their entire bodies in layers. They held no weapons in their hands, but each soldier had two thin swords attached to their hips. They walked seemingly without a cause, with deadpan faces. Casually, they made their way to the three traveling Champions, walking shoulder to shoulder with them. Obsidian shuffled anxiously on Finn's shoulder before leaping off of it and making its way towards the trees.

Some friend you are, thought Finn. *Always leaving before the trouble starts.*

Looking across the river, Finn saw that even more of the soldiers were starting to appear from that side of the jungle as well.

"Who are these people?" Finn whispered into Jade's ear. He popped Finn in the stomach with his elbow but Finn wouldn't stop his pestering. "Who? Just tell me."

"Scouts," Jade finally whispered back. "My father no doubt knows we're here, so be on your best behavior."

"Tell that to Ariel!"

Finn and Jade looked back to see Ariel lifting the flaps of plate armor that encircled the neck of one of the Koosah-moorarian soldiers. The soldier paid her no attention but kept walking forward. Jade hissed at her to stop but she refused to listen.

Soon, the river ended in a magnificent waterfall that fell so far down that the human eye couldn't see where it crashed into the waters below. The sun had descended behind the falls gifting Finn with the most beautiful rainbow he'd ever seen. Even the Koosahmoorarian soldiers seemed to perk up at the sight of it.

"I forgot how beautiful it was," said Jade, looking off to the left.

Finn followed his gaze and nearly stopped in his tracks. The city before him was more than beautiful...there were almost no words to describe it. Before them was a tall gate made of wooden pillars dyed in red paint which stood already wide open, as if waiting for their arrival.

The city of Kimidori was situated on a peninsula surrounded on all three sides by nothing but a long drop. Three large mountains encircled the city, one on the left, one on the right, and one all the way in the back. Over these mountains came pouring down hundreds—if not thousands —of waterfalls, ranging in all sorts of sizes from an entire river exploding over the edge to just mere trickles. All of these waterfalls combined created a gorgeous, pearl-colored mist that covered the outskirts of the city. Finn had been completely satisfied with the two waterfalls he'd already seen but this...this was too much. Did people really live here? It looked more like a paradise than an actual city!

As they walked through the gate, Finn felt them leave the hot, uncomfortable temperature behind. The mist of the surrounding waterfalls was so powerful that it even reached the street that they now walked along in the middle of the city. Soft grass covered the ground across which wagons traveled a very small path, to reduce the amount of green that they trampled.

The dinosaurs were of a variety that Finn was unaccustomed to. Edmontosauruses, of which Finn had only seen drawings, walked freely from house to house. Finn watched their fat tails raise into the air as their long snouts dropped to the ground. Gracefully and without care, the edmontosauruses plucked chunks of grass and chewed slowly. They were in no rush. Life was good.

Their round, heavy bodies walked on two thick back legs and two thinner legs up front. They came in all shapes and sizes. Some were super fat, some were wrinkly and old, and some were big enough to have Koosahmoorarians riding on top of their backs on specially made leather saddles. As for the colors of their skin, Finn saw some that were turquoise, brown, dark blue and even some lighter green ones! While walking by, Finn couldn't help but watch as a little girl painted her very own baby edmontosaurus while her bigger brother pet its head.

"This... is so much more different than Sumetai," Finn said. Jade answered with a grunt. "I don't think I ever want to leave."

"Trust me," said Jade. "You will."

As they walked, Finn suddenly realized that Ariel's hands were no longer on his shoulder. He whipped his head around to look for her and saw her a ways back, helping the little boy and girl paint their edmontosaurus. Somehow, the strange girl had slipped out from behind him, under the eyes of the soldier escort, and had even camouflaged herself amongst the people—even though she looked nothing like them.

Finn was about to warn Jade, but Jade shook his head slowly, not even looking back at him. He somehow knew what Ariel had done. Had this been their plan all along? If so, why hadn't they told him about it?

Finn waited for the soldiers to realize that they were missing another person but they never did. Many were busy accepting gifts from young women and old ladies who exited their houses with baskets filled with delicious smelling breads covered in honeys and jams. Finn's stomach growled, and he licked his lips as he watched a few soldiers take big bites out of the soft-looking pastries.

The homes were built on each side of the road and were constructed with perfect precision. Each house was the same size, the same color, and the space between each house was also the same. The wood was painted in a mixture of black and red dyes, and two oil lanterns were nailed to the outside, one on each side of a black door.

No one paid Finn and Jade any attention. It was as

though armored soldiers escorting strangers through the city was a normal occurrence. Everyone on the streets had a job to do and everyone had a smile on their face. The dinosaurs also seemed to be very happy, performing their duties of pulling carts or farm equipment with not so much as a single roar—or even a sneeze. The drivers of these dinosaurs had no whip in hand and only used whistling noises to direct them. In Sumetai, dinosaurs used for work did not die from starvation or thirst, but from the beatings given to them by their owners. Dinosaurs were merely tools in Sumetai...but here in Kimidori, it seemed, things were different. Dinosaurs were treated more like pets, and Finn liked this. He loved the energy he was feeling. Although, the fact that everything was exactly the same gave him a weird freaky feeling about the place. It was just a little bit *too* perfect.

The familiar screech of pterodactyls made Finn grip Jade's shoulders tightly, but he loosened his hold when he realized that the pterosaurs paid him or anyone else no attention, focusing and diving only on the fish that fell from the waterfall cliffs. The flying reptiles performed this in a circular and orderly fashion, each waiting patiently in line in the air while their brethren got their fish and then flew to the back of the line.

The palace stood at the far end of the road, built with a wide rectangular front entrance and a roof that extended outwards to protect most of the courtyard from the rays of the sun. Standing in front of this courtyard was perhaps the most interesting decoration of all—a twenty-foot-tall, golden statue of which appeared to be the king. His shoulders were back, his chest was broad, and his stomach was flat. In his hand he gripped a mighty sword that he heroically pointed outward.

The soldiers escorted Finn and Jade through the entranceway and into the courtyard. There sat two seats made from the same red wood as the building. Sitting in the tallest of chairs was a wrinkly old man with his black and grey hair tied into a tight bun. To his left, on the second tallest chair, was a woman that looked to be half his age with candy red hair. Her smile was as about as real as the name Lightningsword.

Both of these people, who Finn presumed to be Jade's father and mother, had fair-skin, much different than Jade's black skin.

Finn bent down and whispered in Jade's ear, "Are you sure these are your parents?"

"I never said by blood, did I?"

They both shut up as the king of Kimidori raised his hands and spoke.

"It has been so long, my son!" exclaimed the wrinkly man. His eyes were almond-shaped and his irises were a dark brown. His thick white eyebrows lifted, as well as his arms, as he awaited for his son to embrace him. However, he did not stand up from his throne. Much to Finn's surprise, Jade walked up to his father and gave him a hug.

The mother said nothing but also accepted a hug from Jade. As Jade backed away, Finn noticed that there was another chair to the king's right, only a lot shorter and pushed back a ways. In the chair sat the most gorgeous girl he'd ever seen. She wore light pink clothes that were far too big for her body—her wrists were as thin as twigs. Her hair, a sleek black with highlights of the same candy red as her mother, was also tied in a bun. She wore pink blush on her cheeks and her skin looked so soft that Finn wanted nothing more than to run across the courtyard and rub his face against hers. He wouldn't mind putting his lips against her red-painted ones either.

The girl, who he assumed to be the Princess, caught his gaze and flashed him an angry look. Finn averted his eyes but wondered why this angry look of hers got him excited. What was wrong with him? Why was his tongue swelling up? Why was there no saliva in his mouth? Why had his hands grown clammy? Why did his knees feel weak? What was wrong with his body?!

"Son, why have you taken so long to come back to us?" asked King Whetstone. "Your mother and I thought you dead long ago!" Without warning, the king slapped the shit out of his son's face and then brought him into another hug. Jade turned his face to the side, blood trickling from his lips. He looked at Finn and his eyes said, "I told you so."

What the hell was that? Finn thought to himself. *Did he just slap his son? The son he thought was dead? And why isn't his mother doing anything? She looks more like a wooden dummy than a person!*

"I'm sorry, Father," said Jade, bowing his head.

"Sorry? Sorry for what? You're here now and that is all that matters! PipPip! Oh, PipPip! Dammit, where is that boy?"

"Here I am, sir!" said a young boy with a hideous triangular face. His skin was riddled with pimples and he had one very...very lazy eye. "What can I do for you?"

"For starters, where's that wool sack I gave you to cover that face of yours?" demanded the king.

"It's itchy!"

"Put it back or...or so help me!"

"But why?" asked PipPip, tilting his ugly head.

"Because! Um, because," fumbled the king. "Because it's what's in fashion these days. Now, alert the people that I will be holding a feast in the dining hall to celebrate the return of my son! All are welcome! Well, besides you, of course... I'm sure you're busy, yes?"

"No sir, I'm free. I can make it."

"That won't be necessary," said the king. "I'm sure you're busy."

Before PipPip could argue with him, the king dismissed the boy with a flick of his hand. PipPip sighed, bowed his head, and left.

"Where were we? Oh yes! What have you been doing all of these years? Wait, don't tell me because I already know! You ran off with that pink-headed fairy bitch, didn't you? Don't tell me otherwise because I already know."

Finn watched as Jade tightened his fists by his side, only to release them a second later. The two of them were surrounded by Koorahmoorarian guards and Finn highly doubted he could take down even one of them with his Jigsaw Blade. They looked like they'd been training all of their lives, while he'd been training for less than a year. If you called climbing trees and freezing your ass off in the woods training, that is.

"And who is your Bizarre Blade-wielding friend? He looks more like a squire than an actual Champion."

Finn put a hand to his chest, hurt at the insult. Well, the king was kinda right, he did look scrawny for a warrior.

"This is Finn, Finn Featherstone," said Jade. "He and his Blade just recently communed less than a year ago."

"Is that so? Well, any and all Champions are welcome at my feasting table. What I'm trying to say, Mr. Featherstone, is it would be an honor to have you tonight. Please do excuse my rude comment."

Finn bowed his head because he didn't really know what else to do. "Thank you, Your Highness."

"You're quite welcome."

"Sir," said one of the soldiers who had been part of their forced escort, "the girl has gone missing."

"What?!" cried the king. "How could you let this happen? She couldn't have just disappeared!" The king rethought his words. "Or *could* she? Where was she last seen?"

"I remember seeing her just before we entered into Kimidori, Your Highness."

"Well?" said the king.

The soldier's throat gulped. "Uh, well, what, Your Graciousness?"

"Well, go find her! Go on! Get going!"

The soldier bowed his head quickly, signaled for four of the king's guards to follow him, and they left the courtyard in a rush. Finn turned to watch them leave, then counted the remaining guards.

"You look a little nervous," said the king to Jade. "You know very well that you shouldn't have brought her kind into my Kingdom."

"I thought you might have grown out of that old stigma," said Jade.

"What stigma?"

"The one where you thought all magical beings were evil."

The king's face twisted into a vile angry look, revealing crooked yellow teeth under his white mustache, growing in different directions ending in sharp points. He stroked his long white beard, and with each stroke his face seemed to grow a little kinder. Finn couldn't figure out where to look on this man. It was a hard decision between his jet-black bushy eyebrows and his cannonball shaped gut hanging out of his robes. Strangely, every other part of this man besides his midsection was skinny. Finn looked back at the golden statue depiction of King Whetstone and wondered if the artist that had created it had been blind or too fearful to sculpt the king's true appearance.

With a smile, the king said, "I'm going to let this remark slide just this once because you are my son. However, one more time speaking to me like that, especially in front of your mother, sister, a Champion, and my men, then I will have your tongue pulled, not cut, but pulled from your mouth. Do you understand?"

Jade said nothing, only bowed his head.

Randomly, Jigsaw injected the thought of shoving itself into the king's face but Finn quickly dispersed the idea. Jigsaw must have shared Finn's feelings about King Whetstone. Something about him just wasn't right. He was like an obese snake living in red silk robes.

"Now, I believe you have come here for a reason," announced King Whetstone. "That reason not being to see your mother or myself, but because you *want* something." The king's smile dropped into its true form, the nasty, crooked, yellow-toothed frown. "What is it?" he spat.

"I've come to inherit what is rightfully mine."

The King put his elbow on the armrest of his throne. "You speak of the Phantom Blade?"

"It is the Phantom Blade of which I speak."

"Oh please, drop the formal talk. Why the hell would I give a deserter, the one who turned his back on his kingdom, the most powerful weapon in all of Koosahmoorah? Just saying it out loud sounds ridiculous! It's absurd!"

"Because it's rightfully mine."

"Your rights died when you left with that...*fairy*!" Jade said nothing. "Besides, what makes you think I haven't given the Blade to your brother?"

"Because I know for a fact that Ace has already communed with another weapon."

King Whetstone snorted. "I shoulda known that Nibbles bitch would have used her mage powers to meddle in others' business."

That was all Jade could take. He stormed towards his father with both fists clenched. The guards were on him like flies on mammoth dung. They grabbed him by his shoulders and by his wrists, and one even hugged him from behind, his armored arms squeezing Jade's waist.

The conversation continued like nothing happened.

"The Phantom Blade should have gone to your brother," said the king, drumming his face with his fingers. "Imagine what good he could have brought to our kingdom."

"He left you for similar reasons as I!" shouted Jade. "You're cruel and ignorant!"

King Whetstone sighed and pulled a finger across his throat. The guards were quick and efficient in pulling Jade off of his feet and onto the ground. Everything happened so quickly that Finn had no idea what was going on, but he quickly figured it out when the guards began prying open Jade's mouth as they prepared to pluck out his tongue.

"I warned you," said the King, standing up from his throne. He was almost shorter than Finn. His robe came undone, revealing his disgusting shriveled nudity to the world. "I may be your father, but I am still your king. My threat to pull your tongue was no mere jest." The King walked towards his son, his extra flabby skin jiggling and swinging left and right.

Finn had no choice but to draw Jigsaw. With a mighty roar, the Blade ejected itself out of its magical baldric and into Finn's raised hand. The metal screeched, and smoke poured from its vents as it doubled in size, back to its original girth and length. This awesome display of power took two of the guards by surprise, and they both fell on their asses, their eyes wide with fear.

"Wow!" exclaimed the king while clapping his hands. "Just, wow! Look at that, Yuri!" He turned to the wife who wasn't even paying attention, dead to the world. "Isn't that some kind of Blade?!" He whistled. "Bet that thing isn't clean when it cuts through its victims."

"It isn't," Finn agreed, feeling more like a Champion than he ever had before.

The king put his hands behind his back and put one foot down on his son's chest. The guards who had retreated away from the greatness of the Jigsaw Blade were back on Jade and readying him for his tongue extraction.

"So, what do we do now?" asked the king, looking slightly intrigued by this situation.

"You tell me," said Finn, deepening his voice a little.

The King opened his lips and licked his teeth. He looked down at one of his guards and nodded his head. The guard shoved his hand into Jade's mouth and clamped down onto his tongue.

Finn sprang into action.

31

THE KING'S PROPOSITION

JIGSAW'S TEETH BUZZED MENACINGLY A HAIR'S DISTANCE AWAY from the guard's neck. A drop of sweat popped up above the man's brow and dripped down the side of his face. He did not move a muscle because if he moved just slightly in the wrong direction, then he could say farewell to his neck.

The King's mouth had fallen open. He, too, didn't move, his foot still on his son's chest. Jade looked from Jigsaw, to his father, and back to the Blade. There was a sort of stalemate going on and most of the power rested on Finn's shoulders—or, at least that's what it felt like.

What broke the silence was the king's clapping, his mouth puckering as he nodded his head as though he were impressed. To his left, Finn caught the eyes of Jade's sister, and he nearly fell over. He didn't know what she was but she certainly wasn't human. Judging by the beauty of her face he guessed she was an angel. God, how he loved her face.

"Well done, Master Finn, well done. I'm pretty sure that the undergarments of my men here are full of shit! Hell, I might need a bath myself! It's been so long since I've seen the powers of a Bizarre Blade, and for that I thank you." The king clapped his hands once and Finn's eyes flinched. "Say! Here's an idea!" He stepped off his son and walked up to Finn, his face a few inches away. He smelled awful. "Why don't you show off your Bizarre Blade's powers tonight at the feast?"

"I don't understand," said Finn. "Are we in different worlds or something? I'm pretty sure I almost cut the head off one of your guards, and you about ripped your son's tongue out."

The king slapped his knees and laughed, a little bit of spit splashing onto Finn's face. He imagined it burning into his skin like acid. "A mere jest, my good boy! A jest is all it was!"

"But you literally said it wasn't a jest..."

Ignoring Finn's words, the king commanded, "Guards, please, release my son!"

The guards looked at one before slowly getting off Jade, who stood up, brushing the dirt off his leather armor. He blinked a few times, looked up at Finn, and nodded his head slightly in thanks. For some reason, this sent warmth through Finn's chest. Finally, he'd acted! He'd done something without pause! Was he becoming a true Champion? The one he'd dreamt of becoming? Or was this just a fluke?

"Don't just stand there and make me wait!" shouted the King, slapping Finn hard on his chest. "What do you say? Will you show off your goods to my people tonight?"

"Um, I, uh..." Finn looked up to Jade, who shrugged his shoulders. "Sure, I'll do it," he said.

"Great! Great! Wonderful! I look forward to—what the hell is this?" King Whetstone lifted up the saber-tooth leather shoulder pauldrons and quickly wiped his hands on his robe. "This is from a smilodon, yes?" Finn nodded. "Who the hell did you give this skin to? A kill this precious should have been mended by a true leatherworker! Whoever crafted you this mess should really have their tongue ripped out."

Finn looked up at Jade but he would not return his gaze.

～

THE KING INVITED Finn and Jade to rest in his palace, and had his guards escort them to their own private guest room. Although the King had made it feel like a suggestion, the guards had formed around both of them tightly, making sure that neither of them snuck off. Finn couldn't shake the feeling that he was more of a prisoner now than a guest.

The room he was put in was the most luxurious living quarters he'd ever seen. The walls were covered in soft blankets. In the corner stood a nightstand with some sort of incense that had already burned halfway. It was as if King Whetstone had planned this all along.

The bed, plump and full of feathers, lay on the ground in the middle of the room, its sheets already pulled back and ready for Finn. In the opposite corner was a small planted tree with water running down its leaves from a wooden pipe that jutted out the side of the wall above it. Whoever had designed this room must have been a genius.

As Finn entered the room, he just about stepped on a basket that was filled with all sorts of colorful fruits. There was a note on top of the gift basket but he discarded it without reading it. He sat his dirty self on the floor in front of his bed and ate every last piece of fruit.

～

SEVERAL HOURS HAD GONE by since Finn had last seen Jade

and the King. A pretty female servant had come and fetched him for a bath. She'd also undressed him, which was a scary yet exhilarating experience. Finn wondered if all the women of this Kingdom were so beautiful.

The bathing experience was one he would never forget. The water was at the perfect temperature, if not a little too warm. From the steam that wafted up into his nose, he could tell that they had put soothing smelling oils into it, which just added to the overall relaxing effect. After washing himself, he'd fallen asleep, only to awaken when his nose drifted beneath the surface of the water. He came up coughing and almost jumped out of his skin when he looked up to see two angelic Koosahmoorarian girls standing in front of his bath.

"Can I help you?" he asked them, wiping the water from his face. He rubbed his eyes to make sure he wasn't dreaming.

"The king sent us," the shorter one said.

"I don't need any help bathing," said Finn. "I can manage all by myself." His eyes darted to Jigsaw, his heart jumping into his throat at the idea of someone stealing it. He relaxed when he saw it still standing where he'd laid it up against the wall.

"We aren't here to help you bathe, but to help you relax," said the taller one, a sly grin on her face.

Finn was about to ask them what they meant when both dropped their robes, blinding him with their bodies. He wasn't quite sure, but he thought he felt a tear fall out of one of his eyes. He stared at them for a few moments before dropping his head. This wasn't right. He couldn't do this.

"I'm sorry ladies, but I'm tired." The truth was he was just too nervous to do anything. Besides, what if they had diseases?

"What's wrong with us?" said the shorter one, grabbing her robe and covering herself.

The taller one did the same. "You don't like us?"

"No! No, no, no, no!" exclaimed Finn, waving his hands in the air. "It's not that, it's just. Well..."

"He's a virgin," whispered the shorter one to the taller one.

"Or he prefers the same sex," whispered the other.

Finn raised an eyebrow at them. "You know I can hear you, right?"

"We will be back with your desired sexual partners, Master Featherstone!" said the taller one, turning to leave.

"No! I don't want any sexual partners. I just want to relax."

The two girls looked at each other and started to cry, holding on to one another while their robes slipped from their hands and onto the wet floor. Finn shielded his eyes because...because...well, it just didn't feel right!

"Ladies! Ladies! Why are you crying?"

"Because!" sniffed the short one. "If we leave without you being satisfied then we will surely be beaten!"

"Beaten so badly!" said the tall one.

"Well," said Finn, looking at his bath. "Why not just stay here and we can pretend I'm satisfied with that?"

The two girls looked at each other, then back at Finn. "No nasty time?" they asked in unison.

"What? Nasty time? No, no nasty time. Just, talky time."

The two girls went from crying to giggling, leaving their robes on the floor as they both jumped into the bath, splashing Finn right in the face. They swam right next to him and sat down on the underwater bench, their skin touching his. It wasn't the heat of the bath that made Finn's cheeks warm.

They asked him about how he'd gotten there and he told them the whole story. However, he did leave some parts of his tale out, like his diarrhea of doom as well as his interaction with the millipede. The girls were *oohing* and *aahing* at just the right points of his story, making him get even more dramatic in his telling. He even got comfortable enough to put his arms around them, which made him feel like a god!

"And here I am now! With you two. Feeling very naked and very confused."

"What a great story!" said the short one, resting her head on his shoulder.

"You really *are* a Champion, Master Featherstone!" said the tall one, also resting her head on his shoulder.

The sound of steps came from the changing room and Finn looked up just in time to see Jade's sister staring at him through the doorway. Her placid face seemed to turn angry as she stormed off towards the exit.

Not sure why he was doing it, Finn yelled for her to wait. He crashed through the bath and rushed towards where she'd left. He looked down the hallway, but she was nowhere to be seen. This was probably for the best because his gooch troll was exposed for the whole world to see. Not only that, but whether it was the sunlight or the naked girls in his bath, his troll had turned to stone.

~

THE KING VISITED Finn a half hour before the great feast. He asked him how he had enjoyed his entertainment and Finn didn't lie when he said he had a great time.

"That is wonderful to hear! Also, I will have you know that I have taken the liberty of sending your crudely crafted armor to my finest leatherworker! By tomorrow morning, you will have a set of leather armor suitable for a Champion such as yourself! Tell me, you did kill this saber-tooth yourself?"

"I did," Finn said, leaving out the fact that he'd been extremely lucky.

"Please, do me a favor and tell us this story at the table tonight! Think of it as repayment for the leatherwork! I believe you will find tonight a most joyous occasion. I also have a proposition for you and my son which I think you will be very interested to hear."

"And what is that?" Finn asked.

"Patience, my young Champion, patience! All in good time!" The king snapped his fingers and four young boys around the age of ten ran into the room, each holding a handful of red plate armor. "Please wear this armor tonight while we wait for your smilodon armor. We can't have you coming to dinner in your bath towel, can we?"

"Uh, thank you, Your Highness," said Finn, watching as yet another boy came into his room, this one carrying a tall rectangular mirror.

"Oh please, don't worry about calling me 'Your Highness'. 'Your Graciousness' will do just fine. See you at the feast!" The king turned and left through the door.

The boys placed the mirror against the wall and took off Finn's towel. They worked fast and efficiently as they attached the armor to his body. Finn looked into the mirror at his now half-naked body and saw someone that he did not recognize. This person was not as pale as he once was. Not only that, but the stranger in the mirror had muscle!

Finn flexed his arm and couldn't help but poke at it with his finger in disbelief. When did it get so hard? He let his hand run down his abdominal muscles which had never been visible in the past, but now bulged through his skin.

His chest muscles had squared up and he could make them bounce a little if he concentrated. The jaw of his face looked to have also lost some fat, and it looked more defined and even a little manlier. His curly hair had grown longer than he was used to, but he kind of liked the way it looked as it rested on his shoulders, which also looked to have developed from his time in the woods.

"I look like a warrior," Finn whispered to himself.

"What was that, mister?" said one of the boys, placing the chest piece over Finn's head.

"Nothing," said Finn quickly.

Finn waited for the servant boys to leave before looking again at himself in the mirror. The armor was half plate and half leather. The shiny red shoulder pauldrons connected to one another and Finn's head poked out between them. The top part of his torso was covered in the same colored plate while his stomach and waist were shielded by thick dark red leather. The skirt was made from chainmail but the leggings were fully plated.

Finn couldn't help but jump around the room in his new armor, trying his best not to shout out in excitement. If Obsidian had been there with him the raptor might have thought its owner had gone crazy. Or, the exact opposite. The microraptor might simply have regarded Finn's behavior as normal, which it was—Finn acknowledged that he was a strange individual.

The armor felt a little heavy and made it hard for Finn to breathe, but he didn't care. He looked like a professional Champion! He performed a few poses in the mirror, each one manlier then the last. He slipped the Bizarre Baldric over his head and snapped Jigsaw to it. A small squeak of glee escaped his mouth.

A knock at the door came and Finn opened it to see the

same woman who had undressed him. She eyed him up and down with more interest than when she'd first met him. She lifted her hand as if she was going to touch his chest, but quickly dropped it with a blushing smile on her face. She led him through the corridors which were decorated with candles and paintings, paintings that were almost to his father's quality of work. Almost.

The woman stopped him at two tall rectangular doors. She opened them slightly and Finn heard her whisper something to someone. She closed the doors and waited a good minute before opening them fully. She gestured for Finn to walk in.

The massive room was filled to its limit with occupants already tearing into the abundance of food that covered the five long tables. On the far left sat three thrones exactly like the ones in the courtyard. The king and his daughter both turned to Finn as he entered.

"Introducing! Finn Featherstone!" cried a man to Finn's right. "Bizarre Blade-wielding Champion from Sumetai of the Shimoshimo Kingdom!"

An awkward silence followed as everyone stared at him, most of them halfway through shoving chunks of food down their throats. One person clapped, followed by the rest of the congregation going completely mad with excitement. Food was thrown from one end of the room to the other. People stood and danced with mutton sticking out of their lips. Those still seated banged their eating utensils on the wooden tables as they chanted, "Finn! Finn! Finn!"

When the King stood up, the occupants of the feast went quiet. He looked at Finn and gestured to the chair next to him, the chair his wife, the Queen, should have been seated at. Finn dared not say no to the king's suggested seating, even though it was the last place in the eating hall that he wanted to sit.

King Whetstone pet Finn on his shoulder pauldrons as he walked up the stairs and onto the platform. He turned and had to remind himself to breathe. There were just so many people here! And all their eyes were on him. He felt like he was going to be sick.

"Greetings, people of Kimidori!" shouted the King. "It is I, your King, who has bestowed upon you this great feast in celebration of the return of my son, as well as to welcome our Champion friend here!"

Finn looked down and caught Jade's eyes who sat amongst the people he had been born to rule. No one paid him any attention. A few elbows even knocked into him as people cheered excitedly.

"As we eat, I have been promised by our young Champion friend a display of his Bizarre Blade's power! I hope you all will join me in enjoying this once-in-a-lifetime view of..." He paused here for dramatic effect. "THE JIGSAW BLADE!"

The crowd went into a frenzy. Even more food was flung across the room, as well as full tankards of ale. Women tore off their clothes, as did the men. People danced, while others spat their drinks into the air, and Finn even caught sight of two people strangling each other. This was such the opposite of what he expected from such a precise and quiet people. For some reason, coming to this feast had turned them into animals, and it reminded him of how things were back in Sumetai.

"Say something," the king whispered, bending over and blocking his words with his hands. "Hurry, before these idiots burn down the place!"

The king shoved Finn by his shoulder, being careful not

to get his fingers too close to Jigsaw. Finn staggered forward, barely catching himself from falling off the raised platform. He straightened himself and stared at the slobbering jaws of the hungry beast that was the crowd. He tried picturing them in their undergarments but only succeeded in making himself blush.

What do I say?! thought Finn in a panic. *What do I do with my hands, dammit?! What do I do with my hands?!*

Most of the heads in the crowd tilted as they started up at Finn, expecting some marvelous presentation. If only they knew that the Champion before them was mostly a fraud, a fraud with a semi-powerful Bizarre Blade. He had no tricks up his sleeve, nothing really awesome he could show these people. Jigsaw was, well, it was a saw! Nothing special there. It couldn't make people explode and it certainly couldn't take control of animals. No, it was best used for cutting trees and nothing more.

Finn turned around to look at the king, but his eyes fell on his daughter instead. Her usual uncaring demeanor had changed to...was it, excitement? Wonder? She leaned forward in her chair, her eyes set on the Jigsaw Blade attached to his back. Unlike the crowd, which looked to be becoming impatient, she was just happy to see a Bizarre Blade up close in person. She'd most likely been given everything in life and had become desensitized to most things...but a Bizarre Blade! That was something she rarely got to see, if ever! Or, at least that was Finn's thinking.

Turning back to the crowd, Finn saw that the occupants already returned to their meals with grunts of disapproval, and sensed something spark inside his gut. He felt a little rejuvenated, if not a little more confident in his abilities. Moving his hand slowly over his shoulder, he watched as the crowd fell silent and still. Finn could hear a few of them whispering as he clasped his hand around the grip. He could feel Jigsaw vibrate to life. Finn worried about what he should do first. Should he just reveal the Blade and be done with it? Or did they want more?

Jigsaw answered this question by shoving a few ideas into his head.

That'll work, thought Finn, a sideways smile growing on his face.

The warm feeling of confidence in the pit of his stomach evolved into a revolving ball of fire which rose through his chest, through his neck, and out of his mouth in the form of a war cry. Jigsaw shot out from its magical baldric with a roar, exploding long flames through each side of its vents. The teeth slid across one another rapidly creating a deafening thunder of scraping metal. The people at the very front of the crowd fell off their benches, their cries muted by the shrieks of Jigsaw.

The flames flowing out of the vents grew so large that they turned upward, engulfing the entirety of Jigsaw's blade. The moving teeth dispersed the flames, shooting embers out into the audience. Finn swung the Blade left and right, the fire creating a very satisfying swooshing sound.

Then, something very odd happened.

Finn felt his fist tightening around the leathering grip of Jigsaw—except it wasn't his doing, but the Blade's. Warmth trickled over his fingers and he looked down, afraid that the flames might have become so large that they now licked his hands. What he saw made no sense. Orange magma was oozing out of the vents of Jigsaw and trickling over his hand. He cried out in fear but no one could hear him. No one even noticed his panicked movements as they were all focused completely on the fire-breathing Bizarre Blade.

Finn watched in terror as the smoking magma engulfed

his hand. The pain was strong, but bearable. He tried to relax and calm his breathing as he watched Jigsaw ooze more and more of the orange goo. It was when the magma dried that he realized that it wasn't magma at all...

It was melted steel.

Finn brought his face as close to the dried metal as he dared, his cheeks burning from the smoldering liquid that now crawled down his wrist. He tried flexing his pointer finger and watched with amazement as the metal remelted itself around his joints, allowing him to move them.

A hand clasped him on the shoulder, making him lose concentration. The armor melted once again into a liquid and quickly sucked itself back up into Jigsaw's vents. The Blade went quiet, leaving the temperature onstage swelteringly hot.

"Well done, Champion Featherstone!" shouted the king, taking one of Finn's hands off the Blade and raising it into the air. "Well done, indeed! I asked for a demonstration and you gave us a thrilling presentation, the likes none of us will ever forget! Am I right, people of Kimidori?"

The crowd still remained silent, stunned by Finn's more-than-terrifying demonstration. One person in the very back of the audience, most likely the same person from earlier, started to clap slowly, followed by another, then another. Soon, the entire feast hall was going mad with applause, behaving even more like animals than when Finn had first entered the room. Tables were overturned, men began fist-fights with smiles on their faces, and guards had to kick women with their boots as they tried to make it onstage to get at Finn.

"Enjoy the rest of the evening!" cried the King, turning Finn around and walking him back up to his chair. "Champion Featherstone, you don't know how grateful I am for you making such a spectacular display. Really, you have no idea."

Finn sheathed Jigsaw on his back and it reduced in size without him asking it to. The King's face moved very close to Finn's, and he could smell a very strong scent of alcohol coming off his breath, as well as a strong scent of garlic. The mix of the two smells was making Finn sick and he was afraid he might retch up the fruit gift basket all over the throne—even though he was pretty sure vomiting fruit on the king was punishable by death.

"Between you and me," said the king, sitting down and gesturing for Finn to do the same, "I have been losing favor with the people for quite some time. These animals need displays of power, and as you heard, losing both of my sons has not gone well for me. The people have lost faith in me because I lack a proper heir."

"What about your daughter?" Finn asked.

The King put his frail, bony hand to his oddly-shaped stomach as he let out a jolly laugh. "Not only are you skilled with a Bizarre Blade, but you're funny as well!" He wiped a tear from his eye. "Oh, my boy, we are going to get along quite well. Can you imagine? A woman leading an entire kingdom? It's preposterous!"

Finn felt pressured to laugh and so he threw out a couple of obviously fake chuckles. He looked over the King's shoulder and saw two very evil-looking eyes staring at him. It was obvious that Princess Whetstone did not find this joke amusing. Whatever favor Finn had won with her during his Bizarre Blade presentation had vanished into smoke.

A table was brought out with all sorts of different meats, salads, fruits, and sweet cakes. Finn thought the smell of all of these things might add to his nausea, but was surprised when his appetite was renewed. All anxiety washed away as hunger took its place. Both he and the King ate the food like animals, tearing meat off the bone with their teeth while using their free hand to prepare a spoonful of something else. Finn was pretty sure he ate enough for three people that night.

Between bites, the King went through each scene of Finn's Bizarre Blade display, asking him how long it had taken him to master his Blade. Finn dared not tell the man that he was more of a beginner and basically a stranger to his Blade. It turned out that the King had not noticed the melting steel crawling across Finn's hand, so he kept that one a secret. He would have to experiment with that ability later.

When the King had had his fill, he gestured for his servants to take away the table, even though Finn was still shoving cakes into his face. The Princess hadn't had a single bite but stared off into the corner of the room with her chin rested on her hand. She'd most likely seen quite a few of these savage-like feasts in her lifetime.

King Whetstone stood up, stretched, and walked to the center of the stage. The people had now settled down, their bellies full of good food and ale. They chatted pleasantly with one another but went silent when their King raised his hands into the air.

"People of Kimidori! I have some very exciting news for you all! You have asked me, no, you have BEGGED me to find a resolution to the black beast that has terrorized us for years! I have sent our best warriors to seek out this menace and to make an end of its life, but none have come back. I realize that this was a mistake on my part. I was sending out warriors! But! Instead, I should have been sending out CHAMPIONS!" The King, without turning around, gestured to Finn who had two sweet cakes stuffed into each of his cheeks. "I, your King, give you the resolution to our problem! Champion Finn Featherstone will seek out the black tyrannosaurus rex you people have named Jewels of the Jungle. Champion Featherstone will end this monster's life or die trying!"

Finn was pretty sure he hadn't agreed to any of this.

"Now, Champion Featherstone has agreed wholeheartedly to complete this dangerous task, but I cannot allow him to work for us without compensation, can I?"

The crowd yelled out a big, "NO!"

"What kind of King would I be if I did not offer a proper reward?" he continued. "We have both agreed that the ownership of the Legendary Bizarre Blade of Koosahmoorah, the Phantom Blade, will be passed down to a fit wielder of Champion Featherstone's choosing. Is this not fair compensation for such a heroic task?"

The crowd began to chant Finn's name as he gulped down the rest of the cake. Slaying the smilodon had been one thing, and had nearly gotten him killed. In fact, it should definitely have killed him. The beating heart in his chest should have been torn out by the teeth of the saber-toothed tiger. His body should have been picked clean by scavengers of the woods by now. He had gotten lucky with the smilodon, but there would be no such luck in fighting an overgrown tyrannosaurus rex.

It was suicide, plain and simple.

Finn looked down at Jade, expecting to see someone just as fearful as he was. What he saw, however, was a young man with a focused expression on his face. He caught Finn's gaze and nodded his head.

Apparently, they were going t-rex hunting.

32

FINN'S NIGHTMARE

As soon as the door to his room was shut behind him, Finn let himself fall forward, only half of his body making it onto his bed. No one was there to help him take off his armor and he didn't have the energy to remove it himself. He would just sleep in it tonight.

His stomach gurgled in protest of all the food he'd shoveled into his mouth earlier. He wasn't used to eating so much in one sitting and now he was really paying for it. He knew he should turn onto his side but he felt too heavy to move, so he just shifted his hips a little in order to let out some gas.

It was louder than he expected and, in his exhaustion, he gave a small, delirious laugh. His heart sank when he heard the floor creak just a few feet away from him. It was dark now in the palace, but sometime during the feast someone had come into his room to light a candle. Apparently, that person had never left.

The room stunk and it stunk bad. His stomach turned into knots from his embarrassment. His anxiety gave him the energy needed to lift his head. "Oh my God, I'm so sorry!

I didn't know anyone was in here. I swear that wasn't me. It was this damned squeaky armor, you know how it is—"

A hand shot out from the shadows and clasped onto his neck. Finn sputtered as he tried to cry out for help, but the grip was far too tight around his windpipe. A hand slipped underneath his shoulder and flipped him onto his back which must have taken a lot of strength. The attacker slid his body over Finn's waist and sat atop him, but the armor worked wonders in dispersing the weight around his hips. Either that, or this person was very light.

The smell of sweet cherries filled Finn's nostrils as the assassin dropped his head to his. The candle flicked a glimmer of light over the face of his attacker. Finn gasped.

"Wait, aren't you—"

"Not another word!" hissed Princess Whetstone. "Who are you? What are you *really* doing here?"

Her hand slipped to her belt, and out came a dagger that reflected the candle fire into Finn's eyes. He felt its cold steel press up against his throat. Jigsaw could sense Finn's stress and it growled softly underneath his back, ready to be unleashed.

"I don't know what you're talking about!" Finn tried to sink his neck into the softness of the bed but the dagger followed closely.

"Don't play games with me, *Finn Featherstone,* if that *is* your real name. Who sent you? You're a lackey of Prince Tarek, aren't you? Of course that's what you are. You're nothing more than a hired assassin!"

"If I were the assassin, don't you think the roles would be reversed here?" The dagger pushed deeper into his skin and he could feel a small drop of blood run down his throat. "Okay, okay! Stop that! No more jokes, I promise."

"Then tell me who you are."

The candle shot more light over the girl's face and Finn was yet again stunned by her beauty and aura. Temporarily, all thoughts of the dagger disappeared leaving him alone in an empty room with an angel riding him like an edmontosaurus. His armpits grew sweaty all of a sudden and he wanted nothing more to do than to reach out and stroke her soft hazelnut skin. The fire reflected in her eyes revealed that, beneath the darkness, was a breathtaking color of topaz. Finn gulped and rediscovered the dagger.

"I'm Finn, of the Featherstone family," he choked out. "I come from a father who paints and a mother who was a master gardener. She could make the seed of a date grow even after a week of blizzards. She was known for that."

In the faint light, Finn saw one of the girl's eyebrows twitch and then raise in curiosity. Whatever he was doing, it was working. Or, it was buying him time.

"I grew up drawing and painting, which I do mostly when I get nervous. If you don't believe me, you'll find some of my work in the satchel on my belt. I've even drawn your edmontosaurus, but sadly charcoal sticks can't bring out the beautiful colors of their skin."

"An assassin can be an artist with other tools besides a dagger," she said, her eyebrow dropping, making her appear more serious now.

Finn ignored this and decided to keep going. There was nothing else he could do. He spoke for a few minutes about life in Sumetai and how much he hated the brutality of its people. How he hated the districts in which crime was not only overlooked, but encouraged. He talked about how he wished he lived here in the beautiful city of Kimidori, where the people seemed relatively normal—despite how they'd acted at the feast.

Then, something abnormal happened. The words that

pushed out of him just wouldn't stop. The dam he'd spent years building had finally collapsed and everything was spilling out. Why he confided in the beautiful stranger and not his father, he would never know. The moment was just...right.

"My mother died when I was younger. My father and I now live in a sort of awkward silence. Part of me blames him for her death and I hate myself for believing this, but I can't help but feel the way I do. Even though he now permanently walks with a limp I often wonder if my mother would have been alive if he'd acted just a few seconds earlier.

The dagger's push against Finn's throat lessened but he didn't even notice it. He was in his own little world now.

"What...happened?" asked the girl, her voice now softer, but still holding an undertone of distrust.

Without hesitation, the words spilled out of Finn's mouth without restraint. This was going to happen whether he liked it or not. Even if Princess Whetstone left his room at that moment, he would still continue babbling until he fell asleep.

"My father was commissioned to paint the final race of a very important tournament that the Kingdom of Shimoshimo hosts every year. The merchant that hired him had finally raised the perfect allosaurus for racing and, even though I was much younger, I'll never forget what it looked like. It was not the tallest meat-eater I'd seen, but its purpose wasn't to be tall—it was to be strong, and fast. It had glistening orange feathers mixed with stripes of black that ran down the sides of its tooth-filled mouth, down the sides of its muscular body, and down both of its two legs. I remember watching the dinosaur flex its two hands anxiously as its rider, one of the shortest men I'd ever seen, mounted the leather saddle on its back. The rest of the dinosaurs were a mix of meat-eaters that I'd never seen before but I dared not ask my parents what they were. You see, they were arguing that day but I cannot remember what exactly about. The merchant had grown up in the same village my mother had and therefore had a very strong dialect, so my mother had to go with my father in order to translate. I was too young to stay home alone, so they took me with them. I don't know if you know anything about the Stadium of Athletics in the city of Sumetai, but it is no place for children."

The Princess pulled back her dagger fully now and let it rest by her side as she continued listening to his story. Her silence told Finn that he should continue.

"We were sitting in the stands, which were about twenty or thirty feet high, and designated for the insane and rambunctious betting crowd. I'll always remember how everyone was yelling and spitting at one another. The merchant who had contracted my father's painting skills insisted they sit in the betting section of the stadium as he wanted to place wagers on his own allosaurus. When the canons went off and the jockeys spurred the dinosaurs into action, the rest of my memories kind of melt into a blur. I remember the people behind us pushing against our backs as they leaned forward in the stands to get a better look. Next thing I know, I'm seeing my mother topple forward. I remember seeing her fall through the air, hitting her head on the edge of the stone railing before falling over into the arena. To this day, the cracking of her head still haunts me."

Princess Whetstone could not hide her gasp when he said this. He continued; there was no stopping now.

"My father didn't even notice for a very long time. He and the merchant were so busy wrapped up in talking business that not even the cries of the crowd broke them out of their concentration. It was my tears and my screams that brought my father back to reality. He asked me where my mother was and all I could do was point. I watched him as he stared down into the arena, his bearded gaping mouth quivering. He picked me up and handed me to the merchant, who looked as if he'd just been handed a pile of sloth shit. My father bounded for the stairs and when he made it to the railing he jumped it without hesitation, dropping a good twenty feet. Through my tears I watched as he crawled the rest of the way to my mother who had her legs over her face, her head turned in a way that it shouldn't have been. She could have been dead at this point but I'll never know. The last thing I remember is my father reaching out for her extended hand before the prized allosaurus trampled over her. My mother's body tripped the dinosaur and I remember suddenly being thrown to the ground by the merchant. That day, we lost my mother, as well as the commission."

Finn wasn't sure when he'd started crying but he wasn't surprised. He wasn't even embarrassed. He was barely aware of the girl at all, but the drops of her tears on his face brought him back. Their tears intermingled on his cheek and mixed with the blood on his neck. The Princess looked upset that she was crying. Finn didn't know what overcame him but couldn't stop himself from raising his head. Without thinking, he put his lips on hers, which felt like kissing the softest of pillows. He felt a little wetness on his lips...

His bliss lasted only a second before her palm slapped his face, sending fire through his skin. No matter what she did to him, she could never take away the feeling he'd felt in that moment. It had felt like he was floating, as thousands of dragonflies fluttered in his stomach. The pain in his face only added to the intensity of his emotions.

The Princess jumped off of him and strode off towards the door. She flung the dagger to the ground and it stuck into the wood with a loud *thud*. She turned back to him and shook her head, her face blank as she put her hand to her lips.

She spun back around and swung the door open, but before she could leave, Finn asked her, "What's your name?"

The Princess paused in the doorway, one of her hands still touching her lips. He watched as her shoulders rose shakily. He couldn't tell whether she was furious, or overwhelmed with his story. He was starting to feel stupid about what he'd just done. What *had* he done? Had he just kissed a Princess? That most certainly was punishable by death, he was sure of it, Champion or not.

"Amber," she said. She walked through the door and shut it softly behind her.

Finn put his head to the ground and rested his hand on his forehead. He let a groan escape his mouth as he replayed what had just happened over and over again in his mind. He felt a warmth on his back, bringing his attention back to Jigsaw. When had it stopped growling? It was purring now, sending relaxing vibrations through his body. Finn felt his eyelids grow heavy and he fell asleep with the memory of kissing Amber Whetstone playing in his head.

33

BREAKFAST OF CHAMPIONS

FINN'S HANDS WERE SWEATING SO MUCH THAT HE THOUGHT that they may even start to drip. This was not what he'd imagined waking up to. Not at all.

There he was, with Jade, King Whetstone, and Amber Whetstone all sitting at a circular table that was far too small, in the courtyard in front of the palace. They were eating breakfast together and no one was speaking, which added to Finn's stress—and it wasn't helping that Amber refused to look at him.

Finn felt not only on edge, but was also practically sitting on the edge of his seat. To his left was one of the largest congregations of people he'd ever seen. At the front of the line stood more than fifty, maybe even a hundred edmontosauruses (which they called ed-mounters). These creatures donned leather armor that covered not only their round bodies, but extended over the tops of their necks and down their snouts. The ed-mounters were so tame that they did not even bend down to eat the grass that lay before them, most likely because the soldiers riding them would punish them with the long wooden spears they held. Even a few pterodactyls, it seemed, had stopped by to watch Finn eat his breakfast. He could see them eyeing the table from the roofs of several of the buildings.

Behind the line of ed-mounters were the people of Kimidori. They were all on their knees, bent with their faces toward the ground and their arms out in front of them. It looked very uncomfortable. There were so many of them—Finn wouldn't have doubted it if the entire city was there to watch him break his fast with fresh jelly and toast. He wasn't so sure he liked this sort of special treatment, there was just too much riding on his shoulders. He wasn't an elegant person and he damn sure wasn't royalty.

When they had all finished eating, King Whetstone broke the silence with a loud cry of excitement, and Finn felt like his skin was going to crawl off his body. Even Jade, the great Champion of Arbitration, flinched at this drastic change in noise. Amber, however, remained still.

"GOOD!" cried King Whetstone. "Good, good, good, good, good." He stood up while shoving a lemon-flavored pastry into his mouth. "Champion Featherstone, my boy, look what has arrived for you!"

Finn turned to see PipPip walking out of the main entrance with a pile of armor draped over his body. The boy panted as he struggled towards the table. The king cut him off and lifted one of the armor pieces off the very top. He placed his hand inside what looked like a helmet and turned it around for Finn to see.

At that moment, Finn forgot about the incredibly large number of people kneeling behind him. Resting over King Whetstone's hand was the face of the smilodon he had slayed. The eyes were replaced with marbles, and the teeth had been polished to the perfect shade of white. The helm had been crafted in a way so that the wearer would have his face looking through the gaping mouth of the beast with two dagger-sized teeth resting by his cheekbones.

"Well?" asked the king, gesturing to the helm with a smile. "What do you think? Does my leatherworker do amazing work, or does he do amazing work?" He turned the helm to his face and studied it. "Perhaps his skill might even be considered...godly, to some."

Finn couldn't believe his eyes. Never before had he seen something so...so...magnificent! This was even better than the red-plated Koosahmoorarian armor he'd worn the night before (which he had, in fact, slept in). He hadn't known what he'd expected to come from King Whetstone's leatherworker, but it sure wasn't this.

"I love it," said Finn, standing up and bowing his head. He wanted to put the armor on right then and there.

The king's eyes sparkled. He dropped the helm back onto Pippip, who nearly fell under the added weight, and made his way back over to Finn. "It pleases me so much, Champion Featherstone, that my leatherworker's job was enough to suit your fancy." He turned Finn around and gestured for him to sit back at the table. "I cannot wait to see you in that armor, and I'm sure you're even more excited than I, but there are a few more things we must discuss. More business, I'm afraid."

Without even being asked, Amber stood up, bowed, and left the table. King Whetstone paid her no attention, and was instead complaining to a servant about his slowness when it came to pouring him more wine. Finn, on the other hand, watched her go, and enjoyed doing so very much. The way her hips moved hypnotized him. He only stopped watching her when he felt the heat of Jade's gaze at the side of his face.

"Son, let's get straight to it," said the king, turning back to the table, his eyes on Jade. "You and I have never seen eye to eye, or, at least you never gave me a chance to—"

"Ten years was enough," interrupted Jade.

The king sighed. "I see this is going to be a not-so-easy conversation. Tell me, Jade, do you understand the importance of a king having a proper heir? Do you understand its effects on the confidence of a king's people? What do you think my people are thinking now? A king with no son, and a wife that can no longer bear children? Tell me, son, what do you think will happen when I become even older than I am."

"You will die."

"Exactly, but not in the way you think. There will be a coup and I will be killed." Before Jade could smirk at this, the king added quickly, "And who do you suppose will also be killed? Why, your mother, of course! And don't forget poor little Amber. Oh, she'll be killed—or worse! She'll make an excellent trophy wife to the highest bidder!"

Jade stood up so fast that the table nearly toppled over. The guards were on him within a second, but they did create a wide gap around Finn and Jigsaw. King Whetstone did not look surprised at this outburst, but merely sat there looking up at his son, daring him to do something.

"Just sit down, Jade," Finn whispered to him. "Can't you see we're a little outnumbered?"

Jade didn't look down at Finn but kept his gaze set on his father. Finn let out a small sigh of relief when he finally did sit down. The guards backed off, but reduced their original distance by half.

"So? Are you going to answer the question?" asked the king.

Jade took a deep breath, and through gritted teeth said, "Without an heir...the people lose trust in their king."

"So we are in agreement," said the king. "I *need* an heir."

"I won't do it," spouted Jade. "There's no way in hell I would ever sit on your throne. Not even if your blood ran through my veins...or on the ground."

King Whetstone snickered, "How poetic of you, my son. But do not worry, for I wouldn't have you sit on my throne if you were the last wannabe Champion left in the world!"

Finn grimaced at these words and expected Jade to have yet another tantrum, but he did nothing. He just stared into his father's eyes as if they were having a inaudible conversation. The tension at the table was high, but somehow Finn still had an appetite. Although it was unsuitable timing, he reached out and grabbed another loaf of toasted bread and began spreading honey on it with Amber's dagger that he'd plucked from the floor of his room.

"I'll repeat what I said," said the king. "I *need* an heir just like you *need* the Phantom Blade."

Jade's eyes narrowed. "What are you saying?"

"I'M SAYING THAT FINN MUST MARRY MY DAUGHTER IN EXCHANGE FOR THE BLADE!" screamed the King.

The toasted bread fell out of Finn's mouth and onto his lap, his mouth hanging open as he stared at King Whetstone in disbelief. The table fell silent for a few moments as the words sunk in.

The King threw his hands into the air in frustration. "God! Why is this so difficult? I dropped so many hints throughout this morning's breakfast and no one seems to have any sense! No sense at all!"

"No way," said Jade, slamming his fists on the table. "That won't do. Finn is not marrying my sister."

The king shrugged his shoulders. "You have no real choice in the matter," he said flatly.

While the king and his son continued their childish argument, Finn couldn't take his mind off the prospect of marrying Amber Whetstone. How wonderful that would be! What a dream! She was sassy, she was sexy, and best of all... well, the first two sort of summed it up. Sexy and sassy and he liked her. He liked her A LOT. He would definitely marry her, as their kiss had put a fairy's spell over him.

Jade rubbed his forehead with his thumb and index finger, both of his eyes shut and his elbow on the table. Would he really risk the lives of everyone he loved based solely on the idea of Finn marrying his sister? Did Jade detest him that much?

"Unfortunately, my son, it is not your decision to make. It is mine. You forget too often who the ruler of this powerful Kingdom is. And so," said the king, turning to Finn, "Champion Featherstone, will you do the honor of marrying my—"

"Yes!" exclaimed Finn, accidentally interrupting the king. He felt the blood rush to his pale cheeks and he was positive everyone could tell. Thank God Amber wasn't there to see him.

Jade stared at Finn, his mouth so wide open that Finn could see his uvula hanging in the back of his throat. The king was busy clapping his hands, giggling while he rocked in his chair.

"Oh goodie! Goodie, goodie, goodie!" He stood up and grabbed Finn by the hand. "Come with me, my boy, let us make it official."

Finn was forced up, and he dropped his toast back onto

his plate. The king strode him to the center of the courtyard and raised his hands, and all the people looked up. Their eyes fell on Finn, and he became aware that crumbs covered his mouth and chin.

"My people! Champion Finn Featherstone has accepted my offer to marry my daughter, your Princess, Amber Whetstone! And so I give you!" He took a step to the side and gestured to Finn. "Your future King of Shimoshimo!"

Finn squeezed his cheeks together—and not the cheeks on his face, afraid that morning's strong tea combined with his fear might spark mother nature. He could feel his teeth start to chatter as thousands of people jumped to their feet, cheering. Fireworks were shot off somewhere in the distance sending the pterodactyls flapping into the air, screeching as they made their escape from the loud noises.

Guards rushed to the front of the courtyard to keep everyone back as a happy riot (if there was such a thing) erupted in the streets of Kimidori. King Whetstone was bent over laughing, his hands on his knees. He used Finn's shoulders to pick himself up and Finn saw that tears of joy were in his eyes.

"Oh, my dear boy, you have saved my ass. Do you know how hard it is to find a rightful heir? The people won't just accept anyone, you know. I've been practically begging Champions to come to my dining halls but none thus far have answered my letters."

"Wait," said Finn, scrunching his eyebrows together. "Did you set this all up? Is that why you had me display my Bizarre Blade at the feast?"

"I have chosen well! You aren't so dumb after all!" The king danced a happy little jig, jiggling a lot of extra skin in the process, before turning and walking Finn back to the table.

"But now, you will hand over the Phantom Blade, right?" asked Finn. He was very ready to get out of this city as something wasn't quite right mentally with the king.

"Why, of course, Champion Featherstone! But, there is the matter of killing that damned tyrannosaurus rex before we complete our little deal."

34

THE T-REX WITH A NECKLACE

Sweat trickled down from the back of Finn's neck to the top of his asscrack.

The smilodon armor looked nice, sure, but he hadn't expected how hot it would be to wear it. Sure, it protected more of his body than the style Jade had created, but now it felt like wearing a portable sweat lodge. There would have to be modifications done in order for this armor to be wearable longterm, but as of now it was bearable.

Finn had stood in front of a rectangular mirror while the same servant boys from the night before strapped on his armor. The experience would have been a lot nicer if King Whetstone hadn't made him to try on the armor in front of the entire city.

The helm had fit perfectly over his head and he felt a sense of security from the two canine teeth protecting the sides of his face. Wind flaps had been cut through the top of the helm all the way to the back for better airflow. These flaps had been sewn into all the armor pieces, but there was just one problem...there was no damned breeze in the jungle! The humidity was nearly intolerable and Finn guessed the armor would feel better once he was out in the open.

The chest piece covered the top of his torso, leaving his lower stomach exposed. The shoulder pauldrons were made from the paws of the smilodon, as were the boots. Upon first touching the claws, Finn noticed that they did not feel like the actual claws he'd pulled from the smilodon. He was wondering why this was until the King draped over him a necklace made from the original claws. It was a nice touch, and it was useless, of course, serving only a purpose of aesthetics, but Finn loved it.

The skirt was no longer a skirt but leggings that wrapped around each of his legs, strapping to the backs with very thick leather cord. At first, Finn was afraid that he wouldn't be able to bend down, but that wasn't the case. The leatherworker had added some sort of flexible material beneath the skin as well as cutting small slits at the joints in order to allow for better bending and movement. All in all, Finn was able to do everything he was able to do naked with only a little more effort.

The snow-white fur had been cleaned of all mud and debris that it had accumulated during Finn's time in the jungle. The fur was also brushed with some sort of oil that made it an even brighter white under the sun. As if the armor wasn't beautiful enough, the leatherworker had sewn the furs in just a way that the black stripes of the saber-toothed tiger now slashed diagonally across Finn's chest. It was a breathtaking sight to behold.

Finn now looked like a true Champion. He wasn't as tall as Bryce. Or as strong...or as muscular...or as handsome... but damn, he looked good! Not only that, but he could tell that this armor could take a few beatings and even a few cuts. He felt more confident wearing it, but the humidity of the jungle...it was like he was swimming in a sea of his own sweat.

"You're not marrying my sister," said Jade without even looking at Finn. They had traveled a decent distance away from the city now and as far as Finn could tell, no guards followed them.

"Why?" demanded Finn. "In my opinion, I'd make a great brother-in-law."

Jade did not laugh. He'd probably been expecting Finn to agree with him but that was the thing: Finn did *not* agree with him. Sure, he didn't know the girl, but he still liked her. No, he *loved* her, he was sure of it. He couldn't keep her out of his mind. She was the first thing he thought about in the morning and the last thing he thought about before bed. Was that not love? Yeah, okay, it was most likely a case of strong lust but he didn't care. Never before had he been liked by a female...well, that hadn't really changed but was he going to decline a marriage proposal to the most gorgeous girl he'd ever seen? No, no he was not. He was pretty sure he'd give his left foot to have her.

Am I really that desperate? he thought to himself. *I'm a Champion, for God's sake! I can have any girl I want!* Still the thoughts of Amber and their first kiss were at the top of his mind. Sometimes he would even rub his top and bottom lips together and imagine it was her lips he was kissing... yeah, he was pretty desperate.

"Can we please stop walking right next to the river," complained Finn, after slipping in a particularly muddy spot. He was trying the best he could not to dirty up his new armor but who was he kidding? A day out in this jungle would ruin just about anything.

"It's dangerous, yes," agreed Jade. "But it's a risk we need to take. The days are quickly passing us by, and we need to get back before Constantine keeps his word and puts everyone to flame...if he hasn't already. Going through the jungle will just slow us down."

"Ariel agrees with Finn," came Ariel's voice from above.

Finn and Jade stopped and looked up at the trees. Finn could feel himself sinking ever so slightly into the mud as he looked through the dense leaves and branches for a pink-headed girl, but he just couldn't find her. He gave up and turned his attention back to the river, expecting a gargantuan crocodilian to burst out of the flowing green rapids. He'd already decided he wouldn't save Jade. Nope. He would just throw himself out of the way.

Finn was so busy picturing Jade getting swallowed by the crocodile that he didn't hear the rustling in the trees. He shouted when the girl landed on his shoulders, taking him to the ground. His head splashed into the river and the strong current flowed up his nostrils. Fear shot through him, not only because of the crocodile which had just basically been hand-fed a human head, but because he'd inhaled a good amount of nasty river water.

He yanked his head out of the river, shooting what seemed like half the river back out of his nose. He could taste it coming out of his mouth, mixed with a good amount of mucus. His eyes watered and all Ariel could do was laugh. He didn't think he'd ever been as miserable as he was at that moment...but he was sure something would top it sooner or later.

"Are you crazy!?" Finn managed to shout at Ariel, who was getting hugged tightly by Jade.

Ariel's hair was coated in a black mud, as was the rest of her body. She looked like a mad swamp witch, but somehow

Finn still found himself attracted to her if not by her beauty then by her eccentric personality.

Jade grabbed onto Ariel's face and inspected it for injuries. "You've been out here this entire time?" he asked. "Why not hide somewhere in Kimidori?"

"You know that there is no safe place in Kimidori for Ariel," Ariel said. "No, the jungle was a much safer place. Ariel would rather take her chances with the dinosaurs and venomous snakes than with your father, she thinks."

"What did you mean when you said you agreed with me?" asked Finn, wiping his nose and standing up, being careful not to slip in the mud and take another bath.

"Oh, yes," said Ariel, pointing a finger into the air. "Ariel has been watching the rivers very closely and there has been much activity. MUCH. It is best to stay clear from them."

"But—" Jade tried to interject, but Ariel hadn't finished yet.

"Ariel has also taken the liberty of placing meat she stole from Kimidori all over this section of the jungle. If Ariel's guess is correct, King Whetstone will have proposed we kill Jewels in exchange for the Phantom Blade. No?"

Finn tilted his head "Well, yes, but how did you—"

"Ariel has been seeing more and more Rexie tracks and much of the meat has been eaten! If Ariel had to guess, she would guess that Jewels isn't far from here! Ariel suggests we get into the trees and wait."

"When?" asked Jade. "Now?"

A terrible roar shook the leaves above them, sending vibrations through Finn's bones. A chill ran down his spine as the three Champions gazed at each other in horror. None of them had to guess which dinosaur had made the noise. Even Finn, who had never seen a tyrannosaurus rex, could tell it apart from the other cries of the carnivores he had heard.

"I think now is a good time," said Finn, running to the nearest tree. If there was anything he was good at, it was climbing trees. A year ago he never would have been able to say that.

He could hear Ariel and Jade climbing up behind him, and a moment later they had caught up to him. He tried his best not to kick any bark in their faces by slowing down but Ariel's head pushed against his feet as she tried to hurry him up.

The three of them climbed to the highest limbs that Finn felt certain could hold all of their weight. Once they'd all taken a seat, they tried to look down at the forest floor but a leaf-covered branch blocked their view. Jade cut it off with his dagger.

Below them, Finn could make out the footprints of where they had been standing, as well as the jumbled mess of mud where he had fallen due to Ariel...being Ariel. He waited with his hands tight on the branch, expecting the roar again, only this time a lot closer. What happened instead was even more menacing.

The limb beneath their backsides shook softly. They could hear the sound of cracking pieces of wood and brush being uprooted from the ground. The leaves in front of their faces began to shake with each step of the approaching behemoth. They sat high enough that Finn could look out over some of the other trees. At first, he saw nothing, but swallowed hard when he saw a black line of parting trees that was etching closer and closer to their particular tree, the steps growing louder and louder.

Ariel took Finn's hand as well as Jade's and held them

tightly on her lap as they awaited the terror of the jungle of Koosahmoorah. Whatever Finn had been expecting, it hadn't been the sound of jingling metal which he now heard. The shaking of the limb under his butt was getting to a point where he thought he might fall off...until it stopped without warning.

This was the first time that there was silence in the jungle. No bugs chirped. No distant dinosaurs made a peep. Not even the wind dared rustle the leaves on the trees. It seemed that even the river was doing its best to keep its crashing turbulent waters calm for a moment. All Finn could hear was breathing. Deep and heavy breathing. A smell of bloodied meat, a smell that was familiar to him from skinning the smilodon, drifted into his nose. He, Jade, and Ariel exchanged glances before looking back down.

And there she was.

To say Jewels was no ordinary t-rex was an understatement. All she had to do was stand there, completely still. She had no need to growl, nor to roar. She didn't need to threaten with grasping claws or spreading lips. She didn't even need to open her mouth! The feeling of fear and dread were instant and diarrhea-of-doom inspiring. Finn felt as though he were seconds away from death even though there was no possible way Jewels could get to him from where he sat.

Then...she looked up at him.

Her eyes were big, black, and wet. Finn could see them wavering and moving as she inspected whatever it was that watched her from above. She was aware of all things at all times. She was a hunter, a scavenger, and most importantly of all...she was the queen of this jungle, and she knew it.

Tyrannosaurus Rex

Jewels dropped her head and took a step out of the jungle's edge, shaking Finn back to life with her first heavy step. The majestic monster made noises Finn did not think were possible to come out of such a thick and burly creature.

She was chirping.

With every chirp, Finn could see the back of the t-rex's lips shake, only revealing parts of the teeth that he knew to be conical in shape and strong as hell. Finn wondered if she was communicating to other living things around her. Was she warning them? Or was she merely just talking to herself as many humans did?

Jewels walked to the edge of the river and made another series of chirps, some louder than others. She bent her head low and all three Champions flinched when she spun around with amazing speed, slashing her tail through the water. She did this a couple more times before returning her face towards the water, looking at herself in the reflection.

No one in the world could have denied Jewels' beauty. She was a midnight black with her feathers reminding Finn very much of Obsidian's, only that these were less greasy looking and more... furry? Was that the word? The feathers were also much denser around her neck, making it look as though she had a mane. At the very top of her head, the feathers were almost non-existent, but a few small ones remained. It was here that a small white stripe started and ran down her spine all the way down her tail.

The sound of jingling metal came from the beads of jewelry that hung from her luscious mane of feathers. Stuck in the leathery skin of her neck were the decorated spearheads of hundreds of past failed attempts to hunt down this black beauty. Jewels looked as if she wore a necklace that cost her a couple castles worth of ammonite chips. From up there in the tree, Finn could see the colors of gold, blue, green, red, and orange, all clinking together in the breeze making a strange sort of wind chime.

Jewels bent down her head as if to take a drink of water but just stood there, her snout inches away from the river. She waited there a few moments before spontaneously moving to the side without warning. The three Champions shouted out their surprise as a massive crocodile exploded out of the river.

The crocodile landed flat on its belly, its mouth snapping together with a sound that could only be mimicked by a canon. The river's current splashed over its spiny green back and there seemed to be a sort of awkward pause. The crocodile had missed its target.

Finn looked over at Jade with a evil glare, a glare that said, "And you had us walking near that!" Jade did not dare look over at Finn, and Finn was sure it was because he didn't want to recognize the fact that he'd been wrong. Dead wrong.

"A deinosuchus!" exclaimed Ariel, putting her hand to her mouth. "It's... beautiful."

The deinosuchus, as Ariel had called it, spread its mouth a few inches, a loud hiss breezing through its teeth as it retreated slowly back into the water. Jewels took a few steps back just in case the crocodilian tried any funny business. She was smart. Too smart. Finn wondered why she didn't attack it in return; wouldn't that have been an easy meal? Or was this part of her intelligence? Why go after a meal that could potentially kill you when there were so many other easily edible animals out in the jungle? Like, the three humans sitting in the tree above you, perhaps? They would be mighty easy to get a hold of once they climbed down.

Seeing that it would be impossible to take a safe swallow of water at this particular section of the river, Jewels let out a few more chirps and made for the jungle. She was careful to keep her thick tail from swooping over the river. Seriously, how smart could a dinosaur be?

Loud squawks came from nearby, and Finn knew exactly what had made them. Obviously, Obsidian wasn't as intelligent as Jewels. Perhaps it had spent too much time with Finn and was getting too relaxed. Either that, or it didn't notice the nine-ton monster beneath them. Obsidian flapped its wings loudly as the raptor glided over to Finn and landed on his shoulder.

"Shut up!" hissed Finn, putting a finger to his lips. Obsidian took this as its owner trying to talk to it so the raptor obliged him by cawing even louder. The young Champion tried to grab the raptor by its beak, but it evaded Finn's every effort.

Finn was so preoccupied with trying to shut up his little friend that he didn't see Jewels hugging their tree. Ariel poked his shoulder and pointed down to the ground. Finn followed her finger and a small "EEEP!" noise escaped from his throat. Jewels had laid her head flat on the tree, along with half of her body, her small arms pushed down against her stomach. White wisps of breath puffed from her nostrils as she stared at them with unblinking eyes

Even Jigsaw, known for its ferocity in the most fearful of situations, had fallen silent.

35

BIENVENUE CHEZ LA FAMILLE T-REX

THE WILD EYES OF THE T-REX SEARCHED THE TREE HUNGRILY, knowing that three edible beings lurked somewhere above her snout. Question was, how could she get them and were they worth her time?

With a few frustrated grunts, Jewels pulled her boulder-sized head off the tree, sending a shower of bark to the jungle floor. With one last look up at the three Champions, Jewels made her way back into the jungle. They waited for quite a long time, listening as best they could to make sure the t-rex had truly left.

"We need to go after her," Jade said, breaking the silence.

Finn's mouth dropped. "You have to be kidding me. Did we not just share the same experience? That thing will murder us! I'm pretty sure she doesn't even have to touch us to kill us. In fact, I about nearly died up here, just from her glancing up at me!"

"That's your problem," said Jade, pulling his feet under himself and kneeling on the limb.

"Ariel, you can't possibly think it a smart idea to go after that monster."

Ariel shrugged. "We have no choice. This must be done in order to save Mother Nibbles and the others."

She too jumped to her feet and followed Jade, who hopped to the nearest branch. Finn watched them leap to the next tree and then to the next. He was stunned that they would so bravely choose to go after quite possibly the most terrifying dinosaur that ever evolved. He wracked his mind and could not come up with a more ferocious animal. He would even rather take his chances fighting the mindless massive crocodile than face Jewels.

But why then was he jumping to the next tree with Obsidian gliding by his side? Why did he swing from one branch and catch the next? He was a Champion, that was why, and he too had said the oath of the Champions of Arbitration. He wasn't sure whether or not he regretted the brand that rested on his chest, but still he did not take the oath lightly. He'd never taken an oath before and was surprised to find that it was within his character to uphold it. He was pretty sure the old Finn would have made a rude gesture at the backs of Jade and Ariel, made his way back to Shimoshimo, and lived on the streets.

However, there he was, easily catching up to Jade and Ariel who paid him no attention. They knew he would come. Jigsaw purred softly on his back, making him feel like he'd made the right decision even though he knew deep down he would not leave this jungle alive. Nope, he was literally a swinging t-rex treat begging to be swallowed whole. Jewels could even use Jigsaw to clean her pinecone sized teeth if she wanted to.

Obsidian flapped from tree to tree, its beak bloody from a recent kill. Finn felt ashamed and embarrassed that his little raptor companion had given away their position; the microraptor was his responsibility. If Obsidian was going to stick around, it needed to be taught some valuable commands, starting with how to keep its beak shut...but was it possible to teach a stubborn dinosaur new tricks?

Finn wasn't paying attention and about slammed into the back of Ariel but she sidestepped and his stomach crashed into the branch, forcing the air from his lungs. He tried pulling himself over the limb without revealing he'd hurt himself, but it was impossible.

Jade pointed down at a clearing in the jungle, and once Finn's vision focused he could see a small cave with two hopping animals. He squinted his eyes, and gasped at the sight of two miniature black tyrannosaurus rexes snapping at each other and letting out cute little roars. A fluttering insect took their attention from their mock fight and they chased after it, only for Jewels, their mother, to clear the forest line and push them back towards the cave. She stopped, her head flinging upward to sniff the air. Suddenly, she let out an earsplitting roar, paralyzing the Champions with fear.

Jewels lowered her head to the ground and began sniffing. Clouds of dust shot into the air as she made her way to the side of the cave, not visible for the Champions. Finn watched her come to a halt, her rear end pointed into the air. A small squeak came from her direction as she nuzzled out from behind the cave yet another small black t-rex only this one looked to be the runt; it also looked to be dead. As to how it died Finn had no idea.

Ariel put her hand to her mouth and laid her head on Jade's shoulder, as he patted her mud-matted hair. At the corner of Finn's eye he could see that she was crying. He turned his attention back to the t-rex and watched as she stared down at her dead baby. After a few minutes of contemplation, she pushed the baby from her home and to the forest's edge, leaving it to be eaten by other small scavengers.

The other two baby t-rexes continued their game of fighting while their mother walked to the middle of the clearing. She raised herself onto the very front parts of her feet and Finn readied himself for a roar he would not soon forget.

But no roar came.

A breathy and shaky sort of whisper blew from Jewel's mouth. Finn was no dinosaur, but he could sense her sad energy, so much so that he found himself fighting back tears. Jewels continued to do this for more than ten minutes, and Finn couldn't help but shed some water from his eyes.

They watched the family of t-rexes for the rest of the day from the safety of the trees. Finn didn't know whether or not Jewels was aware of their presence. If she did know that they were there, watching her, then she made no sign of it. He wondered if her baby's death might have lowered her awareness...or maybe it raised it.

Obsidian had been utterly silent after hearing the mother's sad call. The raptor stood motionless on Finn's shoulders for hours, looking down at the mother t-rex with curiosity. Finn wondered what was going through the microraptor's head. Maybe this reminded the raptor that it should try and find a mate. Maybe it felt scared or anxious. Maybe, just maybe, it felt a little sad for Jewels. Either way, Finn was having trouble reading the blue-eyed raptor.

Only half the sun showed its face when Jewels called for her babies to come with her into the cave. Finn was surprised to see them actually listen, curling up next to her and covering their faces in her thick mane of feathers. They bit at her a few times, wanting her to play, but she chirped angrily at them to stop. The playful nips began to slow down, as did the babies' energy. Soon, the tyrannosaurus family had fallen asleep.

"I don't think I can kill her," Finn admitted, his voice sounding strange to himself after such a long time without speaking. "I just can't do it."

"Ariel agrees, we cannot harm this beautiful creature."

"That was never the plan," said Jade, starting to make his way down the tree.

Finn scooted himself down the limb and waited for his turn to descend. "What do you mean?"

"I mean, I never planned to kill Jewels."

"Champions of Arbitration aren't killers for hire," agreed Ariel, hopping down onto the forest ground a few feet from Jade.

Taking his time with each step, Jade made sure each was more silent than the last as he made his way to the baby t-rex's corpse. Finn watched as he pulled out a dagger and cut off the very tip of its black tail. He stood up and was about to walk back with his prize when he bent down again and plucked some fallen feathers from the ground. The king would never know that there was more than one black t-rex in the jungle. Finn had to admit, it was a good idea.

Climbing down carefully from the tree, Finn stepped onto the ground just as Jade was returning. "You both could have let me know we weren't going to try and murder this t-rex in her sleep," said Finn. "I don't feel like we're really working as a team, especially when the plans are being kept secret."

"They aren't being kept secret," said Jade nonchalantly. "You're just too much of a fool to figure them out yourself."

Ariel gasped, putting both hands to her mouth. Finn felt his blood rise to his forehead and cheeks, embarrassed to be spoken to in such a way, especially in front of a girl. He might have let it go if it had just been him and Jade, but no, this had gone too far.

It was unlike him to feel such a strong sense of anger. He'd been made fun of most of his life, and he'd gotten used to it. Maybe he'd been pushing it to the back of his mind and Jade's words had been the leaf that broke the wooly mammoth's back. Usually, the anger dissipated and Finn would return to normal and forget anything had ever happened...but now was different. He wasn't going to take Jade's shit. Not this time. If it hadn't been for him, they wouldn't have even been given this quest by King Whetstone, and Jade would still be a Bizarre Blade-less Champion.

Finn stepped in front of Jade who was about to pass him. "You need to apologize." His voice was low but not quite a whisper.

"Apologize for what?" asked Jade, standing up straight and looking down upon Finn with a face that said he knew EXACTLY what Finn was talking about.

Finn had never been good in verbal arguments, and didn't know how to respond. So he tried his best. "You called me a fool and I didn't like it. Take it back."

Jade snorted. "You *are* a fool. What's even worse is that even you know that you're a fool. That's why your little feelings are hurt. I promise when we get back to Kimidori you can cry into my sister's robes while she strokes your perfect green locks."

"That's what this is about, isn't it?" demanded Finn, stepping in front of Jade as he tried to walk past him again. "It's because you don't want me to marry your sister. Well, I didn't ask for this, Jade! You accepted this quest just as much as I did, and in doing so, it's like you gave your sister's hand to me willingly."

Jade gritted his teeth and Ariel tried to step between them. "Ariel thinks we should calm down. Our voices are getting a tad bit loud, don't you think?"

Neither Jade nor Finn paid her any attention. This was an argument long in the coming. If Jade had a problem with Finn then it needed to be settled there and now because he wasn't going to take any more shit from this Champion wannabe. It was *he* who had the Bizarre Blade, not Jade. Jade should have been on his knees, bowing to Finn and begging for forgiveness because, at that moment, Finn was feeling less attached to the idea of saving the Champions of Arbitration. He could simply go on to Sumetai and look for his father right then and there. Why wait?

"You're not worthy to marry my little sister," spat Jade, raising his chin and baring his teeth. "You're not even worthy of being the towel she wipes her royal ass with."

Finn didn't mean to shove Jade like he did. He certainly didn't mean to put as much force into the blow as he did but, well, he did. Jade went flying backward, his back slamming into the tree with a loud *THUD*. Ariel used a hand to cover her eyes because she knew that the point of reasoning was long gone.

"That felt good," said Finn, balling his fists and breathing in deep through his nose. "That felt *really* good."

"Oh yeah?" asked Jade, wiping his lips and checking his hand for blood. "Then you're really gonna like what happens next."

Jade tore from the tree, his head bent low, and tackled Finn by his waist. They spun a few times on the ground and Finn ended up on top. Obsidian glided to the nearest tree, squawking loudly as it did so. Finn wasn't sure what came over him as he smacked his fist in the side of Jade's mouth. Jade shifted his hips and pulled one leg up with the flexibility of a snake, hooking his ankle around Finn's throat, and yanking him backward. Jade performed a series of ground fighting techniques, ultimately pinning Finn down on his stomach.

"Ha! How's that feel? Still feel good?" asked Jade, sitting on top of Jigsaw and shoving Finn's face into the dirt. Finn tried moving but it was impossible. He was now a human knot, his arms and legs maneuvered in a way he never thought possible. Jade lifted his head and pushed it back down into the ground multiple times, and Finn was afraid his nose might break once again.

Sensing real danger, Jigsaw warmed Finn's lower back as it vibrated itself awake. Without Finn telling it to do so, the Blade shot out a glop of sludge directly into Jade's face, making him cry out and reach up for his eyes. Feeling that he was now able to move, Finn swiped his elbow around and caught Jade in the jaw.

A few more twists and turns on the ground, and Finn and Jade were back up standing. Jade used one hand to wipe most of the sludge from his face and spat some out of his mouth.

Finn readied himself to charge at Jade, wanting nothing more than to punch him again in the mouth, when Ariel ran past them screaming, "RUUUUUN!"

Finn closed his eyes and gulped. Slowly, he turned his head in the direction of the cave, his heart beating rapidly. He already knew what he was about to see when he opened his eyes.

Jewels stood there, looming large only about ten feet away from them, her belly rising and falling with each breath. The energy Finn felt now was not that of sadness nor hunger, but that of anger! Finn's eyes tore towards Jade, who stared up at Jewels with a dropped jaw. Between his belt and hip dangled the dinosaur tail he'd cut from the baby t-rex.

"Oh no," whispered Finn, looking back at Jewels. *She thinks we killed her baby.*

Jewels took a stomp towards them, the sound of shallow and inconsistent angry breaths pushing through her nostrils. The blackness of her eyes now seemed to have taken a red tint, and her mouth began to open. Her pink tongue was a stark contrast to the black-feathered mane that was now growing larger in size as she lifted her feathers up. Soon, the mother t-rex had become nearly double her size, a feature some dinosaurs had in order to promote fear amongst other dinosaurs. Finn was pretty sure that he was feeling those effects himself, as he thought at any moment he might have a heart attack.

A mighty roar bellowed from the depths of Jewels' throat, sending a burst of wind into the face of Finn and Jade. Slobber and bits of meat pelted their bodies as the roar continued to flow from the t-rex. They should have been running at that moment but something about this beast kept their feet planted. They were stunned. How could something so terrifying possibly exist? Weren't humans created to reign over the animal dynasty? Why then did Finn feel like nothing more than the smallest creeping insect in the jungle?

Something grabbed onto Finn's armor from behind and pulled him backward. Finn turned, snapping out of his shock, and saw Ariel and Jade already sprinting away. He took off after them, his feet moving faster than they ever had before. He managed to dodge, dip, duck, dive, and dodge through all the obstacles the jungle threw at him. He even was able to make it past Ariel and Jade, who continued running behind him. His ears began working again and he realized that he was screaming.

The hardest part of running through the jungle at that moment was not the slapping limbs or the tripping vines, but the incredible quakes Jewels pounded through the ground. There were many points where Finn thought he might topple over, but luck was with him that day...as lucky as you could get when running from a freakishly huge t-rex.

He dared not look back because he knew that if he did he would be eaten. Simple as that. However, it seemed being eaten was inevitable, as the last thick brush he pushed through had him slipping through the mud, barely catching himself before taking a dip into the river.

Finn put his hand to his heart, trying to calm himself down. He gazed back at the jungle and then back at the river and it looked as though he had a decision to make.

Should he become crocodile dung? Or t-rex dung?

36

BETWEEN THE HAMMER AND THE ANVIL

LOOKING BACK AT THE JUNGLE, FINN COULD SEE THE TREES spreading apart as the ferocious t-rex mother charged towards him. He had the idea to drop and start slathering himself up with mud in hopes that it would cover his scent, but who was he kidding? That wouldn't work with Jewels and he knew it.

Jade was the first one out of the jungle, and it was one of the few times Finn had actually seen him look afraid. He was now faced with the same predicament as Finn, sliding through the mud and towards the river. Which stomach did he prefer to be digested in? Even if—and that's a big if—they made it into the water without the giant crocodile clasping its maws on one of their legs, no swimmer was strong enough to swim across without being swept away.

Running down the beach of the river wouldn't do any good either because the mud made it too slippery. Jewels, on the other hand, had nice claws sticking out of her feet which gave her better traction. No, their only option was to stand and fight.

Ariel stopped at the edge of the jungle, looking at the

river, then back at the t-rex, which was almost upon them. Any second now, Jewels would leap from the trees with the half-fairy screaming in her mouth.

"Come on, Ariel!" yelled Jade.

"We need to fight together!" shouted Finn. He reached behind him and found an already-vibrating Jigsaw ready for some action. He pulled it out in front of him and the Blade elongated to its normal size (maybe even a little longer and thicker? It was hard to tell).

"Ariel has an idea!" she cried back, glancing up at the trees above her and back down at the ground. She scrunched her face in concentration as she searched for whatever it was that she needed. In two seconds (which seemed like two years to Finn) she cried out, "AH-HAH! You're perfect!"

Ariel gave a big smile as she lifted a long thin stick covered in leaves into the air. Finn was now convinced that she'd officially gone crazy.

The pink-headed girl leapt from the forest's edge, rolled in the mud, and jumped up to her feet with the stick in one hand and her Flutter Blade in the other, her insect eyes bulging from her head. Finn watched as her antennae twitched as she smelled the air. She put her face close to the water, sniffed, moved further down the river, and sniffed again.

Why Jade was letting her do this was beyond Finn. They should be coming up with a battle plan! Or, at least TRYING to run down the beach! Jewels was almost—

The t-rex's head poked out from the jungle, big clouds of air shooting from her nostrils. The most terrifying aspect of Jewels wasn't her black-feathered mane, or her immense teeth, nor was it the skull image that formed on the top of her head from the few white feathers that grew from her face. No, it was the fact that she *knew* they were trapped. She *knew* they couldn't run down the beach and she *knew* they couldn't get past her. It was her intelligence that froze Finn's beating heart and made him want to throw up. It was all over now. She'd found a meal for her remaining two babies.

"Get ready!" cried Ariel from down the beach.

Finn looked to his side and noticed that, having been preoccupied with the colossal t-rex staring at him, Jade and Ariel had made it a good distance from him. He started to sprint towards them and Jewels took this as invitation to reignite the chase—but this time it would only last seconds.

Ariel lifted the leaf-covered stick and popped the top of the river. Nothing happened. She did it again and again, and still nothing happened. Finn was saying a prayer as she struck the top of the river a fourth time, and he never expected his prayer to be answered by a ginormous crocodile exploding out from the river, its nose pointed at the sky. Everything seemed to move in slow motion as the mighty deinosuchus fell, its snout slapping on the edge of the river, the rest of its body sticking out of the water.

That's when everything made sense—well, as much sense as using a crocodile as bridge made. Still, it was Finn's only chance of surviving and he wasn't going to stop running now. Ariel was a genius!

The crocodile erupting from the river had taken Jewels by surprise, and she had stopped running when her jaws had only been a mere foot away from snatching Finn off his feet. Now she continued, but at a more cautious speed—she, too, did not want to be caught in the deinosuchus' gaping maws.

"Hurry, hurry!" shouted Ariel, her eyes shrinking down to normal size. She was already hopping onto the back of the crocodile which did nothing to stop her. All it did was open its mouth a little wider and hiss a little louder.

Jade was next and was already running towards the end of the crocodile's tail when he turned to look over at Finn. Of course, when Finn got close to the crocodile it decided to swing its head towards him, its lifeless eyes begging him to come just an inch closer. Jade saw all of this and...he kept running. He shook his head and made his way for the other side of the river.

Finn was on his own.

Looking down, Finn saw a small stone protruding from the mud and picked it up. An idea came to him and he thought it might just work. What other options did he have? If he could throw the stone across the crocodile's head for it to land on the other side, maybe it would swing its head the other way, giving Finn the opportunity to hop on top of its back!

Finn pulled back his hand and threw as hard as he could. The speed was perfect! However, the accuracy...was not. The stone popped the crocodile in the eye, making it shake its head vigorously. Now, not only did he have to jump on a half-blind, oversized crocodile, he had to do it while it convulsed in pain!

Jewels' roar behind him put fire under his feet as he ran towards the spastic river monster. He screamed, "OOOHHH MMMYYYY GOOOOD!" the entire way, Jigsaw bouncing in the air with his pumping arms. He jumped at the last moment and soared into the air, feeling lucky that he hadn't slipped in the mud. The crocodile's head swung around and clipped Finn's leg, so that he fell on his side directly on one of the crocodile's tall, pointed scales which dug into his ribs.

Jigsaw slipped from his hands.

The world paused around Finn as he felt Jigsaw slip

from his grasp. He could not hear the crocodile slapping its face into the water. He could not hear the roars of a frustrated t-rex. He couldn't even hear the screaming of his ribs which may or may not have been broken. All he could hear was the soft sad hum that Jigsaw made as it left his fingers.

Quickly, Finn stood himself up, balancing as best he could on the frantic deinosuchus. He looked over to the river's edge and saw both Ariel and Jade screaming at him, waving their arms and telling him not to jump. Finn scanned the river for any signs of Jigsaw, while his heart hammered in his chest and sweat dripped in his eyes, making it hard to keep them open. He would stay put on the crocodile as long as it took to find it, because he was *not* leaving without his Bizarre Blade.

There! He caught a glimpse of one of its three chains swinging out of the whitewater. Without a second's thought, an ounce of hesitation, or an inkling of how to swim, Finn jumped into the water.

As bubbles shot up his nostrils and his head spun between his legs, Finn couldn't help but wonder what Ariel or any other Bizarre Blade-wielding Champion would have done in this circumstance. Maybe some of them would have let it go and some might have jumped in after it. Some might have gotten to the other side of the river and ran after it along the beach. Either way, Finn now realized how important this Bizarre Blade was to him. Without this sword, he was just Finn Featherstone, the normal plain-looking young adult who could paint and draw decently well. He was the old Finn Featherstone who'd never climbed a tree nor even held a weapon of any kind. Without the Bizarre Blade he was a nobody and would always be a nobody. Worst of all, he had no destiny without his Blade.

Jigsaw *was* his destiny, and he would not let it just wash down the river.

It didn't take long for Finn to suck in his first small breath of water. He was busy flopping his hands aimlessly at his sides and kicking his feet like a maimed fish. He didn't expect for drowning to hurt the way it did. Something flashed red in his vision and he tried his best to shove his hand toward it. He closed his eyes and wagged his fingers out in the open water, hoping another crocodile wouldn't see them as swimming snacks. It took everything in him not to add to the water collecting in his lungs, even though his mind was doing a great job of persuading him to breathe in more water.

His fingers clasped onto something metallic and he gripped onto it with all his strength. His head beat the bottom of the river...and he felt air touch his feet. He realized that he had been swept away to an area of the river in which was shallow enough to stand, so he pushed down his legs and forced his head out of the water. A thick choking sound, a noise he didn't know he was capable of producing, came from his mouth as he tried to cough out the water from his lungs. His long hair hung heavily in his eyes and snot ran from his nose almost as fast as the river.

But he'd caught his Blade.

Jigsaw was still being pulled by the rapids and it tugged Finn hard enough that he fell to his knees, still unable to breathe. He felt hands under his armpits as he was dragged from the river. He was placed on his back and felt hands pushing just above his naval. The water that shot out of his mouth was thick and warm and it felt like he was exhaling, even though he wasn't. Above him stood Ariel, her muddy hair falling into his face. Her eyes were wide but the words coming out of her mouth made no sense to Finn.

She put him on his side, where he vomited up even more water that he'd swallowed. They let him stay like that for the better part of an hour. His throat was sore, as were his forearms from holding on to Jigsaw for so long. He turned over onto his other side and laid his head on the Blade's face. Jigsaw pushed warm air into the wind, which blew over Finn's body. He must have dozed off at some point because when he awoke, it was dark.

Ariel was screaming at Jade. They were facing each other on opposite sides of a fire. Jade had his head almost between his knees as his sister or romantic partner or whatever she was gave him a scolding Finn never thought possible from such a sweet girl. Then, he remembered her tantrum the very first time he'd met her. Still, it was strange to hear the odd girl speak so normally and like an adult.

"Ariel wants to know what kind of Champion of Arbitration leaves another Champion to die? Who are you? Are you really Jade, or are you an imposter? Ariel has never been more disappointed and disgusted with you then she is right now. You should feel ashamed of yourself. Just because Finn was right for Jigsaw and you weren't doesn't give you any right to just leave him to die. He took our oath, remember? Or are you too narcissistic? He's one of us now, and as far as Ariel is concerned, you just left a brother to die."

Finn pretended to be asleep as Ariel went quiet. Jade said nothing but kept his face toward the ground, both arms rested on his knees.

The next day Jade was silent as they made their way back to Kimidori. Ariel disappeared into the jungle before the Kimidori guards once again arrived to escort them to the royal courtyard, where King Whetstone waited for them. When he spoke, he spoke with slurred words; obviously he'd already been drinking.

"Well done, Champions, well done indeed." King Whetstone stood up from his throne, wobbled a little, and made his way to them. Finn didn't have a good feeling about this, as the number of guards surrounding them had tripled. The King hiccupped. "Are you just going to keep me waiting? Where is the proof you have slain this giant pest of mine?"

Jade said not a word. He reached into his pouch and produced the baby t-rex tail. He popped it up in the air a few times before tossing it to his father. It hit the man in the chest as he tried to catch it, but ultimately it landed on the ground. A few of the guards gasped and began to whisper, expecting the king to order the two Champions arrested for their rudeness, but King Whetstone was either too fascinated with the tail or too drunk to care. He reached down and scooped up the tail, marveling at it as if it were a piece of gold.

"Tell me, how did you kill this beast when all of my most prized warriors could not?"

Finn's hand went to the back of his head and he scratched. He'd never been a good liar, nor had he ever been good at creating stories. With speaking not being an option, Finn pulled Jigsaw from its baldric and pointed the Blade into the air. The king's mouth opened into a big smile as he clasped the tail with both hands.

"I should never have even asked! Of course, it was the Bizarre Blade-wielding Champion who took down such a chaotic and dangerous beast! Champion Featherstone, you have my thanks. Here, please take this as a token of my gratitude."

The king tossed back the dinosaur tail not to Jade, but to Finn. He caught it and put it in his satchel without even glancing at it. Again, the guards gasped as King Whetstone bowed his head to Finn. Even Jade looked unpleasantly surprised by this and perhaps even a little hurt. Finn wondered if Jade wished that he'd been the one to which his father gave so much positive attention.

"Now what?" was all that Finn could ask. "Can we get that Phantom Blade now? We're kind of in a hurry."

"In a hurry? For what? You haven't held up the rest of the deal! You must marry my daughter before I" —he hiccupped—"hand over the Phantom Blade! Don't tell me that a Champion is backing down on his word?"

"N-No! No, never," stammered Finn, feeling a little guilty at the excitement he felt in his stomach. It was most likely wrong to marry a girl that didn't like him, but oh did it feel so good to know she'd be his. Still, he had to ask, "But are you sure that your daughter wants to be married to me? Doesn't she still need to make that choice for herself? This just doesn't feel right…"

It wasn't just the king who laughed at this, but all of the guards as well. Many of them slapped their steel knee plates as if Finn had just told the best joke ever. King Whetstone rose from having buckled over and wiped a tear from his eye. "Oh, Champion Featherstone, you never cease to amaze me. Who knew you were such a jokester!" The king put two fingers in his mouth and whistled twice.

The courtyard palace doors were pulled open by two servant girls, and standing in the middle of the doorway was Amber Whetstone. Finn shoved Jigsaw's tip into the ground and leaned on it to keep his knees from melting underneath him as he laid his eyes on the most gorgeous sight he'd ever beheld. King Whetstone clapped his hands together as Amber made her approach.

She wore a dress made of long red silks that blew in the wind. Her black hair was tied into a tight half-bun, the rest of her hair flowing freely in the breeze. Two fresh pink flowers had been placed just above each ear, which perfectly matched the blush on her cheeks. Black eye makeup brought her almond eyes to sharp points, and the small amount of white powder around her face made the topaz color of the irises shine.

King Whetstone was still clapping when she walked up to Finn. She was the same height as him, give or take half an inch. She stood on her toes and pushed her face towards his. Finn pulled back his head a little but it wasn't enough to evade her lips on his. At that moment, the world seemed to disappear around him as fireworks shot off in his mind. He felt his toes curl in his saber-toothed tiger boots and he gripped Jigsaw's leathery grip just a bit harder. The Blade sensed this feeling of bliss and hummed a song Finn hadn't heard since waking up in the Champions of Arbitration village.

When their lips parted, Finn was sure he saw some interest in those eyes of hers. She might not have loved him and she might not even have liked him, but he was positive she'd sensed the energy that flowed from him through his kiss. He didn't know this girl, but he damn sure did want to.

The king clasped his hands together. "Oh, how beautiful! You two make a fine couple! That will be all, my dear."

Amber bowed her head, her eyes not leaving Finn for a second. She backed away a few steps before turning and walking back to the palace doors. Finn watched her the entire way, the swaying of her hips driving him mad.

The king had been watching him watching her. "Ahh, yes, young love. There is nothing like it. Now, back to business. I understand you two are in a sort of hurry; well, I assure you that the feeling is mutual. The faster I get an heir, the greater my chances at keeping my head attached to my neck. I will arrange the wedding for tonight. We can make it quick and sweet, and you two can be on your way."

Jade walked away without a word. Three guards trailed him but kept their distance. Finn watched as he left. He wanted to feel bad for Jade, he really did, but he could not. Anytime he tried to feel sympathy for the young Champion of Arbitration, the memories of him leaving him to die on the beach circulated through his mind, and he wasn't sure whether or not he'd ever be able to forgive him for that. Hopefully, Nibbles would be able to reassign Finn to another professor and another team of Champions for him to work with. He and Jade were just not compatible and would more than likely end up killing each other.

37

A BEAUTIFUL SORT OF MADNESS

The commencement of the wedding was captivating. The ending, however, was a catastrophe.

Just as King Whetstone had promised, the ceremony was quick and to the point, but still very beautiful. By the end of it, Finn was covered in all sorts of flower petals that had been thrown into the sky. He shook hands with and was congratulated by at least two hundred people he'd never met. Women cried tears of joy, and children played chase in the grass. Music was being played by foreign squeaky wind instruments that Finn had never heard of and never wished to hear again.

The best part about the whole wedding was the very end, when he was asked to kiss his bride. Finn surprised himself by making the first move. He pushed his head forward, placing his lips on hers. At first, she'd raised her hands in surprise, her eyes wide open. Finn lifted a hand and placed it to the side of her face like he'd seen other men do. For the first time during any of their three kisses, he felt Amber relax and slightly push back into his face. He pulled back and took his lips from hers, only for her to kiss him once again. Sparks of electricity ran through Finn's body and he had to mentally focus on reducing the excitement of his gooch troll.

Finn was being handed a glass of bubbling green juice when King Whetstone stood on the wooden stage that had been built in front of the palace doors overnight. He lifted his hands into the air and shouted, "Ladies and gentlemen! I have an announcement to make, one that will surprise you all! It has come time for me to honor my agreement with Champion Featherstone and Prince Whetstone by handing over the most prized possession of the Koosahmoorah Kingdom, the Phantom Blade, which hasn't be drawn nor viewed by the public eye in over a century!" The king clapped his hands and the palace doors opened behind him. The drummers situated around the stage banged their drums, adding to the suspense, as two guards carried out a long, thin box. It must have been heavy because both men were trying very hard not to show strain on their faces. The long chest was placed in front of King Whetstone. He raised his hands once again into the air so the sleeves of his robe fell down to his elbows. He bent down and opened the chest latches with two clicks.

The crowd, including Finn, fell silent. A light, coming from inside the chest, flashed onto the king's face and a few tears fell from his eyes. He stood back up, wiped his face, and gestured to the side of the stage. Out from a side door came Jade, dressed in the same red plate armor that all the guards wore, except a little shinier from a recent polish job. He walked up the stairs and took a knee before his father. Finn, feeling moved from the ceremony, felt goosebumps grow on his arms.

"Jade Whetstone," announced his father. "I know we have never seen eye to eye and may never get along. It has always been that way and it very well may likely remain that way forever. I hope you believe me when I say that I still feel honored to be alive to see the day that this ancient Blade is placed down into your hands. Although you may not like me and maybe not even love me, I am still proud to hand this treasure down to you."

Jade bowed his head as his father put both hands into the chest and slowly pulled out the Bizarre Blade known as the Phantom Blade. Jigsaw purred on Finn's back, recognizing that there was another one of its kind very near to it. Finn's jaw dropped as he mouthed the word, "WOW!"

Black and grey smoke wafted from over the lid of the chest. It wasn't like a smoke from a fire but had a more ghostly effect to it, as though the smoke was alive. The king's face lit up as he pulled the Blade out from the chest. The entire city of Kimidori was present for this and wouldn't have missed it for the world. This was their chance to get a glimpse of the Blade that had protected them for so long. Everyone, including Finn, gasped at the magnificence and elegance of the Blade.

In the King's hands lay a sword with a very thin and very long blade, even longer than Jigsaw's. There were no vents from which the eerie smoke spewed, but rather it crawled from the bottom of the Bizarre Blade from an unknown source and rose into the air. The steel looked more like a mirror, reflecting back the awed faces of the audience. The cross guard was small and circular, the hilt long just like Jigsaw's—except instead of leather wrapping it had black and red silk fabric. The pattern of this fabric was crisscrossed, leaving a diamond of open space, exposing the material of the hilt itself underneath.

Jade hadn't even lifted his head to see his new Bizarre Blade. Finn figured it must have been some sort of custom for him to blindly accept whatever was placed in his hands, which rested in the air palm up. The king raised the Phantom Blade into the sky and all of the citizens bowed their heads. Finn tried to do so but he was too late as everyone was already lifting their faces back up to marvel at the royal exchange.

With swift movements, King Whetstone used the Bizarre Blade to slit his palm. He spun the Blade around and also cut his son's palm. There was a pause as the king held the Phantom Blade in one hand while he clasped bloodied hands with his son. Jade, without looking up, raised his free hand, and the Bizarre Blade's handle was placed into it. At that moment, a strong wind gusted from the stage and over the spectators. Finn could sense a strong power in the air as the Bizarre Blade was transferred from one owner to the next. Finn couldn't help but feel giddy at having the opportunity to feast his eyes on such a rare ceremony, and he wondered if Monk E. would ever believe him.

Standing up, Jade finally looked down at the Blade. His face didn't show any sign of surprise as Finn had expected, but instead it looked as though he'd just been handed a quest rather than a weapon. He bowed to his father and gripped the Phantom Blade with both hands. A servant walked onto the stage holding a Bizarre Baldric and placed it over Jade's head. Finn, as well as the citizens, were all hoping Jade would give it a few practice swings. Everyone groaned when he just twirled it around and snapped it onto the baldric resting on his back. Jade was a spoiler of fun through and through.

He turned back to his father and both of them bowed together. King Whetstone placed his hands back into the air and cried out, "You have been given a most sacred and burdensome responsibility. Take this Blade and go forth!

With it, you will accomplish many a great thing, and so it is to you that I say—" The king's words melted away as he looked up and over the crowd. His mouth dropped and his lips began to shake. He pointed a finger behind all of the onlookers. "By the gods! WHAT THE FUUUUU—"

Chaos erupted in the courtyard as Jewels burst through the congregation, smashing her body into the golden statue of King Whetstone, sending it to the ground where it cracked and shattered into a million pieces. People darted left and right, screaming at the top of their lungs as they tried to find an exit. Taken by complete surprise, Finn shook his head, unable to believe what he saw, and just stood there, dumbfounded.

A hand grabbed him by the wrist and pulled him out of the way, just before Jewels' mouth clamped down around him. Finn looked at who had saved him and it was none other than Amber—his wife. Finn opened his mouth to thank her but was interrupted by the cries of the elderly. Amidst the chaos, Jewels had caught a little old lady by the scruff of her self-knitted coat and had lifted her into the air. She looked up at the mouth that carried her but instead of fear there was anger. "Let go of me, dammit!" She swung her cane upward and caught Jewels in the eye, making her open her mouth in a roar of pain.

Finn bounded towards the falling old lady and dropped to his knees, sliding and catching her at just the last moment. The old lady looked up at him, her eyes magnified ten times by her glasses. A whiskered smile on her face made Finn think she was about to thank him. Instead, she started beating him with the cane, the smile turning to an evil frown. "Let go of me, dammit!"

Finn shoved the old lady off of him and made a run for it back to Amber. Finn took her by the hand and they sprinted as fast as they could away from the commotion. They slammed into body after body and were not making much headway—the panic in Kimidori was so great that no one could escape! Finn looked back and watched as Jewels tore into the citizens, her black feathered mouth red with fresh blood. She wasn't even killing to eat, but killing to kill. Finn imagined that they were like ants to her and she was just squishing the ones that got in her way.

One guard poked the leg muscle of Jewels with his spear. She turned around and chomped down on the upper half of his torso. The man's screams echoed from the vertical cave that was Jewels' mouth as she crunched him in a single bite. She let go and out plopped a lifeless crushed body, the plate armor covered in holes from Jewels' teeth from which blood poured through like a human water fixture. Jewels continued to do this—plucking poor citizens from the ground, crunching them, picking up another, crunching them as well, all the while her tail slammed into people, sending the unlucky Koosahmoorarians flying through the air twenty feet away.

Finn and Amber ducked as a guard flew over their heads after being batted by Jewel's tail. His body spun on the ground a few times, his tongue flopping out of his mouth as he rested on his side. Just by looking at the sheer size and amount of muscle the t-rex had Finn was sure that Jewels had more than enough strength in her tail to kill on impact.

Instead of running, which apparently wasn't working, the two of them overturned a table to use as a shield and waited for openings in the panicking crowd. Finn scanned the people for Jade but couldn't see him anywhere. He tried yelling out his name but it was easily lost in the screams of everyone trying to get out of the way of Jewels' rampage—

which had now turned towards the architecture of the courtyard.

Jewels tripped on a particularly dense group of people, and fell headfirst into King Whetstone's palace. Even over the noise of all the citizens of Kimidori, Finn could hear the screams of King Whetstone. Finn turned and saw the man on his knees in the courtyard, his hands outstretched to his palace, which slowly crumbled before him. He was crying, his head rolling between his shoulders. Suddenly, he turned, locked eyes with Finn, and mouthed the word "YOU!"

"You need to get out of here," yelled Amber into Finn's ears.

"Not without you!" Finn shouted back.

Amber grabbed Finn's face, forcing him to look at her. Her gaze was alert and serious, although she now looked a little crazy. Her bun had come undone long ago and now her hair was a beautiful sort of madness. The white powdered makeup and her red lipstick had smothered all over her face, more closely resembling war paint than makeup. Finn liked her better this way.

"My people here need me, and your people need you."

Finn bit his bottom lip, his eyes shifting to the guards that the king was rallying up. Amber was right, he needed to get out of there as soon as possible...but he just couldn't leave her in this mess. No, he had to do something to help her or else his conscience would never let him live it down.

Then, a terrible, TERRIBLE idea came to him. One that would surely get him killed, but it was worth a shot.

"I'll see you again, yes? I know we haven't known each other for very long but I—" Amber interrupted him with a kiss and he took this as a yes.

Turning his attention back to Jewels, Finn ran out from

their hiding place—*towards* the t-rex, not away from it. He could hear Amber screaming his name from behind but he ignored it. His hand fell to his satchel, and out he pulled the little dinosaur tail, its skin now greyed with age.

Finn whistled as loudly as he could and Jewels turned around to face him. The sunlight revealed her slit pupils and he could see them widen as she focused entirely on him. Finn gulped and wiggled the tail out in the air for her to see.

"Come on! Come and get it!"

Jewels happily complied.

38

HANG TOGETHER OR HANG SEPARATELY

FINN HAD THE FORTITUDE TO WAIT UNTIL HE RAN PAST AMBER before starting to scream. Jewels charged after him, doing an excellent job of crushing any person unlucky enough to be in her way. Finn looked over his shoulder and realized that if he didn't do something quick, she would catch up to him in a matter of seconds. How he wished he'd thought this plan through before jumping into it.

Getting away from Jewels would have been easy if he could just plant Jigsaw into the ground and have it pull him away, which, in retrospect, he probably should have done back in the jungle the first time she was chasing him. However, now that wasn't an option, because Jigsaw would probably kill more people than Jewels already had! The only useful ability Jigsaw had now was giving Finn an excellent calf workout with its heavy-ass weight.

Finn could smell Jewel's breath, fresh with human blood, reach his nose as she gained on him. He could feel her presence right behind him and his eyes flinched as every second passed, thinking each was the moment he would be bitten. A big puff of air blew through his helm and ruffled his hair, and Finn closed his eyes as he ran, expecting every passing moment to be his last.

"Give me the tail!" Finn heard Jade's voice call out to him.

Finn turned and saw Jade running right beside him, the Phantom Blade held in his hand horizontal to the ground. A dark smoke seeped out of Jade's skin and his eyes were completely black, making him look, well, like a phantom!

"Give me the tail!" he repeated, holding out a hand, and Finn eagerly accepted his offer. It had been his dammed idea to cut the tail off anyway.

As soon as the transfer was complete, Finn jumped to the side with as much strength as he could muster. He turned back to see Jewels take a bite directly at the spot where her prey had just been, her pupils dilating as she watched Finn hit the ground some feet out of the way.

It was Jade now who whistled and yelled, "Hey! Over here!" He held up the tail and taunted her with it.

Jewels' face snapped forward, her nostrils widening as she breathed in Jade's scent. She was on the move in an instant, a deep growl bellowing from her lips. Finn watched in amazement as Jade took off with amazing, inhuman speed, his legs blurring with their movement. Finn didn't know exactly what the powers of the Phantom Blade were, but speed most certainly was one of them.

Jade did his best to shove people out of the way before Jewels trampled them, but was only successful half the time as there were just too many of them. Finn had to keep covering his eyes as frantic citizens were either squished by the t-rex's massive feet or slammed into the air by her thick muscular tail. Black feathers floated down from the sky, mixing with the blood puddles on the ground.

King Whetstone was not going to be happy.

Speaking of the king, Finn heard him screaming from a distance behind him.

"There he is! Seize him!"

Finn poked his head up as best he could above the crowds of rushing people and saw at least fifteen guards trying to maneuver through them in order to get to him. Their trouble traversing through the chaos would be Finn's key to escaping this hellhole. He turned back to see Jade leading Jewels down the center of the city and back towards the jungle. How Jewels made it all the way to the palace courtyard without being seen would always remain a mystery.

Using the unfortunate path of dead people left behind by the tyrannosaur, Finn ran right behind it, but still kept his distance just in case. He tried his best to hop over most of the bodies but accidentally stepped on the backs, bellies, and faces of a few. When this happened he'd always whispered a "sorry," to himself, as well as said a little prayer. As he ran, he hoped that Amber, now being his wife, would not be in trouble because of his and Jade's lie. Hopefully, her being a blood relative of the king would spare her from any punishment.

Although this was not the time for laughing, Finn found himself chuckling at how much his life had changed. First, he was put in the army against his will. Then, he stumbled upon a Bizarre Blade and accidentally became its owner. After that, he took an oath and joined a secret society of Champions that upheld the peace. Months later, he was married to a Princess. And now he was chasing after the largest meat-eating dinosaur he'd ever seen. The whole thing sounded ridiculous in his head but it was his life now. This was the life of a Champion.

JADE DISAPPEARED INTO THE FOREST, leading the enraged mother t-rex out of Kimidori. Once again, he'd left on very bad terms. Finn was on his trail, but took a turn after a few minutes and made his way to the river. This time, however, he stayed clear of the water, knowing damn well what lurked within it.

"Ariel is up here!" yelled Ariel from a tree.

Finn stopped running and fell to his hands and knees, panting. No amount of oxygen seemed to be fulfilling his lungs' desires. Ariel plopped down onto the ground beside him and sat. Yet again, she was covered head to foot in dried mud, and her eyes were in their dragonfly form. The small clear wings attached to the Flutter Blade's cross guard flickered as its owner sniffed the air.

"Ariel saw and heard the whole thing," she said, reducing one eye to normal but leaving the other be. Finn wished she wouldn't do that—it really creeped him out.

"But...how?" he asked her between desperate breaths.

"It is one of Ariel's Blade's powers! Ariel takes all attributes from the dragonfly and can use them at will. Ariel is not a Master of the Flutter Blade but she can use many of its functions."

"So, you can see really far and hear very well?"

"Precisely!" she said, winking her normal eye.

Finn turned away, tired of looking at the hideousness of Ariel's deformed face. He'd already seen enough atrocities for one day and just wanted to concentrate on getting his heart to beat less than six hundred thumps a minute.

A swoosh of wind brushed against Finn's face. He looked up to see Jade standing a few feet away from him, the grey smoke curling around his shoulders and into the air. He twirled the Phantom Blade in his hands a few times before returning it to its baldric, and the smoke disappeared.

"Did you kill Jewels?" Finn asked him.

Jade shook his head. "No. Like Ariel told you, the Champions of Arbitration are no hired killers. We try and preserve life as much as possible."

"It makes Ariel wonder if we should have killed Jewels in the first place..." Ariel's face fell to the ground. "So many lives could have been saved this day. Ariel feels much grief in her heart."

Jade bent down and lifted Ariel's chin. "We made the decision we thought best, Ariel. All actions come with consequences, some consequences we can guess and others are simply impossible to see."

Ariel moved her head from Jade's hand, and Finn could tell she was still pretty upset with him. "But we must take responsibility for all of our actions. We are the cause of the deaths of so many Koosahmoorarians."

"I'm not saying we shouldn't take responsibility for our actions, but I will not stand by and let you believe for one second that it was our fault that so many people died. We did not know. We cannot read the future. We made the decision to preserve life and that is something we should all feel pride in. Let us not forget the deaths of those today, but neither should we feel a tremendous amount of guilt. Let us pray for them and never forget."

Finn nodded his head and sat back on his butt. "I agree with Jade. We all saw that family of t-rexes; none of us could have lifted a Blade to end them. We did what we thought was right."

Ariel's frown slowly turned to that of a sad smile. She put one hand on Finn's shoulder and the other on Jade's foot. "Thank you both. Ariel feels a little better. She just needs time."

The three Champions remained in silence for a while, considering the tragic events of the past day. Finn, feeling a little depressed himself after seeing so many bloody deaths, felt his spirits lift upon hearing the familiar squawking of Obsidian who, as per usual when all the fighting was over, swooped down onto his shoulder. Clasped in one of its talons was a stem filled with crowberries which he knew to be Finn's favorites.

"And where have you been?" he asked the microraptor, taking the fruit stem from it. Obsidian answered him with a gaze that he couldn't read. "Am I supposed to think of this as some sort of peace treaty?" He jingled the fruit in front of Obsidian. "You always leave when the going gets tough. Some friend you are."

"That's so mean!" shouted Ariel, her hands going to her mouth. Her other eye shrunk, a hiss of air escaping from the edges of her stretched eyelid. Some of that air got in Finn's mouth, making him gag a little.

"Obsidian knows I'm joking," he said, wiping the top of his tongue with part of his armor. "We always talk like that to each other."

Jade smirked. "Is speaking to dinosaurs one of your skills now?"

"As a matter of fact, it is!"

"Boys!" Ariel cried in frustration. "You both realize that we're about to go and face a small army of mercenaries, right? Led by a cruel man with a Blade that can null our Blades' powers? Do either of you think arguing will aid us in saving our family?"

Finn drug a hand over his face. "It's not me who starts the bickering!"

"Oh, don't worry," Ariel said, looking up at Jade. "Ariel sees this." She turned her gaze back to Finn and pointed a finger at him. "But you're not making it any easier with your choice of words. We all need to realize that there are lives at stake, lives that are very dear to us. If we are to save them we must work as a team."

Finn gritted his teeth. Ariel was right. If they wanted to save Nibbles, Silver, Doctor Skeleton, Gauze, Mary Flowerfield, and all the students that lived in the village, then they would need to pull together their physical and mental resources and work together. Sure, he wasn't as close to these people as Ariel and Jade were, but they had saved his life. They had helped him by answering his questions about his Blade and opened his eyes to more of the realities of the world around him. Even Silver, although basically having tried to kill him, had helped Finn to become better acquainted with his Blade, even though he was still very far from even being an intermediate wielder.

These people, these Champions of Arbitration, had taken him in as one of their own. Finn would never forget this kindness, as he'd never felt so welcomed by anyone. He'd always been the outcast, had always felt like a loser. Nibbles, on the other hand, didn't see him this way. She saw promise in him.

Personal feelings aside, it was the job of a Champion to protect others and fight for what was right. At least, that was what Finn thought all Bizarre Blade wielders were supposed to do, but apparently there were cruel, power-hungry wielders like Constantine Firefurnace. This was why the Champions of Arbitration had been created, and this was all the more reason why Finn needed to help Jade and Ariel save their family, the family he too was now a part of. And, if his father was truly in danger, he needed to settle this crisis first, and as soon as possible, before venturing back to Sumetai.

If Finn was to accomplish all of this, he had to be the bigger man.

"Jade, I'm sorry I'm not the person you wanted to marry your sister. Although I didn't mind marrying her for selfish reasons of my own, it still doesn't take away the fact that she's your little sister. I know deep down that if there had been another way to get the Phantom Blade, I would have done that for you instead."

"There's always another way," spat Jade.

"And if there had been I would have been all ears," said Finn, trying to remain calm and collected. "I'm sorry this is the way things turned out. I never wanted to hurt you or upset you. That was never my goal. If anything, I would very much like to be your friend as I only have a few in this world. You and Ariel have done a lot for me, and for that I thank you with all my heart. I thank you also for saving me from the jaws of Jewels back in Kimidori. You could very well have just left me there to die."

"Ariel saw this as well," she said, nodding her head with closed eyes. "Finn had the option to escape by using the powers of Jigsaw, but in doing so would have killed many innocent people with the teeth of his Blade. Ariel does not know what was going through Finn's mind, but it seemed he was ready to take the teeth of the tyrannosaur rather than cut a path of human flesh to safety. However, it was through a combined effort that you two were able to rid Kimidori of the destructive and angry Jewels. You both put your lives on the line to save as many innocent people as possible and Ariel cannot understand why the two of you cannot be friends. The three of us could do so much good for this world...if only we could be a team."

Jade didn't look at either of them, his face barren and emotionless as he looked down through the trees toward the river. Finn could see him biting down as his cheek muscles flexed. He was thinking about something.

"I'm sorry," he said in such a low voice that Finn almost didn't hear him.

Finn nodded his head, thinking that was all he was going to say. He was just about to stand up when Jade continued with words that were clearly difficult for him to say.

"I want to thank you, as well, for saving my life back at the falls when I was drowning. Although it was your fault in the first place, Ariel tells me you spent more time than you should have in effort to revive me. I'm gonna say this just once...but it means a lot to me."

"Ariel thinks there is one more thing you need to apologize for."

Jade sighed but took Finn by surprise by actually looking at him this time, "Look. I didn't mean what I said about you not being good enough for my sister to even wipe her ass with. Not only was that disgusting and immature of me, but I was wrong. Even though I think it's ridiculous that you said yes to marrying someone you've hardly even met, I don't think you're the worst person my father could have arranged to marry my sister. Sometimes I even think the Jigsaw Blade made the right decision in choosing you."

"Ahhhh, isn't that sweeeeeet?" cooed Ariel, ruining the moment. "Now! Kiss and make up!" Both Finn and Jade looked at her with raised eyebrows. "Or shake hands, whatever you prefer."

Finn stood up and extended his hand. Jade stared at the peace offering for a moment and looked as though he might not accept it. With a grunt, he clasped hands with Finn.

They stood there awkwardly for a moment, and then, not knowing what else to do, Finn brought a very stiff Jade into a hug. He could feel Jade's muscles harden under his fingers but was shocked when they relaxed and he hugged back.

They weren't best friends, but at least they weren't enemies.

Ariel clapped her hands together, stood up, and joined in on the hug. She put her mouth close to Finn's ear and said, "Alrighty, so what's our plan to save the village? Ariel says we gut that son of a bitch using Jigsaw!"

Jade gasped. "Ariel!"

She giggled. "Sorry, Ariel got excited."

Finn felt Ariel's face get closer to his and he knew what was coming. He tried pulling away but wasn't fast enough.

A wet tongue shoved itself into his ear.

39

PLAN B

AFTER ARRIVING AT THE OUTSKIRTS OF THE VILLAGE, JADE AND Ariel were quick to come up with a plan and everyone, for the most part, knew their roles. One thing was for certain— and that was that nothing was for certain. The outcome of that day was veiled, except for the fact that blood would be shed.

Finn wasn't quite comfortable in killing yet, and left the duties of taking out the mercenary sentries to Jade and Ariel. The Phantom Blade turned out to be more than perfect for the job. As far as they all knew, its powers included increased speed, increased jumping abilities, invisibility (although not completely invisible as the smoke gave him away) and the dampening of the sounds of movement.

There were a few drawbacks to these abilities, however. For one, the Phantom Blade could give you immense speed with little jumping ability, or the wielder could go half and half. So, the way Jade had explained it to Finn, the Blade allowed him to be amazing at one ability or great in two, or above average in three. Finn guessed that the more time

Jade spent with his Blade, the more he could push the limits of its abilities.

Still, watching Jade sneak up behind unsuspecting mercenaries was breathtaking. When using the Blade to sneak, his feet disappeared altogether, replaced with only wisps of smoke. There was no snapping of sinister twigs, no rustling or crunching of pesky leaves. The Blade turned Jade into a quiet apparition of deadly proportions, leaving the mercenary scouts with no chance of survival. The powers of this Blade combined with Jade's already-honed subterfuge skills, not to mention the jungle's natural hiding spots, gave him a godly advantage.

Ariel's Blade allowed her to see and hear anything at great distances and she could do both at the same time without the reduction of power of the other. Not only that, but the Flutter Blade made her light on her feet and she could even sprout small wings that allowed her to cross small distances. As of now, she didn't think her flying ability was good enough to aid them in any way. Her body wasn't the only thing that could be reduced in weight, but also the Blade, which paired nicely if you knew how to use a light sword which apparently, she did.

It was weird for Finn to watch Ariel kill. She seemed such a sweet and kind girl, although very odd. Still, she killed without hesitation, and even looked to be in a hurry to do so. Her family's life was on the line and these killers and kidnappers for hire were holding her back from getting to them.

When the two Champions finally returned to the top of the tree where Finn sat, he saw that Jade didn't have an ounce of blood on him, while Ariel was covered in it. The combination of the blood, her huge shiny blue eyeballs, twitching antennae, and her elongated tongue licking one of her own ears made her a horrid sight to behold. Finn doubted he'd ever get used to this form of hers. Times like these made him happy he'd obtained Jigsaw and not the Flutter Blade.

Finn wasn't surprised when Obsidian left his shoulder to go off hunting right before the action started. He swore the dinosaur could sense his energy just as much as he could sense the raptor's energy, and he knew that Finn was about to be in danger. It was probably for the best, as the microraptor would really just end up getting in the way.

"Are we all set?" asked Jade. "Everyone know the plan?"

Finn shook his head. "I'm still not sure I like it."

Jade produced a coil of rope he'd managed to steal from one of the storage houses in the village. "Constantine won't let Ariel and I get close if he doesn't see you. He sure as hell won't trust us if he sees that you're not bound."

"Yeah, yeah, I understand," said Finn. "I'm just not excited about playing the prisoner. What if he kills me on the spot?"

"Then he kills you on the spot," answered Jade with a shrug.

Finn rubbed his face. "That wasn't the answer I was looking for. And what about your Phantom Blade? He's gonna wonder where you got that. He might even try and take it."

"Got that covered already," said Jade, pointing a thumb at the Blade on his back, which disappeared into grey smoke.

"Oh, that's no fair," complained Finn. He was pretty sure Jigsaw couldn't do anything fancy like that. In fact, none of the abilities of Jigsaw were fancy or elegant—they were the exact opposite: loud, deadly, crude, and literally abrasive.

Ariel pet Finn on the head, some of the blood from her

fingers getting into his hair. He tried to shake her off but she kept on petting him. "Don't worry, Finn. Ariel will tie the knot in a way that it will easily come loose. All you have to do is push against it and you'll be free!"

Seeing Finn wipe away the blood from his hair, Jade snapped his fingers and said, "Hey! That's a great idea. Ariel, wipe some blood on his face. Make it look like we roughed him up a bit."

"What? No, no, no, no, no, no thank you. I'd rather—"

Ariel slapped him across the face, her wet hand sliding across his cheek painfully. Before he could scoot down the branch away from her, she slapped him again on the other side.

"Okay! That's enough!"

Jade reached over and lifted Finn's face by his jaw, studying him. He used his fingers to move the blood around a little before nodding his approval. Finn about gagged as he smelled the blood on his face, but quickly covered his mouth before doing so.

Jade gave the thumbs up to his teammates. "Alright, let's go."

ENTERING the village was easier than Finn had thought. He wasn't sure what he expected but it certainly wasn't seeing lounging and laughing mercenaries that barely paid them any attention. One finally stopped them and asked them their business.

"Are you kidding me right now?" asked Jade, gesturing to Finn, who was all tied up. "We've brought the Jigsaw wielder, just as promised."

"What?" asked the mercenary, scratching the side of his

head. A few seconds later he exclaimed, "Oh yeah! Come with me. Constantine's been waiting on you three, I think."

As they reached the center of the village, the three Champions gasped at what they saw. The pile of students, teachers, and Nibbles hadn't moved an inch from where they'd been put on the day this all started. They were panting from the humidity, and looked like they hadn't been released since Jade and Ariel had been let go. Some of the younger students, children really, were bent over the ropes that crossed their bellies. Their dry mouths hung open and it didn't look like they were breathing.

Just then, a stench hit Finn's nose, and he realized that Constantine hadn't even let his prisoners relieve themselves, so they had to do it in their pants and on each other. This brought Finn's blood to a boil. To think a human was capable of letting another human suffer to this extent—it was sick. He couldn't imagine what Ariel and Jade were feeling at that moment.

"What kind of cruel animal does this?" asked Ariel under her breath, her voice shaky from hurt and anger.

Finn could feel Jade's grip on his arm tighten as he forced his face forward. Finn caught a glance from Silver who had, at first, looked like he'd been asleep. His eye now focused on the three of them, and squinted as if he tried to figure out their plan. He gave the slightest of nods towards Finn.

Constantine was seated at a table they'd pulled out from one of the treehouses. It looked banged up, as if they'd merely tossed it out of the door instead of lowering it with ropes. Terrible brown scabs riddled the man's face, and the holes bitten into his cheeks had turned a dark purple from infection. It looked as though he'd tried, to no avail, to cover up his hideous face with powered makeup that didn't match his pale skin tone. He wore an array of brightly colored clothes—pink and purple, to be exact—stolen from the closets of the students and professors.

The Highborn wiped his mouth with a clean cloth napkin as they approached. He waved at them to come closer as he finished his mouthful of food, making sure to cover his mouth with his hand. Just like with any Highborn, manners were always important.

The three Champions waited patiently for Constantine to swallow his dinner. He stood up with open arms, a fiendish smile on his face. "Well, look who it is! I can't actually believe you held up your end of the bargain! Damn, looks like I lost the bet." Constantine grabbed a small pouch off his belt, jingled the ammonite chips that were inside, and tossed them to a nearby mercenary who grinned with delight. "After you two left," continued Constantine, "I started to think, and soon I felt like I had been fooled. Four days went by and I was sure you weren't coming back. You don't know how close I was to setting your pile of friends over there on fire. Tell them how close we were, Jeremy."

The mercenary who had escorted the Champions nodded his head. "I was holdin' the torch and everything!"

"But then," said Constantine, sticking his pointer finger into the air, "a brilliant idea came to me! So brilliant that it gave me chills! I would stop feeding and caring for your friends and let them all die of dehydration. I would win either way! If you showed up then you still got to save your friends, and if you didn't show up then I would have upheld my word and killed them off in one of the most painful ways possible."

Jade's grip on Finn's shoulder was starting to hurt, but he refused to tell him so. Ariel's arm touched his and he could feel her shakiness. They needed to calm themselves if they were going to make this plan work; otherwise, their attitudes would ruin everything.

"Jeremy, do me a favor will you? Go cut our prisoners loose."

"But boss, won't they try and fight us if we do?"

"Do as I say, Jeremy. Trust me on this."

Jeremy shrugged his shoulders and walked over to the pile of slowly decaying people. He spun a dagger out of a sheath on his calf and started to cut away. One by one, each of the prisoners fell flat on their face, including Nibbles. The only four remaining on their knees were Silver, Doctor Skeleton, Gauze, and Mary Flowerfield, but soon, they too began to dwindle. One by one, the Champion professors fell to the ground, defeated by their body's needs for water and food. Silver was the last to drop. Finn could see the dark red and purple imprints running across each of their arms and he wondered how tightly Constantine had tied them up.

"I've upheld my end of the deal," said Constantine, gesturing his hand palm up at the villagers. "Now, hand over Mister Featherstone along with his Blade, and I will be on my way."

Constantine reached for Finn but Jade pulled him back. "And how do we know if they're alive?"

Constantine groaned. "Jeremy, will you please?"

Jeremy lifted his foot and kicked Nibbles hard in the stomach with the tip of his black boot. The old lady moaned and curled like a dying bug. Finn figured this would be the time Jade would lose his nerve and attack Constantine right then and there, but the Highborn was ready. While their attention had been turned away, Constantine had brandished his Nullify Blade.

"Now, hand him over," the Highborn demanded, his smile fading.

Jade shoved Finn over to Constantine who grabbed him by the hair. Finn grunted as the man squeezed his locks in his fist, sending tendrils of pain down his face. Still, Finn did not say a word. He kept going over the plan in his mind, repeating the visualization of how everything was going to proceed.

The plan was rather simple. Finn would become disruptive, taking Constantine's attention away from Jade, who would have his invisible Phantom Blade in his hand by then and ready to cut the Highborn down. Luckily Nullify Blade's abilities were currently shut off seeing as how the Phantom Blade had remained invisible up until that moment.

If, for some reason, this plan did not work, then they would go to plan B. If things went south, Finn would free himself by pushing against the ropes with his arms. It would then be entirely up to him to shove Jigsaw through Constantine's back. It would be his first kill that wasn't by accident, but he was pretty sure he was ready. It was his life or Constantine's.

Constantine backed away with Finn before shoving him to the ground beside him. "You Champions of Arbitration are far too trusting! Did you really think I would just let you all go? HA! NEVER! Not when I can take hold of four Bizarre Blades! Oh wait..." The Nullify Blade began to sparkle as Constantine activated its powers. Finn could feel a force of energy push against his face, and even a little through his armor, as the Nullify Blade performed its magic. "Well, well, what is this?"

With a puff of smoke, Jade's Phantom Blade lost its invisibility and appeared. They'd been found out!

Jade, no longer able to activate his Blade, unsheathed his weapon and thrusted the razor-sharp tip right at Constantine's gut. Even though there was no magical power behind the attack, Jade moved insanely fast with deadly accuracy. Constantine surprised them all by sidestepping and knocking the Phantom Blade off its path, sending it right for Finn's face.

Finn shut his eyes and prepared for a sword to enter his forehead but Jade pulled back at just the last moment.

"Mindless morons!" screamed Constantine, raising his Blade into the air. "Come to my aid!"

Despite the lazy outer demeanor of the mercenaries, they came sprinting towards their leader with a ferocity Finn hadn't seen since their attack on the Shimoshimo army caravan all those nights ago. They surrounded Jade and Ariel in a wide, thick circle, effectively separating them from Finn and his captor. There had to be around twenty of them, maybe even thirty, all with long thin swords held in their hands as they readied themselves to strike when given the order.

The plan had failed. However, Finn could still uphold his end. He could finish all of this with Jigsaw, with or without its powers. This was the perfect time for him to finally take the reins—it was his time to become a Champion! It was time for plan B!

"Ah-hah!" shouted Finn, standing up and puffing out his chest, "I have you now!" He pushed against his bindings, opening his hand wide and readying it to grab hold of Jigsaw, but there was just one problem.

The ropes didn't come undone.

Constantine turned towards him with one raised eyebrow. Finn tried again, pushing against his bindings with all his strength. The ropes whined against the pressure but refused to loosen. He was stuck.

Finn looked up at Constantine whose smile revealed both of his abnormally long canine teeth. Finn muttered an,

"Oh shit," and took off running, which, with both arms tied to his waist, resembled more of a sad trot.

"Kill these two!" commanded Constantine, gesturing his head towards Ariel and Jade. "I'll take care of this one." He pointed his appearing and disappearing Nullify Blade in Finn's direction and sprinted after him.

40

—

OPEN YOUR EYES

CONSTANTINE'S TALL AND THIN BODY GAVE THE IMPRESSION that he was neither strong nor athletic, but he damn sure was. Finn had forgotten that this man had once been Second in Queue right behind the great Bryce Smolder, and there was a reason for that. He was a beast in human form!

Finn found himself a hiding spot behind one of the thinner trees. He stopped and listened for a few moments and started rubbing the back of the ropes against the rough bark of the tree. He'd do this for a few seconds, stop and listen, then continue again. Luckily, he'd been bent at the knees when the Nullify Blade swooshed through the entire trunk of the tree, only a few inches above his head.

As the tree creaked and began to fall over, Finn watched as a few strands of his green hair dwindled to the ground in front of his face. He stood and turned, meeting Constantine Firefurnace eye-to-eye. To this Highborn, this was a game to achieve his revenge, a game he'd already won, and Finn was just adding to the fun of it.

"Hi," Finn said, and with nothing else to do, he kicked as

hard as he could, sending dirt right into the Highborn's stupid face.

Constantine hadn't been expecting this and was too late to block the attack. "My eyes!"

Finn didn't hesitate, but took off once more. His heart beat hard in his chest and sweat dripped into the cracks of his eyes, stinging them and making it hard to see. He swung the hair out of his face and looked for a tree to climb, only to come to realize he couldn't climb! So, he kept running and running, taking random turn after random turn. It didn't take long before he had gotten lost...which gave him an idea. The more lost he got, the more of a chance he might have of getting away! The longer he could keep Constantine out of the village, the more time it gave Ariel and Jade to kill off the mercenaries...or die trying.

Finn broke through the forest and entered a savannah with tall yellowish grass that he could hide himself in. Memories of one of his father's famous warnings popped into his head. *"Don't ever go into the long grass! You never know what's lurking!* However, given his current circumstances, Finn knew his father would understand.

Dropping to the ground in the middle of the field, Finn laid himself on his back and listened. He shut his eyes and calmed his breathing down as best he could. He listened to the wind and felt it glide through the grass and over his sweaty face. Some of the smaller pieces of grass tickled the sides of his cheeks and part of him wished he could just take a nap.

I wonder how Jade and Ariel are holding up, he thought. *I sure hope they're alright.*

He was sure they'd be fine. It was *he* who had the smallest chance of survival. Jade and Ariel actually knew how to fight. As for Finn, he knew how to swing his Blade and make a little bit of fire come out of it which he couldn't even do because Jigsaw's abilities had become nullified.

The wind pushed the smell of sweet nectar into Finn's nose, calming him. He figured that if he died today, then at least he and his mother would be reunited. He imagined all the stories he would tell her, even though she already knew them. When he used to cry when he was younger, father would tell him that mother was always there, always watching over his shoulder. That she was his guardian.

Words entered his mind, the voice a mixture of more than one person.

Open your eyes.

What? Finn asked the voices.

Open your eyes.

He opened his eyes and his breath caught in his throat. There stood Constantine, lurking over him, the Nullify Blade held high over his head, his eyes wide with madness. "Enjoying the weather, Champion?"

Constantine dropped the Blade down, cutting through the wind with amazing speed. Finn was done for, he knew this, but still his instincts made him roll over onto his stomach. He closed his eyes and prayed that the Blade would miss him, but his luck had run out.

The Nullify Blade crashed down onto his body with so much force that Finn's face was pushed hard into the dirt. He waited to feel the sensation of being sliced open, but it never came. What he felt was more like being bludgeoned by a heavy hammer, and he heard the sound of metal clanging against metal. Then, he remembered that Jigsaw was still attached to his back.

Open your eyes.

Finn opened his eyes and saw the bindings of his rope had fallen to his side. He felt the heaviness of the Nullify blade being lifted by Constantine as he prepared for another attack. With nothing else to lose, Finn the Champion jumped up to his feet and brandished Jigsaw.

Finn pointed his Blade at Constantine, who did the same to him. "No more running," Finn said, his lungs still recuperating from the air that had been knocked out of them. "Let's fight like Champions."

Constantine chuckled. "This should be interesting."

Then, he attacked.

41

THE GORGONOPS

Fighting with Jigsaw, without the use of its abilities, felt like swinging around a useless and excessively heavy metal sword, one that was far too large to be considered efficient in swordplay. Not only that, but it severely limited Finn's stamina.

The Nullify Blade, on the other hand, was not as large nor as bulky as Jigsaw, and Constantine used this to his advantage. He swung with precision and speed, his skills with the sword obvious by the crisp and perfect movements of his feet, as well as the elegance with which he tried to chop his enemy's head off.

Finn was quite the opposite.

Constantine thrusted his Blade at his chest and Finn, without the strength to move the Jigsaw Blade in time to block the attack, dove out of the way. He spun on the ground and jumped back up onto his feet—but Constantine was already there waiting for him. The Highborn spun his sword around his body and swung the Blade horizontally, a strike meant to leave Finn literally half a man.

At the very last second, Finn fell onto his backside, the

Nullify Blade whistling overhead and easily slicing through thick chunks of long grass. He kicked Constantine hard in the shin and tried swinging Jigsaw at his legs but the High-born shoved his own Blade into the ground, blocking the strike. The impact of the two Blades sent tremors through Finn's bones, making his teeth chatter and his skull hurt.

Constantine cursed, bending down to rub his shin. As he did so, his eyes locked with Finn's. The whites of his eyes had turned red, and he no longer blinked. He was done playing games and looked ready to finish what he'd started. Finn swallowed hard and turned on his hands and knees as he tried to make his escape. He felt a front kick to his ass and fell face-forward into a pile of the freshly-cut grass. He spun around just in time to put Jigsaw between him and the piercing strike of Constantine's Blade.

A shrieking sound penetrated the air as Jigsaw's face blocked the Nullify Blade's thrust, and a wave of energy exploded outward from the two Blades, pushing both Finn and Constantine's hair backward. The energy couldn't be seen but it definitely could be felt. The tip of the Nullify Blade rested inches above Finn's heart with only Jigsaw there to protect him.

Finn tried reaching out to Jigsaw through his thoughts, hoping the magical sword might have some sort of idea of how to defeat the world's top Champion, but there was only silence. Apparently the Nullify Blade did more than cease the abilities of Blades—it put them to sleep as well.

Constantine lifted his Blade into the air and drove it back down on top of Jigsaw. They were met with another rush of energy, and Jigsaw slipped slightly out of the way as Constantine lifted his sword once again for another attack. With almost zero fighting experience, Finn turned his thoughts to the only lesson he'd really ever had in how to fight, from his dad. Something about being seconds away from death really made the memory so very clear. He could see with fine detail his crippled father standing over him with a white-whiskered smile on his face. Finn remembered when he'd come home, having been beaten up by the bigger kids of the neighborhood.

"Remember, son!" his father had said, bending down with a wet rag to clean Finn's battered face. "You don't come from a family of physically gifted men, so we have to protect ourselves the only way we know how."

"And how's that, Father?"

Finn's imaginary father chuckled. "Well, we have to fight dirty!"

"I'm not following you," Finn remembered saying all those years ago.

"I don't know how much more obvious I can be! Kick 'em in the damn stones, son!"

The memory disappeared in a puff smoke and drifted away in the winds of Finn's mind. Constantine's Blade, held high up in the air, now fell—seemingly in slow motion— once again at Finn's chest. Drool dribbled out the sides of his mouth and he looked much like the saber-toothed tiger, desperate to finish off its prey.

Finn took his father's advice (he really had nothing to lose at that point), lifted his boot, and smashed his heel into Constantine's stones. The strike was more successful than Finn had thought it would be. The two of them rested there, completely still and quiet. Constantine bent over, the Nullify Blade sliding into the dirt a few inches away from Finn's body. His lips puckered and his eyes crossed. A tiny squeak escaped from between his infected purple lips. Finn's foot was still connected to the man's testicles, but he quickly retracted his leg when he swore he could feel the man's jewels hanging over his ankle.

Standing himself up, Finn lifted Jigsaw into the air. A thought pushed through his mind...and he gasped when he realized it had come from Jigsaw! His Blade had awakened! Constantine must have accidentally ceased the abilities of the Nullify Blade now that he was, well, more preoccupied with his damaged dangling bits!

Jigsaw exploded with life, its vents roaring as its teeth became blurs of motion. Finn surprised himself when he swung the Blade right at Constantine's face. He was even more surprised by the excitement he felt thinking he might actually get out of this alive! He would be the savior of the village!

Constantine, on the other hand, refused to go down that easy.

It took only half a second for Jigsaw to be put back to sleep, its teeth going still instantly. Finn was mid-swing and prayed he would at least cut the man with his attack, but he didn't even get that! Constantine, with only a little more strain than usual, lifted his Nullify Blade into the air and blocked Jigsaw.

Again, energy radiated from the two connected Blades as the two of them pushed against each other. Over the past months, Finn's strength had greatly improved, but it was nothing compared to that of the Highborn after a lifetime's worth of training. It wasn't long before Finn's stamina dwindled and the Highborn began overpowering him, little by little. Soon, Jigsaw was shoved into Finn's face and the bodies of the two Champions were pressed together.

Finn put his hand to the back of Jigsaw's blade, and pressed against it with all his strength, trying to push

Constantine back. Unfortunately, the Highborn expected this.

Using Finn's momentum against himself, Constantine sidestepped, and Finn toppled forward. With instincts and finesse that Finn did not know he had, he whirled around with Jigsaw over his head and blocked an oncoming overhead strike by Constantine. The force of this blow brought Finn to his knees, into a very weak position.

"At least you will die knowing that you were a Champion!" cried Constantine, his voice two octaves higher than usual, making him sound insane. Finn didn't have to see his face to know he was smiling. "Even though it wasn't for very long, that is still more than most people would get to say!"

Before Finn could respond, the Nullify Blade slid down Jigsaw's teeth towards his exposed hands. Since Jigsaw had no cross guard, Constantine's Blade brushed over his fist. Finn shut his eyes as he waited for the return attack that would cut him right in half.

But it never came. Finn opened his eyes and saw that Constantine had taken a few steps back, an evil smile spread across his face. He felt warmth on his hands.

Jigsaw fell from Finn's grasp as pain shot up his right hand. He looked down to see a nub of white bone wiggling where the pinky finger should have been. Vomit rose in his throat as his body began to tremble terribly.

"I'll just let you enjoy that for a moment," said Constantine, holding the Nullify Blade out before him with one hand, preparing to finish Finn off. He used the other hand to brush the remaining long blond hairs back over his head and behind his ears. A little bit of sweat glistened on his forehead. "Now you know how it feels to be mutilated! I'm sure by now you've noticed that I, too, am missing a few of my digits." He put out his left hand and wiggled his remaining three fingers. "I was once beautiful, you know! I used to have a full set of gorgeous locks! Women flocked to me, always desiring my attention. Now, Bizarre Blade or not, who could love a hideous face such as this? No one, I tell you, no one! I'm a monster!" Constantine's voice shook as though he was about to start crying. Softly, he rubbed the hole at the side of his cheek. "Now that you have felt some of my pain, it is time I end your pathetic life. You're no Champion. You never were one."

The intense pain in Finn's hand had crawled throughout his body, paralyzing it with shock and agony. He turned to the side and his nausea poured onto the ground in the form of half-digested breakfast. He knew he could no longer fight. This was it. He was finished. He'd done all he could, but now was his time to die. He looked down at the ground, and the sight of his exposed pinky bone made all the blood rush out from his face. He bent his head down and cupped his red hand to his chest.

"Give Bryce my regards."

Finn didn't flinch and honestly, wasn't very worried. He almost welcomed what came next. Thoughts of his mother, not the trampled, messed-up form of her, but the beautiful woman he remembered tucking him in at night, formed in his imagination. He could feel her warm kiss on his forehead and her soft hands brushing through his hair. He remembered her angelic voice as she recited him bedtime stories and sung him soft lullabies. The sensation of her touch became so strong that Finn could have sworn that she was kneeling right there beside him.

Open your eyes, he heard his mother say.

I don't want to. I'm ready to see you.

Open your eyes, said the combined voice of his mother and...someone else, someone familiar.

Please, let me join you.
Open your eyes.

A non-existent hand lifted Finn up by the chin and the sounds of the world around him seeped into his ears. He heard the wind rustling through the trees and through the grass. He heard insects chirping and the running water of a nearby river. Then, he heard a shriek that he'd heard so many times before. It took him a few seconds to realize what it was.

Finally opening his eyes, Finn gasped at the sight of Obsidian ravaging Constantine's already destroyed face. The man screamed as the dinosaur pecked and scratched its target with a ferocity Finn had never seen before. A white ball hung from a red tendon out of the Highborn's eye socket, his mouth curled in horror as he swatted at the mess of black feathers that shredded the skin of his once-handsome appearance.

A lucky strike by Constantine sent Obsidian spinning through the air and landing unconscious—or dead—by Finn's legs. The blood rushed back into Finn's face and he gritted his teeth. He balled both of his fists and the intense pain only fueled his anger as he stood himself up. He could feel both of his eyes rolling upward as his eyebrows connected into one. Sweat dripped down his back as he lifted Jigsaw into the air, which ignited into a show of fire, distorting the air around it with its fumes. Jigsaw's teeth buzzed to life as a deep roar erupted from Finn's mouth. Jigsaw had never felt so light.

Finn took off towards Constantine, who had fallen to his knees trying to grab onto his dangling eyeball but kept screaming every time he touched it. Seconds before his death, the Highborn looked up and pleaded, "No, please, not like this!"

Jigsaw soared through the man's neck so fast that not a single drop of blood stained its iron-grey face. The teeth went silent and the fire sucked itself back into the hilt. Constantine's screams stopped once his head dropped into his own lap.

Constantine's body fell.

~

Finn had no clue how long it had taken Jade and Ariel to find him, only that he was now being dragged backward through the grass. They laid him onto his back underneath a tree not too far away and Ariel resided over him, her hand in his. She was speaking, but all Finn could hear was his own pulse ringing in his ears. He tried moving his hand but it did not cooperate. It felt as though sand were being poured over it, and this feeling began to crawl up the rest of his arm.

He shut his eyes and when he opened them again, the sun had moved out of sight, leaving a sky of violet, blue, and pink. He could feel the wind running over his face and shivered a little. He felt cold but somehow at peace. He let his eyes drift to the left and found Jade sitting beside him. Finn wanted to say something but moving his lips was not an option. Just moving his eyes took an incredible amount of energy.

He felt his mouth being parted but not by his own will. Something was pressed to his lips and in poured a warm, licorice-flavored liquid. It was soothing at first but as Jade massaged his throat and the liquid poured down into his stomach, he felt a burning sensation. He coughed as he tried to breathe but it felt like trying to inhale fire. His eyes watered as he felt the strange liquid flow through his veins in every direction.

At first, he felt nauseous and thought his stomach was being eaten from the inside out. When this feeling finally died down, he was left with a cool sensation as if he'd just drank a gallon of minty water.

"What was that crap?" Finn asked, finding the energy to wipe his mouth. He did so with his right hand, and felt the gauze brush against his face.

"Ariel wasn't able to save your finger," said Ariel, her eyes red from crying and her face covered in dried blood. "Ariel is so sorry."

Finn slowly shook his head. "It's okay. I don't have much need for it. At least, not that I can think of— wait, where's Obsidian? Last time I saw—"

"Obsidian is just fine," said Ariel with a soft smile. "Ariel saw it glide into the trees sometime after we dragged you here. It left only when he knew that you would be okay."

Finn let out a relieved breath. "Thank God...I thought I lost him. And how are the others back at the village?"

"You should worry about yourself," said Jade. He was on his knees and looking down at Finn. Smoke wafted over his head. "If it wasn't for Ariel, you'd be dead."

"And if it wasn't for Jade's newfound tracking abilities, you would also be dead," added Ariel with a quick nod of her head.

"Thank you both."

"Don't thank us," said Jade. "You're the one to thank. You took on an aged warrior, one who actually knew and deserved to swing a Bizarre Blade. That's an achievement, if you ask me."

Finn couldn't decide whether that was a compliment or not but he decided to go with it anyway. "Thank you? But seriously," he said, sitting up. "How is everyone? Are they okay? And what happened to Constantine's Blade?"

"We couldn't find Constantine's Blade," Ariel said with a frown. "Jade and Ariel looked everywhere for it but we think it may have relocated itself, as we are not vile enough to wield it." She paused here, closing her eyes. "As for the villagers...not everyone made it. A few of the younger ones passed away from lack of water. The rest survived, including the professors and mother Nibbles, but they will need more than the concoction Ariel has just given to you. Ariel thinks many days will be needed for healing and to bring nutrition back into their bodies."

"Speak for yourself," came a harsh voice that could belong to no other than Silver.

Everyone turned around to see a very tired-looking, one-eyed albino leaning against a tree. He looked even paler than normal which Finn had previously thought impossible. Both of his cheeks were sunken in, and his neck looked to have closed in on itself. His eyes carried heavy purple bags and he looked like he no longer fit into his clothes. Finn felt as though if he blew on the man, he would fall over.

"You should be lying down, Master," said Ariel, rushing to his side. Silver, however, put up a hand to stop her.

"Don't give me orders. That's my job, remember?" Silver coughed and it sounded wet. "Where's Constantine?"

"Right here." Jade stood up and pointed to the ground behind him.

Finn looked over and saw a decent amount of blood in the grass just above the headless body. Flying insects had already made their way over, attracted by the smells of a soon-to-be rotting corpse.

"Why did you drag the body right next to me?" Finn

asked, wondering if anyone had any decency. "Could have dragged him somewhere else, you know."

Silver ignored him and instead used Finn's head as support as he bent one knee to examine Constantine. A few feet away was the head—they had thankfully turned the face around so they wouldn't have to look at it.

"Open his shirt," commanded Silver, and Jade did so right away, moving Constantine's arm off his chest and unbuttoning his bloodied orange vest. Silver nodded. "Just as I thought."

Jade tilted his head as he stared at whatever it was Silver was looking at. "What does it mean, Master?"

Ariel stepped over Finn to get a good look for herself, accidentally stepping on him in the process. "What kind of creature is that?" she asked. "Ariel has never seen anything like it!"

Curiosity bubbling, Finn shoved his face between Jade and Ariel. Just below Constantine's left collarbone was a black tattoo of a head of a beast that he also had never seen before. Whatever it was, it had the canine teeth of a saber-tooth, the head of a dire wolf, and the skin of a lizard. The large piercing eyes gazed forward with such power that it felt like it looked right into your soul.

Gorgonops

Chills ran up Finn's arms, not because of the tattoo, but because of the look on Silver's face. His usual angry and confident demeanor was replaced with a look of anxiety, his eyes darting left and right as he knelt, deep thought.

"This isn't good. This isn't good at all," he said. He looked at Ariel. "Nurse everyone back to health as fast as possible, beginning with Nibbles. She's going to want to see this."

"But Ariel doesn't understand, Master. What's wrong? What is this?"

Silver swallowed, his eyes dropping back to the tattoo. "This is the mark of a Gorgonops, an extinct ferocious animal. It was branded onto the members of a secret society of heinous individuals, which was supposed to have been disbanded long ago. However, it seems they've returned."

"What do they do that makes them so heinous?" asked Ariel.

Silver shook his head, pulling his eyes off the tattoo and looking down at the ground. "Not much is known about the

Gorgonops. As far as I understood they've all been dead for hundreds of years. Apparently, we were wrong."

"Who's we?" asked Jade. "You and Nibbles?"

Silver nodded. "As well as the other professors. Not even we know a whole lot about this group, just enough to keep them in the back of our minds just in case...something like this were to happen."

Jade crossed his arms over his chest. "Don't you think it would've been important to instruct your students about this? We almost died because of this man!" He pointed down to Constantine's corpse.

Silver moved with speed that Finn couldn't believe considering what he'd just been through. His fist shot out, smacking Jade across the jaw and sending him onto his ass. "Realize who you're speaking to, boy." Silver breathed heavily. "Don't you ever put this blame on my shoulders! Never again, do you hear me?"

Jade didn't answer him, but just stared.

Silver's shoulders slumped as he let himself lean back against the tree. He looked over at Finn, and instead of anger on his face there was pity. "You need to go back to Sumetai."

A lump formed in Finn's throat, and at that moment he forgot about Constantine, his Bizarre Blade, and even his missing pinky. "You heard something about my father, didn't you?"

"Yes."

"What did you hear?"

"Not much, but I know there isn't much time. Certainly not enough time for you to wait for myself and the others to heal. No, you will need to go to Sumetai by yourself. Find your father and bring him here. I can't guarantee his safety in our village but it's better than him staying in Sumetai."

Finn stood up and dusted off his pants. There was no thinking about what needed to be done because his mind was already made up. He had already lost his mother, and he would not lose his father. This time, he was old enough to do something about it.

"You realize you will most likely die," Silver said, his face still pointed towards the ground.

Finn swallowed. "Of course. But if I can survive being chased by a t-rex and cross a river on the back of a giant crocodile, then maybe I can do this."

Silver raised an eyebrow, not understanding what Finn was talking about.

"And he won't have to do it alone."

Finn turned to Jade who had also stood up. Half of his body was covered in the grey smoke that crawled over him in waves, disappearing a foot above his head.

"You don't have to do this," said Finn, shaking his head.

"Of course I do," argued Jade. "You're one of us now."

"And Ariel will go too!"

"No Ariel," said Jade. "You have to stay here and nurse our people."

"He's right," agreed Finn.

Ariel sucked in her lips. "Fine. Ariel will care for her people but will meet up with you two as soon as she is done."

Both Jade and Finn nodded.

Silver pushed himself off the tree and stood a little straighter. Did Finn see a little bit of respect in his eyes? "I'm sorry, Finn, but I don't think Jigsaw will be enough to face the evils that will inevitably stand in the way of you saving your father. None of us know what we're dealing with here."

Finn ignored Silver's words, turned towards Sumetai, and started walking. He didn't look back but he could feel his Master's eyes on him. He could hear Jade right behind him.

Sticking his good hand into his leather satchel, Finn pulled out a leaflet he'd all but forgotten about until that very moment. What these pages held could be the answer to all of his problems. If Jigsaw wasn't going to be enough to save his father, then he knew something that would. He opened the leaflet to page one and began reading.

The Golden Blade is a Blade like no other. The Champion who wields this Blade will have the power to change the world. He or she will be able to craft their own future in any way they desire. All foes will kneel to this awesome power.

Here is how you find it:

The End

Does Finn Featherstone trade in the Jigsaw Blade for a more powerful and shinier Blade? Does he reach his father in time to save him? Find out in *The Golden Blade*! Read Now! (Oh! And the cover is friggin' sweet. Check it out!)

STAY INFORMED

Get a Free Book by visiting Stevie Collier's website www.
StevieCollier.com. You can email me at Stevie.Fiction@gmail.com. I also created a special Facebook group
called "Collier's Conquerors" which you can find @
facebook.com/groups/colliersconquerors This group is
specifically for readers, where I show new cover art, do give-
aways, and run contests. Please check it out and join whenever you get the chance!

For updates about my new releases, as well as exclusive
promotions, visit my website and sign up for the VIP
mailing list. Head there now to receive a free copy of
Cambion.

www.StevieCollier.com

Enjoying the series? Help others discover the beginning of
The Bizarre Blade Series by sharing with a friend!

Stevie Collier is a bestselling Fantasy author unlike you've ever read before (whether that's good or bad he doesn't know). He writes books that are true to himself... which means they're eccentric and weird. Most people describe his work as Unique, Odd, Hilarious, Bizarre, Wacky, Action Packed... and different... kind of like the author himself!

When Stevie isn't writing high fantasy, you can find him at the gym pumping iron or running with his spoiled white Siberian Husky named Spartacus.

He loves watching movies (Horror is his favorite even though it scares the bejeezus out of him) along with a lot of anime. Not to mention that he is an avid gamer when he has time! (He is currently dying a million times playing Sekiro on PS4).

Stevie grew up with way too many creative ideas in his head

and so he had to make a decision. Either sit and write down all his stories... or allow his brain to explode fantasy all over the walls.

facebook.com/steviecollierauthor

instagram.com/steviecollierauthor

DEDICATIONS

This entire series is dedicated to my little brother, "A" Collier. He picked up his first Jurassic Park T-rex at the age of five and never let go! Now, he's studying for his PhD in Paleontology and I couldn't be more excited for him. "A", this one's for you!

To my loving mom, thank you so much for putting my aspirations above that of even your own and believing in me in whatever I chose to do. You're the best mom ever and will always be my number one fan, always.

To my dad, who believed in me so much that we became lifetime business partners. I'm so excited to see where we take our businesses together and already see us fishing on exotic beaches one day with the family!

To my grandparents, thank you so much for being the most supportive grandparents ever! I know Fantasy novels aren't your cup of tea but I can't help but be so inspired by your loving words every time I visit.

To my loving girlfriend, Lisa. I'm so appreciative to God for sending such a miraculous and amazing person into my life. Without you, these books wouldn't be half as good as they are. Thank you so very much. I can't wait to see where the world takes you.

To my friend/honorary little sister, Valerie, thank you so much for being there for me when others were not. You've kept me strong and on track. You're an amazing friend.

To Mrs. Olsovsky for believing in me and my writing. When I was getting into trouble for writing horribly dark stories in Catholic school, you were the one who secretly told me to keep writing and that I had talent. Thank you for the push!

To Mr. Walker, thank you so much for being such an inspiration to me. You taught me the value of investing in my future. I often think of you and your wonderful life lessons (and for teaching me how to use my common sense.)

To Andy Peloquin and the Yanez Family, thank you so much for being by my side every step of the way. Without you guys this series wouldn't have reached the success that it has. Again, thank you so much for believing in me. I'm glad we're friends. Another big thank you to my PR guy, Mike. You rock, dude, seriously... you do.

Last, but certainly not least... a big thank you goes out to God, my creator! Thank you for gifting me with such amazing ideas! I love you and appreciate all the blessings you rain down onto me. (I'm sorry for the crude humor found throughout this book lol).

37889528R00253

Made in the USA
San Bernardino, CA
05 June 2019